SEIZE THE RECKLESS WIND

JOHN GORDON DAVIS was born in what was then
Rhodesia of English parents and educated in South
Africa. He became a member of the Seaman's Union,
spending his university vacations at sea with the Dutch
whaling fleet in the Antarctic, and on British merchant-
men. He took degrees in political science and law and
joined the Rhodesian Civil Service before becoming a
barrister in Hong Kong. After the success of *Hold My
Hand I'm Dying*, to which this book is a sequel, he
decided to become a full-time writer.

JOHN GORDON DAVIS

Seize the Reckless Wind

HARPER

HarperCollins*Publishers*
77–85 Fulham Palace Road,
Hammersmith, London W6 8JB

www.harpercollins.co.uk

This paperback edition 2014
1

First published in Great Britain by HarperCollins*Publishers* 1984

A catalogue record for this book
is available from the British Library

ISBN: 978-0-00-757441-4

FOR ROSEMARY

I am deeply indebted to Malcolm Wren of Wren Airships Ltd. and his staff for all their patient instruction in the science of airships, and to Kevin McPhillips, Harry Green, Lynn Wilson and Michael Owen for taking me literally under their wing and allowing me to learn at first hand about the air frieght business.

All the characters in this novel are, however, fictitious.

PARIS 1897

It was a beautiful morning. The Eiffel Tower rose up into a cloudless sky. Crowds thronged the Champs-Elysées and the cafés, bonnets and parasols and top hats everywhere, and carriages were busy. A parade marched towards the Arc de Triomphe, the people cheering and flags waving. Then there was a new sound above the applause, and a blob came looming over the treetops, spluttering. It was a man flying a tricycle.

His name was Alberto Santos-Dumont. It was one of those newly-invented De Deon motor-tricycles; but the steering was connected to a canvas frame behind, like a ship's rudder, and the engine turned a wooden propeller. Above this contraption floated a big egg-shaped silk balloon of hydrogen, from which the tricycle with the incumbent Alberto were suspended.

Alberto sailed low over the crowds, and all faces were upturned, delighted and waving. The air-cycle went buzzing and backfiring round the Arc de Triomphe, then it headed over the rooftops towards the Eiffel Tower. It rose higher and higher, then sailed ponderously round the mighty tower to roars of applause.

Whereupon Alberto wanted a drink. He came looming down towards the boulevards, spluttering between the treetops, making horses shy. Ahead was his favourite café. Alberto brought his flying machine down lower, and steered it towards a lamppost. He threw down a coil of rope, and his friends grabbed it and tied it to the lamppost. Alberto's engine backfired, and died. The balloon-cycle was moored, hitched above the cobblestones like an elephant.

Alberto jumped down, and walked jauntily into the café, smiling and shaking hands.

ENGLAND 1929

Those were the days of glory and empires, when the statesmen of Europe carved up the world, planted their flags and brought law and order, and Christianity, to the heathen. Everything was well ordered, and if you looked at an atlas much of it was coloured red, for Great Britain, not red for communist as it would be coloured today. The world was full of adventure; and the vast wild places teemed with animals, the seas were full of fish and whales. This was only yesterday, only in your father's day, and maybe in your own. The world was beautiful, and there were no oilslicks on the seas, no oil fumes hanging in the air, no pollution blowing across oceans to make acid rain in faraway places. In those days there were some dashing young men in flying machines, but it was before the age of air travel.

In a field outside the town of Bedford stood two great hangars. Inside one of them, hundreds of men were building a great airship, as long as two football pitches put end to end, great frames of aluminium covered in canvas, and its huge gasbags were made of ox-intestine, to be filled with hydrogen. The ship was being built by the government and it was called the R 101. Across country, in Yorkshire, another airship was being built by a private company for the government, and it was called the R 100. The R 100 was finished first, and she flew on her trials to Canada and back, to much acclaim. There was great urgency to finish the R 101 so she could carry the Secretary of State to India and back in time for the Empire's Jubilee. But when the R 101 was tested, she was sluggish. So they cut her in half and added a whole new section to hold another huge gasbag. But there was not time for all her trials before she left.

It was a cold, rainy afternoon when the R 101 took off for India, with her famous personages aboard. She flew over London, and down in the streets people were waving madly. It was dark when she flew over the Channel, and the rain beat

8

down on her. As she flew over the coastline of France the captain reported by radio to London that his famous passengers had dined well and retired to bed.

That was the last communication.

It is not known for certain why it happened but near Beauvais the great ship came seething down to earth out of the darkness. There was a shocking boom and the great frame crumpled and a vast balloon of flame mushroomed up, and then another and another, and the huge mass of buckled frames glowed red in the ghastly inferno.

There were only six survivors. The world was horrified. And, after the Commission of Inquiry, the other airship was dismantled in her hangar, and broken up with a steam-roller, and sold for scrap.

NEW JERSEY, AMERICA: 7 MAY 1937

In the late afternoon the monster appeared.

It came from the Atlantic, looming slowly larger and closer towards the skyscrapers of New York. It had huge swastikas emblazoned on its tail. It was over seven hundred feet long, a leviathan filled with seven million cubic feet of hydrogen. The sun shone silver on her mighty body, and down in the concrete canyons the people stared upwards, awed, and the passengers gazed down on beautiful Manhattan, the Hudson with steamships from all around the world, the Statue of Liberty, Long Island fading into distant mauve, America stretching away in the lowering sun. Her sister ship, the *Graf Zeppelin*, had made one hundred and thirty trans-Atlantic flights in the last nine years, but people never tired of seeing such massive beauty sailing so majestically through the sky. She was called the *Hindenburg*, and she was the newest prize of the German airfleet. She could carry seventy passengers, sleeping in real cabins and dining in a saloon at real tables with real cutlery, strolling along promenade decks, looking down on to the countrysides gliding quietly by below, so close they could even hear a dog bark and a train whistle.

There was a big crowd awaiting her at the Lakehurst airfield in New Jersey; the ground crew, people to meet the passengers, pressmen, sightseers. The sun was setting when she came into sight. She came through the darkening sky, slowly becoming larger and larger, the captain slowly bringing her down, and the crowd broke into a mass of waving.

The mooring mast was a high steel structure. The ship came purring across the airfield towards it, headed into the breeze, a wondrous silver monster easing down out of the sky; a rope came uncoiling out of her nose; the ground crew ran for it. There was the sound of an explosion; for an instant there was a hellish blue glow, then a great flame leapt upwards.

It exploded out of the stern, and in a moment most of the airship was engulfed in barrelling fire. Instantly half the canvas was gone and the frame glared naked in the sky; the flame mushroomed enormously upwards, yellow and black, and the stern began to fall. There was a second explosion and more flame shot up, the great ship shook. All the passengers knew was the terror, and the deck suddenly lurching away beneath them, and the terrible glare, and the heat. Now the flaming ship was falling to earth in a terrible slow-motion, stern first. There was a third explosion and the airship hit the ground, a blazing mass of frames and flames. The crowd was screaming, people were running to try to help and the radio commentator was weeping, *'Oh my God . . . It's terrible . . . I can't watch it . . . All those people dying . . . Oh my God this is terrible . . . '*

Some people leapt out before it hit the earth, some managed to fight their way out as it crashed. They came staggering out, reeling, on fire, twisting and beating themselves, roasting and crazed. The night was filled with flame and weeping and shouting.

PART 1

PART 1

CHAPTER 1

It is always hot in the Zambesi Valley. From the hard escarpments the valley rolls away, descending through many hills, stretching on and on, mauve, fading into haze, like an ocean, so vast you cannot see the escarpments on the other side. It is a wonderful, wild valley, with elephant and lion and all the buck, and the river is hundreds of yards wide, with sandy banks and islands, and hippo, vundu fish as big as a man, big striped fighting tiger fish, and many crocodiles. The mighty river flows for thousands of miles, from the vast bushland of Angola in the west, over the Victoria Falls – the Smoke that Thunders – through Rhodesia, and Mozambique, and out into the Indian Ocean in the east. The river flows through many narrow rock gorges on this long journey, and where it twists and roars through the one called Kariba it is the home of Nyamayimini, the river god. It was at the entrance to this god's den that the white man built a mighty wall across the river, to flood a huge valley to the west and create an inland sea.

For those were the days of the 'winds of change' that swept through Kenya to the rest of Africa, and the big brave days of Federation and Partnership between white go-ahead Rhodesia, black copper-rich Zambia and poor little Malawi; partnership between the races, equal rights for all civilized men, big white brother going to help little black brother, economic and political partnership, white hand clasped with black hand across the Zambesi. And the white man built the wall across the mighty river to create electricity for the industries that were going to boom, and the inland sea was a symbol of this new partnership. There were the political ones, black men in city clothes who came to the valley and told the Batonka people that the story of the flood was a white man's trick to steal their land, and that they must make war; but the wall slowly went up and the great valley slowly, slowly drowned and died. And with it a whole world of primitive wonder. It was heart-

13

breakingly sad. One day all of Africa would die like that, under the rising tides of the winds of change.

And very soon the partnership died as well, because by the nature of things it was a partnership between the white rider and the black horse, and because the winds of change moaned that there must be One Man One Vote and that the rider must be black. And the political ones, who had been to Moscow and Peking, swaggered through the bush calling the people to meetings, telling them that they must join the Party and take action. Action, boys, action! Burn the schools and burn the missions, burn the diptanks in which the government makes you dip your cattle, stone the policemen and stone the people who are going to work in the factories, burn the huts of the people who do not take Action, maim their cattle and beat their wives and children – and when we rule the country every man will have a white man's house and a bicycle and a transistor radio. And great mother Britain had lost her will; she dissolved the partnership and gave independence to black Zambia and black Malawi because it was easier and cheaper to give away countries than to govern. But she refused independence to white Rhodesia, because that too was easier than to shout against the winds. And the white men in Rhodesia were angry, for they had governed themselves for forty years and they feared that if they were not independent Great Britain would give them away too, and so they declared themselves independent, as the American colonies had done two hundred years before. Thus the white men made themselves outlaws, and the winds of change howled for their blood, and began to make war.

In the third year of that Rhodesian war, when a new election was coming up, Lieutenant Joe Mahoney, who was a lawyer when he was not soldiering, almost won a medal for valour, but do not be too impressed by that because it happened like this:

The truck carrying his troopers was trundling along the escarpment of the Zambesi valley when suddenly there was a burst of gunfire, the truck lurched and Mahoney, who was standing at that moment, fell off the back. He landed with a crash on the dirt road, but still clutching his rifle. For a bone-jarred moment all he knew was the shocked terror of being left in a hail of gunfire; then he collected his wits, scrambled up and fled. He fled doubled-up across the road, and leapt into the bush, desperately looking for cover, when suddenly he saw terrible terrorists leaping up in front of him.

Leaping up and running away, terrorists to left of him, terrorists to right of him, all running for their lives instead of blowing the living shit out of him. For Mahoney, in his shock, had run into their gunfire instead of away from it; all the terrorists saw was the angriest white man in the world charging at them with murder in his heart, and all Mahoney knew was the absolute terror of running straight into the enemy and the desperate necessity of killing them before they killed him, and he wildly opened fire. Firing blindly from the hip, sweeping the bush with his shattering gun, the desperate instinct to *kill kill kill the bastards before they kill me*, and all he saw was men lurching and crashing in full flight – he went crashing on through the bush after them, God knows why, gasping, Joe Mahoney single-handedly taking on the fleeing buttocks of the Liberation Army – he ran and ran, rasping, stumbling, and through the trees he saw a man, fired and saw the blood splat as the man contorted; then Mahoney threw himself behind a tree and slithered to the ground, on to his gasping belly; then his own boys were coming running through the trees; and he sank his head, heart pounding, sick in his guts.

He had just killed seven men all by himself, and he was a hero. Maybe the whole thing had taken one minute.

For the next two days they tracked the rest of the terrorists. The tracker walked ahead, flanked by two men to watch for the enemy while his eyes were on the ground; the troopers followed behind, eyes constantly darting over the bush, every muscle tensed for the sudden shattering gunfire, ready to fling themselves flat. For two days it was like that, stalking through the endless bush under the merciless sun, slogging, sweating, and all the time every nerve tensed to kill and die – and oh God, God, Mahoney hated the war, and hated himself.

15

Because Joe Mahoney, QC, Africa-lover, African lover, just wanted to kill kill kill and get it over, with all his stretched-tight nerves he longed for contact, so that he could go charging in there and get it over with . . . But for what?

Because the enemy were murderous bastards who brutalized their own tribesmen, burned their huts and crops and schools and maimed their cattle, terrorizing everybody into submission because that is the only law Africa respects? Because they were smash-and-grab communists, their heads stuffed with the nihilism of Moscow and Peking who are dedicated to the destruction of the West, to the wars they were waging and winning in the rest of Africa and Central America and Asia and the Middle East, winning by default because the West was now so pusillanimous and gutless? Ah yes, when he reminded himself of these matters Joe Mahoney did not feel so bad. 'What are you fighting for, lad?' he sometimes asked round the fire at night, when the theory is you should be a father-figure to your men, though he really asked it because he wanted to ease his conscience.

'For my country, sir.'

'Against the communists, sir.'

'Anything else?'

(And, God knows, was that not enough?) There always ensued a rag-bag discussion in which half-digested evidence steamrollered itself into gospel truth, tales of barbarity mixed with contempt. How the fucking hell can they rule the fucking country, sir? Usually Mahoney just listened like the magistrate he used to be when large tracts of the world were still governed by the impeccable Victorian standards of the old school tie, a good grasp of Latin verbs and the ability to bowl a good cricket ball. Sometimes he interrupted them with something like: 'Gentlemen, I know we're all in the bush getting our arses shot off without the comfort and society of our womenfolk, but do you think we can uphold some of these standards we cherish by not making *every* adjective a four-letter word?'

But usually he just sat there and listened, his dulled heart aching, for Africa. Because Africa was dying, bleeding to death from self-inflicted wounds. And his heart ached for his troopers too, because Africa was all they had and they were going to lose it, and they did not realise that it was really a black man's war they were fighting and dying for. 'For my country, sir, because how the hell can they run the country, sir?' Oh, it was true. But they thought they were fighting a white man's war, for the white man's status quo. And, if so, was it a *just* war? Had the white man given the black man his fair share of the sun? And, if not, could this war be won? To win, must not the army be the fish swimming in the waters of the people? Was not the real battle for hearts and minds?

The next afternoon the spoor led to a kraal of five huts. The troopers silently surrounded the kraal, while the tracker did a big three-sixty through the surrounding bush, looking for the terrorists' spoor leading out. After fifteen minutes he found it.

'How old?'

'A few hours,' the tracker said. 'They left about noon.'

Mahoney turned and ran back to the kraal, while his men kept him covered. 'Where is the headman?' he shouted.

The African woman looked up, astonished. An infant with flies round his nostrils stared, then burst into tears. People came creeping out of the huts, wide-eyed, young and old, in white man's tatters. 'Are you the headman, old gentleman?' Mahoney demanded.

The man was grey-haired. 'Yes, Nkosi.'

'Some terrorists have been to your kraal today. How many?'

The old man was trembling. 'I have seen nobody, Nkosi.' Everybody was staring, frightened.

Mahoney took him by the elbow and led him aside.

'Their spoor leads into your kraal. Where were they going?'

The old man was shaking. 'They did not say, Nkosi.'

'What did they want from you?'

The old man trembled. 'They ordered my wives to cook food.'

'How many men?'

'I think there were ten.'

Mahoney took a big, sweating breath. 'If anymore come,

17

you have not seen me. When I leave now, you will obliterate my spoor in your kraal. Understand?'

Mahoney turned and left. The soldiers started following the spoor again, hard.

When darkness fell they were less than two hours behind the terrorists. With the first light they started again.

After an hour the spoor split into two groups.

'They're looking for more kraals. For more food.'

Mahoney divided his men. After an hour the spoor he was following turned. It headed back towards the old man's kraal.

When the terrorists got back to the kraal they ordered the women to cook more food and they sat down to wait.

'Have you seen any soldiers?'

'No,' the old man mumbled.

Everybody had their eyes averted. Then a child spoke up boastfully: 'Yesterday a white soldier came.'

First they beat up everybody, with fists and boots and rifle butts, and the air was filled with the screaming and the wailing. Then they threw the old man on his back. They lashed his hands and feet to stakes. They staked his senior wife beside him. Then the commander thrust an axe at the eldest son: *'This is how we treat traitors to the Party! Chop your father's legs off!'*

And the women began to wail and the youth cowered and wept and so they threw him to the ground and kicked him, and then the commander picked up a big stone and he held it over his mother's face: *'This is how we treat people who do not obey!'*

He dropped the stone on to the old woman's face. And her nose broke and she cried out, spluttering blood, half-fainted; he picked up the stone and held it over her again, and dropped it again. Her forehead gashed open and she fainted, gurgling blood. The commander shouted: *'Now chop your father's legs off!'*

And the boy wept and cowered, so they beat him again. And the commander held up the stone again: the old woman had revived, her face a mass of blood and contusion, breathing in gurgling gasps, and when she saw the stone poised again she cried out, cringing; and the man dropped the stone again. There was a big splat of blood and she fainted. The commander shouted: 'Tie wire around his testicles!'

They pulled the boy's trousers off and tied a long wire tight around his scrotum so he screamed, then they yanked him to his feet in front of his father and thrust the axe in his hand.

'*Chop well! For each chop we will pull your balls and drop the stone on your mother's face! Now chop!*' And the wire was wrenched.

The boy screamed, and the wire was wrenched again, and he lurched the axe above his head, his tears streaming, and the old man wrenched at his bonds, and the commander slammed his boot down on his throat. '*Chop!*' he roared and the wire was wrenched and the boy screamed again, and they wrenched the wire again and his face screwed up in agony, and he swung the axe down with all his horrified might. There was a crack of shin-bone and the leg burst open, sinews splayed, and the old man screamed and bucked and the commander bellowed.

'*One!*'

And he dropped the stone on the woman's face and the wire was wrenched so the boy screamed through his hysterical sobbing, and he swung the axe on high again and swiped it down on the other shin, and there was another crack of bone, and another gaping wound in the glaring sunshine, white shattered bone and sinews and blood, and the commander shouted.

'*Two!*'

And he dropped the stone again and the wire wrenched and the boy screamed, reeling, and he swung the axe again at his father's legs.

'*Three!*'

And another crash of the stone, and another wrench of the wire. '*Four!*' And again. '*Five!*' And now the boy was hysterically swinging the axe, out of his mind with the horror and the agony, and there was nothing in the world but the screaming and the blood and stink of sweat under the African sun. Altogether it took the boy nine swipes to chop his father's legs right off, but his mother was dead before then, suffocated in her own blood.

The troopers heard the screams a quarter of a mile away. They came running, spread out. Mahoney saw the old man writhing, the youth reeling over him with an axe, the terrorists, and he thought the youth was one of them – and he fired; then his men opened up, and there was pandemonium. The cracking of guns and the stench of cordite and the screaming and the scrambling and the running.

A minute later it was almost over. The women had fled into a hut. Three terrorists lay dead, three others had dived into a hut, but they had been flushed out by the threat of a hand-grenade. Mahoney knelt beside the groaning old man in the bloody mud, aghast, holding two tourniquets while the sergeant gave the man a morphine injection. He could not bear to look at the two stumps, the splintered bones sticking out, the severed feet. After a minute the man fell mercifully silent. Beside him lay his wife, her head twice its normal size, her lacerated eyes and nostrils swollen tight shut, her split lips swollen shut in death.

Then Mahoney got the story from the weeping women. He stared at the youth he had shot, and he felt ringing in his ears and the vomit rise in his gut. He walked to the back of the hut, and he retched, and retched.

When he came back the sergeant had lined up the terrorists. They were trembling, glistening with sweat. Mahoney could feel his men's seething fury for revenge.

'Shoot them, sir?'

Mahoney stopped in front of the three.

'Or let the women shoot them, sir?'

'Chop their legs off too, sir?' a trooper shouted theatrically.

Mahoney looked at the three. One had his eyes closed in trembling prayer.

'You savages,' Mahoney hissed.

Silence. He could feel his men seething behind him. The commander said, 'I demand the Geneva Convention.'

Mahoney blinked. 'The Geneva Convention?' he whispered.

Then his mind reeled red-black in fury. *'The Geneva Convention?'* – he roared and he bounded at the man and seized him by the neck and wrenched him across the kraal to the corpses. He rammed the man's head down over the stumps of legs: *'Did the Russians teach you this Geneva Convention? And this?'* He rammed the head over the woman's pulped face. He seized up the bloody axe and shook it under the man's face: *'Is this your Geneva Convention?'*

For a long hate-filled moment he held the cowering man by his collar, and with all his vicious fury he just wanted to *ram* the axe into the gibbering face. Then he threw it down furiously. The sergeant grabbed the man. 'Shoot them, sir?'

The three terrorists stood there, terrified. Mahoney stared at them. Oh God, to shoot them and give them their just deserts. Oh, to shoot them so that the weeping kraal members could see that justice had been done. Oh, to shoot them so that all the people in the area would know that the white man's justice was swift and dire.

'They're going to be tried for murder and hanged. Radio for a helicopter.'

And oh God, God, he knew why Rhodesia could not win this war. Not because these bastards outnumbered them, not because Russia and China were pouring military hardware into them, and certainly not because they were better soldiers; but because the likes of Joe Mahoney could not bring themselves to fight the bastards by their own savage rules; Joe Mahoney could not even shoot the bastards who chopped people's legs off. Instead he had to hand them over to the decorous procedures of the courts, where they would be assigned competent counsel at the public's expense, presumed innocent until proved guilty. They would have a lengthy appeal and thereafter their sentences would be considered by the President for the exercise of the Prerogative of Mercy.

And Joe Mahoney knew that he would soldier no more, that he was not much longer for God-forsaken Africa.

21

CHAPTER 2

The town of Kariba is built on the hot valley hilltops above the great dam wall, and the inland sea floods into these hills to make many-tentacled bays and creeks. Along this man-made coastline are hotels and beaches. The army barracks is on the hilltops overlooking the vast blue lake that stretches on and on, over the horizon, reaching into the faraway hills. Way out there was a safari lodge for tourists, which Mahoney partly owned. In those days of war, Kariba was an alive little town. At nights the hotel bars were full of soldiers happy to be back from the bush alive, and Rhodesian tourists who had almost nowhere else to go because of the war, so the air throbbed with dance and music, and talk and laughter. Mahoney was always happy when he came back to Kariba: it was an end to weeks of confrontation with death, and exhaustion, an end to running, and fear, and sweat, and thirst. But when he came out of the bush that last time, trundling down the hot hills of the escarpment back to his barracks, Joe Mahoney was not happy, because he loved somebody who did not love him.

'But I do love you,' he heard Shelagh say. 'It's that I can't live with you anymore . . . I've got to be my own *person*. If I didn't fight every inch of the way you'd just steamroller my needs underfoot. I'm an *artist*, which means delicacy, whereas you bulldoze your way through life, like you go into court and bully the witnesses and bully the other lawyers and come out dusting your hands – I've *seen* you in court.'

'You can stop work altogether and paint all the time.'

'But I don't *want* to stop work, I'm *me*, I don't *want* to be dependent on you! God, why must women be housewives and second-class citizens and even change their names – put "*Mrs*" in front, like we're somebody's sexual property? . . .'

But he ruthlessly pushed Shelagh out of his mind – he had had six weeks in the bush to get used to the idea. He showered and drank three bottles of beer while he wrote his report.

22

Then he drove to the officers' mess to buy a few more to take with him. It was a small mess and as he walked in the first person he saw was Jake Jefferson, the Deputy Director of Combined Operations; he turned away, but Jake looked up, straight into his eyes. 'Hullo, Joe,' he smiled.

Mahoney stopped. 'Good afternoon, sir.' He shook hands. 'What are you doing here?'

'Jake's the name, off duty. A few days' fishing. With my son. What'll you have?'

Mahoney felt his heart contract. He desperately wanted to see the lad – just to *see* him – but yet he didn't think he could bear it. 'Nothing, thanks, I'm only buying a few for the road. Barman,' he called.

Jefferson looked at Mahoney while he made his purchase. 'I hear you made quite a kill?'

'Luck.' Mahoney wondered how the man really felt about him. He then heard himself say, although it was the last subject he wanted to bring up: 'And how is your son?'

'Top of his class,' Jefferson said, and Mahoney wondered for the thousandth time how the man could have no doubts. The barman mercifully came back with his change and he picked up the bottles.

'Well, excuse me, Jake, good to see you.'

'Look after yourself,' Jefferson smiled.

Mahoney walked out, clutching his beers, into the harsh sunlight, trying to look as if nothing had happened. His old Landrover had 'Zambesi Safaris' painted on it. He got in, started the engine, and drove off hurriedly, in case the boy should arrive. He got out of sight of the mess, then slowed, letting himself feel the emotion, and the confusion. Then he took his foot off the accelerator entirely, his heart suddenly beating fast. His vehicle rolled to a stop.

Walking towards him was an eight-year-old boy, carrying a fishing rod. Mahoney stared at him, eating him up with his eyes: the blonde hair, just like his mother's, the same eyes and mouth . . . The boy came level with the Landrover and Mahoney knew he should not do it, for his own sake, but he couldn't resist it. 'Hullo, Sean.'

The boy turned, surprised. 'Hullo, sir,' he said uncertainly.

23

Mahoney smiled at him. 'Do you know who I am?'

The lad looked embarrassed. 'I'm not sure, sir.'

'I'm Joe Mahoney, a friend of your father.' He wanted to say, *And your mother*. 'I haven't seen you for a couple of years, I should think.'

'Oh,' Sean said. 'How do you do, sir?'

Mahoney felt shakey. 'You've grown,' he laughed.

'Yes, sir,' the boy smiled, and Mahoney wanted to cry out *Don't call me sir!*

'Your father tells me you're top of your class?'

'Yes, well, this year, sir.'

Mahoney felt his heart swell. 'Keep that up. And how's the rugby?'

'Well, I'm in the Under Nines A team,' the boy said, 'but I'm better at cricket than rugger so far.'

Oh, he wanted to watch him play. 'Your dad says you're going fishing?'

'Yes.' The boy held up a can. 'Been buying some worms. We're after bream, though we won't have much luck until later.' He looked as if he wanted to get going.

Mahoney said: 'Well, do you trawl for tiger fish while the sun's high?'

'Yes, sir, I've caught five tiger fish in my life.'

In your life . . . And oh, Mahoney longed to be with him, teach him all about life. How he wished he was taking him fishing this afternoon. Sean said earnestly, 'I'd better go now, sir; my father's expecting me.'

'Well, have a good time, Sean.' Mahoney reached out his hand. The boy hastily transferred the rod and with the feel of the small hand Mahoney thought his heart would crack. 'Look after yourself, my boy.'

Sean pumped his hand energetically once. 'Goodbye, sir.'

'Goodbye,'Mahoney said. And it really was goodbye.

The boy strode resolutely on down the road towards the officers' mess. Mahoney sat, watching him in the rear-view mirror, and the tears were burning in his eyes. He whispered: '*And keep coming top of the class!*'

*

He drove slowly on, out of the barracks, shaken from seeing the boy; up the winding hills; to the little cemetery at the very top.

He got out of the Landrover. The sun was burning hot. The Zambesi hills stretched on and on below, into haziness. It was a year since he had been here. He stood, looking about for some wild flowers. He picked one. He walked numbly into the cemetery.

The headstone read: *Suzanna de Villiers Jefferson*.

Mahoney stood in front of it. And maybe it was because he was still tensed up from seeing the boy, and from the bush, but it was all unreal. He whispered: 'Hullo, Suzie. I've come to say goodbye.'

But Suzie did not answer. Suzie only spoke to him when he was drunk nowadays. He did not often speak to her now either, even when he was drunk, because it was all a long time ago, and he loved somebody else now. He stood there, trying to reach her. He whispered: 'I'm going to tell the people what I think, Suzie. The truth. And they're not going to listen to me, so then I'm going to leave.'

Suzie did not answer.

Mahoney stood there, waiting. There was only silence. He knelt on one knee, laid the solitary flower on her grave. He closed his eyes and tried to say a small prayer for Suzie to the God he was not sure he believed in. He whispered: 'Goodbye, Suzie, forever . . . ' And suddenly it was real, the word 'forever', and he felt the numb tension crack and the grief well up through it, the grief of this grave high up in these hot hills of Africa. The heartbreaking sadness that he would never come back, to these hills, to this valley, to that mighty river down there, to this Africa that was dying, dying, to this grave of that lovely girl who had died with it: suddenly it was all real and he felt the tears choke up and he dropped his head in his hands and he sobbed out loud, and he heard Suzie say: 'Come on now, it's not me you're weeping for, or the boy, is it, darling? It's for yourself; and for Shelagh.'

And he wanted to cry out loud, half in happiness that Suzie was there and half in protest that Shelagh was over, and Suzie smiled: 'Well, you always wanted a soulmate. And you got one, in spades. But you're still not happy. Will you ever be happy, darling?'

'You made me happy, Suzie.'

She smiled, 'Ah, yes – but I wasn't clever enough for you, I couldn't argue the problems of the world with you, and it's not me you're weeping for now.'

'Oh God, forgive me, Suzie . . . '

She smiled, 'Of course, darling. Didn't I always forgive you everything? But what about our son?'

And Mahoney took a deep breath and squeezed his fingertips into his face in guilt and anger and confusion. He whispered fiercely: 'He's safe, Suzie, he's *safe* and it would be *wrong* for me to interfere.'

Suzie did not answer; and suddenly she was gone. And Mahoney knew very well that she had never been there, that the conversation had not taken place, but in his heart he almost believed it. He knelt by her grave, trying fiercely to control his guilt and his grief. For a long minute more he knelt; then he squeezed his eyes and took a deep breath. 'Goodbye, Suzie . . . ,' he whispered. He got up, and walked quickly away from her grave.

He drove slowly down the hot, winding hills. He felt wrung out; and when he got to the lakeshore he just wanted to turn left and start driving up out of this valley on to the road to goddamn Salisbury, three hundred miles away, and start telling the people what they had to do to save the country, *tell* them and then get the hell out of it – wash his hands of goddamn Africa . . .

But he was going to Salisbury by air, and he had two hours to wait.

He did not want to hurt himself any further: but he had to say goodbye to the *Noah's Ark* too. He drove slowly to the harbour.

There she lay on her mooring, long and white, her steel hull a little dented where drowning animals and treetops had hit her.

Mahoney sat, looking at her. The brave *Noah's Ark* . . . He

26

was leaving her too. He picked up a beer, got out of the Landrover and walked on to the jetty. There were a number of rowboats tied up. He rowed out to his *Ark*.

'Hullo, old lady . . . '

He clambered aboard her. He stood on the gunnel, looking about. It was a long time since he had used her, because of the war. He stepped over to the wheel, held it a moment. Below, fore and aft, were the cabins and saloon, locked.

He sat down behind the wheel, with a sigh.

And oh, he did not want to sell her. He had bought her to keep forever. She was part of his Africa, a symbol of this great valley that had died, she had been here from the beginning – that was why he had bought her. For in those brave days of Partnership, when the waters began to rise behind that dam wall, the wild animals retreated into the hills, and slowly the hills became islands as the water rose about them, thousands of hilltop islands stretching on and on; and the animals stripped them of grass and bush and bark, as all the time the waters rose higher, and they crowded closer and closer together; and now they were starving; and eventually they had to swim. But they did not know which way to swim to get out of this terrible dying valley, so they swam to other hilltop islands they could see, and they were already stripped bare. The animals swam in all directions, hooves and paws weakly churning, great emaciated elephants ploughing like submarines with just their trunktips showing, starving buck with heads desperately stuck up, desperate monkeys and baboons and lions. Many, many drowned. The government sent in the Wildlife Department men, and volunteers like Joe Mahoney, to drive the animals off the islands with sticks and shouts and thunder-flashes, to make them swim for the faraway escarpments while they still had strength, heading them off from other islands, trying to drag the drowning aboard. The animals that would not take to the water they had to catch, in nets and ambushes and with rugby tackles, wild slashing buck and warthog and porcupine, and bind their feet and put them in the boats. For many, many months this operation went on as the waters of Partnership slowly rose and more hills became islands and slowly drowned: and the motherboat of the flotilla was this *Noah's Ark*.

Now he sat behind her wheel on the great lake, eyes closed; and he could hear the thrashings and the cries and the cursing and the terror, the struggling and the dust and the blood, and the heartbreak of Africa dying. And he remembered the hope: that all this was going to be worth it, that out of this dying would come the new life that Great Britain promised. But it had not come. And now the valley was dead. There were now new cries and screams under the blazing sun, new blood and terror. Partnership was dead, and this grand old boat was all that was left of those brave days, and she also was going to be left behind.

CHAPTER 3

There was military transport to Salisbury, but Mahoney and Bomber Brown and Lovelock and Max and Pomeroy flew back to the city in Mahoney's Piper Comanche, with a crate of cold beers. Bomber did the flying because he did not drink and because Mahoney did not like piloting any more. In fact he downright disliked it. He had asked Lovelock to fly the aeroplane, but Lovelock had shown up at the aerodrome brandishing a brandy bottle and singing, so Mahoney had asked Bomber along. It was a squeeze in the Comanche with five of them, and there were only four sets of headphones, but they made Lovelock do without so that they could not hear him singing, only see his mouth moving. Pomeroy could have flown the plane, for he was an aircraft engineer who also had a commercial pilot's licence, but Pomeroy was accident-prone and tonight he was throwing one of his back-from-the-bush parties and he had already started warming up for it. Pomeroy was a sweet man but when he drank he tended to quarrel with senior officers. Mahoney had represented him at several courts martial. 'But Pomeroy,' he had sighed the last time, 'why did you make it worse by assaulting the police who came to arrest you on this comparatively minor charge?'

'I *didn't*,' Pomeroy protested – 'they assaulted *me*. They send *six* policemen to arrest me? An' they say, "Are you coming voluntary?" An' I said, "Voluntary? Nobody goes with coppers *voluntary* – you'll 'ave to *take* me." An' they tried. *Six* police? That's downright provocation, that is . . .'

But the army put up with Pomeroy because he was such a good aircraft engineer, like they put up with Lovelock because he was such a good flier. Lovelock always looked the same, even when he was sober; amiable and lanky and blonde and pink, not a hard thought in his head. He was one of those English gentlemen who had never done a day's work in his life because all flying was sport to Lovelock, like golf. The Royal Air Force had finally had enough of him. The story was that he was bringing in this screaming jet for an emergency landing and he had the choice of two airfields: *'For God's sake, man, which one are you going for?'* his wing commander had bellowed over the radio. 'Which one has the pub open, sir?' Lovelock had asked earnestly. The RAF had fired him. So he got a job with British Airways, and the story was that when he was getting his licence on 747s he rolled the jumbo over and flew her along upside down for a bit, for the hell of it, and got fired again. Now he flew helicopters for the Rhodesian army, and the terrorists fired at him. It was said Lovelock may look like a long drink of water but he had nerves of steel. Mahoney's view was that he had no nerves at all. He had been flown into combat only once by Lovelock, and that was enough: goddamn Lovelock peering with deep interest into a hail of terrorist gunfire, looking for a nice place to put his helicopter down to discharge his troops, had given Mahoney such heebie-jeebies that he had threatened to brain him then and there. Now Lovelock's head was thrown back, his mouth moving in lusty silent song:

> *'Oh Death where is thy sting-ting-a-ling . . .*
> *'The bells of Hell may ring, ting-a-ling . . .*
> *'For thee, but not for me-e-e— . . .'*

Max shouted in his ear: 'Louder, Lovelock, we can't lip-read.'

'I can't hear you,' Lovelock shouted apologetically, 'I'm not a lip-reader, you know.' But they couldn't hear him.

Mahoney smiled. He had a lot of time for Max. Max was a

29

Selous Scout, one of those brave, tough men who painted themselves black, dressed in terrorist uniform and went into the bush for months spying on them, directing the helicopters in by radio for the kill. Max still had blacking in his hairline and he was going to Pomeroy's sauna party tonight to sweat it out and run around bare-assed. Bomber said to Mahoney over the headphones: 'Do you want to fly her for a bit?'

'No thanks,' Mahoney said, 'I don't like heights.' And he heard Shelagh say: 'I don't know why you bought the wretched thing. As soon as we're airborne you say "Have you had enough, shall we go back now?" Why don't you *sell* it? But no, it's like that *Noah's Ark*, and your safari lodge – you just like to *have* them.'

'What else is there to do with money? You can't take any out of the country.'

'You could buy a decent house in the suburbs, like a successful lawyer, instead of living behind barbed wire on that farm.'

Oh, he could buy a *lovely* house in the suburbs for next to nothing these days, he could have lovely tennis courts and clipped lawns and hedges in the suburbs instead of his security fence; and he could also go right up the fucking wall. Mahoney took a swallow of beer to stop himself thinking about Shelagh as the aeroplane droned on across the vast bush, and Pomeroy said: 'Why don't you sell the bleedin' thing if you don't like flying?'

'But I do love you,' he heard Shelagh say. 'It's just that you're so *stubborn* . . . ' He said to Pomeroy: 'I'm going to. And the farm, if I can get anything like a fair price.'

They all looked at him, except Lovelock. 'Is this Shelagh speaking?' Max said. 'Are you getting married at last?'

'No,' Mahoney said grimly, 'I'm going to Australia.'

Max glared at him. Then looked away in disgust. 'Here we go again. He's taking the Chicken Run again.'

It was a stilted, staccato argument, over the rasping headphones.

I am proud to be a rebel, said the T-shirts, *I am fighting for my country*. And by God they could fight! And the government told them, and they believed it, and it was almost all true, that they were fighting for the best of British values, for the impeccable British standards of justice and efficiency that had gone by the board everywhere else; the rest of the world had gone mad, soft, kow-towing to forces of darkness it had not the guts to withstand, and subversion of trade-unionism and communism that was rotting the world – the Rhodesians were the last bastion of decency and sense, the last of the good old Britishers of Dunkirk and the Battle of Britain, they alone would fight for decency and commonsense in this continent of black political persecution and incompetence, this rich continent that could not even feed itself any more since the white man left, this marvellous continent that had gone mad with One Man One Vote Once. And anybody who does not stay to fight is taking the Chicken Run.

'*Their fair share of the sun?*' Max echoed angrily over the headphones. 'The African has his share of the sun but what does he *do* with it for Chrissakes? He lies in the shade and sleeps off his beer and watches his wives scratch a living! He doesn't *want* to work for anything more – he's *incapable* of anything more! How can you hand over the country to people like that? What was his share of the goddamn sun before the white man came? Tribal warfare and pillage!'

Mahoney rasped: 'A whole new generation of blacks has grown up who wants more than that, and two guerilla armies are massing across the Zambesi to get it—'

'And who're these armies fighting for? A handful of wide-boy politicians, and if they win because people like you take the Chicken Run the poor bloody tribesmen will get even less of the sun because the country will sink back into chaos!'

'And how the hell are you going to beat these armies—'

'By blowing the living shit out of them!'

'– if we don't win the hearts and minds of the people?'

'*We've tried to win their hearts and minds for Chrissake! Schools and hospitals and agricultural services and diptanks – who paid for all that?*'

'But we didn't give them *Partnership!*'

'*Partnership?*' Max shouted. 'We *gave* them Partnership and

31

Britain sold us down the river for thirty pieces of silver! We've still *got* Partnership here – the blacks have got fifteen seats in Parliament out of a total of sixty-five!'

Mahoney shouted, 'Hearts-and-minds Partnership, Max! The educated ones can vote but do we pay the *un*educated ones a decent wage, the factory workers and farmboys who're the basis of the economy? Do we make the black man who's got a tie and jacket and a few quid in his pocket and wants to take his girlfriend on the town? Do we make him feel like a Rhodesian? Do we hell! Do the black kids at school feel the sky's the limit if they work hard? And do we make the poor bloody tribesman feel like a Rhodesian, that we're doing everything to improve his lot?'

'Oh *Jesus!*' Max shouted. '*How can a handful of whites do more? We do ten times more than the rest of Africa where their own black governments cannot even feed their people! Oh Jesus, somebody stop me from braining this bastard!*'

'*I'm going to a better land, a better land by far,*' Lovelock's mouth bellowed silently.

When you love somebody and she doesn't love you any-more . . .

Mahoney tried to thrust Shelagh out of his mind as he drove into Salisbury from the airport, and he was almost successful because he was still angry from his shouting-match with Max, and he had had six weeks in the bush to get used to the idea, and few things unclutter a man's mind so well as the constant prospect of sudden death: but when he saw the familiar outskirts, he was coming home home home, and every street shouted *Shelagh* at him; and, when he stopped at wide Jamieson Avenue, all he wanted to do was keep going, across the big intersection into the suburbs beyond, just swing his car under the jacaranda trees with a blast on the horn and go running up the steps and see her coming running down into his arms, a smile all over her handsome face, everything forgiven and forgotten.

But he crunched his heart and turned right, into central Salisbury.

The city rose up against the clear sky, the new buildings and the old Victorians, the streets wide enough to turn a wagon drawn by sixteen oxen, and all so clean. It was home time and the streets were busy, people hurrying back to their homes and clubs and pubs and cocktail parties. Many were carrying guns. There was the big old High Court where he earned his living, the prime minister's office opposite, the Appeal Court beyond, Parliament and Cecil Square with the bank that kept his money – it was his hometown, and he loved it, and, oh God no, he did not want to give it away.

He parked outside Bude House, left his kit-bag but took his rifle. He took the lift to the seventh floor, to Advocates' Chambers. The clerk's back was turned; he hurried down the corridor, past the row of chambers, into his own.

His desk held a stack of court briefs, tied with red tape. He propped his rifle against the wall and started flicking through briefs.

'I saw you dodging past me. Welcome back.'

He turned. It was the clerk. 'Hello, Dolores,' he smiled. 'I'm in a hurry.'

'Is Pomeroy all right?' Pomeroy was her ex-husband.

'Fine. I flew back with him.'

She relaxed, and turned to business.

'Well, unhurry yourself, you've got lots of work there, first one Monday.'

He sighed. 'But I'm not going to wake up till Monday! What is it?' He scratched through the briefs.

'Company Law,' Dolores said.

'But I'm no good at Company Law and I'm going to sleep till Monday!'

'It's a fat fee.'

'What good is money I can't take out of the country?'

Dolores leant against the door and smiled wearily. 'Here we go again. Where to this time?'

'Australia.'

She shook her head, then ambled into the room. 'But only *after* you've run for parliament, huh?' She sighed and sat down on the other side of the desk, and crossed her plump, sexy legs.

He was flicking through the briefs. 'That's right.'

She looked at him. 'You'll be a voice in the wilderness.'

'I'll at least do my duty. And make a hell of a noise while I lose.'

'So we should just give up everything we've built? Just hand it to savages on a platter?'

'There's a middle course. And if we don't take it, it'll be our heads on that platter.'

She sighed bitterly. 'How goes the war? Are we really losing?'

'We're thrashing them. But we can't keep it up forever.' He put down the briefs and crossed his chambers and closed his door. He sat down heavily. He dragged his hands down his face. 'Dolores, we're going to lose the war, this way. Not this year, not next, but soon. By sheer weight of numbers. And the rest of the world is against us, the whole United Nations.'

'The United Nations,' Dolores said scornfully – 'that Tom and Jerry Show.'

'Indeed,' Mahoney sighed. 'But that's where the economic sanctions come from. We're outlaws, Dolores. And we cannot win unless we also win the hearts and minds of our own black people.' He spread his hands wearily. 'The answer is obvious. We've got to make a deal with our own moderate blacks – bring them into government. Form a *coalition* with them, and unite the people, black and white. Have a wartime coalition, with black co-ministers in the cabinet, and meanwhile write a constitution that guarantees One-Man-One-Vote within the next five years.' He spread his hands. '*Then* we can turn to the world and say, we are truly multi-racial, so stop your sanctions now! And then we can get on with winning this war against the communists. As a united people.' He looked at her wearily. 'That's the only way, Dolores.'

She said bitterly: 'What you're saying is we must fight the black man's battle for him, so that within five years he can rule us with his usual incompetence.'

Mahoney cried softly, 'For God's sake, either way you slice it, it's a black man's war we're fighting. Because if we carry on this way we're going to lose and we're going to have the terrorists marching triumphant into town and ruling *all* of us, black and white, butchering all opposition. We must act *now*, while we've still got the upper hand and can bargain to get the best terms for ourselves under the new constitution. Next year will be too late.'

She was looking at him grimly. He smacked the pile of court-briefs. 'I'll do these cases, but don't accept any new work for me. I'm starting my brief political career.'

She sighed deeply and said, 'You and your sense of duty – I hope it makes you learn some Company Law before Monday.' She stood up wearily. 'Come on, I'll buy you a beer.'

He shook his head. 'I've got to work, Dolores. And sleep.'

She looked at him. 'It's Shelagh, isn't it? You want to wonder who's kissing her now.' He smiled wanly. 'She's just not *worth* it, Joe! Heavens, snap out of it, you could have just about any woman you wanted.' She glared, then tried to make a joke of it. 'Including me. Pomeroy says I should have a fling with you, get your mind off Shelagh.'

He smiled. 'It's a pretty thought.' He added, 'Are you going to the party?'

'Hell no, it's Vulgar Olga's turn tonight.'

'Why do you put up with him?' Mahoney grinned.

'Just because I divorced him doesn't mean I've got to stop *sleeping* with him, does it? One may as well sleep with one's *friends* . . .'

But he did not set to work. He went down the corridor to the library, found Maasdorp on Company Law, slung it in his robes bag, picked up his rifle and left. He started his car, then sat there, wondering where the hell to go. He did not want to go to Pomeroy's house and swim bare-assed and hear how he couldn't get spare parts for his aeroplanes; he did not want to go to Meikles and see the one-legged soldiers drinking, nor to any bars and feel the frantic atmosphere around the guys going into the bush; nor to the Quill Bar and listen to the journalists talking about how we're losing the war; nor the country club and listen to the businessmen crying about sanctions. The only place he wanted to go was Shelagh's apartment.

*

But he did not. He drove through the gracious suburbs with the swimming pools and tennis courts, on to the Umwinzidale Road. The sun was going down, the sky was riotously red. He drove for eleven miles, then turned in the gateway of his farm; he drove over the hill. And there was his house. He stopped at the high security fence, unlocked the gate, drove on. He parked under the frangipani tree, and listened. He heard it, the distant, ululating song coming from his labour compound. It was a reassuring sound, as old as Africa, and he loved it.

It was a simple Rhodesian house that he'd built before he had much money. A row of big rooms connected by a passage, a long red-cement verandah in front, the pillars covered with climbing roses, then thatch over rough-hewn beams. It was comfortably furnished with a miscellany which he had accumulated from departing Rhodesians. He went into his bedroom, slung down his bag and rifle. The room was stuffy but clean; he looked at the big double bed, and it shouted Shelagh at him.

He turned, went to the kitchen, got a beer. He was not ready for work yet. He opened the back door, and stepped out into the dusk.

It was beautiful, as only Africa can be beautiful. The smell and sounds of Africa. The lawns and gardens were surrounded by orchards. He had planted a eucalpytus forest and beyond were sties in which a hundred sows could breed two thousand piglets a year. Stables, chicken runs. He had nearly a thousand acres of grazing and arable land, plenty of water from bore-holes. It was a model farm. He did not make much profit, but what else had he been able to do with his money, except buy more land, start more projects? Beyond his boundaries was African Purchase Area, where black farmers scratched a living. Once upon a time he had cherished the notion that he could help them, by being an example, but that had not worked out. The wide boys from the towns had sabotaged that, burnt his house, killed his prize bull, and Samson – good old Samson, who had been with him on Operation *Noah* – had hanged for it. It was a model farm, but who would want to buy it now? And what good would the money do him? When he emigrated he could only take a thousand dollars.

Mahoney turned grimly towards the swimming pool. And, oh, he did not want to emigrate. He did not want to leave this marvellous land and go and live with the Aussies, where there was nothing important to do except make money. . . .

Suddenly he realized something had changed. He stopped and listened. Then he realized: the singing had stopped.

Not a sound, but the insects. Automatically, he wanted his rifle. He turned and started towards the labour compound, through the orchards.

From fifty yards he could see the huts. He stopped amongst the eucalyptus. He could see his labourers around the fire, their wives and children, silent, staring. He walked closer.

An old man was kneeling near the fire. In the dust were some small bones. Mahoney had never seen the man, but he knew what he was. He was a witchdoctor.

Mahoney stood there. What to do? The practice of witchcraft was a crime, but he did not like to interfere in tribal customs. He stood in the darkness, waiting for the man to speak: then his foreman glanced up. '*Mambo* . . .' he murmured.

Everybody turned, eyes wide in the flickering firelight.

Mahoney called, 'Elijah, please come to my house.'

He turned. The old foreman followed him.

Mahoney walked back through the trees, and stopped outside the kitchen. Elijah came, smiling uncomfortably. Mahoney clapped his hands softly three times, then shook hands. He spoke in Shona: 'I see you, old man.'

'I see the Mambo,' Elijah said, 'and my heart is glad.'

'I have returned and my heart is glad also.'

Mahoney squatted on his haunches. Elijah squatted too, and they faced each other for talk as men should. And the ritual began. It was an empty ritual because Elijah knew the Nkosi had seen the witchdoctor, but it was necessary to say these things to be polite. 'Are your wives well, old man?'

'Ah,' Elijah said, 'my wives are well.' The Nkosi did not have any wives, so Elijah said: 'Is the Nkosi well?'

'I am well. Is Elijah well?'

'Ah,' Elijah said, 'I am well.'

37

'Are the totos well?'

'Ah,' said Elijah, 'the totos are well.' The Nkosi did not have any children, so Elijah said: 'Does the Nkosi sleep well?'

'I sleep well. Does Elijah sleep well?'

Ah, Elijah slept well. Are the cattle well? Ah, the cattle were well; but tnere is drought. Are your grain huts full? Ah, there is drought, but there was grain in the huts. Are your goats well? Yes, the goats were well . . .

Everything was well. Business could begin. 'Old man, is there sickness in the kraal?'

Elijah knew what was coming, and he looked uncomfortable. 'There is no sickness, Nkosi.'

'Are any of the wives barren?'

Elijah said, 'The wives are not barren, Nkosi.'

'Are there any witches living amongst us?'

'Ah!' Elijah did not like to talk about witches. 'I know nothing of witches, Nkosi.'

Mahoney sighed. Once upon a time he had been a young Native Commissioner in charge of an area the size of Scotland or Connecticut. How many men had he sent to jail for this?

'Old man, there are no such things as witches who cast spells to make people ill, or barren, or their cattle sick, or their crops to die. There are no such people as witches who ride through the sky on hyenas in the night.' He made himself glare: 'And it is a crime to consult a witchdoctor to smell out a witch, because stupid people believe him, and they banish the woman he indicates, and she is homeless. And very often she takes her own life. That is a terrible thing, old man!'

Elijah said nothing.

Mahoney breathed. 'The cattle are thin.' He looked up at the cloudless sky. 'How much have you paid the witchdoctor, to make the rains come?'

Elijah shifted uncomfortably. It was no good to lie. 'Each man paid thirty cents, Nkosi.'

Ten men, three dollars, his labour force had just been defrauded of three dollars. What was he going to do about that? Make the witchdoctor give the money back? Drive him off his property? He sighed. No. It would shock and embarrass

38

Elijah, terrify his labourers, show contempt for the peoples' customs which he certainly did not feel. He looked up at the starry sky again. 'I see no clouds.'

Elijah stared at his bony knees. Then he said uncomfortably: 'Does the Nkosi remember my bull, which he wanted to buy for two hundred dollars?'

Mahoney remembered. It was a good animal. He had offered several times to buy it, because he needed another bull and Elijah's land was over-grazed. The old man shifted. 'I will sell him to you for fifty dollars . . . '

Mahoney looked at him. '*Fifty?* Why? Is he sick?'

'Ah,' Elijah said, 'he is very sick.'

Mahoney sighed. He did not want to buy more cattle, if he was emigrating. He said, 'Have no more to do with witch-doctors. Where is this bull?'

'I have brought him to your cattle pen,' the old man said.

Mahoney got up resignedly, fetched his rifle, and followed the old man to the cattle pen beyond the eucalyptus trees.

The animal was sick all right. It was very thin, its head hanging. Mahoney knew what was wrong with it; because the native land was overstocked, it had eaten something bad. It would not live. He said wearily, 'Fifty dollars?'

He counted out the notes. Elijah clapped his hands and took them. Mahoney regretfully walked to the bull's head. He raised the rifle. There was a deafening crack, and the animal collapsed.

'Cut it up, and hang it, then put it in my deep freeze, as ration-meat for your family.'

'Thank you, Nkosi!'

Mahoney looked at the dead bull; the blood was making a tinkling sound. He said, 'Elijah, your land is over-grazed. You could have sold this animal last year for *two hundred* dollars.' He looked at him. 'Why did you not sell him to me then?'

Elijah looked genuinely surprised, then held up his hand. 'Nkosi, how much money have I got in my hand today?'

Mahoney looked at him. 'Fifty dollars.'

Elijah held up the handful of money, and shook it.

'And if I had sold him to you last year, how much money would I have in my hand today?'

Mahoney stared at him. Then shook his head, and laughed.

The sky was full of stars. From the labour compound came the sound of a drum, the rise and fall of singing. The Company Law brief was spread on his study table, but Mahoney sat on the verandah of the womanless house, staring out at the moonlight, listening to the singing; and, oh no, he did not want to leave his Africa. Maybe he should have stayed a Nature Commissioner in the bush, with people who needed men of goodwill like him; to help them, to judge them, to show them how to rotate their crops and put back something into the land, how to improve their cattle; someone who knew all their troubles, who attended their indabas and counselled them, the representative of Kweeni, Elizabeth the Second, by the Grace of God, Queen, Defender of the Faith . . . Maybe that was his natural role, to serve – and God knows thev'll need men like me for the next two hundred years . . .

'And if I had sold him to you last year, how much money would I have in my hand today, Nkosi?' Oh, dear, this is Africa. *Today!* Today the Winds of Change have driven the white man away. Today we have his roads and railways and schools and hospitals. Today we have fifty dollars . . . And tomorrow when the roads start crumbling and the sewerage does not work any more, that has nothing whatsoever to do with today.

Joe Mahoney paced his verandah in the moonlight. It was so sad. Africa was dying, but not in the name of Partnership anymore like in those big brave days of *Operation Noah*, but in the name of Today. And tomorrow the new prime minister will be President-for-Life of a one-party state and there will be no more One Man One Vote, and the roads will be breaking up and the railways breaking down. And he heard Max shout: 'Then why the hell do you want to give them more power?'

'Because that's the only way we can win the war and hang on to just enough!'

But that is only half the godawful story of the dying of

40

Africa, Shelagh. The other half is even more godawful. Because the African counts his wealth in wives and cattle, and in daughters whom he sells as brides for more cattle – his standing is counted by the number of children he has. Twenty years ago there were *two* hundred million Africans in the whole of Africa, today there are *four* hundred million, in twenty years there'll be *eight hundred million – and they can't even feed themselves now.*

So what's it going to be like in twenty years? But even that's not all. What about the forests these starving millions are going to slash trying to feed themselves? What about the earth that's going to turn to dust because they've sucked everything out and put nothing back? What about the rain that won't come because the forests are gone? And what about the wild animals? Where are they going to go? The African word for game is *nyama*, the same word as 'meat'!

Suddenly, out of the corner of his eye, he saw a man. He turned. Another figure followed. It was Elijah, followed by the witchdoctor. Elijah raised his hand. 'The nganga wishes to speak with Nkosi.'

Mahoney sighed. He thought the man had gone. 'Let him speak, then.'

The witchdoctor came forward, dropped to his haunches, his hands clasped. He shook them, muttering, then flung them open. The bones scattered on the ground.

Mahoney stared down at them. And for a moment he felt the age-old awe at being in the presence of the medicine-man. The witchdoctor looked at the bones; then he picked them up, rattled them again, and threw them again. He stared at them.

He threw them a third time. For a full minute he studied them; then he began to point. At one, then another, muttering. Mahoney waited, in suspense. Then the man rocked back on his haunches, closed his eyes. For a minute he rocked. Then he began. 'There are three women. They all have yellow hair . . . But the first woman is a ghost. She is dead . . .'

Mahoney was astonished. *Suzie*. . . .

'The second woman has an unhappy spirit. This woman, you must not marry.'

41

Mahoney's heart was pounding. The witchdoctor could know about Shelagh from Elijah, but not about Suzie.

'The third woman . . .' The witchdoctor stopped, his eyes closed, rocking on his haunches. 'She has the wings of an eagle . . . ' He hesitated, eyes closed. 'She will fall to earth. Like a stone from the sky . . . '

Mahoney tried to dismiss it as nonsense; but he was in suspense. He wanted to know why he must not marry the second woman.

The old man rocked silently.

'And you too have wings. You will go on long journeys, even across the sea. You have a big ship . . . ' The man stopped, eyes still closed. 'You have spirits with you . . . But you do not hear them . . . ' He was quite still. 'There are too many guns.'

Guns? Mahoney thought. Too right there were too many guns. But ships? He waited, pent. But the man shook his head. He opened his eyes, and got up. Mahoney stared at him.

'Nganga,' he demanded, 'what have you not told me?'

The man shook his head. He hesitated, then said: 'The Nkosi must heed the spirits.'

And he raised his hand in a salute, and walked away in the moonlight.

Mahoney sat on his verandah, with a new glass of whisky, trying to stop turning over in his mind what the witchdoctor had said. But he was still under the man's spell. *'This woman you must not marry . . .'*

Suddenly he glimpsed a flash of car lights, coming over the hill, and he jerked. He watched them coming, half-obscured by the trees, and his heart was pounding in hope. They swung on to his gates a hundred yards away, and stopped. He got up. The car door opened and a woman got out.

Mahoney came bounding down the steps and down the drive.

She stood by the car, hands on her hips, a smile on her beautiful face. He strode up to the gates, grinning. 'Hullo,

42

stranger,' Shelagh said. He unlocked the gate shakily. She held her hand out flat, to halt him. 'Why didn't you come to see me?'

'You know why.'

She smiled. 'Very well . . . What do you want first? The bad news or the terrible news?'

He grinned at her: 'What news?'

She took a breath. 'The bad news is I'm pregnant.'

Mahoney stared at her; and he felt his heart turn over. He took a step towards her, a smile breaking all over his face, but she stepped backwards.

'The very bad news is: I've decided not to have an abortion.'

And, oh God, the joy of her in his arms, the feel of her lovely body against him again, and the taste and smell of her, and the laughter and the kissing.

Later, lying deep in the big double bed, she whispered: 'Ask me again.'

He said again, '*Now* will you marry me?'

She lay quite still in his arms for a long moment.

'Yes.'

The moon had gone. He could not see the storm clouds gathering. They were deep asleep when the first claps of thunder came, and the rain.

CHAPTER 4

And so it was that Joe Mahoney got married, stood for parliament, and bought a Britannia cargo aeroplane.

The wedding was the following Friday, before the District Commissioner in Umtali, a hundred and fifty miles from Salisbury. The bride wore red. Nobody was present except the Clerk of Court, as witness, and Mahoney had such a ringing in his ears that he went temporarily deaf. Afterwards they drove up into the Inyanga mountains, to the Troutbeck Inn, where they spent a dazed weekend. On Monday Mahoney got rid of all his cases to other counsel, and started his short political career.

He was standing as an independent. He had posters printed, bought radio and television time. He chose the most prestigious constituency to contest, so he would make the most noise. He made many speeches, visited over a thousand homes, had countless arguments. Not in his wildest dreams did he expect to win; his only interest was the opportunity to tell people the truth. He didn't expect his message to make him popular. 'Let's make it a grand slam!' the government propaganda cried. 'Let's show the world we are a united people!' *Let us BE a united people!*' Mahoney bellowed. '*White and Black united to fight the enemy!*' He drew good crowds, much heckling, and few votes. On polling day the government won every white seat, and there was cheering.

Thus Joseph Mahoney did his duty, then washed his hands of Africa and prepared to emigrate to Australia; but ended up buying a big cargo aeroplane instead, which happened like this.

In those days there were many sanction-busters, men who made their living by exporting Rhodesian products to the outside world in defiance of the United Nations sanctions against Rhodesia, and Tex Weston was one. He was a swash-buckling American with prematurely grey hair, a perfect smile, and a Texan drawl that he could change to an English accent in mid-word; he owned a number of large freight airplanes which plied worldwide, changing their registration documents like chameleons. Tex Weston made a great deal of money by dealing in everything from butter to arms, with anybody. Today it might be ten million eggs, tomorrow hand-grenades. Tex Weston talked a good, quiet game, and claimed he owned a 'consultancy company' in Lichtenstein which devised plans for clandestine military operations for client states and put together the team to do the job. In the Quill Bar, where Mahoney did most of his drinking with the foreign correspondents, they called Tex Weston 'The Vulture', and nobody knew whether to believe him, although it was suspected that occasionally the government employed foreign professionals

44

to carry out operations against the enemy in other countries. But it was undeniable that Tex Weston was once a major in the American Green Berets, that he was a supplier of arms to Rhodesia, that he knew all about aircargo, and that the Rhodesian government sorely needed the likes of him to bust the sanctions.

Now, on the day after the election, a Portuguese sanction-busting aeroplane was shot up by terrorists as it took off from a bush airstrip, and made an emergency landing in Salisbury. The next day Mahoney was in the Quill Bar, waiting for his wife to finish school and trying hard to spend some of the money he could not take with him to Australia, when Tex Weston sauntered up to him. 'I hear you're leaving us for Sydney. I fly Down Under a bit, and sometimes need an understanding lawyer.'

Mahoney smiled wanly. He wondered whether Tex Weston didn't find it a disadvantage being so good-looking. Men distrusted him for it. But he was one of the few people who quite liked the man.

'You'd better get one who understands some Australian law. I've got to re-qualify first.'

Weston shook his head sympathetically. 'How long will that take?'

'A couple of years. Of pure fun.'

Weston smiled. 'What about money? You're only allowed to take a thousand dollars, aren't you?'

Mahoney wondered whether Weston was about to offer to do a bit of smuggling. 'Shelagh'll get a job teaching. And we'll buy a bit of jewellery here and flog it there.'

'You never get your money back on that sort of thing.'

'As long as I get *some* money back.'

Tex said, 'Tell you what. There's this Portuguese cargo plane that got shot up. The owner's lost his nerve, he's selling her cheap: twenty-five thousand pounds, payable in Rhodesian dollars. She's in good condition.'

Mahoney looked at him, taken aback.

'What do I do with a bloody great aeroplane? I've just sold my little one.'

Weston said, 'Fly her to Europe, sell her there. You should

45

make a profit. But even if you lose a bit, you'll have got twenty-odd thousand pounds out. Which is better than it sitting here in the bank until the communists shoot their way into town.'

'But I can't fly a big aeroplane!'

Tex laughed. 'The co-pilot's still aboard, wondering about his next job. Pay his salary and he'll fly you to Kingdom Come. Out-of-work pilots come pretty cheap.'

Mahoney's mind was boggling. 'But how do I go about selling an aeroplane in Europe?'

'There's plenty of brokers – planes are for sale all the time.' He shrugged. 'She's a good buy. The Britannia is an excellent workhorse. She's worth double, I guess.'

'But even fifty thousand sounds suspiciously cheap for a big aeroplane.'

Tex shook his head. 'A popular misconception. Planes are like ships. In Singapore there're hundreds of freighters going rusty. You could pick up a good one for a hundred thousand dollars.'

Mahoney was staring at him. 'And what is fuel to Europe going to cost?'

'A few thousand pounds. But you can get a cargo to cover that; Rhodesians are screaming to export. My agents will get you a cargo tomorrow.' He added, 'She's a bargain, but have your pal Pomeroy check her over.'

Mahoney wondered why the great Tex Weston was being so nice to him. 'If she's such a bargain, why aren't you buying her?'

Tex smiled. 'I've already got twenty. What do I need the hassle for? But it's different for you, you're an emigrant.'

The next week, Joe Mahoney and his patched-up Britannia took off for Lisbon with a cargo of tobacco. Mahoney had three big diamond rings and three enormous gold bracelets in his pocket. The pilot was a fifty-year-old American with a gravelly voice called Ed Hazeltine. Pomeroy had put up five thousand pounds of the price, for a piece of the action. Dolores, his clerk, had put up two thousand pounds. Pomeroy was co-pilot and engineer, though he was not licensed for Britannias. Mrs Shelagh Mahoney was not aboard: she would join her husband later, in Australia, when he had sold the aircraft, rings and bracelets and found them a place to live.

When they were over the Congo, in the moonlight, Mahoney said: 'What're you going to do when we've sold her, Ed?'

'Look for another sucker who owns airplanes,' Ed rumbled. He added: '*If* you sell her.'

'You think that'll be hard?' Mahoney demanded.

'Britannias?' Ed said. 'Nobody can make a living with these old things, except bus-stopping around Africa where nobody else wants to go.'

When they got to Lisbon there was a telex from Tex Weston offering to buy the aircraft for ten thousand pounds.

'The bastard,' Mahoney said.

He spent that day telephoning aircraft brokers all over Europe, but nobody wanted an old Britannia this week. He spent the next day selling a gold bracelet and feverishly telephoning freight agents, trying to find a cargo, because the most terrifying thing about owning an aircraft is how much it costs on the ground. The next day it took off for Nigeria with a cargo of machinery. Mahoney felt he had aged years. As soon as they were at a safe altitude he said grimly, 'O.K., Ed, start showing me how to fly this thing.'

There was no cargo for the return flight awaiting them in Nigeria, although the Lisbon freight-agent had promised one. In desperation Mahoney went to the market place and bought seventeen tons of pineapples, as his own cargo.

'So now we're in the fruit business?' Pomeroy said.

'We've got to pay for the fuel somehow.'

'Where to, boss?' Ed said.

'To wherever they like pineapples. To Sweden. And stop calling me boss.'

'We ain't got enough fuel for Sweden, boss.'

'To England, then,' Mahoney said.

As soon as they were airborne he climbed back into Pomeroy's seat. 'O.K., Ed, now you've really got to teach me to fly this bloody awful machine.'

'Boss, you can't operate this airplane with your private pilot's licence, you've got to go to aviation school.'

'*Start teaching me, Ed!*'

PART 2

PART 2

CHAPTER 5

It was a hand-written letter, in a brisk scrawl:

> The Managing Director
> Redcoat Cargo Airlines Ltd
> Gatwick Airport, England.
> Dear Mr Mahoney,
>
> I read your letter to *The Times* about the escalating
> costs of aviation fuel. I will shortly be floating a
> company to build aircraft which will be very econ-
> omical on fuel, and I am seeking all the moral support
> I can get. Plainly it is vital to build these aircraft in
> (to quote your *Times* letter) a hostile world of oil
> bandits holding us to ransom with ever-increasing
> fuel prices, a world full of poor countries plunging
> deeper into poverty and despair because of oil prices,
> becoming ripe for communist takeover as a con-
> sequence. I would like to meet you. Rest assured I
> am not asking you, or Redcoat Cargo Airlines, for
> money. I will telephone you.
>
> Sincerely,
> (Major) Malcolm Todd

The telephone call, from a coin-box, was equally brisk. So
was the meeting, in a pub called The Fox and Rabbit.
Major Todd thanked him for coming, bought him half a
pint and got straight to the point, as if rehearsed. He was
a grey-haired man, mid-fifties, with a cherubic face and
bespectacled eyes that seldom left Mahoney's; he stood very
still while he spoke:

'I have a Master of Science degree and until the year before
last I was in the Royal Engineers. Five years ago I was given
the task of formulating a plan for moving British troops to
various battle-zones in Europe, North Africa and the Middle
East; I had to assume that the Channel, Gibraltar and Suez
were blocked by enemy navy, our airforce fully engaged in

challenging enemy airstrikes, and that all ports, airfields and railways in Europe were in enemy hands.'

Mahoney was intrigued. The Major went on: 'After considering every form of transport – and of course all methods of breaking blockades – I and my staff concluded that the quickest, cheapest and safest system would be the transportation of troops and armour by airship.'

'By *airship*?'Mahoney interposed.

'Yes. We calculated that an airship with a lifting capacity of seven million cubic feet of helium – not hydrogen – could airlift almost a thousand men, at a hundred miles an hour, at a fraction of the fuel cost of any other vehicle, exposing the troops to less vulnerability-time en route. Remember that all airfields are assumed to be in enemy hands. An airship, however, can hover anywhere, like a helicopter, and lower its troops by scrambling net.'

Mahoney's mind was wrestling with the image of being flown by airship into a hail of terrorist gunfire. The Major glared at him. 'You're thinking that because of its size an airship is vulnerable. But we're talking about the airship as a troop *carrier*, not as an assault vehicle. As a carrier, it is no more vulnerable than a troop ship, or a train, or a convoy of trucks, and it goes much faster than all of them! A paratroop plane is also a big target for modern weapons, and when hit it crashes to earth with all her men! Whereas an airship, even if badly holed, would sink *slowly* as the gas escaped, giving the troops an excellent chance of survival.' He paused briefly. 'But there is another big advantage. Whereas your poor bloody paratrooper must often fly to his drop-zone through airspace dominated by the enemy, the airship can take a safe, circuitous route because it can stay airborne for days. To reach a battle zone in Germany, say, troops could be flown into the Atlantic, avoiding the Channel, swing over north Africa, and approach Germany from the east – even attacking the enemy from behind.'

Mahoney was fascinated. The Major continued:

'Plus the advantage of costs. Such an airship would, on today's prices, cost only about ten million pounds. A big troop plane, say a 747, costs *sixty* million pounds. The government, therefore, could afford to buy six airships in place of one 747.

Expressed another way, it could afford to *lose* six airships before it cost the same as one 747. And the airship is really no bigger target for today's weapons than a 747.'

Mahoney was intrigued – and almost sold on the Major. 'What did the Army say?'

Malcolm Todd glowered. 'My report was well received by the General Staff, but it'll be years before it is implemented because of damn-fool politicians.' He took a breath. 'So, I decided to retire and devote myself to the resurrection of the airship *commercially* – as *cargo*-carrying and passenger aircraft. I formed a private company to consult aeronautical designers. We now have all the necessary designs. With modern technology we can build perfectly safe airships.' He burrowed into his raincoat pocket and pulled out a large envelope, which he slapped on the bar. 'Here is a summary of our achievements – please read them.'

He looked at Mahoney. 'From your letter to *The Times*, it's obvious that you're concerned about the under-developed nations and how oil costs are crippling them.' He tapped the envelope. 'The airship is their answer. Uses a fifth of the fuel. It would enable them to exploit remote, mountainous, desert and jungle regions where there are no roads or airfields: the airship could simply hover to deliver the mining equipment or whatever, winch up the produce, and carry it away. It would revolutionize their economies!'

Mahoney was grappling with the enormity of the idea. 'Marvellous,' he agreed sincerely. He left out, 'If it works.' He had a feeling he would get an earful from the Major if he said that. 'But what do you want from me?'

The Major suddenly looked thoroughly uncomfortable. 'Not money.' He cleared his throat. 'But, in short, until I float my company on the Stock Exchange, I'm flat broke. All my savings, and my military pension, have been used up in research and in buying a lot of important tools and equipment that have come my way cheaply.' He cleared his throat again. 'I'm not asking for money, but Redcoat Cargo Airlines owns a chunk of farmland near Gatwick Airport, which has an old cottage on it, in disrepair. I would like to rent it.' He blinked. 'I confess I will be unable to actually pay any rent until happier days come along. But meanwhile I undertake to make the cottage fully functional again.' He smiled for the first time. 'I am an engineer, and as good with my hands as I am with my head.'

CHAPTER 6

It was a windy, overcast day, and Joe Mahoney was grateful for it, though he detested the cold. He even wished it would come pissing down with rain. He stood in the goods-shed and watched the forklift crossing the tarmac towards his aeroplane. It stopped at the open tail, lifted the crate into the plane. A second forklift was trundling back for another.

'Slow down,' Mahoney said to the superintendent, 'she's half full already.'

The super smiled. 'It's your money.' He called, 'Have a smoke-oh, Bert.'

'But be ready to look busy when they arrive.'

Mahoney turned and paced through the bleak corporation shed. It was packed with cargo, consigned with different airlines. The whole cold place was filled by plaintive cheeping and all the cargo was dominated by thousands of stacked cardboard cartons holding two hundred thousand day-old chicks. Mahoney walked to the nearest stack, lifted a lid. One hundred fluffy, yellow chicks cocked their little eyes up at him, cheeping. He looked at them. They were twenty-four hours old and they had not yet taken their first morsel of food or drop of water. They were still living off their body fluids, but in twenty-four hours they'd die without food and water.

Mahoney took one out. It sat in his hand, little wings hunched, completely unperturbed. Mahoney smiled sadly at it. In three months it would have its head chopped off. It was enough to turn you vegetarian.

His walkie-talkie radio rasped: 'Here they come, Joe!'

He hurried through the shed, straightening his tie. 'O.K.,' he yelled, 'get those forklifts working!' He strode on to the tarmac.

54

Coming past the row of hangars were two black cars. The second car was a Rolls Royce, flying the Ghanaian pennant. In the back sat three black gentlemen.

The leading car came to a halt. It had two white men in it. Mahoney put on his most charming smile, and opened the door.

'Good day, Mr Pennington! Welcome to Redcoat!'

A dapper little man, Mr Pennington looked thoroughly peeved. 'This is Mr Johnson, PCC's house-magazine photographer.'

Mahoney shook hands. 'Well,' he said brightly, 'your cargo is nearly all loaded!' He pointed.

'I thought', Mr Pennington said, 'that you would be ready for take-off by now.'

'Well,' Mahoney said, 'all airlines use the Corporation's shed and labour, so sometimes we *do* have small delays.' He strode towards the other car as it came to a halt. He flung open the door. 'Good day, Consul-General! Welcome to Redcoat!'

A large black gentleman climbed out. He shook Mahoney's hand amiably. 'This', he said, 'is the head of our Information Department, and our photographer.'

'How do you do.' Mahoney took the Consul-General's arm. 'You have met the publicity director of PCC, of course?'

'Indeed, sir!' Mr Pennington's manner had changed entirely. 'I'm sorry it's such a miserable day but it's a very important one for PCC. We hope this is only the first of many contracts with your government.'

'And Redcoat will always be ready to fly your goods,' Mahoney got in cheerfully, rubbing his hands. 'Well, gentlemen? Do you want to take your photographs immediately, or after some refreshment?'

'But you haven't finished loading.' Mr Pennington's manner had changed again. 'We need a picture of the plane taking off!'

Mahoney's heart sank. 'But isn't it better to get photographs of the forklifts working, more action and all that?'

Before they could answer, he turned to lead the way to the

55

aircraft. Mr Pennington hurried up beside him. 'Mister, er . . . ?'

'Mahoney.'

'Whether or not Redcoat get any more contracts from us depends on prompt delivery. These fertilizers are urgently needed in Ghana and they were supposed to fly out yesterday.'

Mahoney wanted to say: Listen, Mr Pencilton, I'm sorry about the delay but if you knew Africa you'd know that it doesn't matter a damn that your fertilizers are late because in Accra they're going to sit for weeks while corrupt officials haggle with other corrupt officials about who gets what rake-off. Instead he said, 'Mr Pennington, our motto is "*The Redcoats Are Coming*" . . . We *deliver*. To out-of-the-way places with strange-sounding names. More, Better, Cheaper, Faster . . . '

It was an excruciating hour, standing in the cold, a fixed smile on his face as they posed for the photographers, shaking hands with each other, under the wings, on the forklifts, on the flightdeck. All the time Pennington whispering complaints that the loading was *still* not finished, that Redcoat better pull up its socks. Mahoney assured him Redcoat would. For an hour the handshaking exercise went on. Then the last crate was loaded, the tail closed, the plane crammed with PCC's fine products. 'Well,' Mr Pennington said, 'I presume you're now ready for take-off and we can get our final photograph?'

'Indeed,' Mahoney said. 'And while we're waiting for the crew, would you join our staff in a few drinks? They're all waiting to meet you!'

'Mr Mahoney,' Mr Pennington said testily, 'I thought the crew were ready!'

'Any moment now, Mr Pennington.' (He so nearly said Pencilton.) 'They only sign on duty shortly before take-off because they're only allowed to do so many duty-hours a month, by law. They'll be arriving any moment. This way please, gentlemen . . . '

56

It was a big galvanized-iron hangar, but it never had an aeroplane inside it because it was full of engines under repair, plus Redcoat vehicles, spares and gear. Redcoat Cargo Airlines had only two aircraft and they were never on the ground long enough to squeeze them into the hangar, and it would have been a financial disaster if they had. Redcoat stayed afloat only because its aircraft stayed aloft, by being repaired the moment anything went wrong, in the middle of the night if necessary, out on the tarmac while the new cargo was being loaded. The other engines in the hangar belonged to other airlines whom Redcoat serviced in a desperate effort to pay its way. Every time he entered the hangar, Mahoney, for whom engines were one of life's mysteries, wondered where the money came from. He had intended showing his customers the hangar and explaining what a wonderful success-story Redcoat was, but Mr Pennington was having none of that. Over the first cup of tea in the corner office, he got Mahoney aside.

'I would like a word with the managing director.'

It was on the tip of Mahoney's tongue to say the boss was out. 'I *am* the managing director.'

'I see . . . ' He drew himself up. 'This shipment was supposed to leave yesterday, then it was put off until this morning. Now it's four o'clock.'

The hand-shaking exercise was in danger of degenerating into a hand-wringing exercise. Just then Dolores exclaimed: 'Oh dear, it's started raining!'

'Oh *dear*!' Mahoney cried, turning to the window.

'*Damn!*' Mr Pennington said.

'I'm afraid', Mahoney turned sadly to the Consul, 'that you won't get your photograph of take-off.' He brightened: 'But never mind, we took some last week, specially for you!'

Like a conjurer, Dolores produced a pile of glossy photographs. 'Taken in sunshine,' Mahoney said, 'much better.' It was a photograph of the Britannia taking off, not the Canadair CL44. He waited with baited breath.

57

Mr Pennington looked at the photograph with distaste. 'Good,' said the Consul, who didn't think much of the English climate. 'Don't you think?'

The moment the Rolls Royce disappeared out the gate, Mahoney went racing across the tarmac, into the Corporation shed.

'*O.K.*,' he shouted, '*get her unloaded! And load the chicks!*'

CHAPTER 7

On one side of the road was Gatwick Airport, acres of building, hangars and carparks: on the other side was the pub called The Fox and Rabbit; down a wooded lane stood Redcoat House, in tranquil isolation. Beyond, the company's farmland ran up to a hill, behind which was the home of the managing director of Redcoat Cargo Airlines. A plaque by the front door of the House was inscribed with an impressive list of companies all beginning with the word 'Redcoat'. But Redcoat House was an old barn. It wasn't even legal. The land was not zoned for commercial purposes. The municipal council had been threatening Redcoat for two years, but Mahoney kept stalling them. One day the council would get Redcoat out, and it was going to cost a lot in legal fees, but it was a lot cheaper than renting legitimate premises. So was the use of Tex Weston's hangar, but the price was that Weston insisted on being on the board of directors, and that the rent be in the form of Redcoat shares.

That worried Mahoney. During the first year, Weston was so seldom in England that he did not matter; but then he began to show up more frequently. As a director, he was entitled to know all business details. Mahoney began to get the feeling that the man was biding his time.

'Fire him off the bleedin' board,' Pomeroy said.

'Then what will you use for a hangar?' Shelagh wanted to know.

'He won't kick us out,' Pomeroy said. 'We're no threat to

to his routes. We even hire his engineers if I can't cope, like.'

'We've got to get our own hangar,' Mahoney said. 'He's got nearly twenty-five percent of the shares already.'

'What'll we use for money?' Shelagh said. 'You and your grandiose schemes.'

'Earn it.'

'*Earn* it! We've only got two aircraft and they're working flat out – and we're still broke!'

'We've got to get rid of that Britannia and buy another Canadair.'

'But the Canadair costs a hundred pounds per hour more to run!'

'But it carries ten tons more cargo.'

'Good God,' she cried, 'where're we going to get the money? We couldn't sell that Britannia – that's how we're stuck in this godawful business! Listen – you said we were going to stay in just until we had enough money to get out.'

'That's why we've got to find another Canadair,' Pomeroy said.

'God! Next you'll be trying to build one of Todd's airships . . .' She got up and walked out of the board meeting.

Dolores shot Mahoney a sympathetic look. Pomeroy and Ed avoided his eye.

That afternoon, after a great deal of hesitation, Mahoney telephoned Shelagh's psychiatrist, and made an appointment to see him that night, at ten o'clock. Then he drove slowly home, to dress for dinner at his Inn of Court, where he was a goddamn law-student again.

It was a beautiful cottage, two hundred years old, with a thatch roof and low beams and small windows; it needed a lot doing to it. The garden was overgrown but completely surrounded by woods, which cut off the airport noise. Mahoney parked the car, and entered the kitchen door with a heavy heart.

'Shelagh?'

She was bathing, and did not hear him. He walked through

59

the living room, up the narrow stairs, down the corridor to Catherine's room, calling, '*Is this where the beautiful Miss Mahoney lives?*' There was a squeak and a toddle of little girl across the room, all curls and smiles, arms outstretched. Mahoney picked her up, and hugged her and kissed her, and his eyes were burning at the thought of losing her.

He left ten minutes later, in his only decent suit. It was grey pinstripe, which was unfortunate because his Inn of Court required black. Shelagh was still in the bath; he called goodbye, got into the car, and drove slowly through the woods on to the road for London, thinking.

He parked and walked into Holborn, through an arch, into the courtyard of Gray's Inn. He walked grimly across into the cloakroom. He took a gown, paid the clerk, signed a register, and walked into the Inn. It was crowded, students finding places at the tables, a clamour of voices. Half the students seemed to be African. He muttered to himself: 'I thought more than three constituted an Unlawful Assembly . . . '

At the top of the old hall was a dais, where the benchers dined. Below were rows of tables, the length of the hall. There were stained-glass windows and high beams. Mahoney walked up an aisle, and sat down at the first empty place. 'Good evening,' he said.

He was sitting between a portly black gentleman and a thin Indian gentleman. Opposite sat a fresh-faced Englishman, and a pretty Chinese woman.

'I think you happen to be Mr Senior of our mess tonight,' the young man said, 'if you're·sitting in that place.'

'Oh, very well.' He reached for the strip of paper and printed his name. He got the names of the other three and printed them in order of their seniority within the mess: Mr Fothergill, Mr Obote, Mrs Chan. He then asked for the names of the people in the messes immediately to right and left of his, and printed them, in order of seniority. Just then there was a loud knock, and all the students stood up.

The door opened, and in walked the benchers, a solemn single file. The senior bencher said grace. Everybody sat down and the tucker began.

Waiters went scurrying down the aisles thumping down

tureens of soup. As Mr Senior, Mahoney started ladling. The wine steward passed with two baskets.

Mahoney filled the glasses and picked up his elaborately: 'Mrs Chan, Mr Fothergill, Mr Obote, lady and gentlemen of the best, your good health. May you live long, plead well and judge with humility.'

He drank solemnly to that. After a minute Mr Fothergill proposed his toast to the mess. They smiled politely. They resumed their soup. Mr Obote picked up his glass.

'Mr Mahoney, Mr Fothergill, Mrs Chan, I wish you good health.' He added with a twinkle: 'May your children be as numerous as the stars in the sky, and your goats and cattle even more numerous.'

Mahoney laughed and slapped the black man on the shoulder. 'Thank you, Mr Obote!'

Mrs Chan piped up, blushing: 'Mr Mahoney, Mr Fothergill, Mr Obote, I wish you good health and happiness.'

Mahoney took a weary breath and muttered, 'Let's get it over with.' He leant forward and addressed the mess to his left. 'Mr Senior of the Upper Mess, may I interrupt your scintillating conversation by proposing a toast?'

'Why, certainly, Mr Senior, if you can tear yourself away from the illuminations of your own mess.'

'With difficulty, Mr Senior.' He read from the list: 'Mr Johnson, Mr Patel, Mr Patel, and Mr Patel – may your cups run over with happiness and may your seed, both severally and jointly, be more numerous than the stars in the sky, your progeny even more fertile, and theirs after them, and your herds even more prolific than the whole damn lot of you put together.' He added, 'All this in your lifetime.'

He drank. The two messes were laughing, except Mr Fothergill. Mahoney then turned the other way and said, 'Mr Senior of the Lower Mess, may I pray your silence while I drink to your sterling health? . . .'

And so on. *Lord*, Mahoney thought, *this is supposed to train lawyers?*

Finally they were through the dessert and on to the coffee and port. Then the shouting started.

'Up, Junior!'

61

But Mr Junior of the lowermost mess, the person closest to the door, studiously ignored the call.

'*Up Junior! . . . Come on, Junior! . . .*'

For five minutes the shouting went on. Finally Mr Junior stood up. Except Mr Junior was a woman. Immediately the jeering and bellowing began.

'*Mr Senior,*' Ms Junior shouted across the hall, '*may we have permission to smoke?*'

The boos and jeers drowned her. Mr Senior of the uppermost mess studiously ignored the request.

'*Louder, Junior!*'

Ms Junior shouted again and the boos and jeers doubled.

'*On the table, Junior!*'

Ms Junior was looking very embarrassed, though she was smiling. She climbed on to her chair, put her hands to her mouth and bellowed.

'*Mr Senior, may we have permission to smoke?*'

'*Shut up, Junior!*' '*Louder, Junior!*' Mahoney put on his spectacles and looked at Mr Senior of the uppermost mess. He was sipping his port as if nothing was happening. Mahoney looked at Ms Junior, and he felt sorry for her. She was about thirty, ten years older than the youngsters ragging her, and Mahoney thought she was beautiful. She had tawny hair in a bun and her embarrassed smile was wide. Now she was clambering up on to the table. She was tall, with good legs.

'*Mr Senior!*' she bellowed – but Mahoney could only see her mouth moving. He sighed. This was supposed to teach law-students the art of public speaking? Mr Senior was looking up as if he had just noticed something.

'I beg your pardon, Junior?'

Laughter and sudden silence. She started again: '*May we*' – and the gleeful catcalls burst out again.

'Smoke?' Mr Senior said, looking puzzled. 'Oh, very well.'

The woman climbed down off the table, and blew out her cheeks.

Mr Mahoney began to get up. 'Well, Mrs Chan and gentlemen, excuse me . . .'

'One moment, Mr Mahoney, please!' Mr Fothergill said.

He stood up. He bellowed: 'Mr Senior in Hall!' The hall fell silent. Fothergill shouted: 'I have two serious charges to make against Mr Mahoney . . . Firstly, when proposing a toast to our mess, he first addressed Mrs Chan, who is Junior of our mess, instead of first addressing me. Secondly, he is wearing a grey pinstriped suit.'

Mr Fothergill sat down, grinning.

'Mr Mahoney,' Senior in Hall intoned, 'how do you answer these weighty allegations?'

Mahoney stood up.

'Mr Senior,' he shouted, 'they are as weightless as the area between Mr Fothergill's ears.' (Laughter.) 'Surely it is customary, even in those dark corners of England which Mr Fothergill hails from, to address a lady first? If I am wrong, I am glad to be so, and my only regret is that I had to toast Mr Fothergill at all.' (Laughter.) 'As to the second charge, my suit is not grey pinstripe, but a white suit with a broad grey stripe in it. I am in the ice-cream business, you see.'

He sat down midst more laughter. Senior in Hall passed judgement.

'On the first charge you are cautioned. On the second, you are fined a bottle of port.'

Mahoney signalled to the waiter . . . At the next table a young man was standing and shouting:

'Mr Senior, I have a most weighty complaint. This gentleman – and I use that in the loosest possible sense of the word – stole my bread roll!'

'Goodnight, everybody,' Mahoney whispered to the mess. He turned, bowed to Senior in Hall, and hurried out. He handed his gown back. As he emerged from the robing room, the beautiful woman was coming out of the hall.

'Well done,' he smiled at her sympathetically.

She rolled her lovely eyes. 'Isn't it a laugh-a-minute?' He caught a trace of an Australian accent.

Mahoney hurried on through the courtyard, out into Holborn. He half regretted that he had not struck up a conversation with the tawny Australian. But what was the point?

He got into his car, and sat there a minute, not relishing what he had to do now.

The house was in Hampstead, but the consulting-room was small. 'It's very good of you to see me so late, Dr Jacobson,' Mahoney said.

'The name's Fred.' He was unsmiling. 'I don't know what you expect of this meeting. Every patient's problem is confidential, so I can't tell you what's *wrong* with Shelagh – if anything. You're not really consulting me as a patient, so' – he looked at his watch – 'the quickest will be if I ask you questions, like you do in court. I warn you, some of them may be painful.'

'That doesn't matter.'

'Oh? O.K. Why's your marriage on the rocks?'

Mahoney was taken aback. *On the rocks!* This expert thought it was that bad?

'Shelagh hates living in England,' he said.

'Why? And what can you do about it?'

Mahoney sighed. 'The weather. The people. She feels they're narrow. The cost of living . . . Our house. My job.'

'And?'

'And', Mahoney said, 'she misses her job in African Education.'

'The last thing you mention. Because you consider it unimportant? And why aren't you living in Australia, like you promised?'

Mahoney had to control his irritation with the man.

'Look, I couldn't sell the Britannia, so I set up the cargo company as insurance and went to Australia and had a good look. And I decided against the place. They're nice people but they've got nothing to worry about except keeping up with the Joneses.'

'And why haven't you re-qualified as a lawyer?'

'Because', Mahoney said wearily, 'I'm in the airline business whether I like it or not. I have to make it work. Look, I'm pretty bright, but I had to go to aviation school to get my commercial pilot's licence – as *well* as run the airline.'

'It's a big undertaking, to become a pilot.'

'It's *not*. There're a lot of exams, but any fool can learn to fly; some people fly solo after eight hours! On the big ones you just got to remember which bloody buttons to press.' He added, 'I only fly as co-pilot anyway.'

'To save a pilot's salary. Away half the time. What kind of life is that for a woman?'

'But most pilots' wives survive. Look, I'm not flying for fun. They're bloody dangerous machines. And boring.'

'Why haven't you sat any of the law exams yet? Shelagh says they're easy.'

'Shelagh's not a lawyer, to my knowledge.' He shifted. 'No, they're not hard, and I'm exempted a lot of the exams. But it's still a pain and I'm tired out when I get home. Listen, I'll re-qualify. But I'm not a steam-driven genius.'

'How much did you earn in Rhodesia?'

Mahoney sighed. 'Sixty thousand dollars a year. A hundred thousand, if I worked my ass off.'

'And it's all sitting in the bank back home?'

'I spent most of it.'

'What on?'

He shrugged. 'The farm. A boat. I don't know. Booze. Women. I was a bachelor.'

'And now you only earn housekeeping money. Is that fair? Why don't you at least take your family home to Rhodesia where you can earn a decent living?'

Mahoney sat forward. 'Rhodesia is finished. The whites have lost their chance to make it a multi-racial society, there's no point defending a doomed situation just to earn money which you can't take out when the blacks turn the country into an intolerable mess.'

'And you're not a racist?'

Mahoney shook his head. 'No, I am a realist. Is there one African country which isn't misgoverned? That's not prejudice, it's fact. Look, Shelagh taught in the Department of African Education, so all she met were nice black children eager to learn. And she's British, brought up here; she doesn't *know* about the vast mass of primitive ignorance out

65

in the bush. She thinks they're noble savages who just need a bit of education and one-man-one-vote to turn them into western democrats. She thinks the Russians are sincere people, that we're all the victims of American propaganda.'

'You haven't a high regard for her opinion. Do you think you qualify as her soulmate?'

Mahoney sighed.

'I like to read, but I haven't much time. But Shelagh? – she writes poetry. She's into long walks in the woods when it's pissing with rain. Women's Lib. Now she's into meditation. I simply haven't got the *time*.'

'No, you're the breadwinner, the Victorian husband who says: "*This* is what we're doing, *here* is where we'll live, *I'm* the man in this house" . . .'

Mahoney stared at him. 'You think I'm like that?'

'I'm suggesting *Shelagh* sees you like that . . . So, you don't like Australia, and Shelagh must accept your life here.'

Mahoney took a breath. 'You may not appreciate this, but being a Rhodesian makes me British to the goddamn core. Rhodesians may be a bit slow off the mark making the reforms people like me wanted, but the Rhodesians – even including Ian Smith and most of his cowboys – the Rhodesians *are* the last of the British! The last custodians of the good old British values in Africa. Like hard work. Incorruptible public service. Good judges. Good police. Good health and education services. And' – he held up a finger – 'a Victorian *civilizing* mission.'

'*Victorian* . . .' the psychiatrist murmured.

Mahoney held up a hand. 'Ah yes, those good old values are old-fashioned in today's milk-and-water egalitarianism and the world-owes-us-a-living ethic. But I was brought up to think and feel British – I *feel* like an Englishman. I don't *want* to be Australian or American – so if Rhodesia is finished, I'll come back to the land of my forebears.' He added, with a bleak smile: 'In fact, God is an Englishman.'

'And you want to run an airline instead of being a lawyer.'

Mahoney sighed. 'In Rhodesia I was a big fish in a small pond. But here there'd be many lean years before I built up a reputation. And I don't know much Law, never did.

A seat-of-the-pants barrister, that's me. And now I have to make that airline work because all our capital's in it. And it *is* working. All around airlines go bankrupt, but we're making it! Because we're lean and work hard. O.K., we only get housekeeping money, because we've got to pay off mortgages on our aircraft, and homes. Do you know what our aviation fuel-bill is? One and half *million* pounds a year! Cash on fill-up. No credit. Our pilots carry five thousand pounds with them on each trip, to fill up. And the banks that lend us that kind of money want it back at the end of each week. How do we do it? By working *hard* . . . Once our mortgages are paid we're going to be well off. But right now we're two weeks away from bankruptcy at any given moment. It only needs those OPEC bastards to hike the price of oil unexpectedly, or we lose two engines, or we've got an empty plane, and we're broke. So we have to *work* . . .'

He massaged his brow. 'And', he said 'it's worthwhile work! Britain *has* to export. We're helping British goods go worldwide, at cheaper rates. And we specialize in out-of-the-way places the big airlines refuse to serve, and we bring back products that otherwise wouldn't be sold! Shelagh sees us as a trucking company, but aren't we helping the economy? And isn't economics the key to Africa's backwardness – a man will never grow more than he needs to eat unless he can sell his surplus and buy something else with his money.' He sat back. 'Isn't that better than arguing Carlyle versus The Carbolic Smokeball Company, which any fool lawyer can do?'

'So *you* haven't washed your hands of Africa – but Shelagh must! And now, far from going back to Law, you're talking about airships.'

Mahoney slumped back.

'Airships . . . ,' he sighed. 'Airships don't even *exist*, except these mickey-mouse Goodyear blimps.' He shook his head. 'I'm very interested in the *principle* of airships, because they would revolutionize the Third World economies. But', he smiled wearily, 'all I've done is lent a tumble-down cottage to a guy called Malcolm Todd. That's a far cry from spending Shelagh's housekeeping money on an airship.'

The psychiatrist put his hands together. 'So what are you going to do to get her back? That's why you're here, isn't it, at forty quid an hour, which you can ill afford?'

Get her back? Oh God! And Cathy . . .

'Well,' the psychiatrist demanded, 'do you love her?' He answered himself. 'Of course, you adore her, don't you?'

Mahoney breathed deep. 'Yes.'

'And does Shelagh love you?' He answered again: 'Yes, when you were the young big-wheel lawyer around town? Then she realized you were also a dictatorial Victorian bastard who didn't go too much for transcendental meditation, so she began to cool off you? Tell me, what did you love about her? Her mind? Didn't you find her a little way-out for you, a bit too arty, undergraduate? She didn't even like to get drunk with you.' He leant forward. 'It's her *body*, isn't it?'

Mahoney shifted.

The psychiatrist said, 'You're *hooked* on her body. Her *loins* . . . And Joe Mahoney had never been rejected before, he'd always been the one to love 'em and leave 'em. And you couldn't *bear* the thought of her screwing somebody else, could you?'

'Is that unusual?'

'So when she comes back to you the last time, you marry her. Why? Because she's pregnant? Did you think that marriage would change your relationship? Is that the advice you would have given a client?'

'Probably not,' Mahoney sighed.

'Exactly. But your heart ruled your head – as always, I suspect.' He added: 'And now you're being illogical. You're the Victorian, but instead of kicking her out, as a Victorian would – or giving her a hiding and taking on a mistress for good measure – you're a supplicant.'

Mahoney stared at him. '*Me? A supplicant?*'

'Oh, you don't walk around with a hang-dog expression begging her favours – in fact the opposite, you doggedly lay down the law – but mentally you're trying to figure out how to get her love back, and you badly want to make love to her. Right? Tell me – how's your sex life?'

Mahoney didn't answer.

'Exactly,' the psychiatrist sighed. 'How can you be a confident lover with all that? And remember the old rule-of-thumb: a woman who's getting well laid will forgive her man anything. But if she isn't . . .'

CHAPTER 8

The summer went that way. Afterwards, he did not remember much about the days. They were all work work work, chasing cargo, juggling overdrafts, worrying about engines, schedules. It was the nights he would remember. Redcoat preferred to fly out at night because there was less time waiting on the runway for permission to take off, burning fuel, and it allowed Mahoney to do some office work during the day. You have plenty of time to think and feel, flying through the nights.

And he remembered the Africa at the other end. Redcoat always tried to arrive after sunrise, in case they had forgotten to switch on the runway lights, or they were off at a beer drink. They parked on the apron and let the warm, fertile air of Africa flood in, and the swarm of cargo handlers, and they broke out the beer while they talked to their agent, changed money at blackmarket rates, got the good news or the bad news about the cargo that had or had not shown up; then went bumping into town over broken roads to another run-down hotel. If Mahoney didn't have to buy twenty-five tons of bananas or pineapples as his cargo, he usually walked downtown through the broken-down shops and chickens and derelict cars and children with flies around their nostrils, and went to a pub and drank beer which would have cost three pounds a bottle if he had changed money at the official rates but cost thirty pence at the blackmarket rates, and he watched Africa go by. And he loved these people, and he despaired. He thought: in ten years Rhodesia is going to be like this. And he thought: I

69

wish Shelagh were here . . . Twelve hours later they took off again, into the African night.

And maybe it was because of the droning beauty of the night, flying home, home, home, but when he saw the desert begin to change down there, and then the coastal mountains of the Mediterranean begin, and then faraway lights, and just a few hours ahead was the Channel and England – every time it seemed that all the pain and anger had been purged by those two days away, that none of that was important, all that mattered was love and life, and in a few hours he would be bouncing up the track to his home, and he wanted to walk in the door and shout:

'*Hey, I love you! What's all this nonsense? Life is beautiful and you're beautiful and our daughter's beautiful and this house is beautiful!*'

And she was running down the stairs, her hair flying, and she flung her arms around him, and told him that she had come to terms with herself and she was going to live with him happily ever after.

She said: 'Please sit down. I want to say something.' She was standing at the kitchen window, her back to him.

He sat down slowly at the table. She took a breath.

'While you were away, I made up my mind. About my life.'

He started to say, Your life is with me – then stopped himself.

She said: 'I'm going back to Rhodesia, Joe. You know my reasons . . .' She shook her head. 'I don't like England. I don't like this business you're into. I want my work – my *real* work, teaching Africans. My *own* money—' She paused. 'I've written to the Education Department and asked for my job back. They've agreed, though I forfeited all my seniority because I left. I've also written to the university, enrolling in a part-time arts course.'

His heart was knocking. It was unreal.

'You're not taking Cathy away.'

She said, 'I am. I've taken legal advice. A court will always give custody of an infant to the mother. You obviously couldn't

70

look after her.' She turned around and faced him.

His heart was hammering, but he also felt a numbed, deadly calm. He did not think she had seen a lawyer, but she was right about Cathy. *Time*, he still had time to work on this. He said, 'Rhodesia is not a safe place for Catherine.'

'Nonsense, people are having babies out there all the time. The war is not in Salisbury. It'll be over long before the fighting gets near town, you said that yourself. And why should anybody hurt me, I'll be teaching *their* people . . .' She dismissed that, then added uncomfortably: 'We have to discuss money.'

He stared at her.

'You want to talk about money at a time like this?'

She said defiantly: 'I'm sorry, but we must clear the air. We don't want to go through this again tomorrow. Besides, you're flying tomorrow.' She took a breath. 'I own twenty-five percent of the shares in Redcoat. Admittedly you gave them to me, but didn't I work, even while I was eight months pregnant?' She took a breath and looked at him squarely. 'I want your assurance that you're going to support us.'

He was incensed. It crossed his mind to say that he wanted those shares, he would buy them from her, but, oh, maybe they were a key to keeping her and Catherine with him. He said softly, 'You're leaving me. You're taking my child away, and you want to talk about money in the same breath?'

'I've got to be my own person, Joe!' she cut in tensely. 'I'll bring Cathy back for holidays. Or you can come and see us. Listen, you needn't even *send* money; you've got thousands frozen in the bank in Rhodesia. Or you could sell the farm, and the safari lodge, and the boat. I'll supervise it all for you.'

He could hardly believe she was saying this. For a moment he almost despised her.

'I didn't sell the farm because I couldn't get anything like what it's worth. And the situation is worse, now, and the safari shares aren't worth anything.'

'Please yourself. But the market can only get worse.' She waited, guiltily defiant.

He sat there, feeling sick in the guts. Not yet the grief, the

71

final pain; what he needed was *time* – to figure out if there was one last card to play.

'Please sit down,' he said.

'My mind's made up, Joe.'

'Sit down, please.'

She did so. She had never looked so beautiful. He took a deep breath.

'Please don't interrupt me.' He looked at her. He felt gaunt. 'This has been coming a long time, and I have also reached a decision.'

She waited, grimly. He said, 'Give us one more year, Shelagh. In one year the airline will be on its feet, we'll have a good income, in foreign currencies. *Then* we can go back to Rhodesia, and take our chances. We won't be dependent on frozen Rhodesian assets. You can go back to work then – to university – anything. But . . .' He shook his head. 'If you leave me now, it is finished, Shelagh. You cannot come back. I will give you only enough money to support Cathy properly. No more, no less. I will not pay you to desert me.'

Her eyes flashed, but he held up a hand. 'Let me finish.' He looked at her steadily. 'If you leave, you must take everything of yours with you. I will pay for its freight. Anything of Cathy's can stay here. But I want absolutely nothing of yours to remind me of you, especially not any pretty clothes, not even a hairclip.'

She flashed, 'You're trying to make it difficult for me!'

He said, 'No, I'm trying to protect myself against pain.'

She jumped up. 'Very well! I'll go and start packing now.'

She strode out of the room.

He sat there, staring across the kitchen. It was still unreal. He felt exhausted. He got up, and walked slowly out of the kitchen. Through the living room. Up the stairs. He could hear Shelagh in the bedroom, pulling out suitcases. He walked on, into Cathy's room.

She was playing on the floor, a mop of curls on her beautiful little head, and her infant face burst into smiles.

72

'Hullo, my darling . . .'

He picked her up. He held her against him, her tiny arms around his neck, breath on his cheek; and he felt his heart turn over. And then up it came, the grief.

CHAPTER 9

Flying. One of the best things to do when you are unhappy is to fly. Fly away into the sunset, every moment hurtling you further away from your pain, into a different world: the unreality of crossing continents, high mountains down there, seeing faraway lights and oceans; one moment flying through black cloud, the next through moonlight or sunshine, from the countries that have rain and snow to the countries that have sunshine and flowers; within hours, from great cities to countries that have only jungles and deserts; and you look down and realise there is an infinite amount of life apart from your own, all those millions of people down there living and dying and loving, and millions of other creatures whose lives are just as important to them – and the skies stretching on into infinity, *not contained by anything*, holding millions of other worlds: and you realise just how small one human being is, how unimportant one heart-break, and maybe for a moment you will almost glimpse the whole cosmic picture and what a minute, insignificant part of it your troubles are.

But flying is also one of the worst things when you are unhappy. Because there is nothing to do but sit there, and stare out of the perspex at the night, every moment your aeroplane hurtling you further away from the place you really want to be, your home and wife and child who are busy leaving you, and when you get back it'll be two days nearer, and all you want to do is get this aeroplane to the other end and discharge the cargo and fly, fly back home before it is too late and walk in the front door and say . . .

Say what? Please don't leave? . . . I love you? . . .

'Hullo,' he said.

'Hullo. You're back early! Have a good trip?'

'Is Cathy asleep yet?'

'Yes, don't disturb her, please. Did you have a good trip?'

Oh Cathy. He just wanted to be with her. Each day was precious. 'The homeward-bound cargo didn't show up.'

'So. More pineapples, is it?'

'No pineapples, either. Tomatoes. Can I get you a drink?'

'One day you're going to find yourself stuck with twenty-eight tons of rotting tomatoes. Did Dolores find a buyer?'

'Yes.'

'God, you take chances.'

'Will you have a drink if I light a fire?'

'No, it's too early. You go ahead.'

Oh God, he did not want to stay in the emptying house, and he did not want to go out. 'Would you like to go to The Rabbit? I'll ask one of the Todd children to babysit.'

'No, you go ahead. I'm awfully busy.'

She was very businesslike. The paintings were the first to go, and the walls shrieked at him. For days the paintings stood stacked: then, when he came back from a trip, they were gone.

'Malcolm Todd built me some crates. The rest I farmed out, for safe-keeping.'

For safe-keeping? Till when? And despite himself he felt the hope rise. He heard himself say, 'You could have left them here.'

'Oh no, you told me you wanted no reminders.'

She was punishing him. Then she said: 'Actually, I've left two you might like. That one of Cathy. The other is that old one of the farm.' She added, 'If you don't want them, just chuck them.'

He felt his eyes burn. 'Thank you. Yes, I'd like them.'

'Well, make up your mind where you want to hang them.'

Off the shelves everything systematically came, all her books and ornaments and knick-knacks, packed into cartons; out of her wardrobes came her clothes, neatly packed into trunks and suitcases, depending on whether they were winter or summer clothes.

74

'It'll be summer there now. The winter stuff can come by sea.'

Maybe she was expecting him to break, tell her she could leave all her things, come back whenever she chose, and her house and all would be waiting for her. And God knows there were times during that long bad month when he almost broke and said it.

He spent every moment he could with Cathy. He hated coming home to the heartbreakingly emptying house, and he was desperate to be with her. He told Dolores to re-arrange his flights, so he could get home before she went to bed. If it was raining, he played with her in her room, to have her to himself. But he could not bear the sounds of packing going on and whenever he could he took her out. She was not yet two but he loved to talk to her, to figure out what was going on in her little head. Sometimes he took her to the park, to play on the swings and roundabouts, but she always got over-excited there, and he preferred just to walk with her down the lanes, carrying her on his shoulders, or holding her hand as she toddled along. Sometimes he drove into the village to buy her icecream and to show her the shops. Christmas was coming, and it crunched his heart. Christmas, but no Cathy, and no Shelagh. For that reason he did not like the Christmassy shops, but Cathy thought they were wonderful and he relented, taking her inside on his shoulders so she could see everything, and he always ended up buying her something. He liked to think of her out playing with them in sunny Rhodesia. And oh God, he just hoped that she would remember him when she did. But no, she would not; she was too little to remember these heartbreaking days, when she was leaving her daddy. He took her to see his aeroplanes, tried to explain them to her, hoping she would remember something, he desperately wanted her to remember as much about him as she could. 'I'm your daddy, my darling, and I will always love you, always, you can *always* turn to me, for the rest of your life . . .' But no, she did not know what was happening to her little life and to her daddy, and it made him feel desperate. She would grow up without him, and get to love some other man as her daddy, and that man could never, *never* feel the love that he was giving her . . .

75

At last he had to take her home to the heartbreaking cottage in the woods, to the sights of packing. And he sat with her while she bathed, watching her; and, oh, the feel of her small body as he soaped her, her little ribs and back and shoulders, then rubbing her dry while she giggled, and clutching her to his breast. And, after he had kissed her goodnight, he did not know what to do. With all his heart he longed to walk up to her mother, just take her in his arms and tell her he loved her, and their daughter, please don't leave me. But he could not. Neither could he go and sit with Shelagh while she went about her packing; he did not want to let her out of his sight either, but he could not bear the house, so sometimes he went down to The Rabbit.

One night Danish Erika, who owned the joint, said: 'I hear Shelagh's leaving.'

He felt his heart squeeze. 'She's only going for a holiday.'

'Uh-huh,' Danish Erika said. 'Nice work, if you can get it. So, you'll be a bachelor. Well, when you start dishing it out, remember your friends.'

He pretended she was joking. At Redcoat House Dolores said, 'If Shelagh's only going for a few months, how come Malcolm crated up her pictures?'

'She needs them at her summer course at the university.'

She followed him into his office. She said: 'The council served a summons on us yesterday, to get us out of here. They're sick of you stalling them.'

He looked at the summons. He hardly cared. The hearing was months hence.

'We'll wait till the last moment, enter an Appearance to Defend and ask for an adjournment.'

'Then where do we go?'

'To the Town Planning Tribunal. Then to the appeal court. Stop worrying, we've got years here.'

She looked at him sympathetically; then sat down on the corner of his desk. 'Joe? It's all for the best.'

He hated people knowing.

She said quietly: 'This, too, shall pass . . .' She sighed: 'I should know; I feel much better since I washed my hands of Pomeroy.'

He didn't say anything.

'All right,' she said, 'I'll mind my own business.' She stood up. 'But you *are* my business, remember.' She added, challenging. 'Where's the beer-swigging, womanizing, life-and-soul-of-the-party I used to know?'

'O.K., Dolores,' he said.

'O.K. But, boy – how the mighty are fallen!'

In the second last week he came back from Accra and the carpets were gone. They were hers. The living room looked very bare. She said, 'It looks a bit sad, doesn't it?'

'Yes.'

'The bedroom ones I sold. I need the money. The living room one, Malcolm wrapped up for me, for shipping.'

His throat felt thick. 'I'd have bought them from you.'

'Oh no. You told me.' She added, 'You'll probably notice that all your shirts have now got buttons on. I had a blitz.'

He was taken aback. 'Thank you, Shelagh.'

'And I've stocked the deep-freeze. I opened an account for you, so don't forget to pay it. The bill's on the spike.'

He was touched. 'Thank you.'

She said, 'Well, I'm going up to Mom and Dad this afternoon, back by Monday night. Do you want to come? I'll be driving through the Lake District; I haven't seen it for years.'

The bloody Lake District. 'No, thanks. I don't want to intrude on your parents' last weekend with you.'

'Very well, please yourself. You always do.'

After they left, he went slowly upstairs, with a glass of whisky. He stood in the bedroom doorway. The bare floor shrieked *Shelagh* at him. He walked slowly to her wardrobe.

It smelt of her, that faint, woman-body smell of powder, perfume. Only three garments hung there. Dresses she would wear before she left. All her shoes gone, her sexy high heels, her boots, summer sandals, all gone into those

77

cardboard crates that had disappeared. To fly, fly away, a whole life flying away, off to another continent, for other lovers to know. Her dressing table had almost nothing on it. He pulled open her underwear drawers. There were just two pairs of panties left. Gone were her stockings and suspender belts, her slips and bras. Into one of the suitcases to fly, fly away, to other lovers.

He turned slowly out of the naked room. He walked down the passage, into Cathy's. He stopped. Almost everything of hers was gone. Off the floors, the shelves, all her toys and colouring books gone, the pictures all gone off the walls: just one teddy bear left on her neatly-made bed. The room was empty, childless. He walked slowly in, and laid himself down on her bed, and he put his arm across his eyes; and his heart broke, and the tears ran silently down his face.

That long, bad weekend he just wanted to turn his face to the wall, to be in a dark place, to hide. On Saturday Dolores telephoned to ask if he was coming in, but really to find out if he was all right. He just sat in the kitchen, staring at nothing, drinking beer. Saturday night was very bad. He woke up at three a.m. He got up, tried to work, but he couldn't. Finally he got a beer and sat in the dark kitchen again. On Sunday there was a persistent knocking on the door. Finally he got up and opened it; there stood Dolores, in her tracksuit.

'Is there anything I can get for you? A barbecue chicken?'

'I'm O.K., Dolores.'

'You look like hell. Shall I get a relief pilot for tomorrow?'

'No, I'll be all right.'

'When this nonsense is finally over.'

Then she put her arms around him, and held him tight; and with the feel of her womanness and sympathy the tears choked him, then suddenly she kissed him. Hard and fierce, as if she wanted to bite him, then her fingers went to her zip and she said, 'I guess we've got to do this – for your good. *And* mine.'

He backed off, half shocked, half guilty, and wanted to

protest that everything was all right with his marriage . . .

'If you're worried about being my boss, don't be; I'll pretend it never happened.' She unzipped her tracksuit and came towards him. He held her again, rigidly. He closed his eyes. 'I'm sorry,' he said.

She stared at him, then slumped against the table, her magnificent breasts free.

'Wow! I don't know any man who'd knock back an offer that strong. Are you really that hung up on her? Or do I need a bath, I've been jogging, dammit!'

'Dolores . . .'

'But you went to bed with *her*.' She nodded in the direction of The Rabbit.

He stared. 'She told you that?'

'No, but the word's out.'

He felt absolutely unreasonable panic. 'Well, the word is wrong! God, what a town.'

'There's more adultery here than there are passengers. Pomeroy loves it.' She held up her hands, and got up. 'O.K., I'll go now.' She looked at him sullenly. 'Can't I buy you a beer at The Rabbit? Come on, they'll be singing Christmas carols.'

Christmas! 'I'm fine, thank you for coming.'

'I wish I had,' she said. 'More important, I wish *you* had . . .'

She left, jogging through the forest, and blew him a truculent kiss. But an hour later she was back, in her car, and a little tipsy. 'I want to put my case again.' And she unzipped her tracksuit purposefully; but just then there was a knock on the door. He went to it, with relief, while Dolores hastily zipped up; and in walked Val Meredith, whose husband sometimes flew for Redcoat. In fact he was flying one of the Redcoat planes right that moment. 'Hullo, I've come to invite you to Sunday lunch.' Then she saw Dolores smiling at her icily. 'Woops, sorry!'

After she left Dolores said, 'Not Val Meredith, is it?'

'No,' he sighed. He wondered how the hell Val Meredith knew Shelagh was away.

'O.K.,' Dolores said, 'the Florence Nightingale in me is

cooled.' She got up to go, fed up. 'But do you see? What fun life could be?'

He took a deep breath. 'Dolores? . . .' Then he shook his head. 'Forget it. I don't want to know.'

She looked at him. 'You mean has Shelagh? . . .' She put her hands on her hips, wearily. 'No,' she said. I haven't heard even a whisper about her playing around. And believe me, I'd tell you if I had.'

He was a bit better on Monday, but Dolores had arranged a relief pilot. He did not work on Tuesday and Wednesday, so he could be with Cathy. He did not want to let her out of his sight. He played with her in her room. He had to go into the village so he took her to a tea-room and bought her icecream, as much as she wanted, so he could have her to himself, listen to her. He did not want to take her home; she would no longer be alone with him. He bathed her and sat with her while she had her supper. Then he had to let her go to bed. He sat with her until she was asleep, just looking at her. Finally, he had to leave her alone, and then he did not know what to do with himself. He sat in the kitchen and drank beer and tried to read the newspapers, while Shelagh cooked dinner between going upstairs to do the last of her packing. They were polite to each other, even kind. Sometimes she just touched him in passing, though she did not want to start anything. She showed genuine interest in the airline.

'We're having a record month,' he said.

'Great. That's three in a row.' She sighed. 'Well, you all deserve it. But, truly, don't buy a third Canadair. Get rid of the Britannia, but don't replace her.'

'We're talking about doing passenger charters with the Britannia.'

'But she's such a mess inside.'

'Tart her up a bit. Quick Change seating, and so forth.'

'But you need wide-bodies for passenger work. Like Freddie Laker.'

'It's easier to fill up a small plane than a big one.'

80

'Don't you think Freddie knows what he's doing?'

'He's a genius. But he'll come unstuck with all these wide-bodies he's buying. Small is beautiful.'

'Remember that if you're thinking of building a bloody great airship, darling.'

It touched him when she used the endearment. Another time she said: 'I really do think airships are a wonderful *idea*. So romantic. It's just . . .' She waved her hand. 'I just don't *believe* in them. For all the obvious reasons. And I think you're . . .' She decided not to finish.

'Wasting my time?'

'Oh, you're wasting *yourself*. You're a brilliant barrister – everybody says so. But you're an incurable *romantic*, darling – your head literally in the clouds.' She sighed. 'You're going to lose every penny you make, and end up a broken man, like Malcolm Todd.'

He smiled. 'I think he's a genius.'

She smiled wearily. 'Of course you do. Birds of a feather.'

They slept in the same bed, but did not touch each other. He lay in the darkness, pretending to sleep, and with all his heart he yearned to reach out and take her in his arms and tell her he loved her, and beg her not to leave. But he could not. Maybe she was also pretending to be asleep, feeling the same. But no. You can feel these things. Maybe she was waiting for him to break, tell her she could come back after she had done her thing, and God knows there were times when he nearly did. On that last Friday morning he awoke before dawn, found himself lying against her, his hand holding her breast; and for a moment, in his half-sleep, he was completely happy. Then he came back to reality, and his heart cracked. He got up, straight away, racked, slammed on the shower, the water beating away his tears. He got dressed, and left the dark cottage. He did not know where he was going; he only knew he could not stay there, waiting for them to wake up and leave. He walked through the woods, down the road, towards Redcoat House. He unlocked the door, and stood there. He could not work. He started walking again. It was getting light when he got back to the cottage. He opened the front door, and her suitcases were lined up. Shelagh was standing there, and he looked at them, and he broke. He leant in the doorway, and the tears rolled down his face, and he reached out and took her in his arms, and whispered, 'Please come back . . .'

She stood in his arms a long moment. Then she said gently: 'Breakfast is ready.'

After that he composed himself. They drove to Heathrow airport, with Cathy sitting between them. They were silent all the way. He checked them in. They had ample time for coffee, but he could not bear it.

He picked up Cathy. He held her tight, and his throat was thick as he said: 'Look after Mommy, won't you, darling?'

Then he turned to Shelagh. Her eyes were clear and steady. He held her tight once, then kissed her cheek.

'Goodbye,' he whispered. 'Good luck.'

She smiled. 'Good luck.'

'Go on,' he said. 'Go now.'

She took Cathy by the hand and turned, without looking at him. He watched them walk away, Cathy toddling along. At the door Shelagh stopped, and looked back, smiled, then waved; then she bent and waved Cathy's hand at her daddy.

Then they went through the door.

He walked out of the concourse, the tears running down his face. He got into his car, began to start it: then he dropped his face into his hands and wept.

For five minutes he sat there. Then he dragged his wrist across his eyes. He did not want to leave the place he had last seen his wife and child, but he made himself. He drove slowly out of the parking block, then into the tunnel. He drove through the tunnel, out at the other end; he drove slowly round the traffic island, and back into the tunnel, back to the airport again.

He went up to the observation lounge. He could see the plane, but not the passengers boarding. He just stood there and watched the plane.

Finally the Boeing reversed out of the bay. He imagined

82

Shelagh and Cathy inside. He watched it taxi, disappear from sight: then it reappeared, roaring down the runway, fast and faster; it took off, and his heart finally broke, and he sobbed out loud.

He watched it go, getting smaller and smaller. Then it was gone, into the clouds.

But he did not want to leave the airport, the last place he had seen his wife and child.

PART 3

PART 3

eat, Romeo Yankee, I have you . . .' And you tell her your compass heading and the slab of air the little guy allotted you and she says, 'O.K.,' but say 'Or she says something like, 'Descend a thousand . . .' . . . . And, boy, you do as you're told. As you're as hell. It gave Mahoney the . . . . Hell, England's so

CHAPTER 10

Now, this is how you fly a bloody great aeroplane. It's simple really: a simple matter of life and death.

First, you've tanked up with twenty-five tons of fuel, which is the combined weight of five adult elephants, to blast your twenty-five tons of cargo (another five elephants) plus fifty tons of aeroplane (ten elephants) through thin air in defiance of gravity. You've filed your Flight Plan, telling the guys in control the route you'd like to fly. Now you're waiting on the runway, engines whining, brakes on, waiting for them to tell you it's safe to go, waiting for a gap in that black sky midst all those dozens of other aeroplanes screaming around on top of each other all wanting to come in, all of you blindly relying on that same little guy in his control room who's looking at his radar set. And then he says *Go*, and, boy, off you go.

Blindly trusting in the blind faith everybody has in everybody else, galloping down the black runway, the lights flashing past, eighty miles an hour, ninety, a hundred, just praying you don't burst a tyre. Then you reach V1, the speed at which you become committed to taking off, you cannot stop now without killing yourself and making everybody very cross. You reach VR, ease back the stick, up comes the nose, and, bingo, you've done it, you're airborne! Lifting up into thin air, you and your twenty-odd elephants. Up up up you go into the blackness where the little guy told you to, aiming for that nice gap he's found for you between all those friendly aeroplanes screaming around in circles up there; but it's O.K. because he's watching you all on his radar screen. Sometimes he screams over the radio, '*Romeo Yankee, left, turn left*' and you holler, '*O.K., left!*' – and some fucking great machine comes screaming out of the blackness, just missing you. But not often, hell no, those guys are good; anybody can make a mistake. And you're on your way to sunny Africa or wherever, and he hands you over to the next control sector. You twiddle that up on your radio and in Paris some dolly-bird says, '*Oui*

– *oui*, Romeo Yankee, I have you . . .' And you tell her your compass heading and the slab of air the little guy allocated you and she says, 'O.K., *bon soir*.' Or she says something like, 'Descend a thousand feet, somebody's coming!' And, boy, you do as you're told. As simple as that. It gave Mahoney the screaming heebie-jeebies.

'Hell, England's easy,' said Ed. 'You should see some of the balls-up airports I've flown into, especially in Africa. Sometimes you have to fly low over the control tower to wake them up.'

'Give me Africa every time,' Mahoney said, 'at least you're the only plane in the sky there. It's going for the gap between all the other guys that gives me the willies.'

'You've got to learn to relax, or you don't do this job.'

'I'm only doing the job, Ed, until we can afford to keep me on the ground, believe me.'

'Well, that may be some time, boss, so you better learn to quit passing me the buck everytime something tricky happens.'

'You're the fleet-captain. Of course I pass the buck; that's what I pay you for.'

'Not very much. You should fly more with the other guys, stop being so dependent on me. Fly as captain for a change.'

'Fly as captain? Never,' Mahoney said. 'Never.'

'Take responsibility. You're quite a good pilot, really.'

'I'm a lousy pilot, I'm only here to make up the numbers. You want to take over some of my responsibilities? You're quite a good co-director, really.'

'Hell, no. Never,' Ed said. 'O.K. – go and work, boss.'

And Mahoney got out of his seat and sat at the fold-away table that Pomeroy had made for him, and he worked on Redcoat business that Dolores had packed for him. She prepared the same lists of SDDs (Suggested Dos and Don'ts) as she had done with his legal briefs in the old days. Nowadays it was: 'O.K., sign encls.' 'Study carefully.' 'Have arranged appt with Bank Mgr for . . .' 'F. says pineapple glut, bananas O.K. this week . . .' 'This is prick who gave us so much trouble over . . .'

And there was the telephone. It went 'bing-bong' on the flight-deck, and that meant trouble because Dolores did not waste money. Engine trouble, or cargo trouble, or crew trouble. 'That engine on the Britannia has gone on the blink again, Pomeroy says he's got to take the whole thing out, at least five days, do you want me to charter an aircraft or do a handwringing exercise?' Oh, God, engines! 'Meredith has just lost the number two engine on the Canadair and turned back to Naples, which means tomorrow's Khartoum cargo . . .' 'Pomeroy has just heard of an excellent second-hand engine going cheap in Cyprus; he must go there immediately to inspect it and this means that . . .' And goddamn cargoes. 'Your homeward-bound cargo has fallen through, but Abdullah in Uganda has got one. Is it worth flying empty from Ghana to fetch it? . . .'

The other big trouble was crew. Hard-luck crews, that's what Redcoat tended to get. Ed Hazeltine and Mahoney were the only pilots in Redcoat's full-time employment. For the rest, Redcoat hired pilots, flight by flight. There were usually plenty, with so many airlines retrenching. The trouble with pilots is they tend to drink, to relax from the unnatural business of defying gravity for a living. *Bing-bong*. 'That cargo of bulls for Johannesburg? Well, Captain Meredith's gone on a bender, he caught a tailwind and got home early and found his wife in the bathtub with you-know-who . . .'

'Then get Mason!'

'Unfortunately, that's who she was in the bathtub with. He's suddenly got two very black eyes and no front teeth.'

'Oh Jesus! Then get Cooper!'

'Cooper's flying for Starlux, Benny's flying for Tradewinds, Renner's flying the Canadair right now, Morley's goofing-off on the Costa del Sol. I assure you there's *nobody* . . .'

'Johnson?'

'Mother's dying.'

'Fullbright?'

'Just got a full-time job with Ethiopia Air.'

'Well, *find* somebody, Dolorés! Even if you've got to drop your knickers and run bare-assed round Gatwick Airport! What are we going to do with thirty bulls around Redcoat House?'

'That's why I phoned, dammit! Sounds like a lot of bullshit to me . . .'

When he got to the hangar the next evening, there was his new captain awaiting him. 'Good evening, name's Sydney Benson.'

Mahoney was taken aback. 'Are you Jamaican?'

'As the ace of spades.'

Mahoney grinned. As he was signing on duty he muttered out of the corner of his mouth, 'You sure he can fly aeroplanes?'

Dolores slapped the desk and burst into smothered giggles. 'Your *face* – it's a *scream*.'

As they walked together through the grey drizzle to the Canadair, Mahoney said: 'Dolores tells me your last job was with Air Jamaica, Sydney. What brings you to England?'

Sydney broke into a little shuffle:

> '*This is my island, in the sun*
> *Built for me, by the English-mun*
> *All my days, I will sing in praise*
> *Of the National Assistance and the Labour*
> *Exchange . . .*'

Mahoney threw back his head and laughed.

After they had settled down on the flight-deck, Mahoney said: 'If you don't mind, I'd like to do take-off.'

Sydney looked at him.

'You don't like spades taking off? Well, I'm not too wild about honkies, either.'

'Not that,' Mahoney smiled. 'You see, I'm managing director and I've a lot of work—'

'And I'm captain of this aircraft, sah, and what I say is *law*. You got that?'

Mahoney sighed. 'Got it.'

'And I also just got fired, right?'

'No. Go on, take off, you're the boss.'

Sydney sat back, with a brilliant smile. 'O.K., you take off, then go'n work, I'll hold the fort, pal.'

After that Sydney often flew for Redcoat, and Mahoney liked to fly with him. The man was an excellent pilot, and bloody funny. It was an asset, too, having a black captain to argue with black officials about dash and blackmail and blackmarket rates. 'How you've *stood* these mothers,' Sydney complained, 'it makes me embarrassed about my pigmentation, and I've always thought nothing was worse than pinko-grey like you unfortunates.' Sydney's wife was a buxom American black lass with flashing eyes, called Muriel, who came to work for Redcoat. *'Don't think I'm going to shoulder the whole white man's burden, I refuse to work more than eighteen hours a day for this pittance!'* Mahoney was rather intimidated by her, Pomeroy was terrified of her, Dolores was delighted with her. 'Works like a black,' Dolores enthused, 'and so *funny* . . .'

Mahoney hardly ever saw Pomeroy or Vulgar Olga these days. Vulgar Olga worked as a barmaid across town and Pomeroy was always inside some engine, covered in grease, going cuss cuss cuss. Sometimes they met at The Rabbit, to talk some business, but Pomeroy was no good at anything except engines, and booze and women, he wanted to leave all that mindblowing management crap to Mahoney. And Mahoney didn't know anything about engines, he wanted to leave all that mindblowing crap to Pomeroy, anything Pomeroy decided to do with Redcoat Engineering Ltd was O.K. with Mahoney as long as it made money. He was very pleased with Pomeroy, and wished he saw more of him. Sometimes Pomeroy took a break and went on a flight as engineer. He amused Mahoney. Pomeroy was a cockney barrow-boy at heart, but now that he had made good he was getting awfully toffy. Pomeroy and Vulgar Olga lived in a chintzy mortgaged house, and when he wasn't inside engines he was socializing with the gentry and he didn't assault policemen anymore now he was respectable. 'Cor-er, marvellous crumpet in the suburbs,' Pomeroy confided. 'Worth all the effort, even thinking of taking elocution lessons, like.'

'And what does Olga think about all the crumpet?'

'Loves it! Old Olga, y'know, she's only here for the beer. I'm even thinkin' of marrying her, we get along so famous. Wot I mean is, you really should come along to some of these toffy parties and get some of this marvellous married crumpet. Biggest club in the world!'

'I've got to work,' Mahoney smiled.

And when he was through with office work, there were the piles of Malcolm Todd's airship material. The principles of lighter-than-air flight, the esoteric formulae he had to grasp, the significance of comparative graphs, Malcolm's screeds of essays and promotional material, all the draftsman's drawings, all the books. Mahoney had the gift of the gab rather than a mathematical turn of mind, so the science did not come easily to him, but being of above-average intelligence he could, with effort, understand it. It also helped to keep his mind off the empty cottage that was waiting for him. And he was fascinated. It simply did not make sense to be hurtling twenty elephants through the night sky in defiance of the laws of gravity when you could float them, riding the air like a ship rides on the sea.

CHAPTER 11

Work, booze, and adultery. And guilt.

Mahoney half-woke feeling terrible, thinking he was late for work, and he started scrambling up when Dolores mumbled: 'Relax, it's Sunday . . .'

He slumped back, his head thudding. He remembered where he was now. Pomeroy's house. Oh God, with Dolores . . . As if reading his mind, she muttered, 'Relax, we didn't do anything.'

But, oh, why hadn't he gone home? Why did he ever drink brandy? . . . Then he remembered: chocolate mousse. . . .

It came back, fragmented. The lunch was clear enough. Dolores was not there then. Wine flowing like water, dropping on to the gins and tonics. Why did he ever drink gin? Then the brandies. They all knew each other very well, except for Mahoney. Mahoney only knew Danish Erika and Pomeroy well, and he knew how his parties turned out. Then the whiskies, getting dark now. Sitting around Pomeroy's fake mahogany bar with all its gear, its erotic curios, all the suggestive talk and laughter and double meanings. Memory began to blur. He remembered starting to feel very drunk. Remembered seeing it was nine o'clock. He remembered Vulgar Olga taking off her clothes for the sauna. Then Pomeroy, then the other women, then Fullbright and Mason. And all this was fine, the naked women were fine, but no way was he going to get undressed and sit in a hot sauna. He didn't give a damn what they did. Once upon a time he'd have filled his boots and maybe one day he would again, but right now no way was he going to get involved, he just wanted to go home. He remembered them calling him a spoil sport, and too drunk to drive, and Erika stealing his car keys. He remembered bumping upstairs to look for a bed; then blank.

The rest was very confused. He remembered waking up, finding himself on the sofa in Pomeroy's bedroom, clothes on. Olga shaking him, telling him to get his gear off and join the action. The next thing, Danish Erika shaking him saying it was four o'clock, time to go home, did he want any chocolate mousse? He sat up, holding his head and feeling like death, and there were the six of them – evidently Fullbright had gone – sitting on the floor stark naked and drunk and disorderly around this big bowl of chocolate mousse and bottles of champagne.

He did not remember how it started because he was too busy feeling terrible; maybe Pomeroy did it because Vulgar Olga squirted champagne at him, or maybe Pomeroy slopped a spoonful of chocolate mousse on Vulgar Olga, but suddenly there were these squeals and there is Pomeroy with champagne all over his face and Olga with chocolate mousse on hers – then Janet Mason splatting chocolate mousse on Pomeroy midst screams of laughter, and then Erika letting Mason have it, and the real shambles began. Sitting pole-axed on the sofa, Mahoney stared in bludgeoned astonishment at the spectacle exploding before him, everybody fighting with chocolate mousse midst screaming and squealing – then champagne squirting everywhere; then Pomeroy screaming and clutching his chocolate-face and the door bursting open and there stood Fullbright, fully dressed and unchocolated, seething with righteous indignation. The battle stopped as suddenly as it had begun, everybody staring at Fullbright, except Pomeroy who was whimpering, clutching his chocolate face.

'*You!*' Fullbright jabbed his pristine finger at Mason – '*And you!'* – at the dark, wailing Pomeroy – *'And you!'* – at an astonished Mahoney – *'stay away from my wife!'*

'I've got chocolate mousse in my eye—' Pomeroy wailed, and Vulgar Olga wailed, *'Oh darling!'*

'You all stay away from my wife!' Fullbright was yelling.

'Somebody stuck their finger in my eye—' Pomeroy was wailing.

'A doctor,' Vulgar Olga was wailing. *'Call Dolores—' 'Nine-nine-nine,'* Pomeroy was wailing at everybody – *'tell 'em I got chocolate mousse in my eye—'* Then Fullbright bounding at his wife as Pomeroy was blindly scrambling for the door with Olga lumbering chocolate-arsed after him, and all four of them colliding in the doorway in a big chocolatey bottleneck. Fullbright was now getting pretty chocolatey himself, and Lavinia Fullbright was screaming at him, *'You bastard—'* And Olga was screaming, *'Get out of the bloody way,'* and then Fullbright went flying through the doorway with Pomeroy exploding after him in a sudden unbottlenecking. He crashed on top of Fullbright, and the whole chocolatey lot of them went crashing down the stairs, crash bang wallop to the bottom in a mad tangled bellowing mess, then Olga was scrambling for the telephone and Pomeroy was blundering around yelling, *'Tell the Eye Bank I've got chocolate mousse in my eye—'*

Something like that. All very confused. Mahoney remembered the front door slamming, Fullbright's car roaring away with Lavinia: then the ambulance wailing, Pomeroy reeling out into the night with a blanket around him, wailing to everybody that he had chocolate mousse in his eye.

Then Dolores arriving, to sort this lot out.

Mahoney got out of bed carefully. He staggered into the bathroom, found a toothbrush, brushed his teeth, turned on the shower. He stood under it, suffering, then scrubbed himself and washed his hair. Then let cold water hammer on his head, trying to knock out the stunned feeling. Cold showers are like flying aeroplanes: they're so nice when they stop.

He dressed, tiptoed down the stairs, feeling a little better. The stair walls were smeared with mousse, and it smelled as if Olga had tried to clean the stuff up with benzene. The living room looked like a battlefield, clothes everywhere. You expected to find bodies. He found his jacket.

He went to the kitchen, got a beer. He took a long swig, then sat at the table, suffering, waiting for it to steady him. But why should he feel remorse? It was their business. Their wives. He hadn't even stuck his finger in Pomeroy's eye. So why should he feel remorse?

It was sick. Marriage, the biggest club in the world . . . None of the desperate wining and dining of bachelorhood, the heavy-duty charm-treatment, impressing her with what a big wheel you are, the hopeful dancing cheek-to-cheek, the worrying, and finally the acid test when you get her home, the protests. But with adultery? All you've got to do is look for the signs. Why do married people talk about sex so much? Oh God, he just longed for his lovely wholesome wife and child . . .

He went to the fridge for another beer. He heard footsteps. Pomeroy tottered in, all hairy and horrible, a bandage around his head.

'Are you in the Black and White Minstrel Show?' Mahoney said.

'Oh boy,' Pomeroy said. He tottered to the fridge, got a beer blindly, slumped at the table.

'Can you work tomorrow?'

'If you don't mind one-eyed engineers.' He lifted the bandage. His eyelid was black and swollen and stitched, his slit of eyeball murderously bloodshot.

'Who was it?'

'I couldn't see because somebody stuck their finger in my eye.'

Mahoney was grinning. 'What did they sat at the hospital?'

'Caused a bit of bovver at the hospital,' Pomeroy admitted. 'Old Olga, you know, you should have been there.'

'What did Olga do?'

'Naked as the day she was born under that blanket,' Pomeroy said, 'and chocolate mousse. Raised a bit of a bovver. She didn't know the black doctor was a doctor, you should have been there. He said, "Medem, is this a case of the pot-i calling the kettle black?"'

Mahoney laughed and it hurt his head. Pomeroy sighed, 'Isn't that Fullbright a prick?'

'You better leave the Fullbrights out of your chocolate mousse parties.'

I'm going to leave you out, an' all,' Pomeroy said. 'Here I go to this enormous expense and pain to cheer you up . . .' He glared with his good eye. 'But no, you're still brooding about *her*.' He got up. 'I'm goin' to the loo,' he said.

The rest is legend. Pomeroy goes to the lavatory, sits down, lights a cigarette, and drops the match into the lavatory bowl. And in that bowl unbeknown to him is the wad of cotton wool with which Vulgar Olga cleaned up the chocolate mousse, all soaked in benzene. And, sitting in the kitchen, all Mahoney heard was a mighty whooshing bang and then Pomeroy howls and comes bursting out of the toilet with his arse on fire. There's Pomeroy running around hollering, '*My arse is blown off*,' and Olga coming running stark naked screaming, '*Oh darling, I forgot to flush it!*' – and Dolores yelling, '*What's wrong now?*' – and Pomeroy hollering, '*Call the ambulance – my arse is burnt off!*' And the women chasing him, yelling, cornering him, trying to inspect his arse while he hopped around hollering.

Then the wailing of the ambulance above Pomeroy's wailing, and in burst the stretcher-bearers, and they're the same guys who came for him earlier. And they load him on to the stretcher, and out the front door Pomeroy goes, red raw arse up and his bandage round his eye, still covered in dried chocolate mousse. And the ambulance boys were laughing so much that one trips down the front steps. All Mahoney saw was a sudden mass of crashing arms and legs and Pomeroy's arse. Then Pomeroy was wailing '*My shoulder!*', and his collar bone was broken.

Mahoney helped Dolores tidy up the house while Olga and Pomeroy were back at the hospital getting his arse and collar bone fixed; then he left. He drove slowly home, trying not to think about bloody Sunday. He was flying at midnight so he had to sleep off his hangover this afternoon. He could have a nice pub-lunch at The Rabbit, then get Danish Erika or Val or Beatrice to sleep it off with him, so what did he have to complain about? What's so tough about being a bachelor? And tomorrow he'd be in Uganda, would you rather be in court tomorrow, worrying about all that Law you never learned? He took a deep breath, trying to stop thinking about Sunday and Cathy, and stopped to buy a newspaper.

He looked at the front page for news of Rhodesia.

SMITH ANNOUNCES 'INTERNAL SETTLEMENT'

The Rhodesian Prime Minister announced in Salisbury today that his government was setting out to seek an 'internal settlement' with the country's moderate African leaders, in terms of which a 'Transitional Co-alition Government' would be formed with them, pending a new one-man-one-vote constitution . . .

Mahoney read the piece with stumbling speed: and for a minute he felt confused elation. Then he slumped. He thought: *Big Deal* . . .

Big deal, Mr Smith . . . You should have done this years ago when I told you to! . . . You think a coalition government now will get you international recognition so economic sanctions and the war will end? *Well you're too bloody late, Mr Smith* . . .

Mahoney took a deep, bitter breath. Because it was too bloody late for such a compromise, because now the Rhodesians were fighting with their backs to the wall, and no way were Moscow and Peking going to rejoice in a nice moderate settlement and let their boys in the bush lay down their arms – Moscow and Peking didn't want a nice moderate black government in Rhodesia, they wanted a communist one. You did not have to be a clairvoyant to see that the war would go on.

And the news of the war was shocking. The next headline made his guts turn over:

TERRORISTS SHOOT DOWN RHODESIAN TOURIST PLANE

A Rhodesian Airways plane carrying over fifty civilian holiday-makers, mostly women and children, from the Zambesi Valley to Salisbury, was shot down yesterday by terrorists using a heat-seeking anti-aircraft missile of Russian manufacture . . .

He felt sick in his guts. He could almost hear the screams as the plane came tearing down out of the sky, the smashing and crashing. Miraculously, ten survivors had crawled out of the terrible wreckage, hysterical, astonished to be alive, and four of them had gone off to find help: then the terrorists had arrived, raped the women, then shot them all. The Selous Scouts were now tracking the terrorists. Meanwhile, another mission station was attacked yesterday, all the missionaries butchered, two of them women, two babies bayoneted . . .

Jesus! He started the car furiously. What do you say about a war like that? You want to bellow to the world, '*What the hell are you supporting communist murderers like that for?*' And he wanted to grab Ian Smith by the scruff of neck and shake him.

He drove angrily home. Through the cow-meadow, through the woods, to the empty house. He thought, And what are you doing about it, coming home hungover from a drunken orgy while the communists close in on your country – with your daughter in it?

He got out of his car, slammed the door. No, he did not believe that Catherine was in danger: the terrorists would never get the towns; they would only ravage the countryside like roving packs of wild dogs. But that would be enough to win the war.

He went inside, put the radio on loud to stop himself thinking about it. He went upstairs, changed into fresh clothes, to go to work at Malcolm Todd's cottage.

CHAPTER 12

By law he was only allowed to work ninety hours a month, to be in good condition to fly aeroplanes; but he could not stay in the empty cottage, so usually he went to Redcoat House and did his paperwork, then worked on drafting the new Civil Aviation Authority's Airship Regulations. The best place for that was the Todds' cottage, so that Malcolm could explain everything, the technicalities, the importance of each part, and Mahoney tried to put it into the legal language that civil servants like to hear.

'Those heaters won't go wrong,' Malcolm said.

'What minimum dimensions must they be to heat all that helium? And snow and ice?'

'Snow and ice will not collect during flight,' Malcolm said, 'because of the slipstream of air around the hull. Snow collects while the ship is stationary, but the heating system will warm the hull and melt it.'

'But if the heater broke down, how do we get rid of the ice?'

'It won't break down. It is simply the heat from the exhaust, piped through the hull and out the other side. That hot pipe is surrounded by a jacket with a built-in fan. The fan sucks cold helium in one end of the jacket, it is heated by the pipe, and blows warm helium out the end of the jacket. Can't fail.'

'But if that fan breaks down?'

'You'd have to send a man inside to fix the damn thing, that's all. With a breathing apparatus because helium contains no oxygen. What scuba-divers use.' He added: 'Helium's not poisonous.'

'Let's make a note . . . And if he couldn't fix the fan? He'd have to go out on top to shovel the snow off? Maybe during flight. What kind of life-lines must we have?'

Malcolm sighed irritably. 'Any fool can fix that fan! And those German boys on the Zeppelins never *wore* life-lines when they went topside to stitch up canvas. But what you must impress on the C.A.A. is we *can* send a man up there to shovel snow off. But if the heating fails on the leading edge of a jetliner's wings you *can't* send a man out – you get iced-up and crash! . . . Bloody cats!' he shouted. '*Get out!*'

A cat fled.

'I heard you shouting at Napoleon,' Anne shouted from the kitchen. 'Poor Napoleon, was the general being nasty?'

Malcolm snorted wearily to himself.

'I heard you snorting wearily to yourself in there, Field Marshal. Isn't it time you boys knocked off, your dinner's getting cold.'

'It's only eleven! We're making history in here, woman!'

Anne recited in the kitchen:

'I always thought it rather odd
That there should be two Ds in "Todd"
When after all there's only one in "God".'

She came into the room. She was a good-looking, weary woman. She slipped her arm around Malcolm's shoulder. 'Come on, old gas-bag, reveille, this man's got to fly aeroplanes tomorrow.'

'Less of the old,' Malcolm muttered. 'He's got to bang the C.A.A.'s head together next month.'

'Our attitude', the very precise, hard-to-charm civil servant said, 'is that we'll believe it when we see it. Until then . . .' Mahoney waited. 'Until then, I'm afraid you can't expect us to do any work on this. People have been talking about bringing back the airship for fifty years – ever since the *Hindenburg*. Nothing has ever come of it. Because the airship proved itself a thoroughly unreliable, dangerous machine. Oh, I'm aware that hydrogen caused those disasters and you want to use helium.'

'The *Graf Zeppelin*', Mahoney said, 'flew between Germany, South America and New York for years without a single accident – even though she was filled with hydrogen.'

The neat man nodded. 'Mr Mahoney, the C.A.A. is a very busy government body which acts as watchdog on aircraft safety, and we're very expensive. If you design a new aeroplane, our experts would check minutely whether it conformed to these safety regulations.' He tapped a thick book. 'Now, we've *got* no regulations on airships. And we've got no aeronautical *experts* on airships, because airships simply don't exist. And I don't know where such people are to be found.'

'I do.'

'I mean expert by *our* standards. And we'd have to put a lawyer exclusively on to drafting the legislation – and *you'd* have to pay for all this. We don't give free legal advice, you know.'

'I know,' Mahoney said, 'I'm a lawyer.'

The man was surprised. 'I thought you were a commercial pilot?'

'I'm both. I went to Aviation flying school a few years ago.'

'I see. How very odd. Then how is it you're a captain already?'

'I own the airline. The major partner. In fact, I only fly as co-pilot, not as captain.' The civil servant looked at Redcoat with new suspicion. 'But, as a lawyer, I've started drafting the legislation to shortcut . . .'

'I need a *proper* lawyer, Mr Mahoney – the C.A.A. doesn't take shortcuts.'

'I *am* a proper lawyer, Mr White. And I *do* understand airships, which your lawyer won't. All I'm asking for is cooperation, so we know what you're worried about.'

'We'll be worried stiff about everything! Good Lord, a monster twice as long as a football field, flying over London in a gale . . . Mr Mahoney, before you ask us for guidance, you'll have to convince us our effort is not going to be wasted.'

Mahoney smacked the pile of files. 'There are the plans, prepared by an expert. And there's my effort so far at drafting the legislation. Now, are you going to read them or not, Mr White?'

Mr White sat back and looked at the ceiling. 'Mr Mahoney, how much is one airship going to cost?'

'Between ten and fifteen million pounds, once we've got a production line.'

'And', Mr White said politely, 'has Redcoat got that kind of money?'

'Not yet.'

'No,' Mr White said, lowering his eyes. 'And the banks won't lend it to you. And where do you propose building such a huge thing? No building I know of is big enough.'

'At Cardington,' Mahoney said grimly. 'There are two old airship hangars.'

'Cardington?' Mr White mused. 'Where the ill-fated R 101 was built? Charming connotations. And will the government lease them to you, do you think?'

'They're a white elephant, and government will be delighted that we're providing employment.'

'*If* the Civil Aviation Authority endorses your plans. And what about airports, Mr Mahoney? You can't land these things at Heathrow. You'll want government to build airports?

Where? At what tremendous cost? That's the sort of thing—'

'That', Mahoney said, 'is exactly the sort of thing I want to talk about. I have here provisional plans for airports, plus full-scale ones for the future, all diligently prepared by Major—'

'Indeed? And who's going to pilot these things? You have been awfully busy, Mr Mahoney, but who is going to instruct the instructors who're going to instruct the trainee pilots? It's a whole new ball-game.'

Mahoney took a breath. 'We are, Mr White,' he said. 'Redcoat.'

Mr White stared. 'But what', he said, 'are your qualifications?'

Mahoney leant forward. 'Mr White, I'll soon know more about airships than almost any man alive. Now, the C.A.A. is going to *have* to allow somebody to test-fly the first airships. And you'll *have* to grant concessionary licences to those test-pilots for that purpose.'

Mr White looked at him. 'I see . . .' Then he scratched his cheek. 'What about the banks? What do they say?'

'We haven't been to the banks yet. They'll want to see that the C.A.A. are taking it seriously.'

Mr White glared at the formidable pile of files. 'The chicken or the egg?'

'Yes,' Mahoney smiled.

Mr White suddenly shook his head wearily, like an ordinary human being. 'You know damn well I'm required to look into this bumf.'

Mahoney put on his most charming smile. 'Yes, sir,' he said.

Cash flow. That's what airlines desperately need, to pay their huge operating costs: and plenty of it. Cash flow, that's what the Civil Aviation Authority insists on seeing in airlines' books, to satisfy themselves that this airline can pay engineering maintenance so their aeroplanes do not come crashing down out of the skies. (So you can't even cheat on your income tax.) Cash flow, that is what bank managers insist on from little airlines who haven't got big shareholders behind them: cash constantly flowing in, to justify the huge amounts of revolving credit the airline needs to keep it aloft from one week to the next: no sufficient cash flow, no more credit, no more airline.

'Five million pounds was our gross cash flow last year.'

'Yes, but our local branch had to lend you over four and a half million while you earned it,' the bank executive pointed out.

It was Mahoney's first venture into the City. He didn't like messing with bank managers, men who could cut off his lifeline at any time, but if he had to he preferred the suburban variety who held Redcoat's purse-strings at Gatwick, not these silver-haired, heavy-duty gentlemen of the City.

'You've earned a lot of interest,' he said. 'We've been good business for Barclays.'

'Indeed,' the banker said, sitting up. 'Mr Mahoney, we are not belittling Redcoat. We respect you as hard-working and ingenious. In fact we're amazed that you've survived, let alone prospered. Your local manager' – he consulted a letter – 'says that, when you first arrived, the airline wallahs expected you to collapse in two weeks.'

Mahoney knew he wouldn't get the money. 'But?' he said grimly.

The banker decided to cut through all this.

'Mr Mahoney, five million pounds turnover a year is a great deal of money to you and me. But to banks, Redcoat is a very small business.'

Mahoney nodded. 'But if British Airways were asking you for fifteen million pounds, it would be different.'

'Obviously it would put a different complexion on the matter.'

'British Airways', Mahoney said heavily, 'lost *eighty million* pounds last year. Redcoat made a good profit.'

'But', the banker went on, 'even if it was British Airways, I would not be financing an airship project. I am a good deal older than you, and I remember the old airships, though I was only a boy. I remember them flying over London, darkening the sky. Wonderful things – but completely impractical.' He

103

shook his head. 'I remember the *Hindenburg* crashing in New Jersey. Our R 101 crashing in France—'

Mahoney groaned. 'Modern airships . . .'

'I know. Will use helium instead of hydrogen. But I took the trouble, when your branch manager referred you to us, to approach a client who is the chairman of one of the biggest airlines in the world.'

'And I bet he's losing money. Well?'

The executive smiled thinly. 'He gave me seven reasons why airships will never work. I'll read them.'

He picked up a letter.

'One. The huge cost of design and development . . .'

Mahoney said, 'They have already been designed by Major Todd and his consultants. The only cost was Major Todd's army career, and the shares he will give in his company to the consultants for their work.'

'Two,' the banker said. 'The slow speed, about a hundred miles an hour, which means it will be very difficult to keep to schedules in high head winds.'

Mahoney shook his head. 'Speed is so unimportant, Mr Hampstead. Who needs speed? Only fat businessmen flying to New York and Tokyo. I'll be flying not them but their *products*. And a hundred miles an hour is a lot faster than ship and rail.'

'Three. The powers of *lift* vary with atmospheric temperatures and pressures. For instance, in the tropics, twelve percent of lift is lost by the heat.'

Mahoney said, 'Aeroplanes are affected too! Who is this guy?'

'Four,' the banker said resolutely. 'The problems of having to fly low. For every one thousand feet of height the helium expands three percent, so you either have to valve it off, which is expensive, or start off your voyage less than fully inflated.'

'Sure!' Mahoney shrugged. 'Who wants to fly high?'

'But what about mountains?'

'Fly around the high ones! Plan your routes.' He shook his head. 'Next complaint?'

The banker shot him a look. 'Five. The environmental

objections to flying a monstrous and noisy machine low and slowly over inhabited areas.'

Mahoney was amazed. That this ignorance, from an alleged expert, was stopping his loan.

'*Noisy?*' he exclaimed. 'It'll make a *fraction* of the noise of a jet! Good Lord – ask the people who live near Heathrow and Kennedy about jet noise! And airships will cause one-fifth of the pollution from engine exhaust!'

The banker looked at him. 'What about this one? Six: the problems; especially in high winds, of controlling a monstrous machine as large as the Albert Hall and as light as a feather?'

Mahoney sighed. There was no point in antagonizing the man. 'All aeroplanes are affected by winds. So are ships. But *air*ships will also *use* the winds, like the sailing ships did, to push them along. They'll fly trade-wind routes. And as for landing in winds, an aeroplane can only tolerate so much cross-wind, but an airship doesn't use a *straight* runway like an aeroplane. It can approach its mast from any direction, so it's always flying *into* the wind when it's docking. And it can fly away and stay up there for days, waiting for the weather to improve. An aeroplane can't do that.'

The banker put the letter down. 'Finally,' he says, 'a 747 can fly five times the number of miles that an airship could in a year – therefore do five times the work. Earn five times as much.' He looked at him with raised eyebrows.

Mahoney sat back.

'Bullshit, sir.' (The banker blinked.) 'Who is this guy? Which airline?'

'I'm afraid—'

'Look, all the big airlines are losing money – British Airways, Pan American, Air France . . . How many failures do you people need? Of course a jumbo 747 can fly five times as many miles a year, because it flies at five times the speed. But at five times the cost of fuel for each mile! And the world's going to run out of fuel! And a jumbo can only fly to big expensive airports – it can't fly to the middle of the Sahara or the Amazon jungle! So add to the cost of a jumbo's cargo the onward transmission of it by road or rail – if they exist! And for every 747 you've got to have at least three crews: one flying, one resting, and one about to take over! Big airlines have six or seven crews.'

'And how many crews for an airship?' the banker asked.

Mahoney held up a finger. 'One.'

The banker looked surprised. 'How?'

'Because', Mahoney said, 'they'll sleep aboard. A ship only has one crew, doesn't it? We'll keep watches, like a ship at sea. A captain and two officers. Plus an engineer. Plus a loadmaster – who'll double as cook.' He shook his head. 'They'll have proper sleeping cabins, bathrooms, dining room – they'll live aboard.'

The banker was silent. Then he smiled, and sat forward. 'It's a romantic notion,' he admitted. 'Young man, may I ask your age?'

'Thirty-nine.' Mahoney had decided to stay thirty-nine for some years.

The banker nodded, for a moment envy flickered on his face. 'You look younger. But will you forgive me if I offer some friendly advice?'

'Go ahead.'

'You used to be a lawyer. And I suspect you were a good one. Now you're an airline owner, and doing it well too. But you're a romantic, I can tell. Which is fine. Enjoy it. But out here in the big bad world of business, it's cold-blooded. Not romantic.'

'So what's your advice?' Mahoney smiled grimly.

'Stick with your proven aeroplanes. Because this real world of business does not lend money on dreams.'

Friends. And lots of them. That's what you need if you're an impoverished ex-army major trying to launch a multi-million pound airship industry. Plenty of good, long-suffering friends, to invest in a dream.

'I'm in, for five hundred pounds,' David Baker said.

'Who's David Baker?' Mahoney said.

'Insurance pal of mine,' Malcolm Todd said. 'He's bought

five hundred shares. And Admiral Pike's buying three thousand.'

'Three thousand! Who's Admiral Pike?'

'Retired Royal Navy. Nice old boy. Sees a great future for the small, non-rigid airship in coastal surveillance. Knows lots of people in the right places. I can pay Redcoat some back rent now.'

'Pay your consultant,' Mahoney smiled, 'he deserves it. Pay yourself some salary too. And take Anne to dinner.'

'A hamburger's all I'll get from the O.C.,' Anne said. 'And we'll talk airships all through it . . . *Piss-off, cat!*' A cat fled.

Malcolm said, 'We can't afford any salaries, but we're paying Redcoat some rent.'

'We'll take shares in your company instead.'

Malcolm smiled. 'You're a bloody good friend.'

'And a bloody good worker,' Anne said.

One advantage of being a barrister, perhaps the only one, is that you train yourself out of sheer necessity to absorb huge volumes of fact rapidly, marshall them correctly, then present them persuasively: middle-aged soldiers, however, are often men of few words, and often the wrong ones. 'There're the facts,' Malcolm Todd tended to say, 'take it or leave it, just look snappy about it!'

'Malcolm,' Mahoney said, 'these guys are big wheels. Captains of commerce. You've got to grab their attention cleverly.'

'I should grab their shirtfronts and bang their thick heads together.'

'Malcolm, explain it to me, and I'll say it for you.'

'It's all written down there! Self-explanatory! Clearly!'

'Clear as mud. Even I can't understand it, and I'm pretty smart about airships, now.'

'Listen to Joe, darling,' Anne called from the kitchen.

'Will you', Malcolm said, 'tell that woman in there to shut up?'

'Malcolm, start at the beginning.'

'You tell him, Joe,' Anne called. 'I couldn't understand that essay, and I'm pretty smart about airships too, now. Boy!' – she rolled her eyes – 'have I heard all about airships . . .'

One advantage of being boss of an airline, perhaps the only one, is that you can give your captains orders, even if you're only the co-pilot. And, definitely, the only advantage of being a pilot at all, in Mahoney's view, was that it gave you plenty of time to think. Being a pilot, in Mahoney's view, was about the most stultifying job an intelligent man could have: flying is vast stretches of intense boredom punctuated only with moments of intense crisis. The more he learned about aeroplanes the more he considered them a dangerous business. As managing director, Mahoney insisted on doing take-offs, even though he hated take-offs, because he wanted his two hours and the nasty congestion of Europe over with, so he could go aft and work: as soon as his two hours were up he said, 'O.K., Captain, I'm off,' and he went to his folding table. He was reworking the screeds of brochures that Malcolm was writing to precondition the public for the launching of his company on the stock market. Mahoney thought he knew everything about airships now, but every time he went back to Malcolm there were new drawings and notes. Then one day he found Malcolm busily reworking designs for small, non-rigid airships, with Admiral Pike. That really worried him.

'We have to have designs of several different ships available to show to potential buyers,' Malcolm explained.

'But these small blimps hardly carry any cargo, Malcolm.'

'Two tons, plus seven people!' Admiral Pike said. 'It's an ideal machine for naval surveillance. Patrolling fishing grounds, for example. Stays aloft thirty-six hours cruising at sixty miles an hour! No aeroplane or naval vessel can match that performance – and it's much cheaper. I'm sure old Ocker Anderson will go for it.'

'Who's Ocker Anderson?'

'Admiral Anderson, Australian Navy, chum of mine. Dinkum Aussie, rough as they come, but a good egg. Can't sail ships, of course, without pranging them into each other, but he's got a lot of clout with the government.'

Mahoney smiled despite himself. He had never met a real, live admiral. The old boy was as ramrod straight with a bristly beard, exactly as an admiral should be..'Ocker will go for it,' the Admiral insisted, 'save risking his precious ships at sea, old Ocker will love that. Those vast coastlines patrolled for him by airships? And the government, you know how jumpy they are about those yellow fellahs in Asia – if there's one thing that makes an Aussie uptight more than suggesting that Donald Bradman wasn't the world's greatest cricketer, it's those Japs and yeller fellahs. Little Johnny Johnson will go for it too.'

'Is he another admiral?'

'New Zealand Navy, nice little chap. I'll buzz down there and bang some sense into them.'

Mahoney was very impressed by all these admirals but he was worried about Malcolm being sidetracked. 'Those are wonderful contacts, but think this through . . .'

'I know,' Malcolm said, 'I don't like these blimps either, Mickey Mouse little things —'

'Mickey *Mouse*? . . .' the Admiral said indignantly.

'– but we've got to get a name for ourselves and the navy wallahs are our most likely first customers. Then, we'll be in good shape to tackle the big rigids.'

'What about China?' the Admiral said, 'their vast coastline, and borders with Russia? It would be an ideal patrol vehicle for those fellahs.'

'Do you know Admiral Wong too? Listen,' Mahoney said worriedly, 'no government will buy airships until they've actually *seen* one. Demonstrated. *That* means you're going to have to build one. Then they might *not* buy! And we're stuck with a white elephant. Stick with the big cargo rigids, Malcolm.'

'Have you', Admiral Pike said frostily to Mahoney, 'got fifteen million pounds?'

Mahoney took a worried breath. 'O.K. . . . . I'm only a shareholder; it's your company, not mine. But *please* don't go off half-cocked. Let me rework your brochures. Redcoat will print them up.'

The Admiral slapped him on the back. 'That's it, young fellah! Good to have you aboard! And I'll buzz Down Under to talk some sense into old Ocker and Johnny Johnson.'

'*Wait*.' Mahoney said. 'Until our literature's perfect and you're properly briefed, Admiral.'

'Right-oh, good thinking! Meanwhile, what can I do? I'll go and see those RAF fellahs, shall I, and talk them into giving us those hangars at Cardington. I know old Air-Marshal Thompson, used to play rugger against him. Hopeless at rugger, he was, couldn't catch a pig in a passage, but he knows a bit about aeroplanes, I suppose.'

'Excellent,' Malcolm said.

When the Admiral had gone Mahoney said: 'Malcolm, be careful of him. Don't get talked into building a blimp *unless* a government has actually ordered it.'

'We may have to.'

Mahoney shook his head. 'Malcolm, it's time we started on the Onassis principle. Go to places like China and Brazil to talk them into giving us a contract to carry their cargo, *then* go back to the banks.' He added soberly: 'Redcoat will finance the trips, by buying some of your shares. Buy yourself a new suit too.'

'The pot calling the kettle black!' Malcolm said.

CHAPTER 13

Except it was much easier for Onassis. Tankers existed. Onassis could contract with the Arabs to deliver their oil and, armed with the contracts, go to the banks to borrow money to buy the tanker to carry the oil to earn the money to repay the bank.

'But there are no airships,' the Chinese girl interpreted.

'There soon will be!' Malcolm said. 'I'm going to build them! Tell them that.'

They were in a panelled office in the Bank of China. Outside were the jampacked streets of Hong Kong, the teeming harbour, hazy in the heat. Mahoney watched the three communist officials. He suspected they understood English. Before they could reply he interrupted: 'Gentlemen, we are not necessarily trying to *sell* China an airship. Interpret that please, Miss Li.' She did. 'We're selling the service of *our* airships to China.'

Miss Li interpreted. The three solemnly smiling Chinese

nodded. One spoke. 'There are no airships,' Miss Li interpreted.

Mahoney soldiered on. 'China needs airships because its the size of the whole of Europe, with inadequate droads, railways, ports, insufficent ships and aircraft. With one thousand *million* people. You could be exporting more than the whole of Europe!'

Malcolm interrupted: 'Near Mongolia, you have huge deposits of coal and iron. But you can't mine it, because it's so mountainous and you have no roads! You can't *afford* to mine it, my dear fellow!'

'Wait, please,' Miss Li said, 'I cannot remember everything.' She interpreted. One Chinese spoke and Miss Li said: 'How do you know this?'

Malcolm looked at her as if she were a raving lunatic. Mahoney trod heavily on his toe. 'Because', Malcolm beamed politely, 'it's in the public library. In the *Encyclopaedia Britannica*. Good Lord, they don't think we're *spying*, do they?'

'The point', Mahoney cut in, before Miss Li could interpret the last bit, 'is that we could fly in your heavy mining equipment, your men, hover, and off you go. When your iron or coal is ready, we come back, hover, load it, and take it away, *direct* to your factory. No roads needed, no trucks, no ships, no airports.'

'But who will fly these airships?' Miss Li interpreted.

'We will! If China wanted to buy an airship we would provide the crew, and maintenance, for a fee. Or we would train *your* crews. Or you can contract with us to deliver your cargo in our airship – which will be much cheaper than any other means.'

One Chinese said in English: 'China has typhoons. Very dangerous.'

Malcolm shook his head. Mahoney said: 'Aeroplanes and ships have to avoid typhoons too. Typhoons move slowly. Airships would fly away from them, or around them. If necessary, the airship can stay up there for days to keep out of danger. Aeroplanes cannot do that.'

'But where is your airship?'

Mahoney groaned inwardly. 'Now, if you look at page

111

twelve of the brochure . . .' It was an impressive, glossy booklet, in English and Chinese characters. 'There I give actual tonnages of cargo China exported last year by air, and what it cost you.'

He paused for Miss Li to translate.

'How do you know these figures?'

'From the *Far East Economic Review*. Now, on the opposite page, I show how much *less* it would have cost China if you had exported that cargo by my airship.'

The Chinese studied the figures, spoke amongst themselves. Then looked at Mahoney inscrutably. He said, 'And *now*, look at this.' He produced a document. 'Here is a Bill of Lading for cargo that Redcoat carried from Hong Kong to Europe only last month. You see what it cost for fifty tons. And whose cargo was it? China's. *Your* government paid for it!' He paused. 'And here is another document. It shows how much less it would have cost you by airship.'

They studied the documents.

Mahoney took a breath. 'Now, what we seek from China is a contract for us to fly her cargo at a guaranteed, attractive price for a specified period. Then I will build the airship to do the job.' He held up another document. 'Here is a specimen of that contract, written in both English and Chinese.'

The Chinese said: 'But how can you do it without an airship yet?' Mahoney groaned. The Chinese smiled: 'We will consider everything.' He added: 'In Peking.' Then: 'Maybe it is better if you build your airships in China?'

Mahoney was taken aback. In China? In a communist factory? The Chinese said, 'Then we could see it.'

Mahoney's mind was racing. The ramifications were enormous. As if on cue all three stood up. 'Thank you,' the official said. 'We will write. *Ho choi*, good luck.'

Outside, the stone lions guarding the bank stood at revolutionary attention. Mahoney and Malcolm walked between them, then round the corner into Statue Square. Ahead was the mighty Hongkong & Shanghai Bank, the big black lions guarding its portals imperialistically recumbent.

'What do you think, Malcolm?'

'What is the sound of one hand clapping?' Malcolm said.

112

Maybe it wasn't so easy for Onassis, either.

In the British Natural History Museum you can find out everything about this plant. With their geological maps, books and atlases you can find out all the proven sites of precious minerals. In the Department of Mines of Canberra and in Ottawa, anybody can, on payment of a search-fee, and with patience, find out registered owners of the mining rights.

'My doctor tol' me I could only drink wine,' Tank O'Sullivan mumbled through his big mouthful of curry. 'So that's all I drink.'

'All day,' his wife sighed.

'Tol' me to quit with the whisky,' Tank explained reasonably to Mahoney and Malcolm, 'so now I only drink wine.'

'All *day* . . . '

'Hey, what's 'at?' Tank jabbed with his fork at a passing waiter. 'I wan' some o' that!'

'That's the sweet trolley, Tank,' Malcolm said.

'Waiter, c'mere!' Tank shouted. His hand shot out and grabbed a chocolate eclair. He opened his mouth full of curry and chomped. ('Tank, dear . . . ,' his wife said.) 'C'mere, waiter!' Tank's big hand grabbed a fruit salad, up-ended it over his curry. 'An' some more of this!' He held up his wine tankard.

The waiter dashed away. Tank reached out for the trolley and his fist closed around some cream cake. 'Yeah,' he chomped thoughtfully through a mouthful of cream cake curry fruit salad, 'bought them claims up in Yukon when gold was thirty-two dollars an ounce. Wasn't worth mining 'cos no roads. Only way was helicopter. Impossible.'

'But when it went up to eight hundred dollars an ounce?'

'Still too expensive,' Tank chomped. 'You know what roads cost? Hey, what's 'at?'

Mahoney looked at his own plate. 'Curried prawn,' he said.

'Why ain't I got curried prawn?'

'Because you ordered curried chicken.'

'I wan' prawns.' His fork stabbed one off Mahoney's plate.

113

'Waiter – bring me some of that!' He stuffed the prawn in with the curried cream cake and chomped.

Mahoney tapped the sheet of paper. 'But even now, when gold's four hundred dollars an ounce, you'll make a fortune if you use an airship to freight your gear up there.'

Tank shovelled thoughtfully. 'Know what's gonna happen to gold?'

'It's going up to a thousand dollars an ounce?'

Tank chomped. 'Two thousand. Paper money ain't gonna count for nothin'. Only thing's gonna count is gold.'

'*If*', Malcolm said, 'you've got it out of the ground in time.'

Tank speared another prawn. Mahoney pushed his plate towards him with a grin. 'I wan' my *own*,' Tank complained, stabbing another one. 'Yeah,' he mumbled on, 'how long's it gonna take you to build?'

'Give us a contract today,' Mahoney said, 'to freight your plant, men and ore, and I'll be back here in eighteen months with an airship.'

Tank shook his big head. 'I wan' my *own* airship!'

'Fine!' Malcolm beamed.

The waiter hurried up with Tank's very own prawns. Tank picked two up in his fingers, tilted back his big head and dropped the animals into his mouth on top of all the rest. 'I ain't gonna spend twenty-odd millions bucks on somethin' I ain't never *seen*.' He looked at them with big brown eyes. 'You build it . . .' he chomped, 'I like it . . .' he chomped, 'I buy it . . .' He picked up another prawn. 'No like, no buy.'

Mahoney said earnestly, 'Will you give us a contract to that effect – plus a refundable down-payment if you don't buy?'

Tank picked up two more prawns and bomb-dropped them into his throat like a pelican.

'Nope. That ain't how Tank O'Sullivan got rich.'

CHAPTER 14

Contacts, people who knew the right people, that's what they needed. And some of them came their way by accident.

Sometimes Mahoney waded through another of those dinners at his Inn of Court. Each time he looked out for the beautiful Australian woman, but he did not see her. Then one night he thought he saw her enter the crowded hall, the leonine sweep of tawny hair, and his heart missed a beat. He put on his spectacles, but she had already sat down. After the dinner there was to be a debate, on the merits of British Colonial Policy, the motion being '*It's an ill wind that blows nobody any good*'. He resolved to stay for the debate, if she did, in the hopes of speaking to her afterwards. He kept an eye on the door.

He listened to the debate with mounting irritation. The student arguing for the merits was apologetic about the old British Empire, but suggested there was *some* merit . . . The opposition spokesman was from Ghana, and he let flow a diatribe against the British, how they had 'enslaved the people', 'ground the faces of the poor', 'bled the economy white'; he ranted about 'travesties of justice', 'raping peace-loving civilizations', 'inadequate medicine', and 'bleeding the continent white' some more. He was very fond of 'bleeding the continent white'. Then the debate was thrown open. There followed a litany of complaints about colonialists in general and the British in particular. Some white students stood up and offered some defence, but always with the preface that colonialism was admittedly bad. Mahoney listened in amazement. There was no *pride* in what England had achieved . . . He'd had no intention of involving himself in undergraduate debate, but finally he stood up.

'Master,' he said loudly, 'I have never heard such balls!'

There was shocked silence and some titters.

'Such *what*?' the Master said dangerously.

'Beach-balls, Master,' Mahoney cried, 'tennis balls, footballs, all share the characteristic that there is nothing inside them except air! Like the empty vessels, Master, which make the most noise! What *appals* me is that at no time in this veritable gale of hot air we've had the misfortune to hear tonight have we met one iota of *pride* from our British brothers about England's achievements in spreading Christian civilization! No *pride*, Master, that Great Britain sent her best sons

115

out to the corners of the earth to bring science and civilization to people who had not yet discovered the wheel! Medicine to people who perished in hordes from simple ailments! Law and order to people who slaughtered and enslaved each other in internecine tribal warfare! Agricultural science to people who only scratched a living from the soil and often suffered from malnutrition! Economics to people who only knew about barter! British justice to places that had no justice at all, where people settled their differences by spear, or at best had only primitive tribunals which admitted the vaguest hearsay evidence and at which the accused had to prove his innocence! We heard no *pride* tonight, Master, in these sons of England who brought all the values of the English public school and Oxford and Cambridge and this very Inn to create an efficient and incorruptible administration where before there was none, to build roads, and railways, and harbours, and airports, where before there was only jungle and desert, who brought the telegraph and radio to places where the only communication was by mouth and by drum – and who brought *democracy*, Master, to places where the chief's word was law!

'Now these are *facts*, Master, not matters of opinion; we heard no acknowledgment tonight of these facts, nor of the missionary zeal of those *excellent* men. All we heard were apologies and *damning* with faint praise!' He spread his hands theatrically. '*Apologies!* What *nonsense* is this? I ask you, Master, has British youth become such a bunch of long-haired, lily-livered, milk-and-water lefties that they feel *apologetic* for the grand deeds of their gutsy forefathers? Alas, it seems so!'

'I think you are becoming rather personal, Mr – er – whatever-your-name-is,' the Master said.

'On the contrary, Master,' Mahoney cried, 'I am making a sweeping and valid generalization! And I'll make another: we have heard not one word of acknowledgment of these benefits from our non-British brothers-in-law tonight – benefits which enable them to be here today enjoying a freedom of speech they wouldn't *dare* employ in their own countries now the British, whom they castigate, have departed, enjoying human rights that they no longer have back home since the Westminster-style democracy the British gave them has been

116

thrown out the window – we have heard not one word about these benefits, let alone *gratitude*. Only *black ingratitude*, if you'll forgive a useful pun—'

The first piece of bread flew, and Mahoney dodged it artfully. 'Master,' he shouted happily, 'they should be damn grateful! They should shout *Hallelujah!* Because if it weren't for British colonial policy they wouldn't be here today – they'd be running around in loincloths!'

He dodged another piece of bread, hastily bowed to the bench as the debate erupted in disorder, and ducked out of the hall, delighted with himself.

God, he enjoyed that . . . He hastily returned his gown to the cloakroom and set off across the dark courtyard. It was not until he was approaching the archway that he remembered the lovely woman. He stopped. But it was too late now. He dared not go back into the Inn now. He sure hadn't won any hearts and minds in there . . .

Then he thought: Faint heart never won fair lady!

He turned and slowly retraced his steps across the courtyard. He waited for five minutes, in the shadows. Students started emerging from the Inn, talking noisily, thronging into the cloakroom. Mahoney stood in the shadows, watching for her. Perhaps she was with somebody. Perhaps she was lingering inside over port. Then he saw her. She was coming out, taking off her gown. She walked into the cloakroom.

Two minutes later she reappeared, alone, carrying a handbag. She wore a smart black suit, black stockings, black high heels and a white ruffle-neck blouse. She looked very sophisticated and purposeful as she set off into the courtyard. Mahoney came out of the shadows. His heart was knocking. He was not much good at picking up women.

'Good evening!' He put on his most charming smile.

'Oh, good evening.' She flashed him a brisk smile and kept on walking.

He said, striding beside her, 'May I introduce myself? I'm Joe Mahoney.'

She said briskly: 'How do you do, Mr Mahoney? I am Tana Hutton.'

117

He caught the trace of Antipodes that he had noticed last time. 'How do you do? Are you from Australia, Miss Hutton?'

'I am.' She glanced at him. 'And you, I gather from your little speech, are from the right wing of the Tory Party?'

He smiled. 'No, Rhodesia.'

'Ah,' she said, as if that explained a great deal. 'And *are* you in the ice-cream business?'

Mahoney laughed, delighted that she had remembered. 'That was the night you were Mr Junior. No, actually I'm in the freight business.'

She said, surprised, 'And why should someone in the freight business be reading for the Bar?'

'Well, I used to be a lawyer in sunny Rhodesia. Are you a lawyer in sunny Australia?'

'No.' She added: 'But my family is in the freight business, too.'

'Really? Which company are you?'

She said, 'It's nothing to do with me – my father. Thoren Pacific Airline – Thoren Shipping – have you heard of them?'

Indeed he had. One of the biggest carriers out there. 'Of course. One of my competitors.' And his spirits sank. So she was *Mrs* Hutton, née Thoren. 'Your father's a politician,' he said.

'Right. You and he would see eye-to-eye. He regards Margaret Thatcher as a dangerous left-winger.' (Mahoney laughed.) 'And what's the name of your company?'

'Redcoat, you won't have heard of us. We've only got two planes.' They were three quarters across the courtyard now. 'And what are you doing reading law? Are you going to practise?'

'No, I'm simply doing it for interest. My father thought a university education was wasted on a woman, but I always fancied myself in a wig and gown. Are you going to practise here?'

'Perhaps. What year are you?'

'I'm in my final year. And you?'

He admitted, 'I haven't taken any of the exams yet.' They were entering the archway to Holborn – it was now or never. 'Mrs Hutton, shall we go to Hennekeys and have a glass of port?'

She said, 'No, thank you, Mr Mahoney, I have an appointment.'

'Oh. Another night perhaps?'

'I doubt there'll be one. I finished my three years of thirty-six dinners tonight.'

'Will you have dinner with *me*? Tomorrow night?'

'I'm afraid—'

He interrupted cunningly, 'Or the night after. Or next week? Next month? *Any* goddamn night?'

She smiled. 'I'm afraid I return to Australia tomorrow, Mr Mahoney, and I've no idea when I'll be back here.' They emerged through the arch, and she looked up the street for a taxi.

'Mrs Hutton, I'm getting discouraged. But perhaps we can be pen-pals?'

She grinned. 'At best . . .' She waved to an approaching taxi. He said urgently: 'Can I drive you to your appointment?'

'Here's the taxi,' she said politely.

He watched it pull up, with resignation. He opened the door.

'Thank you.'

He closed the door regretfully. She spoke to the driver. Mahoney tapped the window: 'Remember to write!'

She laughed, and the taxi began to move away.

He stood in the street and watched it go. He thought, What a lovely woman. What lovely legs. He could see her through the rear window. She did not turn. But, then, she raised her hand, without looking round, and twiddled her fingers over her shoulder.

Mahoney grinned and waved back energetically. He watched the taxi until it was out of sight. Then he turned and walked sadly back down Holborn.

Married, of course. Well, that was the end of that blazing romance . . .

Then he stopped in his tracks. Of course . . . Thoren Pacific. Thoren Shipping. Thoren International Holdings. Mr Thoren was a man to see about airships! At least to get on side. And Thorens had a big office in London. He could probably set up the meeting from here. Furthermore, Redcoat had a flight going to Australia next month.

CHAPTER 15

Every time he flew over this island he was impressed by its vastness, and excited by its huge emptiness, its massive opportunities. Around the endless coastlines was a narrow border of green, then the mauve mountains, then the brownness stretching on and on, fading into grey haze. What treasures lay under that immensity? If only they could dig a canal across it, from the Gulf of Carpenteria down to the Great Australian Bight, and flood the vast heart of this continent, it would change the whole climate, make rain. There were fortunes to be made here.

'Not enough of the right people,' old Erling Thoren said. There was a slow Norwegian accent beneath the Australian. 'Most Australians are soft. Bladdy meatpies and Fosters, they think that is their birthright.' He turned his blue eyes on Mahoney. 'I tell them in Canberra, forget about these bladdy English immigrants, get Americans if you want to develop this country. Now we have forty thousand Yanks. They bladdy *work*.' His eyes twinkled. 'The Australians call them "Septic Tanks".'

Mahoney liked the old boy. He was amazed at the size of the ranch.

'I was a stoker in a Norwegian ship. I jumped ship in Perth. They put me in jail for a week. Then the magistrate said: "That's what we do with naughty boys. Now, do you want to go home to Norway or stay here?" I said, "Stay here." "O.K.," said the magistrate, "but don't do it again."' He laughed. 'So I walked into the outback and bought ten cows.'

'Now how many do you have?'

'Thirty thousand. In Australia we have strikes all the time. Most of the trouble makers are from England. The communists send them out here. It is part of their overall strategy to undermine the West.' He shook his head. 'This country could be like America all over again, I tell them in Canberra.'

'And what do they say?'

'There is no shortage of bladdy fools in Canberra. Votes, that's all most of them want. Changing government here is only like changing deck-chairs on the *Titanic*. I'm an independent, you know – always in opposition.'

'Yes.' Mahoney had done his homework. 'How much land do you have here?'

'Ten thousand square miles. That's not so big. My daughter has more.' He added: 'And she bought it herself, not me. On her tenth birthday I gave her ten cows, like I had. By the time she was twenty she had two thousand. Buying and selling. And a plumber.'

'A plumber?'

The old man smiled. 'She bought some old houses in Sydney. The plumbing was bad. When she found out how much plumbers cost, she went to technical school, then did the plumbing. With her own hands.'

Mahoney liked talking about her. 'Extraordinary.'

'Then she sold some houses and bought more farmland, and sold some cattle and bought more houses. She is a very good builder and buyer and seller. I told her: "Go and *work*, young lady!"' He added, 'She could fly an aeroplane when she was fifteen.'

'And now she is studying Law,' said Mahoney.

Down there he could see the airstrip, over there the red roof of the homestead. The old man brought the little plane down to a good landing. There was a Landrover parked in the trees. They drove to the homestead. Then sat on the old porch, behind the fly screens, drinking beer.

'I keep telling them in Canberra: *Work!* The frontier spirit! But we are in the age of the two-car man, and strikes.'

'What about water?' Mahoney said.

'Dams. A survey showed it was possible to turn some rivers around and make them go through the desert. But', he said, disgusted, 'government said it was too bladdy expensive.'

Mahoney said: 'One day it won't be. When the Chinese invade. They'll just put ten million coolies on to digging canals and tunnels.'

'You think they'll invade us?'

Mahoney began his sales pitch. 'I think it's inevitable, unless

121

you're well-prepared. One thousand million Chinese live just up there. Six hundred million Indians. Two hundred million Japanese. All living on top of each other. The day will come when they have to expand, out of sheer pressure of numbers. Where will they go? Australia's wide open. There's only a handful of you, and you're next door.'

Erling Thoren slapped him on the knee. 'Thank God for somebody with a bit of bladdy sense! We are the most vulnerable nation in the world today, with the possible exception of West Germany. So what do you suggest we do?'

Mahoney wanted to concentrate on Cattle-Air – the military aspects were Malcolm's department. He tapped the thick brochure.

'It's all in there. Australia has about ten thousand miles of coastline to worry about. The biggest in the world. Your maritime belt is two hundred miles out to sea. Multiply ten thousand by two hundred and you get two million square miles of sea that you control – in theory. Against enemy shipping. Against violation of fishing rights. But the Japs could steal your seas blind and you wouldn't know.'

'We *do* know. They've tried stripping the Great Barrier Reef.'

'But', Mahoney said, 'with a small fleet of airships you could patrol your seas economically. Look at this graph.' He opened the brochure. 'A small airship patrolling at four thousand feet, at forty knots, allowing for a twenty-knot wind all the way, would, with his radar, efficiently scan one hundred and thirty-six thousand square miles in forty-two hours, without refuelling.'

The old man nodded. 'That is very interesting.'

'When an airship spots suspicious shipping, it could chase it, at over twice the speed of any ship. It could hover to interrogate it, send men down by ladder to inspect it, and escort it to an Australian harbour. No aeroplane can do that. A helicopter couldn't do it; it cannot carry enough fuel.'

'Yes, I understand everything perfectly.'

Mahoney went on: 'Now, if Australia is invaded, how are you going to get troops across this vast country, in a hurry? By train? Too slow, not enough railways. And the enemy only need blow up one bridge. By road? Same answer. By sea? By the time troopships got up there the enemy would be well-established. So? That leaves the air.'

The old man was waiting patiently.

'But where could your big troop-planes land? How far from the enemy? And the first things the enemy would capture are your jungle airstrips. So – paratroops? But how many would you need? And how many have you got?'

The old man smiled grimly: 'But the enemy would blow your troop-carrying airships out of the sky.'

'They are no bigger target than a ship. A troop-plane is a big target too, for modern weapons. Your airship could even carry its own fighter aircraft, in its belly. An airborne aircraft carrier. The Americans perfected that technique with their old airships.'

Erling Thoren uncrossed his lanky legs. 'Yes, I read your brochure. But what do you want from me?'

Mahoney took a breath. 'You own Cattle-Air. Air-freighting cattle is expensive. I'll do it cheaper for you, when I've built my airship.'

'You've done a good study of the beef industry. What else?'

'I want to convince you of the merit of airships for both military and commercial uses, so that you will be our advocate in Canberra.'

Erling Thoren said, with a twinkle in his blue eyes: 'I have told you how many bladdy fools are in Canberra. And it will not be easy to convince me, either. Go on.'

'That's it.'

The wise old man thought, then shook his head.

'Maybe military airships. Commercial airships, no. Maybe in places like Africa, where they have hardly any airports, so you don't have to change what they have already, only chop down some trees to make a new space.' He turned to Mahoney: 'I have extensive businesses in Africa, you know.'

'Yes, I know.'

'And the communists are going to get the lot one day, unless we fight. Russia wants the Cape sea-route, and Suez, and Panama. Then they'll dominate all the trading routes. They are winning all the wars in Africa, and we do not

123

fight back – except South Africa and the Rhodesians.' He shook his head. 'Whatever we may think of South African politics, we must fight the Russians with them.' He turned to Mahoney. 'I was interested in what you said in your political campaign.'

Mahoney was surprised. 'You know about that?'

The old eyes twinkled. 'I know everything. And what I don't know, I think I know. They do not call me Old Thoren-in-the-flesh for nothing, you know.' He ripped the top of another can of beer. 'Very well, let's talk. But I can tell you now that those people in Canberra won't buy an airship until they have seen one. Nor would Erling Thoren tell them to do so.'

CHAPTER 16

That year went that way. Business was good. Redcoat bought another Canadair. They did passenger charters to the Greek islands in the Britannia, but the competition was fierce with the air-lines selling cheap tickets. For two weeks Redcoat did charters from Morocco, carrying pilgrims to Mecca. They had to fly low over the airstrips to chase the goats away before they could land: then the Arabs came swarming aboard, and just huddled on the floor. Once Mahoney smelt smoke: he flung open the door, and saw the Arabs had lit a fire and were roasting a goat which they had slain on board. He grabbed the fire extinguisher and the foam flew; there was a great surge of pilgrims scrambling over each other, and Mahoney had to admit he wasn't too careful where the foam blasted.

He did not hear from Erling Thoren, but Redcoat did receive a few contracts from Thorens to haul cargo from Africa to Europe, which was gratifying. What he would remember most about that year was the frustration, the work, work, work, and the waiting – for results, for people to reply. And not sleeping properly. When he went to bed he fell asleep immediately, as if his body had just shut down in protest, but he always woke up early, no matter how late he had gone to bed; suddenly he was wide-awake, staring in the darkness, as if he had heard something. He got straight up, got into his tracksuit and set out in the darkness, jogging. He tried to jog three miles — but sometimes he just had to walk a bit, when that pounding in his chest told him he was no longer in the army but a small-time airline manager with a load on his mind, and not as young as he used to be.

Mostly, he had stopped dreaming about Shelagh; but sometimes she still came out of the darkness, beautiful, smiling, and he was happy — then he woke up. And he was filled with emptiness, and he wanted to go back to sleep, to be with her: but he made himself get up. Sometimes he dreamed about the courtroom, and again he was happy, doing work he was good at, and when he woke up he wondered what the hell he was doing running an airline when he didn't even like aeroplanes.

And he dreamed about airships; and they were frightened dreams. He was flying a machine as light as a feather, as huge as a thundercloud; then the winds were wrenching it, the whole massive structure lurching under his feet, his engines screaming ineffectually, and down there were the rooftops of London, people screaming, he was going to be blown on to the rooftops, crumpling, tearing buildings down, and he desperately released all the ballast and then the giant machine was ballooning away into the lashing gale, barrelling up into the blackness, blind, and he did not know where his ship would founder and he would die, in the icy waves of the Atlantic, crashed around, breaking up . . . And he woke up in a cold sweat, and for long moments he forgot all he knew about airships and he was victim of the same fears as everybody. And he felt the icy fear of bankruptcy, losing everything in one mad, dangerous machine everybody said would fail . . .

But he was over the dreams by the time he got to Redcoat House. It was still dark. It felt good to be starting the day so early, getting ahead of everybody else, everything quiet. Often he had caught up on all the paperwork by the time Dolores and Nancy came. Then, usually, he left, so that officially he was not working, and he went to Malcolm's cottage to work on airships. And towards the end of that year there was not much he could do on that: he had finished the Airship Regulations, written all the brochures, only Malcolm could work on the various technical designs: often there was nothing to do but read, sleep and wait for evening, when he could go back to Redcoat House and see what there was for him to do before he flew away again.

Sometimes he went out for a drink. Usually he went to The Rabbit, Danish Erika's pub, with its low beams and log fire, where usually he sat alone and read the newspapers because he did not want to answer questions about airships or what he thought of the situation in Rhodesia. He often wondered what the hell he was doing in a business that didn't let him drink or work as much as he wanted to. The Rabbit also served pub grub, which was better than eating alone in the house in the woods. What he remembered well about those days was the loneliness of eating alone. He did not mind drinking alone, because that gives you time to think; after the third pint it's time to start talking the usual bullshit, and maybe trying to get into the girls' pants: but he did not like dining alone. Then you really remember, and you think what a goddamn mess your life is, here you are eating a Co-op hamburger with a plastic mixed veg alone in your haunted house, about to tackle gravity in your aeroplane again when you're a lawyer who could be back in Rhodesia making fifty thousand pounds a year just by keeping your fingers crossed that nobody threw too many curly bits of Law at you – money for jam, that is. So, as Shelagh said, why are you in the airlines business? Because of the challenge? No . . . Mostly because of the *romance* of it. Of flying to faraway places with strange-sounding names, of being involved in the economy – of being a *trader*. I suppose if I had my way I would really be in sailing ships, Captain Mahoney pacing his bridge. And that's why you're into airships: what really turns you on is that galleon in the skies . . .

In fact, Mahoney need never have eaten alone, nor slept alone. There was an abundance of woman-flesh. He avoided married women: it was not only dishonourable, but unnecessarily hazardous. The law of averages is against you. Don't believe this legend about married women being so discreet, and beware of the lines 'he wouldn't care' and particularly 'he'll never know'. He'll know just as soon as somebody feels bitchy enough, or when *she* finds out *he's* been playing around and yells it in words of one syllable. And there are few sensations more uncomfortable than a guilty conscience. It was unnecessary because there were all the girls who worked at the airport, and the air hostesses.

Sometimes he made a date. Sometimes he took her to dinner, but usually he couldn't afford that so he said, 'I travel so much that when I get home I like to stay there, so how about I cook you dinner?' – whereupon she did the cooking, anyway. And the bedroom close, none of this getting in and out of cars in the bloody English rain, it's unreasonable for her to go home. Sometimes he invited a girl on a flight: that was very easy. 'We're flying to Nairobi tomorrow, do come along, though Redcoat doesn't stay in the best hotels, I'm afraid.' They brightened up the trip. If they wanted to come too often, he only had to say, 'Darling, we're overloaded.' Another good thing, he found, about being a flyer is you always have the excuses that you can't see her until next week because you're going from Accra to Khartoum to Bombay, even if you're only going to Brussels. If she sees you in the street you can say the Khartoum cargo didn't show up.

So he need never have been lonely, and in fact he thoroughly enjoyed himself at times, and new loins are always exciting, new contours and textures and underwear; but what he mostly remembered was the emptiness, once the newness had worn off, and he wanted to get going, to Redcoat House, or to Malcolm's, even up there in his aeroplanes and go, go, go.

And there was always Danish Erika. They had a good relationship, because there was no future in it. 'Relax, Mahoney, I've been married three times and I wasn't faithful to any of them, it's only your *body* I want, and only half the time.'

Half the time Danish Erika's body was in excellent condition. She was a health fanatic, excepting for booze and cigarettes. Every two months Erika disappeared to a health farm where she dried out and ate lettuce. When she came back she was beautiful for a month, a curvy waist and those long Danish legs, her eyes bright blue. After a month she began to look like a bosomy barmaid again, a month later she disappeared again. Sometimes she would telephone and say: 'It's been two weeks, Mahoney. You may be working but you still eat, right?'

'Right.'

'So instead of spending your money in my boozer, go buy a steak, and I'll bring my own wine, thanks very much.'

'You don't like my homemade wine?'

'I prefer my own hangovers to yours.'

Erika dabbled in spiritualism, and claimed to be a medium.

'Each one of us has a guardian spirit. They don't like to make decisions for you, because that hampers your own spiritual growth. But they'll try to help you.'

'You really believe this?'

'Of course. Somebody like you can only speak to them through a medium. But once you've opened up the channel you can talk to them when you like. I speak to Erowan every day.' (Erowan was Erika's guardian spirit, a Buddhist monk who died four hundred years previously.) 'Usually in the morning.'

'What does he look like?'

'Like an ex-Buddhist monk from Thailand.'

'And don't you get kind of uncomfortable waking up and finding Erowan standing there, in his saffron robe and all?'

'Of course not. I love him.'

'And what does he say? Do you say, "Morning, Erowan", or what?'

'I do it in my head. He's *around* all the time. Available. Even if sometimes I've got to wait a bit.'

Mahoney glanced over his shoulder. 'You can't see him now, can you?'

Danish Erika burst out laughing.

'Shall I', she said, 'go into a trance and ask Erowan to call your guardian spirit?'

'No! Please don't bring Erowan to my house!'

She was a good friend. She was always there when he wanted her, pulling pints in The Rabbit. 'Why are you still brooding about her? Forget her, Joe.'

He hated talking about it.

'Any moves about a divorce.'

'No.'

'Maybe you need to talk about it. So, does she write?'

'Occasionally.'

'And?'

And Shelagh was happy. She had her old job, even her old apartment. Catherine was now at infant school. Shelagh was not worried about the war, now that the multi-racial Transitional Government was in operation pending One-Man-One-Vote elections the following year. She wrote: 'Surely, after those elections, Britain will recognize the new black government, sanctions will be lifted and we will win the war. The terrorists will lay down their arms, there'll be no point risking their lives once there's a legal black government. Zambia and Mozambique must recognize us, so the terrorists won't have any bases. In short, the war is all but over! And I see a bright future. Bishop Muzorewa is bound to win the election. He's a good man, a moderate, a man of God, and I'm sure the whites will be welcome. Really, now is the time you should come back and re-establish yourself. There're going to be great opportunities for good men like you. Everything is waiting for you, your law, your farm, your bank account. In fact, if you don't come back and work the farm the new black government will nationalize it. Even Bishop Muzorewa won't tolerate absentee landlords, good agricultural land lying unused. So you must either sell it immediately after the election – you won't find a buyer now – or return. It's no good trying legal dodges like transferring title to Cathy's name, because I have not the time, nor the know-how, to farm it. I've been out once, it's looking beautiful, but very sad. Elijah's a good caretaker, but you cannot leave it much longer. Really, we're now doing exactly as you advocated years ago. How can you possibly justify keeping your back turned on the country *now*?'

Because it was too bloody late now! But oh God, yes, at times he wanted to go back, to his child and his wife and his farm and the work he knew, often he longed to be back on his feet in his wig and gown in that brotherhood of the Bar. He noticed she did not mention returning to *her*, even trying to read between the lines: she wrote like a school mistress advising a wayward pupil whose interests she had at heart. But, oh yes,

129

at times he wanted to go back, to the heat and the skies and the sound of the rain and the smell of the earth and wood smoke, the tall green grass and the mauve horizons, the great Zambesi, and the hippo barking in the moonlight, and the elephants crossing, with the babies hanging on to their mothers' tails, and the sound of drums. Oh God, yes, he wanted to go home and just throw himself down on the warm earth of Africa, where he belonged, and soldier for peace, and throw his lot in with the country . . . And oh yes, he wanted his child.

'Shelagh's fine,' he said to Erika. 'Let's talk about you.'

'Just keeping you on the back-burner, huh? O.K. . . . Has the government given you those hangars at Cardington yet?'

He did not want to talk airships either.

'No. But the C.A.A.'s working on those instructions I drafted.' She was very worried about him losing his money.

'I watch those jets come in, and I can understand that, they've got weight and power behind them, you can control that. But an airship? The mind boggles.'

'A jet touches down at over a hundred miles an hour. An airship docks at *zero* miles an hour. Which sounds safer? It boggles my mind every time I tank up with twenty-five tons of fuel to fly twenty-five tons of cargo, Erika.'

She sighed. 'O.K. I'll leave you to read the papers and pick up the pieces of your life, seeing you're in such an amorous mood. But remember, when you want a piece . . .' She waggled her thumb at herself.

Yes, he could justify it . . . But only with guilt.

He did not want to read about Rhodesia, but that was the first news he looked for. He had washed his hands of Rhodesia, and he felt guilty about deserting his countrymen. The blacks were his countrymen too, and had he not said that the whites should give them their fair share of the sun? And were they not doing just that? And this new Transitional Government of Zimbabwe–Rhodesia cried out to the world:

130

'Recognize us now! . . . We have done everything you wanted of us! . . . Lift your sanctions and let us win this war against the communists!'

But no. The world would not recognize them because the terrorists howled that they would stop the elections and shoot their way triumphant into Salisbury. And the Transitional Government sent out civil servants to explain to the tribesmen about One-Man-One-Vote, how each political party had been assigned a symbol, how one should put a cross next to the symbol of the party of one's choice; to explain about secret ballots, how nobody would know how any man voted with his cross; and they explained that the cross meant something good, it was like the cross of Jesus, a cross of peace, not the cross of some wrong thing like maybe they had learned at mission school: and the tribesmen asked, If we vote with our cross, will the war end? And the civil servants explained that when they had shown the world they could do One-Man-One-Vote with their good cross the war would become like a tree that has had its bark stripped off, such a tree would soon die. Meanwhile the war went on. But it was a black man's war which the whites were fighting now, they were fighting for the new black government that was going to be elected with the cross of Jesus.

And by God how they fought! And how Mahoney's heart ached for them. There were newspaper articles about the superb quality of the Rhodesian trooper, the lads who went into battle in a pair of shorts and hockey-shoes, who went leaping out of helicopters with their guns blazing, who spent weeks tracking through the bush, digging for water, every moment expecting the terrible clatter of guns – the tooth clenched charging into battle when it came: 'They have the faces of children but they fight like lions.' 'They are without doubt the finest bush-soldiers in the world,' said another article, 'and amongst the finest fighting-men the world has ever seen.' And they were Mahoney's men, his friends. What made them so good, these clerks and tradesmen who spent half a year in the bush? It was the Rhodesian spirit, the article said: loyalty and the feeling of Us against the rest of the world; the quality of the British soldier in the days of redcoats and empire, the stiff upper lip and conviction that they had right on their side. . . .

But they were fighting a black man's war now..

And Mahoney's heart ached. Because surely to God, as Shelagh said, now was the time he should go back and join them, now they were fighting for the very thing that he had advocated.

But would he? No. Because now he had too much to lose. And because those brave Rhodesian lads were going to lose . . . Because no way was Great Mother Britain going to give them her blessing and upset the other black countries in the United Nations and Moscow and Peking, oh dear me no. And Mahoney wanted to bellow to the English skies:

'For God's sake are you mad? Recognize us! Do you want those Marxist bastards to win the war?'

But no, Britain would not recognize them, because Moscow and Peking did not want to see any democratic nonsense in Rhodesia. So the war would go from bad to worse until the communists finally ended democracy once and for all – then the West would recognize *them*. . . .

That year went that way. Christmas was coming again, when Malcolm and the Admiral came marching up the lane to his house.

'We've got it!' Malcolm beamed. 'Government's going to rent us the hangars at Cardington! For a song!'

'Told them they were damn lucky to get rid of them!' Admiral Pike exclaimed.

CHAPTER 17

It was a bleak, windy day.

As they drove through RAF Cardington, Mahoney felt a shiver and he wondered all over again what he was doing in the air business. Some people like bare airfields and the brisk, businesslike talk that surrounds them: but Joe Mahoney was a sub-tropical man. He liked palm trees, the earth beneath his feet, and if he were drafted into the services his last choice would have been the Air Force, not only because of his deep respect for the laws of gravity but because he thoroughly disliked bare, windy places: but as he saw the hangars ahead, his distaste turned to awe.

The size of them! The sheer, mindblowing *size* of them. . . !

They were each the size of two football pitches placed end to end. They stood side by side, alone, aloof in their gianthood, grand old relics of the past. They were corrugated iron, painted green, with huge sliding doors.

He stared at them. So *this* was where the R·101 was built fifty-five years ago. Over these same meadows she had made her maiden flights and was found to be sluggish in her buoyancy, and underpowered: this was where she was cut in half to enlarge her to hold another huge gasbag. From this very field the great ship took off on the rainy day of her deadline, with official fanfare, her famous personages aboard, bound for India, only to crash in flames over France that night. And in that very hangar next door had lived the R 100, which had flown to Canada and back, before she was broken up with a steamroller.

It was ghostly. Mahoney was awed that he was about to start the whole mighty business all over again. He could almost feel the presence of those brave airmen of half a century ago who flew on hydrogen bagged in ox-intestines, he could almost see the huge circular sections hanging in the gloom, the tiny figures of the workmen so high that clouds sometimes formed about them. He walked slowly through the vast hangar, and slowly his awe gave way to elation. *He* was going to build a ship *this* big! A ship that was going to ride on the air like a boat. A ship that would revolutionize world trading . . .

'*Now*'s the time for you to go public to get your capital, Malcolm! And for me to make my announcement. In a blaze of publicity.'

Malcolm nodded happily. 'Yes, it certainly is.'

'But', Mahoney said excitedly, '*I'm* going to rent that second

133

hangar, in Redcoat's name. *That* is where you're going to build my airship, Malcolm – in Redcoat's *own* hangar. And Redcoat will also lease from you the tools and presses you use to build her . . .'

Malcolm stared at him. 'Why?' the Admiral demanded indignantly.

'Because', Mahoney said, 'the ownership of the hull during construction is going to reside in *Redcoat*. Every rivet is going to be Redcoat's the moment it's put in.' He turned to Admiral Pike. 'So that if Malcolm's company goes bankrupt while you're building your blimps for naval surveillance in your hangar, my hull can't be sold to pay your debts. It'll be mine, in my own hangar, and Malcolm can still finish building it. And your equipment cannot be grabbed by your creditors either, because I'll be renting them. Or if Malcolm gets a lot of contracts to build airships, I'm not waiting in a queue for hangar space . . .' He clenched his fist in excitement. 'The whole world is going to know our name if Redcoat is the first ship in the skies! *We'll* be the first to establish ourselves – *we'll* be the first to get licences, while the other airlines queue up to train their pilots . . .'

CHAPTER 18

The timing was important. Few people believed in the airship: send polite invitations to attend a press conference next week and people had too much time to think about it and dismiss you as a nutter. Locale was also important. You shouldn't call a big-deal press conference at a joint like Redcoat House, which consisted largely of ventilation.

It was very expensive, but the only place to launch a grand idea was a grand hotel like the Dorchester, and the only way to make sure the press came running was to telephone the editorial desks early in the morning on the day. That's what Mahoney did, and by 10 a.m. the Dorchester was packed with journalists and television crews. Outside stood a row of hired despatch-riders with motor cycles. Dolores ticked off the names as the newsmen arrived, handed them kits of photographs and press releases: when the conference began, she dashed outside and handed the despatch-riders kits to hotfoot to those newspapers that had not shown up: but almost everybody came.

The model airship gleamed on the platform, five feet long, in perfect proportion, with *Redcoat Airshiplines* emblazoned on it. On the wall hung huge photographs of the Cardington hangars, of Redcoat's planes in flight, forklifts off-loading cargo from Redcoat planes all over the world, racehorses in Buenos Aires, oil pipes in Australia: all dominated by a trick-photograph of the model airship flying over the Statue of Liberty in New York, in glorious colour, with the bold caption '*The Redcoats Are Coming*'. On the platform with Mahoney were Malcolm Todd in his Hong Kong suit, Pomeroy and Dolores.

Mahoney stood in front of a bristle of microphones, his heart thumping. He was used to judges and juries and political audiences. But he was making the most important speech of his life, of vital publicity value when Malcolm's shares went on the Stock Exchange.

'I repeat, it is not my argument that the airship is going to *replace* the aeroplane. There will always be jet planes for the high-powered businessmen who've got to get there fast – though they are going to be very expensive. There will always be cargo planes for people who need their goods in a hurry, and are prepared to pay dearly. What I am saying is that the return of the airship is *inevitable* as the price of oil goes up, *inevitable* as oil wells begin to run dry, as the world population relentlessly increases and demands more and more oil for industries, for agriculture, to feed its ever-swelling crescendo of mouths. And the airship is *essential* for the underdeveloped countries, to enable them to exploit their resources in their jungles and mountainous hinterlands where there are no roads or railways or airports or harbours. Airships are *essential* to pull them out of their deadly spiral of debt as each year they pay more for oil with money they've got to borrow because they don't produce enough, because they're too poor to build roads to where their resources are. The airship is *desperately* important to stop these countries plunging into economic chaos, and falling like dominoes to Communist revolutionaries. As they are doing . . .'

He looked at them grimly.

'Ladies and gentlemen, is it not absolutely essential to us of the Free World that the Third World countries develop into strong, middle-class, sensible nations, people who will not be fertile fields for communist revolution, who will naturally *resist* communist subversions? Is it not essential to our whole Western monetary system that these poor countries survive – because have not our Western banks leant them thousands of billions of dollars: and if they cannot repay, will not many of our banks also collapse, and our whole financial system with it?' He paused. 'But apart from our own vested interests in the economic stability of the third world, is it not our *humanitarian* duty to help them struggle up out of the quicksands of debt? And is not the airship, which uses one-fifth of the amount of fuel, the solution to their problem?'

He nodded slowly at them. 'The airship . . . which requires no airports, which can fly from the heart of the Andes, or the Congo, and deliver right at your factory gates, with no gas-guzzling trucks increasing your national debt to the oil dealers. With no noise, no bloody great vehicles clogging up your roads, screaming along highways that had to be specially built for them, no ugly swathes of tarmac cutting across your beautiful countryside, rendering the surroundings uninhabitable. No exhaust fumes polluting your air, blackening your lungs, adding their excrement to the filth of screaming aeroplanes, all of it adding up relentlessly, year after year, to the great shroud of carbon that we're *stupidly* throwing up around our earth, slowly but surely creating a greenhouse effect which is slowly but surely affecting our climates and rainfall, until the day will come that the whole delicate balance of nature upon which our very lives *depend* will be upset beyond the point of no return! Whereupon the oceans will slowly die, the oceans which make the rain – the oceans which cover six-sevenths of our world's surface. They will *die*, because all their organisms depend on the sun's rays, and they will be starved of it, so they will rot, giving off a terrible stench, and they will no longer make the oxygen we breathe, nor the rain that feeds our crops. We will be surrounded by rotting, stinking seas and we will die crowded together on high ground, gasping for air . . .'

Mahoney paused, letting that image sink in.

'Ladies and gentlemen, at the beginning I stressed the safety factor – how *unsafe* aeroplanes are by comparison. I stressed the economic factor: how *stupid* it is to burn one ton of fuel to deliver one ton of cargo, how important it is we *conserve* oil. I stressed the *political* factors: how unwise it is for the world to be dependent on the greed, and political squeeze of the OPEC countries. But, surely, equally important are the humanitarian, and the environmental factors. Of course, the airship will be slower than the aeroplane on long hauls. But speed doesn't really matter. Provided there is a continuous supply of cargo, it makes no difference whether the soap powder or fertilizer takes ten hours or thirty to get from Birmingham to Lagos.' He shook his head at them. 'And why this modern preoccupation with speed, anyway? Only because the speed-merchants have conditioned us to thinking it's necessary, at the cost of polluting the whole world and guzzling up the oil resources.'

He paused again. He had them spellbound, and he knew it.

'All these are irresistibly compelling reasons why the airship must come back, and why Redcoat is going to do just that . . . Ladies and gentlemen, Redcoat Cargo Airlines are proud to announce that they have signed a contract with Major Malcolm Todd, who is about to float a new public company, to build a rigid airship, with a payload of seventy-five tons . . .' He pointed upwards. 'Within two years from today, ladies and gentlemen, Redcoat's airship will be flying over London, with its first cargo. . . !'

PART 4

CHAPTER 19

That winter and spring were very successful.

Success was Redcoat's announcement going around the world, the photographs of Joe Mahoney and Malcolm Todd standing beside their model airship with the magic words Redcoat Airshiplines, the photograph of the airship floating high and mighty over the Statue of Liberty, the Cardington hangars. Some newspapers were sceptical, some had the photographs of the *Hindenburg* bursting into flames over New Jersey, the twisted wreckage of the R 101 in France. But success was the public's imagination being fired, their sentimentality for the old giants of the sky, for romantic journeys, success was the floods of letters, from little old ladies who wanted to invest ten pounds, businessmen who wanted to know more, manufacturers from Birmingham to Boise, Idaho, who wanted to know when. Success was the freight pouring in for Redcoat to haul to Hong Kong and Addis Ababa and Australia and Paraguay. Success was Joe Mahoney having to buy yet another Canadair CL 44 to handle it all. Success was Malcolm Todd's new company going on the Stock Exchange.

Or partial success. Fifty million shares were being offered at one pound each. Not in his wildest dreams did Mahoney expect Malcolm to sell all of them. He would have been delighted if he sold half of them, happy if he had sold a third. With fifteen million pounds Malcolm could build an airship, just. Malcolm sold just over five million shares.

The next week Mahoney's new company, Redcoat Airshiplines, went on the Stock Exchange. Redcoat Cargo Airlines retained fifty-one percent of the shares, and forty-nine percent, fifteen million shares, were offered at one pound each. Mahoney and Pomeroy pledged all their assets, then borrowed some more, and bought half a million. They needed to sell at least twelve million of the balance. They sold only eight million.

'But with our five million pounds we can build a non-rigid,

141

to show Ocker Anderson!' Admiral Pike exulted. The cork popped and champagne spewed. 'Two non-rigids – right?'

'Wrong,' Mahoney said. 'You must keep that money until I've got more capital—'

'No!' the Admiral cried joyously. 'Ocker will buy half a dozen – and so will the New Zealand Navy, and we'll make a million profit on each one! With contracts like that we can start building your big rigid, young fellah – we can buy shares in *your* company, because we'll be rolling in money as we turn out non-rigids like a sausage machine!'

'Malcolm' – Mahoney tried to make himself heard – 'don't build *anything* until you've got a firm contract and seen the colour of the money.'

'But we can't sit on five million quid waiting for you—'

'Let's see the colour of *your* money—' the Admiral cried.

'Shut up, Admiral!' Anne shouted – 'if it weren't for Joe none of us would be millionaires!'

'We still haven't got a bean!' Malcolm sighed irritably. 'It's the *shareholders*' money, it's company capital, woman.'

'But we can start paying ourselves a salary! We're off the rabbit stew!'

'Will you all shut up and listen to Joe?' Dolores shouted.

Mahoney held up his hand for silence. 'I'll have the rest of the money within three months.'

'But we've got the money *now*,' Anne cried. 'Between us we've got thirteen million pounds! That's almost enough for one silly old airship!'

'You don't understand, woman,' Malcolm sighed.

'And don't call me woman in that tone of voice, sergeant, or I'll stick a bazooka up your ass!'

'Anne, you don't understand—' Mahoney began.

'*He* can say it,' Malcolm complained. 'Joe can say it and she flaps her miserable old eyelashes.'

'You tell us, young fellah,' the Admiral said, 'how you're going to raise another six million-odd pounds in three months.'

'Anne?' Mahoney said. 'Malcolm's got five million. But that's his company money. As boss, he can lend it to me, sure, to build my airship—'

'Right! Why don't you lend Joe our five million, you miserable old scrooge?'

'Because', Mahoney said, 'he needs most of it to put his hangar into production. Tools. Labour . . .'

'But we've got most of the tools!'

'And I don't want to borrow from Malcolm for the very good reason that if his company goes bankrupt when my airship's half-finished, I've got to repay him, and then Redcoat goes bankrupt too.'

'I'm waiting to hear', the Admiral said happily, 'how you're going to raise another six million pounds.'

Mahoney took a deep breath. 'Redcoat is buying the other six million-odd shares, Admiral.'

They all stared at him.

'But', the Admiral exploded, 'where's the *cash*?'

'In the banks,' Mahoney said. 'Where it always is.' He looked at them. 'I'll now go back to the banks. But this time from a position of strength. My company's *got* over eight million pounds in cash. And we *got* our own hangar. And next door is Malcolm, with five million pounds, ready, willing and able to start work.' He looked at them. 'The banks will lend me the money. I'll do it the way Onassis did it . . .'

'*Which* bank?' the Admiral demanded. 'And *how* long do we have to wait?'

'A couple of months,' Mahoney said. 'I don't know which bank. I'll keep going through the land till I find one.'

It took him twelve weeks, actually. And he did have to go to almost every bank in the land, and to some beyond. Not all were as impressed as Mahoney with his argument, but the managers treated him with respect because they all knew about him. In the twelfth week he sat in the manager's office of the Hongkong & Shanghai Bank, in Hong Kong. 'This is how Onassis did it,' he said earnestly. He held up two documents, one in each hand.

'In this hand I have a cast-iron contract, between Redcoat Cargo Airlines and Redcoat Airshiplines – giving my airship

143

company the right to carry as much of Redcoat's cargo as she can handle. It therefore *guarantees* the airship company a huge amount of business – huge revenue, out of which I'll be able to repay your loan.' He paused. 'And in this other hand I have another cast-iron contract. It is between my airship company and Malcolm Todd's company. In terms of which his company agrees to build my company an airship – the airship which before it is even *built* has guaranteed revenue. By the terms of *this* contract, Malcolm Todd's company will build an airship for us *at cost*.' He paused for effect. 'Of course, Todd *does* make a profit, but only *after* the airship is flying and earning her keep – and we pay him that profit over a number of years.' He spread his hands eloquently. 'What an *excellent* deal that is for Redcoat Airshiplines!'

The bank manager said, a little suspiciously: 'It's even a better deal than Onassis got.'

'Indeed it is!'

'Why is Major Todd being so kind to you?'

'Because', Mahoney said, 'he needs my business, to get him started, as much as I need him. I'm the only customer he's got at the moment. And he's the only airship builder in the world.'

Late that afternoon Mahoney emerged from the bank into the clamorous heat of Hong Kong, walking on air.

He could hardly believe it . . . Joseph Mahoney had just borrowed six *million* pounds . . .

In only twelve weeks. But even that was too long. Because by that time Malcolm Todd had started building a small, non-rigid airship to show to the navies of the world.

Three days later Mahoney stood in his Cardington hangar, still dazed, and a little hung-over. It was summer again but the wind still moaned between the two vast structures. In Malcolm's hangar, workers were already preparing to assemble the first components of his first non-rigid.

Mahoney walked slowly through his hangar, looking up at the huge ceiling way, way up there; and looking down the length of it; and he was filled with awe all over again.

Joe Mahoney was going to build a flying ship *this* big . . .

And Joe Mahoney owed the bank six *million* pounds . . .

He still could hardly believe it, that all the theory and worrying and work had culminated in this staggering fact. Joe Mahoney, has-been lawyer, who four years ago knew almost nothing about aeroplanes, who was afraid of flying, who only twelve weeks ago was worth a quarter of a million pounds, maybe, on paper – now this very same Joe Mahoney *owed* six million pounds because he had taken it into his head to build a flying machine *this* big. . . .

And how did it feel?

It felt bloody marvellous.

Absolutely terrifying – but bloody marvellous.

CHAPTER 20

Success was Redcoat's name emblazoned on the Cardington roof, the photographs published across the world of the huge circular sections coming together inside the hangar: the in-depth articles, about the future of the airship, about the dashing men who were bringing back the airship, about Redcoat, the swashbuckling young company. Success was the wave of nostalgia for the airship, the letters flooding in, success was invitations to speak at businessmen's luncheons about airships; the switchboard jammed with more freight orders than Redcoat could handle; success was people wanting to use Redcoat on principle because it was a gutsy little airline.

Once a week Mahoney drove up to Cardington. Every time he stared in awe again.

The sheer, mindblowing *size* of it! . . .

Huge circular sections hung from the distant ceiling, gleaming in the scattered lights, fading up into gloom: riveting machines echoing, tiny figures of workmen on the vast scaffolding, cables dangling everywhere: the organized confusion. Mahoney walked slowly through, amazed each time at the ingenuity of his fellow men, people who could start with a vast space and slowly but surely make and bring together this huge mass of material. Where to begin? And he was amazed all over again that *he* was paying for it. Sometimes he did wake up in the night in a cold sweat. But every time he walked into that hangar his awe gave way to excitement again, and pride, and impatience to get it finished and flying through the sky, huge and silver with Redcoat's name emblazoned across it.

'When will you be finished this stage, Malcolm?'

'When I'm done, young man, when I'm done!'

'But are you on schedule?'

'More or less, young man, more or less.'

'But there seem to be less men working than last time.'

'That's because there *are* less.'

'But why have you taken some men off the job?'

'Because I know what I'm doing. You're only being charged for the days they work for you. Now will you please stop worrying and go'n fly your old-fashioned aeroplanes so you can pay for this, and let the real men get on with their work?'

But Mahoney worried about everything and particularly about 'Malcolm's Motorized Balloon'. He stood in the hangar next door and stared at it worriedly. It lay spreadeagled on the canvas-covered floor, a huge mass of egg-shaped, white plastic, fifty yards long and twenty-five yards wide. Wrapped around this mess was a great nylon net, from which the gondola was going to be suspended tight aginst the underside. The gondola was slowly coming together. It was moulded fibre-glass. Technicians were fitting a mass of gear, wires hanging everywhere: and attached to either side were the two engines. Mahoney slowly walked around the spreadeagled mass.

Malcolm's Motorized Balloon . . . Mahoney detested the bloody thing. O.K., it would make an excellent coastal-surveillance vehicle, and he himself had helped try to sell it as much; but oh dear . . . Over a million pounds Malcolm had invested in it so far, on the principle that he had to have a production-line model to show, a bread-and-butter machine to get his company off the ground. Sure, in principle, Mahoney

146

could not quarrel with that: but the hard fact was that it cost a million pounds to create a plastic machine which no government had ordered. He didn't care if Malcolm smothered the skies in blimps, he hoped Malcolm made a fortune so that he could build Mahoney's next airship, and his next, but his considered opinion was that right now Malcolm Todd was wasting precious money and time.

'And when will this damn thing be finished?'

'Next spring. And don't call it "this thing".'

'Why so bloody long? There's nothing to it.'

'There is', Malcolm said dangerously, 'a great deal to it. Now will you please go and fly your gas-guzzling aeroplanes and stop getting in the way of the hired help!'

The summer passed that way. They were good times. But on the other side of the world, in Zimbabwe–Rhodesia, they held their first One-Man-One-Vote elections, and it was the beginning of very bad times, the disgraceful times, of Realpolitik. Shelagh wrote in one of her rare letters:

'Really, I am ashamed to be British these days! The elections were free and fair! Did not Britain send observers, and did not they report back to Westminster that they were? Did not Bishop Muzorewa win the election hands down, and is he not a good man? As you know, I have precious little time for the white politicians of this country, but it must be acknowledged that they have now done absolutely *everything* the world demanded, they have handed over power to a black prime minister who was freely and fairly elected by his own black people – and yet *still* Britain will not recognize him and thereby put an end to this terrible war!'

And, oh, the war was terrible. And now it was truly a black man's war, now it was the black government of Zimbabwe–Rhodesia which the white soldiers were defending against the black terrorists of Moscow and Peking, and the people to suffer most were the simple black tribesmen whom the world insisted have their One-Man-One-Vote. And they cried out:

But I had my One-Man-One-Vote, I made my good cross

147

of Jesus so why do the ZANU men come and beat us and take our food and our women and kill us, and then the white soldiers come and ask us if we have seen the ZANU soldiers and if we do not tell them they will beat us also—

And the politicians in Westminster heard these words, for they are very well informed in Westminster, and they turned a deaf ear, for if they had replied.they would have had to say, Ah yes, my dear black fellow, but you see it's all for the best that we let them kill you because here in Westminster we are concerned with Diplomacy, which means Money and Trade, and if we recognize your black government which you elected we would upset Moscow and Peking and the other black countries which they support, and that would mean we *British* might suffer in trade, and this is called *realpolitik*, I'm sure you understand, dear tribesman-fellow . . .

So out there in the bush the war went on, the terrorists of Moscow and Peking pouring across the vast bush borders, rampaging through the kraals, shouting, Who are the sell-outs who voted for this government? Out there in the bush the clatter of the helicopters, the running rasping gasping gun-battles, the tribesmen running for their lives from cross-fire.

But, Jesus, sir, why're we fighting a kaffirs' war?

Because you're in the Army, lad, because an army fights for its government, and out there are thousands of communist killers, lad . . .

But why doesn't Britain recognize this black government, sir?

Oh Jesus, Britain . . . The same question asked over and over in the seige society of Zimbabwe–Rhodesia: for Christ's sake, haven't we satisfied all Britain's principles, so why doesn't she recognize us now and let us win this war against the communists? . . .

But, no. That would have been bad Diplomacy. Bad for Trade. Bad for business.

Because you see, dear fellow, there are now *new* principles – now you must satisfy the United States as well, dear fellow, because, you see, the President of the United States was elected thanks to the black American vote and he can't upset them, and he can't afford to upset Moscow either, and he can't upset China either because he's trying to normalize relations – *one*

148

thousand million customers for American goods, dear fellow, imagine that bonanza! – and if he upsets the O.A.U. he'll upset the OPEC countries, you see, and of course we British can't afford to upset the Americans. All wheels within wheels, dear fellow . . .

So the helicopters went clattering out over the vast bush and the soldiers were running in, guns blazing; and they were winning every battle. But losing the war. Because there were just too many battles to be fought. Realpolitik was this war going on while Britain tried to persuade the communists nicely to come to a nice all-party conference to arrange another nice election. And Mahoney's heart ached. Because surely to God now was the time he should go back and fight. But no, again. He owed six million pounds. That was Realpolitik too.

And then one day he looked up and Tex Weston was standing in the door. He was taken aback. It was over two years since he had set eyes on the man.

'Hullo, Tex,' he said grimly. 'What can Redcoat do for you?'

'I wondered if I might buy you a drink?'

'I'm sorry,' Mahoney lied, 'I'm off to a meeting.'

Tex strolled in. 'A drink with me would be more reward.'

Mahoney got up. No way was he going to have any deals with Tex Weston. 'What do you want, Tex?' He put on his jacket.

Tex strolled to the window.

'I want to make you an offer you can't refuse.'

Mahoney had his jacket half on. He stared at the man's back.

'I would like to buy some shares in Redcoat Airshiplines.' Tex smiled: 'A drink at The Rabbit?'

Mahoney wanted to laugh.

'There's none left, Tex, you should have bought them when they were on the Stock Exchange. Redcoat's bought up all the ones that were loose.' He indicated the door. 'If you'll excuse me?'

'I'm talking about a great deal of money, Joe.'

149

'Those shares are worth a great deal of money. And they're *mine*.' He added: 'You've already got far too many shares in Redcoat for my liking.' He waited at the door.

Tex strolled through. 'I think you'll change your mind.'

Mahoney walked to the front door. He got into his car, and started it. 'Cheerio, Tex.'

'See you soon,' Tex smiled.

Mahoney reversed out, and drove away. He went once around the airport, then came back. Tex Weston was gone. As he walked into the office, Dolores said:

'What do you think of the news?'

'What news?'

'Didn't Tex tell you? It's not official yet, but he assures me it's true. Are you ready for it? . . . The Rhodesian war's almost over!'

'*Over?*' Mahoney stared.

'Yes! The British have managed to talk everybody into attending a peace conference next month at Lancaster House!'

'Good *God*!' Mahoney breathed.

CHAPTER 21

The rain lashed down. As Mahoney dashed past Malcolm's Portakabin office he glimpsed a young man sitting inside, furtively taking a swig from a beer bottle. Mahoney hurried into the hangar, stamping water off his feet.

'What's happening, Malcolm? There seems no progress on my ship since two weeks!'

'There is', Malcolm said testily, 'plenty of progress. That's the trouble with you buyers, you imagine—'

'I'm the only buyer you've got, remember! How many men have you taken off my ship and put on this thing?'

Malcolm glared at him, then said slowly: 'You and I have a contract. In terms of which you are only charged for the number of man-hours worked. I get no profit until your ship's flying. I get *all* my profit on *my* ship as soon as it's sold. And if you don't like it, go get yourself another builder, chum!'

150

He glared at the older man angrily: then sighed. 'Malcolm? Are you on schedule?'

'How the hell should I know? Nobody's built one of these in fifty years . . .' He glared, then relaxed his shoulders. 'Yes, I think so. You've got to trust me.'

'I trust your *honesty*, Malcolm! . . . It's your *business* acumen I'm worried about.' He sighed again. 'Who's the kid, sitting in your Portakabin?'

'That "kid"', Malcolm said, mollified-grumpy, 'is a fully qualified airship pilot.'

Mahoney looked at him. '*Airship* pilot? But there aren't any.'

'He's licensed in America to fly the Goodyear ships.'

Mahoney groaned. 'Those blimps . . .'

'He's very good. I've hired him.'

Mahoney stared. '*Hired* him?! For God's sake, Ed and I have been granted concessionary licences, *we're* test-flying the blimp for you! How the *hell* can you afford this guy?'

Malcolm said sulkily, 'I'll be fine when this blimp's sold. But I need a fully qualified man to fly her to get her sold.'

'And when will she be finished?'

'In the new year. Say February.'

'That's four months' salary for nothing, Malcolm!' He shook his head. 'Look – has he got commercial licences?'

'The lot. I've seen them.'

Mahoney sighed again. 'Then I'll take him on as a part-timer, I always need pilots. I'll speak to him, what's his name?'

'Martin Lovelock,' Malcolm said. 'Says he knows you.'

'*Lovelock?*' Mahoney cried.

He turned and went hurrying out of the hangar, grinning.

They sat opposite each other in the Portakabin, swigging beer.

'Old Abbie you know, she ditched me again and went home to America. Three years ago now, said I drank too much.'

'What rot!'

'Absolutely,' Lovelock agreed. 'But I did start hitting the bottle a bit after that. Finally, when my contract was up, I followed her.'

151

'The Army didn't fire you for drinking, did they?'

'Lord, no!' Lovelock looked hurt. 'The Army didn't do things like that, we got along famously.'

Mahoney smiled. No, the Rhodesian Army wouldn't fire Lovelock. He thought of Lovelock and Pomeroy kneeling beside their shot-up machine repairing it while the lads tried to hold the terrorists off and Lovelock suddenly saying 'Damn, I've been shot in the arse, how do I explain that to the family?'

'How was the war when you left?' Mahoney smiled.

'We are knocking the daylights out of them. Still are, you know, Tex Weston says, while this conference is going on.'

Mahoney raised his eyebrows. 'When did you see Tex Weston?'

'Saw him in Youngstown, Ohio. That's where I was flying the Goodyear blimps.'

'What was he doing, sniffing around Goodyear?'

Lovelock said, as if it were the most natural thing in the world: 'He's interested in airships. Everybody is, it seems. He told me about you chaps. So I telephoned Mr Todd. Got a job.'

'Lovelock? Goodyear didn't fire you for drinking, did they?'

'Lord, no! I only drink beer, nowadays. And only in moderation. It's Christmas time, you see.'

Mahoney smiled. 'Next month. You didn't fly one of their airships upside down, did you?'

Lovelock grinned. 'Don't think it could be done, centre of gravity all wrong.'

Mahoney grinned. 'Did you really flip that British Airways jumbo over and fly her along upside down?'

'Well yes, I did rather. But there were no passengers, only me and the test-captain, we were all strapped in well.'

Mahoney threw back his head and laughed.

He flipped the caps off two more beers and sat forward.

'What's it like flying an airship, Martin?'

Lovelock took a swig.

'It's easy, really. Much easier than an aeroplane. Just get your sums right before you begin. You're going to enjoy it.'

Mahoney hunched forward.

'Start at the beginning,' he said. 'Tell me everything you've learned.'

CHAPTER 22

It didn't matter a damn to Mahoney what was happening at the Lancaster House peace conference, he had washed his hands of the whole bloody thing: and it mattered so much it was the first news he looked for, it mattered so much it made him furious each time. '*Bloody despicable Lancaster House . . .*' Furious that an honestly elected man had to bargain with the henchmen of Moscow and Peking, furious that Britain made them do it.

'*The bloody piss-weak British and their realpolitik . . .*'

Oh, it didn't matter that the terrorists swaggered and shouted at Lancaster House and objected to everything and made asses of themselves, from the seating arrangements to cease-fire, from constitutional proposals to whether they'd attend the cocktail party, from compensation for land they vowed to confiscate to who would control the army during the election, it did not matter that they threatened to walk out, that they threatened to fly to New York to complain to the United Nations, it didn't matter that they called Lord Carrington 'Comrade', it didn't matter what they finally agreed to because the end result was going to be the same. Oh, Lancaster House was all great British diplomacy, a great job by Lord Carrington, but it didn't matter a damn because when the ceasefire began the terrorists were going to rampage through the bush and the terrified tribesmen would have to vote for them, and Rhodesia was going to have a communist government no matter what was piously done and shouted and postured and swaggered at Lancaster House:

'*Oh, why make a deal with the devil at all?*'

On the ninety-ninth day, a few days before Christmas of that year, the Lancaster House conference ended, with great fanfare. That afternoon Mahoney returned from a three-day flight, and it was front-page news in all the papers: The Rhodesian War is over! A peace agreement had been reached! New elections to be held in February! Well done, Lord

Carrington! A great British diplomatic triumph! . . .

And Moscow and Peking clapped their hands in glee.

And Joe Mahoney went down to The Rabbit to get drunk.
A hand fell on his shoulder. He turned, and stared.

'Good God, Max . . .' he said.

'I've been looking for you.' Max grinned bleakly.

'What the hell are you doing here?'

'The same as you, I've quit.'

They sat in the corner, where nobody could hear them. Max
said grimly: 'I haven't quit, Joe. The government's quit. The
whites have quit. The British quit thirty years ago, though
they've never quit as ingloriously and ignominiously as they
did today.' He looked at him angrily. 'The only people who
haven't quit are the communists. Those bastards will never
quit until they rule the whole world.'

Mahoney nodded, waiting. Max went on grimly: 'But, no,
I haven't quit . . . And nor have a good few other people
with a bit of sense and guts.' Max looked at him. 'Whom I
represent.'

Mahoney stared. 'Who do you represent?'

Max snorted. He looked at the fire, then said: 'Who do you
think's going to win this so-called election?'

'The communists.'

Max snorted wearily. 'So, living in England hasn't entirely
addled your head.' His eyes glinted. 'Of course! Because tens
of thousands of terrorists whom we've been fighting for seven
years are now going to walk into the country free as air and
intimidate the people! Even the British know that. Jesus, do
you think Moscow and Peking have fought this war to let it
go any other way?' He glared. 'But which is going to win
this so-called election – the Chinese-backed terrorists or the
Russian-backed terrorists? Robert Mugabe or Joshua Nkomo?'

Mahoney said: 'Mugabe.'

'Of course! Because the Shona are the largest tribe and
because Mugabe has got more terrorists inside the country
than Nkomo . . . And how're Nkomo and his Russian pals
going to like that? Tell me – do you think this war's over?'

154

'What're you getting at, Max?' Mahoney asked quietly.

'No matter what happens, the war goes on. If by some fluke Bishop Muzorewa and his moderates win, the war will go on, because communists don't go for any democratic bullshit. And if Mugabe wins the Matabele will fight on. And if the Matabele win, Mugabe and his Chinese pals will fight on. The war's not over, Joe.'

'What're you getting at, Max?' Mahoney repeated.

Max looked at him, then spread his arms wide. 'I'm just visiting my old pal Joe Mahoney! Who used to be Rhodesian! Who used to care so much he actually fought an election! Who actually advocated that we have a multi-racial government so we could fight the communists with a united front! And when it finally came about, he was sitting in dear old mother England making himself a millionaire, donchaknow?' He spread his arms again: 'I'm visiting my dear, good, loyal, Rhodesian pal Joe Mahoney who loves 'em and leaves 'em . . .' He glared. 'Have you got a bed for me tonight in that war-torn house of yours?'

'Of course.' Mahoney stood up grimly to fetch two more beers.

Max said, 'No, let's go there. It's best to discuss public business in private.'

Max hunched over his whisky at the kitchen table. He waved at the room and said truculently: 'Nice.'

Mahoney said: 'What public business?'

Max got up. 'Do you want communists to rule your country?'

'Of course not.'

'Well,' Max said, suddenly airily, 'what are you prepared to do about it?'

Mahoney waited impatiently. Max paced, head down.

'Mugabe is a dyed-in-the-wool communist. So? What would a sane man do about him – and all his henchmen?'

Mahoney said, 'And how're you going to get rid of his army?'

Max held up a finger. 'Good point. How would this sane man deal with Mugabe's China-backed army? Well, now . . .

Nkomo is backed by the Russians, sure. But Nkomo ain't no communist. He's used them, but he's a capitalist. Of the two, *he's* the man one would prefer to win this so-called election.'

Mahoney waited.

'And *Nkomo*'s got an army to deal with Mugabe's army . . . And in a straight fight, one Matabele is worth ten Shona.' He stopped and looked at him. 'Nkomo didn't send all his troops into Rhodesia. So that if Mugabe wins the elections, he's got his army intact, to fight on.'

Mahoney waited. Max started pacing again.

'But Nkomo's made a mistake. Because Zambia won't let him use their territory after the election. Nor will Mozambique. So? Nkomo will be a man with an army without a barracks.' He looked at him. 'Without lines of supply. For arms. Ammunition. Food.'

Mahoney said, 'Get to the point.'

Max paced across the kitchen.

'There are a lot of people – including, I would guess, thousands of white soldiers – who would like to help Nkomo get rid of Mugabe.'

'And you're one of them.'

Max looked at him. 'Are you?'

Mahoney said quietly, 'What do you want from me, Max?'

Max paced. 'I should imagine that such people would need help from somebody who had big aeroplanes. A legitimate airline that wouldn't attract attention. And they'd pay very well for such work.'

Mahoney got up. He opened another beer. 'No way, Max.'

Max looked at him grimly. 'No. You've washed your hands of us.'

Mahoney took a breath. 'Max, as you say, Redcoat is a legitimate airline. We're not like Tex Weston's outfit. We don't smuggle, we don't dabble in politics, we don't deal in arms. Or wars. Or treason.'

'*Treason?*' Max whispered.

'Of course! That's what it's going to be once the communists are elected and internationally recognized – and you'll hang for treason in Salisbury Central Prison! But there's another reason, Max. Rhodesia's had enough war! The country is exahusted. We've lost, Max. *Accept* that! We made a number of mistakes over the years, and so we lost the country.'

'*Treason?* . . .' Max whispered. He shook his head in wonder. 'Today you've seen your country handed on a plate to communist bandits, and you talk of *treason?* . . .' He shook his head again: 'Today you've seen your country sold down the river by the gutless British – just like she did with all her other colonies – just like she did with our Federation. But today it was *ten* times worse, because today you saw Britain take a decent, moderate, honestly elected black government and force it to abdicate so she could curry favour with tinpot, bankrupt, black dictatorships! Today she *knowingly* handed your country over to marauding communists who are going to oppress the very black people you used to champion! Who're going to turn your country into a one-party dictatorship and butcher any opposition!' He shouted: '*And you talk to me about treason?* . . .'

'Max!'

'*Oh, Jesus Christ!*' He banged down his glass. '*Goodbye!*' He flung open the kitchen door.

CHAPTER 23

It rained all that winter. It swept down on the two great hangars, drumming, muffling the cavernous banging and whirring of tools in the vast, ghostly lamplight: and it was cold, so that rain sometimes wept down from the mist that formed way up there under that vast ceiling. But in the reborn British colony of Rhodesia it was summer, the bush was green and the sky was blue. It was perfect weather for winding up a war.

Sometimes he caught the newsreels on television, but he hated watching it. Ah, it was a beautiful country . . . He hated seeing truckloads of communist terrorists coming out of the bush singing and swaggering; seeing foreign commonwealth troops in charge of his country while his own army was being disbanded: he did not like seeing the Union Jack flying again under that lovely sky of his, because soon it was going to be hauled down forever, and the last of the British values they had fought for would come down with it. He did not like seeing a British governor in Government House again because this man was going to hand his country over to the enemy. He could not bring himself to listen to the electioneering speeches, the ululating and the bellowing Marxist bullshit: and the television cameras could not see what was happening out there in the bush, the menace of the political ones, did not record them saying, 'Anyone who does not vote for our Party is a sell-out . . . There is no such thing as a secret ballot . . .' And on election day the British Government's observers of fair play and English policemen would not have the savvy to pay attention to the men lounging around the ballot booths, watching, the menacing men whom every voter knew. . . .

Shelagh wrote: 'Everybody is praying that Bishop Muzorewa wins again. The whites are holding their breath while the black campaigning goes on and the British soldiers keep the peace. Actually, for all the whites' fears, I think there is very little intimidation going on – and that Bishop Muzorewa will win. Really, you should be here, to witness history of your country in the making. I am not coyly suggesting that we resume married life, only that you take an interest. I, for one, am proud to see the people I have helped educate – and whose cause you yourself championed – come into their own . . .'

Oh, he could imagine the desperate optimism of the whites that Muzorewa win. And Shelagh, with her blind faith in her fellow men, would not know what was happening out there in the bush.

On the day of the election he was flying to Buenos Aires. He got the news on the B.B.C.:

Mugabe and his China-backed ZANU Party had won the election. And a worried world wondered what was going to happen next.

CHAPTER 24

The winter slowly wept by.

Twice a month Mahoney drove up to Cardington. It was difficult to see from one visit to the next what progress had been made behind the huge scaffolding that stretched away into the gloom – there was so much massive, confused sameness; and every week hundreds of thousands of borrowed pounds dribbling away like sand through an hour-glass. It made Mahoney feverish. Sometimes Malcolm was there, way up on some scaffolding, steamy-breathed, laden with scrolls of drawings and no time for him, sometimes in his Portakabin surrounded by overflowing in-baskets and empty out-baskets and teacups and ashtrays and beer bottles and with no time for damn-fool questions. More often he was to be found in the hangar next door with his great mass of egg-shaped plastic, and often he was not to be found at all because he was at some factory inspecting materials before they were delivered in terms of the legion of sub-contracts he had made. With every visit Mahoney's nerves stretched tighter. Towards the end of that long winter he made himself stay away from Cardington for six solid weeks because he couldn't stand it. Then, one day, when he came back from a long trip, he saw new, tight buds on the trees of England, and it was the beginning of spring, and he drove up to Cardington again.

And he could not believe it . . .

There seemed to be almost no progress in Redcoat's hangar. He strode angrily out into the windy passage.

But plenty had changed in Malcolm's hangar! The gondola-cabin looked finished, polished, gleaming with instruments. The tail fins had been fitted to the huge crumpled envelope, sticking up high, supported by struts. Fifty yards away the nose bulged up, stiffened with batons. The whole mass was slowly swelling, swelling. Beyond stood a phalanx of gas cylinders, as big as a man, a pipe running from one with a hissing noise. Mahoney stared. They were almost finished already . . .

'*Mal-colm!*' he bellowed.

And there he was, coming towards him, his cold-pink face wreathed in smiles. 'I've got a job for Redcoat!'

Mahoney glared. 'Oh yeah? What's happening to my ship? This thing of yours is almost finished!'

'Yes,' Malcolm beamed, 'we've been working overtime. Because . . .' He paused for effect. 'You're going to freight this airship to *Australia* at the end of the month!'

Mahoney stared, amazed. Malcolm went on busily: 'The Australian Navy want to see her demonstrated down there. And if they like her they're going to buy! Admiral Pike's done a wonderful job!'

Mahoney could not believe the man. 'By the end of this *month*?'

'We'll finish her in two weeks if we work double time! Day after tomorrow she'll be fully inflated, hanging up there!' He pointed. 'Then we fit the gondola and engines.'

Mahoney waved his hand: 'But you can't test-fly her within two *weeks* – and not in this weather! You want to wait for perfect conditions!'

Malcolm wasn't to be bothered. 'Perfect conditions in Australia this time of the year! We'll test everything right here in the hangar – run-in the engines, all instrumentation, the works. Except flight. Then we deflate her, disassemble her, pack her in her box. Then off we go in your aeroplane!'

'God!' Mahoney whispered. He wanted to bang his head.

'We reassemble her in Australia,' Malcolm continued enthusiastically, 'and she'll be in mint condition.'

'But she might give *trouble*! . . . She might have all kinds of bugs to shake out before you show her to a customer, Malcolm!'

Malcolm looked at him as if he was a bloody bureaucrat. 'She'll fly perfectly. I thought you wanted to see the back of her?'

Mahoney was exasperated. Malcolm said: 'Joe, I know what I'm doing. If we wait for perfect conditions here we may wait months. The Aussies are keen_*now*. *And* our demonstration

160

will coincide with their Royal Easter Show, when the whole country's in Sydney. It'll be wonderful publicity! Now, are you going to freight her or do I use another airline?'

Mahoney groaned. 'And if the Aussies don't buy? I freight it back again! It would be cheaper to fly the bloody Australian Navy here. Do you know how much this is going to cost you?'

Malcolm smiled: 'You're going to do it for us at cost price, aren't you?'

'Am I, indeed?'

'And I'll pay you the proper price after I've sold the airship! How's that? Between pals?'

'Pals, huh? I don't like to see my pals go bankrupt when they're building *me* an airship!' He rubbed his forehead. God knew he was glad the Australians wanted to see the ship. God knew he was glad to see the back of the bloody thing. But he worried about Malcolm going off half-cocked. 'The cost depends on what other cargo I can get to Australia. Whether I use the Brittania or a Canadair.' He took a breath. 'You sure you're right? And why is nothing happening on my bloody ship?'

'Plenty', Malcolm said, 'has happened.'

Mahoney sighed. 'What's the total weight of your airship? Including engines, crates, everything.'

'Four tons,' said Malcolm, without a care in the world. 'The Navy are providing a mast. They'll build a mobile one on a truck.'

Mahoney said grimly: 'How many men?'

'Myself, two leading hands, and Lovelock. The Navy'll supply the rest.'

'What are the dimensions of the three crates?'

Malcolm told him. Mahoney pulled out a pen, did some calculations. 'Where's a telephone?' He dialled Redcoat House reluctantly.

'Dolores, start looking for a cargo to Sydney. And another load back. Phone all the freight agents. We'll do it cheap. And we'll fly any route, via Africa if necessary, to pick up a cargo.'

Malcolm slapped him on the back. 'That's it, young fellah!'

'You've been with that admiral too bloody much. And I

161

hope you realize you're within spitting distance of bankruptcy if the Aussies don't buy!'

'They'll buy,' Malcolm said happily.

PART 5

CHAPTER 25

When the gorilla was an infant, in the green mountains bordering Uganda, his mother cradled him and suckled him exactly as a human mother does, and she played with him, smiling at him, and fondling him. She taught him what to eat, and if he picked anything unsuitable she took it away from him. If he misbehaved, she disciplined him. He played with other juveniles in the troupe, wrestling matches and king-of-the-castle and follow-the-leader, swinging through the trees. He learned to accept the undisputed authority of the big silverback male who was their leader, and although the old man sometimes let them climb all over him and drop out of the trees on him, one stare was enough to put them back in their place, one sharp grunt enough to put an end to any quarrel. The young gorilla learned how to challenge and posture, to beat his chest with his cupped hands, and give a hooting roar, then rip up vegetation furiously and throw it in the air, then beat the earth with his hand and charge. But there was never any real fighting, for there was land enough for all the troupes, food enough for everybody. For gorillas do not have to use their strength and cunning to feed, they only want to live and let live, slowly wandering from one lush green place to another.

For two happy years this was his life. Now he had stopped suckling, but if there was alarm he still scampered to his mother, and though, at dusk, he imitated the adults and started trying to build his own nest, he always gave up and went to sleep with her. But, for the rest, he could almost look after himself and he was always off playing. That is what they were doing when the black hunters crept up on them.

They were armed with an assortment of white man's rifles and spears and old mining cable which was spliced into big nooses for snares. They were poachers, men who combed the bush, tracking elephant for their ivory, setting snares for rhinos for their horn, and most creatures for their hides; these they sold to middlemen who shipped them around the world as floor mats and piano keys and billiard balls and handbags and watch-straps and aphrodisiacs and fur coats for rich ladies. When the chance came their way they captured animals alive to sell to animal dealers who sold them to zoos.

Now, the trick when capturing gorillas is to kill the adult males and wound the females enough to anchor them: then the youngsters hang on to their crippled mothers and are easily caught. The poachers split into two groups: one went downwind as beaters, circling to the other side of the grove where the troupe was feeding, while the rest hid on the other side. Then the beaters set up a terrifying noise and the troupe of gorillas ran.

They came crashing through the undergrowth on all fours, the females screaming to their youngsters, the big silverback bringing up the rear. He roared and beat his black chest and wrenched up foliage fiercely and threw it in the air, but he could not see the enemy and he went on galloping on behind his troupe, the other males covering the flanks: they came galloping panic-stricken into the open, and the slaughter began.

The poachers opened fire, *crack crack*, and the foremost female crashed, then she scrambled up, fangs bared wildly and screaming for her youngster midst the cacophony of the rifles shattering the jungle. And all about the other females were screaming and crashing and clutching for their babies, and the youngsters were scattering panic-stricken, then galloping back to their bloody mothers; then the first male came thundering out. Roaring and terrified and furious, jaws agape, and the poacher got him through the middle of the face and he sprawled; then the big silverback came racing out. On his hind legs, roaring and beating his shaggy chest, his eyes wild and his jaws flashing, crashing through the undergrowth at the poachers to tear them apart with his teeth, and the poacher aimed between the two furious eyes, and fired. The gorilla contorted, arms upflung, like a man. Then the poachers ran in with their nets and clubs.

The young gorillas were screaming and clutching their mothers. A female staggered up and grabbed her youngster, gargling in terror, and tried to scramble into the bamboo, and

166

a poacher swiped her across the head. She scrambled up again, both arms clutching her head to ward off the blows, her infant clinging to her. The African grabbed its leg and slung a net over it, and he swiped at the mother again. She was reeling. He swiped her and swiped her with all his might, then she fell. He clubbed her and clubbed her to death.

The other poachers were clubbing the other females, and they got nets over all the youngsters. And it was all over. The undergrowth was trampled muddy with blood about the big black furry bodies of nine adult gorillas. Maybe the whole business had only taken five minutes.

CHAPTER 26

The rain beat down, but in the Redcoat hangar at Gatwick there was a holiday mood. Out on the tarmac the Canadair stood loaded with the crates containing the deflated airship, the gondola, the engines and tail fins. Stacked around them were hundreds of long plastic pipes for Chad, the smaller inside the bigger, all lashed down. Everything was ready to go.

Dolores was issuing the flight documents to Sydney Benson. Malcolm's cheeks were flushed from the whisky bottle his men and Lovelock had been passing around since loading their precious cargo. They were joking about the sunshine and bikinis that were waiting for them in Australia. Pomeroy, who was coming as flight engineer, was also in good form. Even Mahoney was in something of a holiday mood: all the tests of the airship within the hangar had gone perfectly. While Sydney finished his documentation, Mahoney left the hangar to buy some tobacco. As he opened the door, he saw Tex Weston getting out of a car.

'Joe!' he called. 'Can I have a quick word?'

Mahoney walked towards his own car. 'Sorry, I'm about to take off.'

Tex called, 'It's about Shelagh. I saw her yesterday in Salisbury.'

Mahoney's pulse tripped. He stopped. 'Is Cathy all right?'

'Yes, Cathy's fine,' Tex said cheerfully.

Mahoney got into his car. 'Come on, then. We can talk while we drive.'

He reversed, then roared out of the compound. His face was throbbing, from an emotion he had thought he no longer felt. 'Well, what about Shelagh?'

The Texan said: 'I bumped into her in Meikles Hotel yesterday. We had a chat. She sends her best wishes to you.'

'Thanks.'

Tex said, 'She's a bit short of money, Joe.'

He felt a flare of anger. He drove on grimly, pulled up in the airport parking lot. 'That's my business, Tex. Not yours.' He got out and started walking, into the concourse.

Tex caught up outside the tobacconist. He said quietly, 'It happens to be my business. Because I'm helping her out.'

Mahoney turned. He felt a stab of angry jealousy. 'Oh?' He strode into the shop, got three tins of Golden Virginia. Tex was behind him.

'I'm buying her shares in Redcoat off her.'

Mahoney froze. He turned slowly and looked at the man.

'You are not,' he announced quietly.

'I'm afraid', Tex said, 'that the deal is already concluded. I've already paid her. I've just come to collect the share certificates.'

Mahoney glared at him. 'Well, I'm giving the money back to you.'

'I don't want the money, Joe. I want the shares.'

Mahoney got his change and shakily stuffed it in his pocket. 'You're getting the money back,' he said.

'You can't do that.'

Mahoney strode out. 'Yes, I can. Because', he said grimly, 'the sale is not legal. She sold them to me. Long ago. When we separated.'

Weston smiled. 'Tell me another one. Have you got a written contract?'

'A perfectly valid verbal one, my friend. I'm a lawyer under this uniform.'

'Then don't make me sue you, Joe, to prove you a liar. I

168

questioned Shelagh closely about this possibility. *I* have a written contract with her.'

Mahoney turned pale. 'Show me.'

Tex held out a photocopy document, Mahoney snatched it. It was one paragraph, handwritten. But perfectly legal.

He stopped. 'You paid twice their value!'

'That's a matter of opinion.'

Mahoney's mind was racing. What was this? He stuffed the document in his pocket and strode on. He flung open the glass door. 'Why do you want more Redcoat shares that badly, Weston?'

'For the usual reasons. I know a good company when I see one. I want a piece of the action. What I can't understand is why you don't want me.'

Mahoney stopped at his car. 'Bullshit. You want airships.'

'Anything wrong in that? You're telling the world what a good bet they are.'

'Well, go and buy your own.'

'Maybe I will one day.'

'But meantime you'll just have a piece of the action, let the brave guys take the risks. Well, you're dead right I don't want you, Tex. Because I don't trust you, and I won't tolerate you as a bigger shareholder than you already are.' He flashed him a brilliant smile and flung open his door. 'Nothing personal.'

He started his car. He rammed it into gear and drove away hard.

Everybody was waiting for him in the hangar office. He strode through them, into his cubicle and grabbed the telephone. He dialled international, then Rhodesia's code, then Salisbury's, then Shelagh's number. His hand was shaking.

The telephone rang, and rang. He looked feverishly at his watch.

He slammed down the phone. He'd have to go through Berna Radio once he was airborne. God! He was in grave danger of losing control of his own company.

As soon as they were over the Channel, Mahoney called Berna Radio. Ten minutes later they called him back.

169

'Victoria Quebec, I'm sorry there's no reply.'

'Please keep trying!' He muttered to himself: 'I've got to get to her before Weston does.'

It was two long hours later, when they had left the dark clouds of Europe behind, that the bell rang. 'Victor Quebec, we have your party.'

'Shelagh?' he shouted.

'Hullo? . . .' a little voice said.

Mahoney's heart turned over. 'Cathy!' he shouted. 'Hullo darling! It's Daddy!'

'Hullo?' Cathy said.

Mahoney felt his eyes burn and his throat thicken; *'Cathy – it's your Daddy, from England, don't you remember me?* . . .'

'Yes,' Cathy said uncertainly, five thousand miles away.

'Hullo, who's this?' Shelagh's voice.

Mahoney closed his eyes. It was a moment before he could respond.

'Joe!' she said. 'What a surprise! I was in the bath, I'm standing here dripping! . . .'

He took a breath.

'Go and put some clothes on.'

'It's all right,' she said, 'it's summer.'

He heard her light a cigarette.

'Darling,' she said, 'cool down. It's not quite like that. Tex phoned *me* yesterday and asked *me* to meet him at Meikles. "To discuss something of mutual interest," quote unquote. He offered to buy my Redcoat shares – after asking how I was financially, et cetera. He made me a damn good offer. I said I would sell, but I had to offer them to you first, gentleman's agreement, and maybe you would want him to pay *you* in sterling and you would pay *me* with Rhodesian dollars you've got frozen in the bank here. He said O.K., he'd speak to you.'

Mahoney felt limp with relief. 'Oh, he's a liar. He said he'd already paid you.'

'He has,' she said.

He blanched. 'He *has*? Then you've sealed a contract, Shelagh!'

'He gave me a post-dated cheque, dated tomorrow.'

'A *post*-dated cheque.' Relief again. So, it was a conditional sale.

'I said I wouldn't cash it until you'd decided whether you wanted the shares.'

Mahoney breathed. 'Shelagh? I want you to tear up that cheque, *now*. And post it back to him, with a letter saying it's no deal.'

'And where does that leave me?' she said.

'I'll buy them.'

'At what price?'

He sighed. 'Shelagh – they're not worth what he offered.'

'Exactly, that's why I didn't think you'd want them at that price.'

He cried, 'For God's sake understand that if Weston buys them I lose control of Redcoat Cargo! And if I lose control of Redcoat Cargo I also lose control of Redcoat Airshiplines, because Redcoat Cargo controls the airship company!'

'Nonsense, Dolores and Pomeroy would always vote with you – Weston could never *out-vote* you.'

'He could! He owns twenty-six percent already, almost the same as me. With your twenty-five percent he'd own fifty-one percent!'

There was a silence. 'So you only want to pay me their book value?' Mahoney took a big breath. She went on: 'Is that fair? You gave me the shares. Didn't I work hard? Aren't I entitled to as much as I can get?'

He sighed. 'I'll give you the same as Weston's offering.'

There was a sullen silence.

'When?'

'I'll write to the bank when I get home. That'll clean me out of Rhodesian dollars. I'll send you the rest in sterling. But you'll have to wait. At least a year – maybe more.'

'A *year*?' she cried.

'For God's sake, Shelagh, I owe six million pounds right now!'

There was a shocked silence. He heard her draw on her

cigarette. 'Good God! . . . .' Then: 'Now you're making me feel guilty,' she said bitterly. 'Why should I feel a shit – they're my shares!'

He prayed.

'But it's a deal,' she ended.

Mahoney was suddenly smiling. He did not know where he was getting the money from. 'Thanks, Shelagh.'

She said: 'But you're not to register them in your name until you finish paying for them. I want to keep some leverage over you. Is that a deal?'

'Yes. Thanks, Shelagh.'

She said, bewildered: 'I just presumed that if you had floated the new company you would have raised the money.'

He said, 'Shelagh, how is it in. . . ?'

'It's fine. You were quite wrong about this government. Joe?'

'Yes?'

'Do you really owe six million pounds?'

It did not seem real to him either. 'Yes.'

He heard her breathe. 'God! . . . Well,' she said sincerely, 'I really do wish you all the luck . . .'

'Thank you, Shelagh.'

Then: 'Well, when you're in the red for that much I suppose a few hundred thousand you owe me for the shares doesn't make much difference!'

'Oh, doesn't it? I guess not.'

She said sullenly: 'You'd better sell the farm now. To pay me. The government's likely to nationalize it anyway. Do you want me to organize it?'

He sighed. His lovely farm . . . 'Yes, please,' he said. 'Put it in the hands of an estate agent. I'll also write to them.'

She said bitterly, 'You may be too bloody late, the government may just tell you what they're paying you for it as it's been lying idle all this time. You should have *listened* to me.'

He sighed. 'O.K. Let me speak to Cathy again.'

'No, she's gone out to play. She's only just discovered the telephone anyway, just gawks hullo into it. Write her more letters if you want, I'll read them to her, you haven't exactly been a doting father.' Then: 'Joe?'

172

He felt a little on his mettle. 'Yes?'

She breathed.

'You're a hell of a guy . . .' She added: 'That doesn't mean anything – just that I think you're a hell of a guy.'

He felt his eyes burn. 'Thanks, Shelagh.'

'And don't tell me I'm a hell of a woman. I know that already.'

It was a beautiful sunset. Thirty thousand feet below, the Mediterranean was in darkness, but the mountaintops of North Africa were still pink and up here the aeroplane gleamed, the wingtips sparkling. Mahoney climbed out of his seat, a smile all over his face. He opened the door and heard the distant bellow of 'Waltzing Matilda' above the hum of engines.

He squeezed through the cargo, towards the tail where Lovelock and the boys were making merry.

It was a beautiful world! And *not* because his wife had almost told him she loved him. But because she most distinctly had not! She'd only told him he was a hell of a guy. And that made him free! . . . Because he didn't love her anymore either! There was only *feeling*. A kind of love that didn't have pain anymore.

Mahoney squeezed into the swingtail, grinning. There was Lovelock, happy blond head thrown back in song, and Malcolm, red in the face, whisky bottle on high. Mahoney took the bottle and took a big swig and threw back his head and sang:

'*Who'll come a-waltz-ing Mat-ilda with meee . . .*'

Malcolm and the boys were asleep. Mahoney put coffee into a thermos jug, added boiling water, picked up three mugs, and made his way back to the flightdeck. Pomeroy pulled a face at him. Mahoney put on his headset. 'What?'

Sydney said, 'We've entered the Chad airspace but no reply from Fort Lamy.'

Mahoney sighed. Oh, Africa! Why hadn't he just emigrated to Australia and gone back to law?

It was still before dawn when the Canadair began its descent, into cloud. Mahoney muttered: 'Isn't it marvellous? I've never met cloud over here before. It's a bloody desert, isn't it?'

The stars were gone. The insrument lights glowed on their faces. Mahoney watched the altimeter and glanced at the chart. He said, carefully and slowly into the transmitter: 'Fort Lamy, this is Victor Quebec 901. Commencing Standard Approach, Descent and Landing Procedure.'

'Any good trying it in French?'

'Do you know French?'

'Nope.'

But he knew exactly where he was. What he did not know was the depth of this cloud he was hurtling through. The altimeter was reading 10,000, then 9,000, then 9,800 . . .

That little altimeter was all he was relying on. He was not worried about that, he had relied upon it countless times: and he was worried stiff about it. It just did not make sense, hurtling tons of machinery earthwards, blind. Then the cloud was thinning out, flashing past: then the earth burst into view. And there it was, exactly where he had expected to see it, the sprinkling of lights of Fort Lamy.

'But where's the bloody airport?'

The town was where it was supposed to be. But over there, where the airport should be, was blackness. 'Asleep! The bastards are asleep again!'

'What do you want to do?' Sydney sighed. 'We got enough fuel to make Entebbe.'

Mahoney said angrily, 'Take over, Syd. You're going to wake the bastards up, that's what! What're we going to do with these pipes in Entebbe? Any obstructions?'

'No.'

Sydney took over the controls. His eye sped over the chart. 'O.K. . . .'

At four thousand feet his artificial horizon dial showed him the slope and localizer flight directors. Mahoney smiled grimly. *Wonderful, isn't it?* 'They go to sleep, switch off the runway lights, but leave the Instrument Landing System pulsing away.'

'Probably a separate generator. Gentleman was too tired to switch it off.'

Sydney flew the Canadair through the blackness by the artificial horizon and the flight directors, bringing her in low. When she was three miles from normal touchdown point he crossed the outer marker and switched his landing lights on. They beamed down into the night like a car's headlamps, but they did not yet show the ground. Ahead there was nothing but blackness; only the flight director on his horizon dial told him where the runway was, only his altimeter told him how high above the earth he was. Then his landing lights picked up the scrub flashing by below. He saw the runway looming ahead. Sydney brought the aircraft down to two hundred feet and he was going to go screaming over the control tower to wake them up as he had done more than once in Africa: he went roaring at the control tower, the earth flashing by beneath, then suddenly his headlights picked up the big truck parked across the runway. His heart missed a beat, he saw another, then another, then all lights in the control tower blazed on and the firing broke out. *'God!'* Mahoney shouted and the roaring plane heaved her nose upwards. Sydney slammed off the landing lights.

'What on earth? . . .'

Mahoney's face was white as he watched the altimeter. Pomeroy said: 'Well, we woke 'em up fine, like. The whole bleedin' army!'

The radio crackled in a flood of angry language.

Sydney rasped into the transmitter: 'Speak English! This is Victor Quebec 901 attempting to land as per filed flight plan!'

There was more guttural shouting.

Sydney climbed the aircraft up, up, well outside rifle-range; then turned into a big holding arc. A stilted voice said in English: 'This airport is under military control and all un-authorized aircraft will be shot.'

Mahoney said angrily, *'We are authorized! We're delivering a cargo!'*

There was a crackling silence.

'From what country?'

'Great Britain! Queen Elizabeth country!'

175

Silence. Sydney said, 'They've gone to find somebody who understands what to do.'

'They probably shot the only guy! And he was never too smart.'

Mahoney tuned the radio for Berna. On top of the Swiss Alps, a radio antenna swung around and focused on the compass bearing of faraway Fort Lamy. 'What number do you want, please?'

In London the Telecom tower picked up the Berna signal, and relayed it.

'Redcoat Control,' Dolores said from her bedside.

'This is Joe. We're holding over Fort Lamy, there's been a military takeover of some kind. We've got enough fuel to hold for two hours, then we've got to head for Entebbe. If that happens, find out what the shipper wants done with these pipes. Got that?'

'Roger.'

'And tell Abdullah out there to start looking for another cargo chop-chop, going anywhere east. And if you haven't heard from us in ten hours get Her Majesty's Government to start asking questions. Got all that?'

'Roger. Shall I call Reuters and try to find out what's happened?'

'Try. Call me back straightaway.'

Thirty minutes later, as the first dawn came over Africa, Dolores called.

'You better get out of there. Reuters don't know the details but civil war's broken out again and Libya has mounted another invasion of Chad . . .'

'Oh that bastard! What about those bloody pipes?'

'You aren't going to land in Chad, are you?'

'Hell, no – we're going to Entebbe! Get on to Abdullah, Dolores!'

He slumped back furiously. 'Get us the hell out of here!'

Oh God, Africa . . .

He was furious about his cargo – these bloody pipes and his cargo from Chad to Perth, *This bastard was costing him thousands . . .*

He sat there seething.

But when the sun was well up, Dolores was back on the telephone.

'Oh you beauty!' he cried. 'What kind of cargo?'

'Livestock, ready and waiting, it's really very lucky!'

'You make your own luck in this life, Dolores! Goodbye!'

CHAPTER 27

The rain came down, drumming on the shanty towns, rushing down the dirt roads. It was steamy, Uganda hot. Mahoney's shirt stuck to his back.

There were bullet holes along the verandah wall, from the days of Idi Amin. The hotel carpets were gone, door-handles loose, windows cracked, furniture rickety. The Victoria used to be a grand hotel. Out there, the streets were pot-holed, gutters clogged. The shops were bare, the telephones and electricity only worked sometimes; and beyond sprawled the shanty-towns, rutted, sodden lanes with refuse and mangy dogs and faeces and pot-bellied, malnutritioned children with flies clustered round their nostrils and eyes: and everywhere the hunger. But the worst had been the airport.

For *there* was the food. Great stacks of grain, the sheds overflowing on to the tarmac: United Nations' food supplies flown from Australia and America and South Africa – but it was not getting to the people. There were United Nations officials scurrying about, plenty of natives to load it on to the trucks. But the roads were very bad and there were not enough lorries, not enough fuel, and no spare parts. So the people were dying.

Oh Africa . . . What has happened to you? Dragged into the twentieth century by the white man, then abandoned. Without the knowhow, without enough good men to lead you: but with plenty of guns. And the gunmen pillage what little you have: and finally the men of the twentieth century come back to help you, and it is too late. But we will not be allowed to *stay* to help you. The world will allow the Vietnamese to stay in Cambodia and the Russians in

Afghanistan and the Cubans in Angola, they would probably even allow Idi Amin to come back to Uganda; but they will not allow the white man to finish the job of bringing you into the twentieth century . . . And maybe it was because he was a little drunk, but Mahoney wanted to go running to the airport and start humping those sacks of grain himself to the people, and feel the rain of Africa beating down on him in a kind of penance.

Because what had he contributed? He had left his Africa, washed his hands of it. Once he had chucked up everything and gone into the Zambesi Valley to help rescue the wild animals, but would he do the same now, to help people? . . .

And there was something else Mahoney did not like about himself.

Abdullah, his Ugandan freight-agent, had been waiting on the broiling tarmac when he climbed down from the Canadair. 'Good day, captain!'

'I'm not the captain, Abdullah, but you did a great job finding a cargo! Everything ready for the morning?'

'Yes, sir! In the shed, sir!'

The corrugated-iron shed shimmered in the sun. Abdullah slid back the door, beaming. It was dark inside. Mahoney felt the heat wafting out. Abdullah switched on a naked light. Mahoney let his eyes adjust. Cargo stacked everywhere. He looked where Abdullah was proudly pointing, and his eyes widened.

'Good God, Abdullah!'

'Yes, *sir!*'

Huddled in a small crate were three young gorillas, staring at him, petrified. Mahoney looked aghast. In the next cage were six antelope, trembling, so closely packed they could not turn, staring at him. Two more cages of antelope.

'Good Lord, Abdullah! What else?'

'Zebras, sir,' Abdullah said proudly.

Mahoney stared. There was a stallion and a mare, their crates built close around them, their legs hobbled. Mahoney cursed and peered further. Two African buffalo, their horns lashed to ring-bolts to stop them smashing their crates, rolling their eyes at him. 'Oh, Lord!' In the corner loomed two big

178

crates. They were plank, reinforced with iron bands. At one end there was an opening, for air. 'What's in there?' There was a crash and a phallic horn lashed up through the opening, then disappeared.

'Rhino!'

'Yes, sir,' Abdullah beamed.

Mahoney turned on him. 'When last were these animals fed and watered?'

'They came last night, sir.'

Have you fed them today?

Abdullah said nervously: 'My son's cutting grass, sir.'

Mahoney jabbed his finger under the man's nose. 'I want grass in here this high!' He held his hand above his head. 'And water. Understand?'

'Yes, sir.'

'Have the cages got drinking troughs?'

'Yes, sir.'

Mahoney strode to the first buffalo's crate. It had a tin trough but the animal's horns were tied, so it could not reach. 'Jesus!' He pulled out his pen-knife. He angrily sawed through the rope. The buffalo wrenched its head free and crashed its horns, so the cage shook. Then it lowered its head and drank thirstily. 'Get that hose!' Mahoney strode on to the next buffalo and cut its horns free. 'What about the rhino?'

He jumped up, on top of the big crate, keeping well clear of the opening. The crate shook and the horn came crashing up. 'Bring me a torch!' He peered down the opening. All he could see was the huge, dangerous, prehistoric head. 'There's no trough in here!' He jumped down, furiously. 'Bring a bucket! And a rope!'

'Please sir,' Abdullah said, 'rhino just smashed the bucket, sir.'

'Go'n buy another one, Abdullah!' Mahoney shouted. *'Two!'* He thrust a five-pound note at him. 'And get the grass in here. And fetch me at the hotel when you've got it all!' He glared. 'Abdullah, you've been my agent three years and you know damn well that Redcoat refuses to carry skins of wild animals. So why did you get me *this* cargo?'

179

Abdullah looked at him in amazement. 'These animals *alive*, sir!'

'Who's shipping them?' Mahoney demanded angrily.

Abdullah gave him a cargo note. Mahoney read it, and snorted. What a way to make a living. 'Have they been quarantined?'

'Yes, sir.' He produced another document. Mahoney hardly believed that.

He screwed up the cargo note. 'No way, Abdullah! I'm not delivering wild African animals to some dumb Aussie with more money than sense!'

Abdullah was staring in consternation. Mahoney threw the note on the floor furiously. Then shook his finger at the worried Indian. 'And fetch me at the hotel!'

He strode across the tarmac. He was disgusted – and bitterly disappointed that he had lost a cargo.

Then he stopped, angrily.

Yes, all very noble. But what was going to happen to these animals if he didn't take them tomorrow? How long would they languish in that stinking hot shed before Abdullah found another aircraft to carry them?

CHAPTER 28

The coast of east Africa dropped astern; ahead lay thousands of miles of Indian Ocean. The droning Canadair's hold smelt of dung and grass. The animals huddled in their crates, lying down to steady themselves, staring, frightened. They all had enough to eat. Abdullah had stuffed the hold with grass. But Mahoney felt frantic about the rhinos. He was talking to his agent in Perth:

'The troughs must be made of heavy iron, so they can't smash them up. Get a blacksmith to work immediately, Mac.'

'It's almost evening here, sport,' Mac said. 'Won't buckets do?'

'*No*, these are *rhinos*, not koala bears! They smashed up

four buckets last night as fast as we lowered them in, and they've simply *got* to drink tonight.'

'Didn't they drink at all?'

'No! So get a blacksmith, Mac, and have those troughs at the airport by dawn. And telephone . . .' He consulted the cargo note, read the Sydney agent's name. 'And tell them to have the transport ready to take these animals to their destination. I'm not having them stuck in a shed for another week.'

'Gotcha,' Mac said.

Pomeroy said, 'And what'll you do if everything ain't to your satisfaction, like?'

Mahoney snorted. What, indeed?

Mac had the two iron troughs at the airport at dawn. Mahoney did not know what he was going to do if this didn't work. He climbed on to the crate. The trough was tied to two lines. He lowered it gingerly into the opening. And all hell broke loose again in there, crashing of iron and wood and the crate shook. But after a dozen tries he got the trough down, right side up. He heaved a sigh. 'Now the hose.'

It was lowered in. And the sound of slurping rose up, like a vacuum cleaner.

Sixteen hours later the Canadair took off again, into the night.

The sun rose again, glinting into the flightdeck, reflected in their sunglasses, easing the stars out of the sky: but down there Australia was still in darkness, without even the pinpricks of earthlings on the Nullabar Desert. Then the sun rose higher, golden red, and in slow, magical moments the vastness of Australia was born. First a mistiness emerging, then suddenly, slowly, the sun was touching the tops of the scrub: for a long minute Australia was a quilt of streaked gold and mauve, young and beautiful: then the sun was truly up, and the vast desert appeared, brown and hard, stretching on and on to the hazy horizon.

The Canadair rolled into its bay at Mascot Airport, Sydney, and Mahoney shut down the screaming engines. He was

181

pleased: a tailwind had cut the flying time by half an hour and saved almost a thousand dollars in fuel. A freight-agent whom he did not know was waiting. As Mahoney came down the steps he saw a woman striding across the tarmac. 'Captain? . . .' she called.

It irritated him to be called that. He stopped halfway down the ladder.

'Thank you for bringing my cargo. Are they all right?'

Mahoney looked at her. She was in a green trouser suit that hugged her hips, the top well open, showing a deep, tanned cleavage. She wore a large picture hat and large sunglasses, and looked as if she were on her way to a garden party. Her hair was golden and hung down her back, and Mahoney thought she was stunning. Then, as she came closer, his pulse tripped as he recognized her. Mrs Tana Hutton, of Gray's Inn fame . . . He came on down the ladder. He had intended saying a hell of a lot to the consignee of these animals. He stepped on to the tarmac as she came striding up. He took off his sunglasses.

'Good morning. The last time we met was at our Inn of Court.'

'Ah, yes.' She smiled briefly, took off her sunglasses. 'How do you do, again, Mr Mahoney? My father recommended I try your airline, but I hardly expected you personally. How are the animals?'

'Did he? That's kind of him.' He was nettled by her manner, and her sheer ignorance of the trauma to which she had subjected the animals. 'They're as well as can be expected. Exhausted. And frightened. And reeking of their own excrement. Also airsick, and hungry.' He looked at her firmly. 'What arrangements have you made for them from here?'

'Haven't they been fed?' she demanded.

'They have,' Mahoney said grimly, 'but only thanks to me. I've got a few other bills for you. There were no drinking troughs for the rhinos so I had to have heavy ones made or they wouldn't have had a drink in three days.'

She turned angrily on the agent. 'I gave express instructions for feed and water!'

Mahoney said, 'Express instructions mean little in darkest Africa, Mrs Hutton. Please remember that in future.'

She looked at him a long moment. 'Thank you. I'll reimburse you, of course. And I happen to be familiar with darkest Africa.' She took a breath and shot her agent another angry look. 'Now, if the lecture is over – can we discuss business?'

'Mrs Hutton,' Mahoney sighed. Hell, he didn't want to antagonize her. And she was even more beautiful than he remembered. 'I don't want reimbursement, put that down to Redcoat's fine service, I'm just concerned what happens to the animals now.'

'That', Mrs Hutton said archly, 'is the business in question. Can Redcoat', she said, 'fly them up to my station?'

'Have you got proper accommodation for them ready?'

'Yes.' She added, 'And fodder for the journey.'

Mahoney felt a bit better about Mrs Hutton again. She looked the kind who would have everything ready. 'Where's your station?'

'Eleven hundred miles north. I have a landing strip, a mile and a half long. Is that enough for Redcoat?'

Mahoney smiled. He'd certainly rubbed this happy customer up the wrong way. 'What about a forklift, for getting the crates down?'

'I've got one of those too.'

'Oh. Good. Have you got a chart of your area?'

'Of course.'

'And your foreman will be on hand to take delivery?'

'That's me. I'll be flying with you. Because, you see, Mr Mahoney, contrary to what you think, I *do* care about the welfare of my animals.' She took a grim breath. 'How much is it going to cost me?' She warned: 'My family's also in this business, remember.'

Mahoney elaborately pulled out a pen. 'O.K., Mrs Hutton. The Redcoats are coming.'

CHAPTER 29

It was a beautiful day. Below was the Great Dividing Range, a long rumpled mass of blue mountains, jig-sawed with farms and forest dotted with far-apart towns. Beyond, the blue ocean rolled towards the best beaches in the world: but to the west the green quickly faded into yellow and brown, and then desert – thousands of miles of scrub and sand going on and on, almost all the way to the Indian Ocean. Every time Mahoney flew over this country, that vast hinterland depressed him. So much of the earth's surface almost useless. And every time he felt an offence against Nature: hurling fifty tons of machine at a thousand pounds an hour across a wasteland with a little bit of cargo.

It was a singularly unsociable journey. Mrs Hutton sat behind them, reading *Vogue* magazine or staring out her window, bored. She wandered off to her animals for a while. Mahoney invited her to don a headset, so she could talk to them, or listen to the news, but she only answered a few polite questions with frosty precision before taking it off. He had asked, 'What are you going to do with these animals, Mrs Hutton?' and she replied: 'Keep them.' He had invited her to go to the swingtail and make herself coffee. 'No, thank you.' He offered her a cigarette, but she preferred her own, thank you. O.K. Mrs Hutton, he thought, this is obviously a case of unrequited lust and anyway I don't like rich bitches who buy wild animals they know nothing about. Now he turned to her and beckoned. She put her headset on, and leant towards him. 'Yes?' Mahoney smelt Caleche and tore his mind off the flash of cleavage. He pointed.

'That's the hill, if we've done our sums right.'

'Correct,' she said. 'Start descending now. From the hill, it's three-forty-five degrees. Seventy-two miles on three-four-five, and you'll hit it on the nose. Is that all?'

Mahoney nodded at the horizon. 'Yes, thank you.' She turned, sat down again, and took off the headset.

Sydney smiled. 'I don't think she likes you, mon.'

Mahoney murmured, 'God spare me from rich bitches.'

'But those tits,' Pomeroy groaned. 'Ooooh . . .'

Sydney grinned, 'You might as well have a rich one and be comfortable while you're miserable.'

The terrain had slowly changed. Stretching all the way to the horizon was a mixture of sub-tropical woodland and yellow-green grassland. Seventy-two miles after the hill he saw the landing strip, a straight, treeless swathe well over a hundred yards wide.

'You want to bring her down, Syd?'

'No,' Sydney said. 'You've got to quit passing the buck to me, mon.'

'I'm the boss,' Mahoney said. 'Bosses are allowed to pass the buck.'

'And I'm the captain,' Sydney said.

'You're approaching too high,' Mrs Hutton said.

Mahoney turned, surprised. She was behind him, headset on again.

'Please don't talk to me now.'

'You're far too high! I know this runway.'

'I'm going to fly over it first to make sure there're no obstructions.'

'There'll *be* no obstructions.'

'Do you mind if the pilots of this aircraft reassure themselves?'

'Suit yourself, it's your fuel you're wasting.'

'Please sit down and strap yourself in!'

Mahoney flew low over the strip, peering below unhappily. There was a windsock, hanging mercifully limp. The runway looked newly bulldozed.

He brought her down with a thump that made him wince. The Canadair bounced ponderously off the dirt, somewhat crabbing, and her wheels hit again. She bounced again and the tail swung to the right. He corrected her, and she hit the earth a third time. Then she settled. He reversed his engines and the machine went screaming bumpily down the strip, to a ponderous halt.

He'd not done that very well . . . He shut down the engines.

Mrs Hutton shot him an amused look. Sydney and Pomeroy were grinning.

He had seen no house. There was a small hangar on the treeline. A Landrover had emerged from the trees, a horseman galloping behind, who turned out to be a beefy, sweat-stained jillaroo with freckles and bouncing breasts, called Angel, and the Landrover's driver another sweating jillaroo whose name Mahoney did not catch but who called him cobber. The horsewoman had galloped off, reappeared driving a forklift. Mrs Hutton had changed into jeans and T-shirt.

'Oooh . . .' Pomeroy groaned.

It was all very no-nonsense. Mahoney was impressed, despite himself. Mrs Hutton did not want his help. She evidently did not trust anybody with the forklift. She manoeuvred the rumbling machine under the aircraft's tail, lined up the fork with the pallet under each crate, her tongue clenched in concentration. The crated zebra rose, kicking in fright. Mrs Hutton reversed carefully away. She went trundling across the strip and disappeared into the trees. Angel put a cargo hook on the next pallet, connected it by rope to the Landrover. The nameless jillaroo ground the vehicle forward, dragging the next crate to the open end.

Mahoney walked across the airstrip, towards the treeline. Mrs Hutton was coming back on the forklift, but she did not look at him. Mahoney walked into the trees, looking. Pomeroy strolled after him, hands in pockets. Sydney followed. Mahoney walked a few hundred yards. Ahead he could make out a stockade. He saw Aborigines.

He walked on, towards them.

It was a stout stockade, made of ten-foot poles lashed vertically together on to crossmembers. Mahoney peered through the gaps between the poles: then he climbed up on to the crossmembers.

It was a square the size of two tennis courts, divided by more vertical poles into eight pens, with concrete drinking troughs. It looked newly built. Below him milled the antelope. They huddled together, staring fearfully about them. They were too frightened to drink yet. The Aborigines were staring at the buck, chattering.

'Jesus,' Mahoney said.

Pomeroy clambered up beside him and stared around.

'And this is it? No bleedin' shade?'

'Except there.' A high observation platform stood at the far end. It had a canvas awning. Mounted on the platform was a video camera.

He heard a diesel engine and turned. Mrs Hutton re-appeared, driving the forklift bumpily through the trees, carrying a crate. She drove round the corner of the stockade. Two Aborigines opened the gate. Mrs Hutton lowered the crate into the gateway. She climbed down from the forklift. The crate suddenly shook, with a bang. She waited till it stopped, then carefully climbed up on top of the crate, and lay on her stomach. She carefully pulled back the big iron bolt. She swung open the crate's door, and scrambled off on to the poles. And there stood the massive hindquarters of the buffalo.

But it did not move. It stood there, rump to the open door, confused. Everybody waited, the Aborigines grinning. Mrs Hutton leant down, clinging to the pole-tops; she gave the rump a poke with her finger. 'Hey!'

There was a snort and a crashing, then the beast came scrambling out backwards. He reversed into the stockade in a cloud of dust, and spun around to face his enemy, flanks heaving. But all he saw was empty stockade. He snorted, frightened, and spun the other way. Angel waved her hat down into the pen, and the buffalo charged. He thundered across in a cloud of dust and Angel whipped her hat away. The buffalo thundered to a stop, and glared, then lowered his head again and charged at the poles. He hit them with a crash and the jillaroo clung, and Mrs Hutton reversed the crate away and the Aborigines slammed the gate shut. Everybody was grinning with excitement.

Mahoney shook his head. 'I can't watch this.'

He jumped down, and strode away. A minute later Mrs Hutton passed him on the forklift and he did not look at her. He was working on what he was going to say to her. He walked

187

grimly through the trees, across the strip, back to his aircraft. He got aboard, went into the flightdeck, closed the door, and sat down angrily.

Three hours later all the animals were in the stockade, except the three gorillas, which were elsewhere.

The jillaroos drove the Landrover and the forklift away. Then Angel manned the video camera. The Aborigines were clustered on the pole-tops. Mrs Hutton looked around. 'Everybody ready?'

She climbed up the first rhino's pen. The jillaroo on the opposite side took off her hat and leaned down, and waved it inside the pen.

The rhino whirled with a snort, then lowered his head and charged at the hat, and hit the poles. On the other side Aborigines started opening the gate. They heaved out four poles frantically, then the rhino heard them making the opening and he spun around, and the Aborigines leapt up on to the stockade, and the rhino charged.

The prehistoric beast came pounding across the pen, two thousand pounds of armoured fury, and he hit the poles on which Mrs Hutton clung, hooking and crashing, wildeyed and murderous; then he backed off and looked up at her, his flanks heaving. He lowered his head again; then he saw the opening, right in front of him. He glared at it, eyes rolling furious red. Then he charged at the offending opening.

He thundered at it so the earth shook, then he skidded to a stop. He glared, head down: then he backed off furiously to charge it again: then realized what he had seen beyond. He snorted, lowered his head dangerously, made a feint charge at it; thundered to another halt. He peered short-sightedly through the hole, rump up, snorting. Then took a heavy, cautious step forward, ready to kill. He stuck his horn cautiously through. He peered left, and right, huffing. Then he suddenly backed off, flanks heaving in outraged suspicion.

Mrs Hutton took off her hat.

She leant down carefully, and waved the hat inside the

opening. And the rhinoceros charged at it. Head down, red-eyed, and the earth shook, and he blundered through the opening, and he was out, and Mrs Hutton's hat went flying through the air. The rhinoceros pounded furiously after it, to kill it, and crashed his sharp horn right through it. He shook his head furiously, and then charged murderously after the hat on his horn, then he saw Pomeroy walking through the trees towards the stockade, with Mahoney a hundred yards behind him.

All Pomeroy knew was that one minute he was strolling along, minding his own business, thinking about Mrs Hutton's tits, the next moment the earth shook, and all he saw was a terrible rhinoceros thundering at him wearing a hat. For a shocked instant Pomeroy stared, then he turned around, wildeyed, and he fled. As fast as his legs would carry him, and he filled his lungs and bellowed '*Heeeelp!*' – and he ran frantically for the Landrover. Mahoney heard him, then saw him, then the rhino pounding after him, and he yelled '*Get up a tree—*' and he tore off his shirt. Pomeroy fled flat out through the trees with the rhinoceros thundering twenty yards behind him, with Mrs Hutton fifty yards behind the rhinoceros, yelling, and Pomeroy reached the Landrover. He threw himself at it frantically and flung himself inside and all he saw was that terrible rhino, head down for the kill, and he slammed the door and the rhino hit the landrover.

The rhinoceros hit at full two-thousand-pound charge, and the front wheels heaved off the ground, and Pomeroy felt the world disappear. The vehicle crashed down on to its wheels again, and the furious beast snorted, red-eyed, be-hatted, and thundered at it again, and hooked with all his Herculean might, and the Landrover rose up, up and Pomeroy clutched wildly, then over it went. He was thrown upside down, and all he knew was red-black stars and the impressive crashing and smashing of stout metal as the rhinoceros got stuck into the under-carriage: then the beast saw Mrs Hutton.

The rhino whirled furiously around, and Mahoney screamed '*Tree!*' – and Mrs Hutton turned and ran at the nearest one, and she tripped and fell. She sprawled on to

189

her face, and the rhino charged at her. Head down and hooves pounding, to ram his horn right through her and throw her over the tree-tops, and Mahoney roared, wildly waving his shirt, and the rhinoceros turned. And Mahoney swerved, desperately swiping his shirt at the animal, and Mrs Hutton scrambled up. The rhinoceros charged and Mahoney threw the shirt at him, and he flung himself at a tree. The rhino charged at the shirt, and Mahoney scrambled frantically up his tree. Twenty yards away Mrs Hutton had clawed her way to safety. On the ground, the rhino proceeded to murder the shirt.

He chased it across the earth, hooking and swiping, then the hat flew off his horn. He skidded to a halt, and glared about him, flanks heaving murderously. He looked up into the tree at Mahoney. He glared at him malevolently, then worked himself up into another rage. He hit the trunk so the whole tree shook; then he turned and went running off at a fast, confused trot, his tail curled up over his back. And he was gone, into his new hinterland.

CHAPTER 30

He was expecting a big homestead, like her father's. Instead, Mahoney found six round huts of white-washed bricks, with thatched roofs. They were dotted along a creek twelve miles from the airstrip. He was amazed: it was like many a bush camp he had seen in Africa. Not dissimilar to the safari place he still had shares in. There was a central hut, just a thatched roof on gum-poles, a cooking fire smouldering in the middle.

Pomeroy was having a little lie-down in his hut; so was Sydney. Mahoney sat in a camp-chair by the creek, freshly bathed, drinking cold Tooheys beer, waiting for somebody to appear, marvelling at this delightful place that was not strange to him at all. Reliving the extraordinary, delightful business of the animals being set free, everybody still shaky and laughey from the rhino incident, the animals blundering out, be-

190

wildered, into their new hinterland, the dust hanging in the hot afternoon shadows. Mahoney thought the whole place was lovely. It wasn't Africa, but it was very likè it; and, oh, it made him yearn for the warm earth between his fingers again, under his bare feet, the long hot days and the noises of the night.

He heard the Landrover bouncing up. Angel called: 'Tana says to grab a few Tooheys and hop in if you want a flip over the spread.'

She had changed into a pair of khaki shorts that showed off long tanned legs, a white T-shirt with BEAUTY WITHOUT CRUELTY emblazoned across her breasts, and IVORY KILLS on the back. Her hair was wet and combed, her face shiny from soap and her eyes were very blue. And maybe it was the booze, or the whole lovely day, but Mahoney was smitten. She said into her head-set, 'You sure you don't want to drive?'

'Quite sure. I only fly for a living, with reluctance.'

'O.K.' She eased the throttle and the engine whined up to a scream: then she let go the brake and the Cessna went racing down the airstrip, bumping, faster and faster; then up, suddenly smoothly up the little aircraft rose.

She climbed, then levelled off. She held out her hand for his can of beer. She took a swallow and passed it back to him. She said over the headset: 'I'm sorry if I was rather cool today, Mr Mahoney. But I'm a bit sensitive to people telling me I don't know what I'm doing.'

He smiled uncomfortably. 'I wasn't my usual charming self, either. I'm sorry.'

'O.K.' She changed the subject. 'So, why aren't you lawyering if you don't like flying?'

It sounded stilted over the intercom.

'That's what my wife wanted to know. I assure you, as soon as I can afford to, I'll quit flying.' He said: 'And, are you a qualified lawyer now?'

'Yes. Wrote my finals last year.'

'Congratulations. So, are you going to practise?'

191

'No. I simply got tired of listening to lawyers I didn't understand.

He smiled. 'Like you got tired of plumbers?'

She grinned. 'He told you that, did he?' She said: 'Like you're tired of aeroplanes and want to build airships?' She added with a smile: 'You made a big impression on my father. He likes you.'

Mahoney was delighted with his credentials. And he was almost madly in love.

It was lovely. The treetops, all the colours, feeling all the bumps and vibrations. The world stretched out, away over there blue mountains. And all the time the long, bare legs of Mrs Tana Hutton beside him, and the good glow of the beer inside him. But conversation was difficult over the intercom.

'Twenty *thousand* square miles you've got here? . . .'

'That's only two hundred miles long by a hundred-odd wide. Not so big for Australia.'

Mahoney wanted to throw back his head and laugh. He was crazily in love with an Aussie sheila who lived twelve thousand miles away who thought twenty thousand square miles was not so big! 'That's bigger than the whole of Ireland!'

'So is the Kruger National Park in South Africa.'

She climbed the aeroplane up, up to ten thousand feet in the crystal clear sky.

'I'm showing you the difference in vegetation. We're a good way from the dry plains here.' She pointed west. The country over there looked grey-green, stretching on and on. She said: 'We're about twenty degrees latitude here. About the same as Rhodesia.' She pointed north-east. 'It gets sub-tropical, over there.'

'How much of this is yours?'

'About as much as you can see now,' she said. 'And over those mountains.' Her hand reached out for his beer, and she took another swig; then pointed again. Dust was hanging in the air. 'Cattle drovers.'

'Yours?'

'A neighbour's. Going to the railhead, crossing my land.'

She eased the yoke forward, and the plane turned down, down.

'How many?'

'About two thousand, I guess.'

'How long to get to the railhead?'

'About a month.'

He said happily: 'They must lose a lot of weight on that drive.'

'Say fifty pounds a head. Maybe much more.'

'Multiply that by two thousand. A hundred thousand pounds of beef sweated off! Fifty tons. What's that cost – half a dollar a pound?'

'Near enough for the ranchers.'

'Fifty thousand dollars lost,' he said. 'Plus the drovers' wages.'

She grinned at him around her mouthpiece: 'I know what you're thinking. I've read your brochures.'

'And all over the country thousands of ranchers are losing the same.' He turned to her: 'You don't believe in airships?'

'Nope.' She smiled.

'I'll show you one soon.'

'I know. At the Royal Easter Show.'

'How do you know?'

'My father knows everything.'

He grinned. 'Will you be there?'

'Oh, yes. Exhibiting my cattle. In my Easter bonnet.'

He sang: 'With all the frills upon it . . .' They laughed.

'How many cattle do you run on this spread?'

'Only a few. I only bought it a year ago. There're some wild water buffalo, and camels. And kangaroos, of course.'

'What are you going to do with these African animals?'

But she was lining the airstrip up. She came droning down. She hit the ground smoothly and only bounced once. The little aircraft came careering to a stop. She shut down the engine, unstrapped herself. Then turned to him.

'You're wondering why I took you up there?'

'I was hoping it was because of my big blue eyes.'

She smiled. 'Come back to the camp and I'll explain.'

The Landrover bounced over the dirt road, back to the huts.

She fetched a bottle of wine from the gas refrigerator, two cans of Tooheys, then led him to the chairs. She sat down, ripped the top off a can, passed it to him, and got straight to business.

'Mr Mahoney, I need a reliable airline to fly fairly large numbers of African wildlife here . . .' She paused. 'And not only reliable, but one that cares about their conditions – whether they spend an extra day languishing in a cargo shed or not. Whether they get fed and watered or not.' She smiled: 'I think you'll do.'

Mahoney took a guarded breath. She held up a hand. 'That's why I took you up. To show you the extent of this place. Its variety, its water. To show you that I know what I'm doing.' She paused, then went on resolutely: 'African wildlife is being driven towards extinction, Mr Mahoney. In fifty years it's going to be gone. And I'm going to recreate it right here in Queensland, Australia.'

She sloshed more wine into her glass.

'I suppose you think that's presumptuous. But my father owns the adjoining station, south. I'll inherit it one day. And the next one, north. And I'm setting the wheels in motion to get the government to declare a large part of Queensland a National Park. It's mostly uninhabited anyway.' She looked at him. 'Do you know how big that it would be? Almost as big as Kenya, Mr Mahoney . . . But even if we only get a *quarter* of that, is that not big enough?'

Mahoney shifted in his chair, but she got up and paced slowly towards the river. He had to tear his mind off her legs.

She said, 'Australia is an ideal environment for all these animals, Mr Mahoney. The climate ranges from tropical in the north, like the Congo, to Mediterranean in the south, and it's very sparsely populated. Whereas from the Congo to Cape Town there're about a *hundred* million people now. There's no zoological reason why Australia hasn't *naturally* got these animals. There are elephants and rhinos in India and Thailand.' She pointed. 'Just up there. And tigers. The only reason

194

Australia hasn't got them is an accident of geography. When Australia split away from Asia, the predecessors of these animals hadn't yet got here. All we got was kangaroos and koala bears.'

Mahoney sat up, guardedly. 'Mrs Hutton, your motives are laudable.'

'But?' she demanded.

Mahoney shifted forward. 'But I know Africa well; I've had a lot to do with wildlife. And I know how they capture wild animals for dealers.' She started to speak but he went on: 'It's a very big, bad cruel business, Mrs Hutton.' He looked at her. 'Often the mother animal is shot in order to capture the baby. And they spend months in cages awaiting shipment.'

'Then you also know about the poachers! That's even crueller, *very* big, bad business indeed! Those bastards have driven the rhino to the edge of extinction, Mr Mahoney. And all for its horn, to sell to Oriental gentlemen as an aphrodisiac, which doesn't work anyway. And you also know all about the African population explosion!'

Mahoney nodded. She sighed impatiently. 'Mr Mahoney, I'm a different political stripe to you – and to my father. I believe One-Man-One-Vote is inevitable, I see it in terms of Nature. Politics is Nature too, because man is a political animal. So they have the right to *mis*govern themselves. But that does not give them the right to *destroy* Nature! Anymore than industrialists have the right to pollute the air. And that is what the Africans are doing to their wildlife.'

Mahoney waited. She stood there, in the sunset.

'The writing's so clear on the wall. It's such a *small* world, and we're running out of everything.' She shook her head. 'In Africa in particular. It used to be *paradise*. Vast vistas of game, all the way to the horizon. And, sure, the black man hunted, but only with his spears, and only for food. And then the white man came, with his law and order, and medicine, and guns . . . *Death* Control, but no *Birth* Control. And the population explosion began. And the rape of Africa.'

He nodded slightly. 'I know.'

'Then before you criticize me for putting these animals through the trauma of transportation . . . tell me, what is

195

Africa going to be like in forty years, when the population has quadrupled yet again? What will have happened to all the animals by then? They will all be *gone. Eaten* . . . Even the Kruger National Park, because South Africa will probably have collapsed under the sheer weight of numbers! Whereas in Australia?' She spread her arms. 'It's a *beautiful* country. And, mostly empty. It could be *paradise*.' She shook her head at him. 'Australia can inherit the earth! Become the guardian of its treasures. . . .' She leaned towards him. 'In fact, that is Australia's *duty*.' She paused. 'Because it's the last place left!'

She sat down again. She was beautiful. He said: 'It's a wonderful thought.'

She insisted: 'Look. Let me worry about how the animals are captured. And I wish to impress upon you that I don't *order* the *capture* of animals. I buy ones that are already caught. All I want to know is whether we can rely on Redcoat.' She added: 'It could be lucrative.'

Mahoney sat up. 'Mrs Hutton, Redcoat is not in the business of turning away work. However, I would *insist* on knowing that we are not aiding and abetting unscrupulous poachers and animal dealers. There's plenty of them out there. It can take weeks, *months*, with the animals in a cage before there are enough to be shipped. We would want to know the circumstances of each cargo. Obviously, we are not prepared to help keep cruel men in business.'

'Of course not! I'm only buying animals already captured.'

He pointed at her T-shirt. 'Ivory kills. It's wrong to buy ivory bangles because it encourages hunters to go out and shoot elephants.'

'Exactly. And that is why I am spending a good deal of my time in Africa.' She added, 'But in three years' time I'll be flying tourists here on safari.'

He hardly believed that. 'I think you'll regret those rhinos,' he said.

'Why? Because they're bad tempered?' She waved her hand. 'Nonsense, there are rhinos in the Kruger National Park and

196

they don't stop the tourists. Besides, *rhinos*, as you doubtless know, are an endangered species. In a few decades there'll be no more rhinos outside of South Africa and Kenya. I'm going to get *more*, to build up a breeding nucleus. This land is huge, and they don't roam far.'

'What other animals have you got here? Any elephants?'

'Six,' she said. 'All adolescents. A male and five females. Again, no trouble.' She added: 'No lions.'

'What are you going to do with those three gorillas?'

'Tomorrow the girls are driving them to my other station, where it's more tropical. They'll be acclimatized then turned loose.' She was through with defending herself. 'Mr Mahoney, my zoologist friends and I know what we're doing. And we don't "order" wild animals. We *rescue* the ones already caught! Now will Redcoat fly my animals, or not?'

Mahoney sighed. He did not like the business of translocating African animals.

'Provided they are animals which are *already* captured – not which you've *ordered* captured – yes.'

She stood up with finality. 'Good.' She held out her hand. 'Well goodbye, Mr Mahoney.'

Mahoney stood up slowly, surprised. 'You're not leaving?'

'Yes, I have to be in Cairns. I'll be in touch with you.'

'But', he protested, 'you haven't finished telling me about this place.'

'Maybe some other time.'

He was bitterly disappointed. 'Every time I see you, you disappear. I thought I'd definitely corner you for dinner tonight.'

She smiled. 'I really must go.' She held out her hand a second time. 'Goodbye, and thank you.'

He refused to take it. 'Will I see you at the Easter Show?'

'I'm sure to see you waltzing overhead in your airship.'

'That's just a motorized *balloon*, I've got to tell you about *real* airships. And', he added cunningly, 'I want to see your prize-winning cattle. Over dinner?'

She said, with a twinkle in her eye, 'Are you very interested in cattle, Mr Mahoney?'

'I'm very interested in their owners.'

She said sweetly, 'Husbands and all?'

He smiled. 'I'm interested in air-freighting their cattle.'

She nodded. 'I suppose, Mr Mahoney, your wife doesn't understand you?'

'Absolutely. She left three years ago, shaking her head.'

She smiled, amused. 'If we run into each other we may have further business to discuss.' She held out her hand a third time: 'Goodbye.'

She got up into the Landrover and turned the key in the ignition. He said above the clatter of the engine: 'Remember to write!'

He stood, smiling regretfully, waiting for her to look back. She did not. But, as she disappeared into the trees, she raised her hand and twiddled her fingers over her shoulder. *Again* Mahoney grinned and waved energetically. Thirty minutes later he heard her Cessna. It flew low over the camp. He stood up. She zoomed straight overhead, heading east. He watched, waiting for her to waggle her wings. She did not. Then the plane was gone, behind the trees.

But she had flown too low overhead. Mahoney sat down again, smiling. And very disappointed.

CHAPTER 31

He was head over heels in love.

Of course he knew he wasn't in love, but it felt like it. He also knew that it didn't even feel like it, it just felt like fun. It wasn't even fun, it just felt frustrating as hell. Anyway, he thought about her all the way back to England. Well, a lot of the way. And there was precious little else to think about flying his goddamn aeroplane for two days. And there was plenty of *her* to think about: boy, they breed 'em healthy in Australia . . . That was it: he wasn't in love, he was in *lust*. It was ten o'clock at night when they landed at Gatwick and he was still so in love with Mrs Tana Hutton that he went straight to The Rabbit and hauled Danish Erika home to bed. He started undressing her inside the front door. 'My, my,' she said, 'Australia certainly agrees with you.'

'I was thinking about you all the way back,' he said.

The next morning he knew it was all ridiculous, of course.

What was the point of being in love with a married *Australian* woman? They've got to be the most *in*convenient kind. As far away from England as you can get. That's why we sent the convicts out there, isn't it? . . .

Mahoney banished Mrs Tana Hutton from his mind.

On his way to the office he stopped for a beer at The Rabbit. On his second beer he went to the public telephone.

'Hi!' Dolores said. 'Are you coming in?'

'Yes. No. Listen, have we got any cargo for Australia?'

'No, should we?'

'Australia, Dolores. That's where we want cargo to. Get on to the freight agents and tell them Sydney.'

'Who is she?' Dolores said.

'Don't talk nonsense. But I want you to find out something. Phone Australia House, she might be in their *Who's Who*. And send a telex to our agent in Sydney, ask him. Her father is a well-known politician, name of Erling Thoren. Her married name is Hutton.'

'This is business, of course, I can tell by your dispassionate voice.'

'Australian, huh?' Danish Erika said after he hung up.

He turned down a siesta with Erika and drove up to Cardington. It was raining hard. He put the blue skies of Australia firmly out of his mind.

It was all nonsense, anyway. She'd never put her grand scheme into effect. Just a sentimentalist with more money than sense. Anybody can buy a few dozen miserable African animals and stick them on their bit of outback. Plenty of people do that, even in England.

I thought you were going to stop thinking about her?

I am! Just watch me.

*

199

The two great hangars loomed ahead in rain. The mere sight of them made him feverish. The enormity of the undertaking, the money . . . He stopped his car at a distance, and stared at them. Was he crazy? And in a ghastly flash he saw his giant machine coming down to her mast through this lashing rain, huge and as unwieldy as the Albert Hall, buffeted by these winds, in terrible peril . . .

He started his car again, pulled up at the Portakabin. Pulled up his raincoat collar. He dashed for the side-door of his hangar.

The rain drummed loud. He walked through the vast place, dripping, peering upwards in the patchy electric lights. He stopped, and stared.

The huge sections of the ship reared up, disappearing down the vastness into gloom amid the confusion of scaffolding. But he could only make out half-a-dozen tiny figures of men working. And the ship looked no nearer completion than two weeks ago. He turned and looked around angrily for the foreman. He was walking towards him from the corner. 'Afternoon, Mr Mahoney.'

'Mr Gillespie, what's happening? There're only six men working!'

'Nine, actually,' the foreman said apologetically.

'But why only *nine*? The other ship's finished and gone!'

Mr Gillespie looked at him with sad eyes. 'The reason, Mr Mahoney, is money. Major Todd's orders. Until the blimp is sold we'll have to get by with just ten of us. The other men we've laid off; they haven't even been paid for their last four weeks.'

Mahoney felt himself go white. 'Not been paid!'

'Nor the ten of us who're still here, sir. But we're prepared to keep working, in the hope that all will soon be well.'

'Good *God*!'

He was appalled. That Malcolm had reached this stage without letting him know. Unless Malcolm sold that goddamn blimp he was bankrupt! And Redcoat would be left with an unfinished airship! How long would those laid-off workmen wait for their money before they cut up rough and started putting Malcolm into liquidation? 'Where the hell's the production manager?'

'He's at the factory, sir, inspecting your new materials before delivery.'

Mahoney turned and strode furiously out of the hangar. He dashed into the Portakabin, grabbed the telephone and dialled.

'Roger, I'm at Cardington! It appears you're almost bankrupt!'

He heard Malcolm's long-suffering solicitor sigh.

'Hardly bankrupt, old chap. So, we owe some wages. But that airship is worth a couple of million.'

'*If* Malcolm sells it. Otherwise it's worth nothing. Why wasn't I advised how desperate things were getting?'

Roger said quietly, 'As I recall, you're not on the board, Joe; you're only a minor shareholder.'

'I have a moral right! I helped Malcolm get started!'

'The crisis', Roger said slowly, 'only came about in the last month, because the blimp took longer than estimated to finish. And Malcolm didn't want to give you any sleepless nights. There was nothing you could have done about it anyway. You had paid up for your materials and he has paid the men who worked on your ship in full; except the ten who've volunteered to continue. I think it is a tribute to him that many more workers were prepared to continue – and that he wanted to spare you the anxiety. He'll straighten it out with you when he gets back.'

Bloody smooth-talking lawyers! He desperately wanted to be reassured. 'That goddamn blimp – I told him he was heading for trouble!'

The lawyer said: 'It is without doubt the most commercial airship he could have started with. *You* weren't offering him an immediate profit on your ship, were you?' He paused. 'Get this in perspective, Joe. If Malcolm had concentrated on his own airship, instead of working on yours, he wouldn't be in this jam now. He's only building yours because he felt he *owed* it to you. He's spent most of his capital on equipment to build *your* ship – not his. You got a marvellous deal. Only when your ship is flying and earning do you start paying him his profit.' He added: 'If Malcolm had followed my advice he wouldn't have touched the deal.'

Mahoney took an angry breath. 'He's been pinching my labour!'

'Not so! The only thing he's pinched is himself, doing two jobs. If he's devoted too much time, for your liking, to his own ship, he'll repay you handsomely soon. Patience is the least you owe him.'

'Patience! . . . I'm paying interest on six million pounds while that airship stands unfinished like a monument to disaster!'

'Well,' the lawyer said smoothly, 'I phoned Malcolm today. And he's very optimistic, the Australians are being very nice.'

'Malcolm's always optimistic! And the Australians are usually nice.'

'Well, I think I can also tell you something else – in professional confidence, of course . . . There has been some very big interest shown in our shares recently. I think we may shortly have a large injection of capital from share sales.'

Mahoney's heart leapt. 'Who is it?'

'I don't know, that sort of thing is often done through nominees.' He added: 'That's confidential. Now I must go.'

'That big?'

Mahoney was slightly mollified. It was dark when he got back to his cottage. There was an envelope under his door. It was a typed note from Dolores:

Re yr strictly business enq re Ms Hutton née Thoren.

    Whos Who lists Big Daddy only. A pretty big wheel; Politics, Businesses incl. Thoren Shipping, Thoren Pacific Airlines, Cattle-Air, Thoren International, Thoren Pharmaceuticals, Thoren Wines and Breweries, some newspapers, cattle stations, numerous African mining & mnfrg interests. Reasonable credit risk.

    Our Sydney agent replies re. Ms H: well-known local beauty(???) & society princess/queen (depending how old the old bag is). Former champion skier. (Tend to fat when they quit.) Tons of vulgar dough. Owns real estate development company, cattle stations, also into food canning. Big Daddy's grooming her to take over Thoren empire. Her own company called Fairwinds, also into travel business. Spoilt little bitch if you ask me.

The bad news is she's divorced from another politician called, surprisingly, Hutton.

The terrible news is we've got a cargo for Sydney next week.

Further info when you stop jerking off. G'night.

CHAPTER 32

As soon as Ed shut down the engines, they broke out the beer. It was a beautiful Sydney morning, the beer tasted marvellous after the the two-day flight – and he *felt* marvellous. He had twenty-four hours' stopover, he was going to have a big Australian steak for breakfast, and a bottle of cold crisp wine, then sleep like a child until late afternoon. As soon as Customs were finished, he set off to the Navy hangar with a spring in his step. It was a beautiful day to be taking a beautiful woman to dinner this night. Mahoney felt so good he wasn't even going to tear a piece off Malcolm for getting himself into a financial jam.

He stopped outside the hangar. And even that bloody stupid blimp was looking beautiful!

She floated in her hangar, gleaming white, anchored to the floor. She was moored to the mast which the Navy had welded to the back of a truck. Mahoney strode inside. Malcolm was under the gondola. 'Good morning, Major!'

Malcolm jerked and bumped his head. 'Joe!' He wriggled out, beaming.

'She's looking good, Malcolm!'

'She's going sweet as a nut.'

'Where's Lovelock? Is he behaving himself!'

'Hullo, young fella!' Mahoney turned. It was the Admiral, striding over in a natty pin-stripe suit, hand out, beaming.

'Admiral! What's happening with the Navy?'

'Beautiful,' the Admiral beamed. 'Old Ocker Anderson's such a good egg, I want you to meet him tonight.'

'I can't tonight, I'm afraid,' Mahoney said happily.

203

'Pity. We're having a dinner aboard his flagship. They're really keen! They've had observers here every day, watching the assembly. And I've been playing elaborate war games with them!'

'War games?'

'You know, big maps. Here's Australia . . . Here's the enemy fleet. Here's your jolly old fleet. What you going to do, old chap? Well, if you had had your airships patrolling here, here and here, the crisis wouldn't have arisen, old chap, you'd have been forewarned and had your ships there, and there, and blown the jolly old Japs to kingdom come before they got to first base! I've worked out a dozen games, all the likely situations, and on paper I won every battle.'

'Excellent, Admiral.'

'Simple, even old Ocker understands. The naval role of the airship is self-evident. And the Ag and Fish boys are *very* interested.'

'Ag and Fish?'

'Agriculture and Fisheries,' Malcolm said. 'The Admiral's given them the war-games treatment too – showed them how we're going to save Australia a fortune. We're having lunch with them tomorrow, can you come?'

'I'm afraid I'll be gone,' Mahoney said.

'Pity,' the Admiral said. 'The Head of Department himself is going to be there. Just give him a rip-top pie and he'll be sweet, *aha-ha-ha*! By the way, we're indebted to you for the good work you've done with Erling Thoren.'

Mahoney's face lit up. 'He's been in touch?'

'He's been *here*,' Malcolm said. 'Once alone, once with Admiral Anderson. He gives the impression of having a bit of clout.'

'And a third time,' the Admiral said, 'with that lovely daughter of his.'

'With his *daughter*?' Mahoney beamed.

'Lovely woman,' the Admiral said. 'Oh, to be sixty again, *aha-ha-ha*! He spoke rather highly of you.'

Mahoney was beaming. 'What did his daughter say?'

'Actually, *she* really checked us out,' Malcolm said.

'When was all this?'

'Yesterday.'

So she was in town and had received his telex! Mahoney was too pleased with life to say anything to Malcolm about his own airship.

Normally, Redcoat crew stayed in cheap hotels. But today Mahoney booked himself into the Town House, one of the best in Sydney. He had breakfast, left instructions to be woken at four p.m., and he went upstairs to bed happily.

He woke feeling fit as a fiddle. He showered cheerfully and shaved carefully. He got a beer from the refrigerator, lit a cigarette, and sat at the telephone and dialled Fairwinds. A female voiced sang: '*Mush*-rooms.'

Mahoney blinked. 'I'm sorry,' he said, 'I'm trying to get a company called Fairwinds.'

'You've got it,' the voice said. 'Just a crossed line, you've got straight through to the Mushroom Department.'

Mahoney smiled. 'Fairwinds sells mushrooms?'

'Only the *spore*, sir, we encourage *you* to grow the mushrooms. Hold on, I'll transfer you.'

He waited. The phone went dead.

He dialled again. 'Fairwinds, g'day,' another voice said.

'G'day,' Mahoney said, in the vernacular. 'Mrs Hutton, please.'

There was a click. '*Mush*-rooms . . . ,' the voice sang.

'Hullo, Mushrooms,' Mahoney smiled, 'we've got that dreaded crossed line again, I'm trying to get Mrs Hutton's secretary.'

'I am Mrs Hutton's secretary today. I'm also handling mushrooms today, the regular mushroom lady is off.'

He smiled. 'But you're only handling the *spore*?'

'Only the spore, sir. We buy *your* mushrooms after *you've* grown them with *our* spore.'

'Ah . . . And what do you do with the fully-fledged, adult mushroom once you've bought it?'

'Can it and sell it, sir. By the ton. How many tons do you want?'

205

'Actually, I was thinking', Mahoney smiled, 'of one can. But there's no rush.'

'I see. Well, what else can I do for you, sir?'

'May I speak to Mrs Hutton, please. This is Redcoat Airlines.'

'Ah, Redcoat . . . England. Didn't you get our telex?'

'No?'

'Mrs Hutton regrets. She leaves tonight for Africa.'

Mahoney's heart sank. 'Oh.' He was bitterly disappointed. He thought. 'Well . . . just tell Mrs Hutton . . .'

The girl sighed. 'I *am* Mrs Hutton. Good afternoon.'

'Mrs Hutton!' he cried. 'This is Joe Mahoney!'

'I know,' Tana Hutton said. 'I got your accent in one.'

He grinned. 'What happened to *your* accent?'

'I turned on my Aussie one when I recognized yours the first time you got Mushrooms. But as you evidently don't eat many, what can I do for you?'

He said, 'Please tell Mrs Hutton I'm expecting her for dinner tonight at eight o'clock, as per my telex.'

'She can't come. She's leaving for Africa.'

'She isn't. She's avoiding me for some mysterious reason.'

'Why should she want to avoid you?'

'Because she's nursing a secret passion for me, and it worries her.'

'Really? . . . Nothing worries Mrs Hutton when she's impassioned. But she is not impassioned at all. And she can see no point in having dinner with a fly-by-night.'

'*Me?*'

'Besides, I happen to be married.'

He grinned. 'You're not very married.'

'Mr Mahoney, for all you know about me, I am very married indeed. And you're a very charming pilot who has a girl in every airport.'

'Mrs Hutton . . .'

'Mr Mahoney, I really am going to Africa tonight. And even if I wasn't, I still wouldn't have dinner with you. No matter how honourable your intentions with my body, we really have no business to discuss – it's all in my telex to you.'

'What is?'

She said: 'I'm going to Africa to buy some more animals. I've asked Redcoat to quote for a flight next week, Kenya to my station.'

Mahoney smiled. 'Provided my conditions about the dealers are met, we'll be delighted.'

'That', she said, 'is why I'm going to Africa. And to make it more worth your while, I've got a cargo for you from my station to Sydney. Cattle I'm exhibiting at the Show. I want an all-in price.'

'You'll get a good one,' Mahoney promised.

'I don't want any favours, Mr Mahoney,' she smiled, 'they won't be returned. And now I really must fly. Where are you staying, by the way?'

'The Town House.' He added: 'Redcoat always stays at the best hotels.'

'Well, they'll give you a good dinner. Goodbye, Mr Mahoney.'

He sat on the bed, a rueful smile on his face. He was bitterly disappointed. He did not know what to believe. Was she really going to Africa? But Joe Mahoney had got the brush-off, loud and clear. 'A fly-by-night.' *Him?* The injustice of it. The sheer, towering injustice of it . . .

He dressed and walked slowly down the corridor towards the elevator. He felt absolutely aimless, but he had half a smile on his face. Because he had made a fool of himself. For ten solid days he, Joe Mahoney, that very same Joe Mahoney, QC, who was old enough to know better, that hell-of-a-guy who had broken more than his fair share of hearts, including his own – had been besotted by a woman he'd met exactly *twice* . . . for ten solid days he had been dithering about her in starry-eyed *lust*. To the point where he'd rescheduled his flights, booked himself into an expensive hotel . . . It was, as he had told himself repeatedly over the last ten days, fucking ridiculous.

He smiled ruefully at himself in the mirror as he waited for the elevator.

Oh, well . . . A man was entitled to a little nonsense, wasn't he? And he'd even got some good business out of it.

The elevator doors opened and he stepped in.

The doors opened on the ground floor, and he found himself confronting a despatch rider with a crash helmet. Next to him stood a bellboy, with a tray. 'Mr Mahoney? This arrived for you, sir.'

Mahoney stared at the tray.

Neatly in the centre of it stood one can of mushrooms.

He strode to the reception desk, a smile all over his face. He telephoned a florist.

He ordered a dozen of their best red roses to be delivered aboard Qantas' flight to Africa tonight, to Mrs Tana Hutton.

'And what do we write on the card?' the clerk said.

'Nothing,' Mahoney said.

'Not even who they are from?'

'No.' Then suddenly he had a brainstorm. 'Change that to *eleven* red roses. And write on the card: "The twelfth one is you." No name.'

He was delighted with himself.

CHAPTER 33

The sky was full of stars. The weather report had promised a cloudless day. A lovely day to start the Royal Easter Show.

'And no wind,' Mahoney prayed. 'Please God no sneaky little wind suddenly slipping around the end of that hangar just as Malcolm walks her out.'

Mahoney lay on his bed at Mrs Hutton's camp, sweating, staring up at the dark thatch. He had not seen her in Kenya the day before yesterday when he had picked up her cargo of animals, and he was not thinking about her now. He had to resist getting up, pacing about. It was important that he rest. Today was Malcolm's big day. If Malcolm did not sell his airship to the Navy today . . .

He looked at his watch. In an hour Malcolm would be walking her out. The air is stillest just before the dawn.

Before dawn Angel came for them. They bounced over the tracks to the airstrip. Before first light the cattle were loaded into Canadair.

Malcolm Todd had not slept all night.

Before dawn three truckloads of sailors arrived at the Navy hangar, in good spirits. There were three officers who had observed assembly procedures from the beginning, twenty days ago. Their admiral would arrive later.

The assembly team had been at the hangar for hours doing final checks and polishing. Everything was absolutely ready. The airship hung in the hangar, gleaming white, fifty-three yards long. Her gondola clung snug beneath her belly, twenty-seven feet long, shining. She was moored to the mast on the back of the truck.

The sailors had fallen in and Malcolm was addressing them.

'This is the most tricky manoeuvre. In the old days, in America and Germany, many accidents happened when walking an airship out of her hangar. A sudden gust of wind can smash her against the door, and ruin her. That's why I've planted a windsock at each corner. To make it trickier, this is a manoeuvre *I* have never done before. In fact, the instructions I'm going to give you now are based on the old Luftwaffe manual of World War One.' He smiled: 'Anybody here read German?'

Polite laughter.

'Now, you are divided into three groups, and you are going to hang on to each side of the airship and the tail. This truck is going to tow her forward: you are going to walk with her, restraining her against any gusts of wind. There will be three speeds: walk; fast walk; and *run*. And: backwards walk; and backwards run. We'll practise it. And you must walk in *step* . . .' He beamed at them: '*Can* the Navy march in step, by the way?'

Laughter.

Everything had been perfect.

There had been no wind at sunrise. The hangar doors were opened. The sailors were in position. Lovelock did his checks with the engineer. He started the engines. Their scream filled the hangar.

The anchoring lines were loosened, and the sailors hung on. Malcolm darted around, checking. Then he stood in front of the truck, put his whistle to his mouth, and blasted the starting signal.

The truck rumbled forward. The big, bulbous airship began to lumber after it, towed by her nose. The sailors walked with her, holding tight to her strong-points, in step.

Malcolm walked backwards in front, eyes darting. On the airship slowly came.

Now Malcolm was passing through the doors. The truck's bonnet rumbled through, then the cab. Then the mast. Now began the crucial time. But there was not a breath of wind in that beautiful sunrise. The big white nose entered the doorway and Malcolm blasted the signal for quick-march, the truck surged and the airship began to emerge into the Australian morning: five yards, ten, fifteen . . . When she was one third out, the truck conked out.

Nobody heard the engine cough, only felt the sudden lurch, and the quick-marching sailors bumped into each other, three men fell and the airship jerked. Malcolm bellowed and the men heaved as she swayed towards the door; they *heaved* and just stopped her in time, gasping. Malcolm was bellowing, '*Engineer!*'

The engineer flung himself under the bonnet, while the sailors clung on. '*How long?*' Malcolm seethed.

'Dirty fuel, sir!'

'*Shove!*' Malcolm bawled.

Every available man got behind the truck and heaved. Grunting, cursing, teeth clenched. It began to roll. They shoved and shoved, grunting, gasping, then suddenly Malcolm felt the breeze.

He looked wildly over his shoulder at the windsock. '*Hold hard!*'

The breeze swirled round the hangar. '*Hold on starboard!*' The ship surged like a sail and the men heaved against it with all their might.

'*Get the Navy truck to tow us!*'

The sun glinted into the flight-deck of the Canadair. 'No news is good news,' Ed said.

Just then the bell went *bing-bong* and Mahoney's heart missed a beat. He flicked the switch.

'We have a call for you from Redcoat House.'

Mahoney closed his eyes in relief. 'Thank you . . .'

A moment later Dolores was on the air. She said, 'Thank God, we've been trying to get hold of you for twelve hours!'

Mahoney's pulse tripped. 'What's the trouble?'

She said, 'Big trouble, Joe. Are you ready for it?' Mahoney's stomach contracted. She said: 'Malcolm's company has gone bankrupt.'

Mahoney felt himself go white. He cried:

'But that's impossible! Malcolm's *here*, about to demonstrate his ship!'

She said: 'They've been forced into liquidation. As I understand it, somebody bought up all the debts and foreclosed. Malcolm's liabilities far exceeded his assets, and the court has ordered a provisional liquidation.'

He was stunned. 'But he only owed some back wages! All his tools and presses are worth a fortune!'

'No, they're all leased to Redcoat in terms of our contract, that's where all his capital went, on tools so he could build your ship. And he hasn't paid for all the materials for that blimp yet!'

Mahoney's ears were ringing. *Oh God* . . . Dolores went on: 'A new company has been formed. They're taking over Malcolm's staff and they're going into production of airships with massive capital.'

Mahoney shouted, 'They can't touch our airship! We own

211

every rivet and we've leased the tools and presses until the job's finished!'

'Yes, that's understood. That's how Malcolm busted himself.'

Mahoney was aghast. All he could see was poor, broken Malcolm, and Redcoat's airship standing unfinished forever. *'Who are these bastards?'*

She said: 'Can't you guess? Tex Weston, in company camouflage.'

Mahoney stared. Of course! He'd stopped Weston getting Shelagh's shares, so he nails Malcolm's company to get airships! Dolores said: 'I think he's going to make you and Malcolm offers you can't refuse.'

'For God's sake stop talking in riddles, woman!'

Dolores said, 'For Malcolm to work for the new company. And for your airship. To take it off your hands.'

Mahoney flared up. Of course! He would be forced to sell the unfinished hull cheap if Malcolm went to work for Weston. Dolores said: 'Are you there? I've told you everything I know. What must I do?'

He was struggling to think straight, his ears ringing.

'If anybody asks, you haven't contacted me yet. You can't find me.'

'Understood.'

He was thinking feverishly. 'Phone Malcolm. Tell him nothing except that I say he must *not* accept any phone calls until I get there.'

'Understood.'

He looked at Ed, white-faced. Then he scrambled up. He lurched through the hold, his hand over his mouth. He just made the toilet before he retched

The Navy vehicle swung in front of the stalled truck. The officer flung himself under the rear with a rope, Malcolm scrambled frantically under the truck with the other end. He began to lash it around the axle, whimpering, fumbling. He felt the truck lurch as the wind hit the ship. *'Hold hard!'* he screamed.

The wind wrenched and the men heaved, straining, grunting, their officers bellowing. The ship came within three feet of the doorframe before they pulled her back, straining, gasping. '*Hold on!*' Malcolm whimpered, teeth clenched, knuckles bleeding, wrestling with the rope. He got the knot tied and the truck lurched again.

The wind came whipping around the opposite side of the hangar and hit the big blimp and the men were caught off step, heaving and yelling and staggering. Malcolm came scrambling out, greasy, bloody, wild-eyed, yelling. '*Heave!*' The blimp lurched within a foot of the doorframe before the men pulled it back. '*Drive!*' Malcolm screamed.

The officer was scrambling out from under the forward truck. The engine roared, and the vehicle leapt forward, and the men staggered as the wind struck again. '*Go!*' Malcolm bellowed.

The truck roared forward and the men lurched into a run. '*Faster!*' Malcolm screamed. The vehicle surged and the men ran frantically, clinging, staggering. The wind struck again: and the airship came lurching out of the hangar. And she was clear.

CHAPTER 34

She floated at her mast, shining in the sun, her gondola gleaming. She looked very impressive. A crowd was gathered around her, newsmen and people from neighbouring hangars. It was a beautiful day to make her debut. But for Mahoney it was dark.

He strode grimly across the tarmac. '*Malcolm!*' he shouted.

Malcolm turned, his flushed face cheerfully expectant. He waved and started towards him. 'Hullo, Joe! I got a strange message from Dolores.' Mahoney took his arm and started towards the hangar.

'I've got bad news, Malcolm. That airship isn't yours anymore . . . '

Malcolm slumped in a chair, his cheeks wet, his face blotchy with emotion. Mahoney sat opposite him, hunched forward.

'He's stolen your company, Malcolm. And it's obvious why he waited! He wanted us both out of the country. And he had to do it *before* you clinched the Australian deal because then you'd probably have enough money to pay your debts. He had to catch you while you were broke!'

'But why didn't he just buy shares? Why did he have to *kill* me?'

Mahoney clenched his fist in exasperation. '*Think* about it, Malcolm. If he bought *shares* he'd be keeping your company alive, to build blimps for the Navy and to finish my airship. He doesn't *want* that. He wants *you* – your know-how, but as his *employee*, to build what *he* wants.'

'But there are other people, there's that university professor—'

'But yours is the only company that's actually *working*! You have *hangars*. Those hangars are about the only place in the world where anybody can build an airship today – without spending millions on erecting them. And he's in a hurry.' He added fiercely: 'O.K., you can fight the provisional order of liquidation, try to prove that you're not legally bankrupt – but are you going to *work* for the bastard?'

Malcolm sat, red-eyed, his face suffused. 'Ten years of my life . . . All my money. My sweat. And just when I'm about to get a big contract . . .'

'No, Malcolm! Think again. He's not interested in building blimps. He could build them in any decent-size hangar. He wants *big* rigids, and that's why he wants to buy my airship. Because its half built and because he needs my hangar too. One of the reasons he didn't simply buy shares in your company is that he'd be stuck with our contract, to build my ship at *cost* price. He doesn't *want* me on his back, so he had to kill our *contract*, and get my hangar – plus my airship. At *less* than cost, because I'd be forced to sell to get rid of a terrible burden if you couldn't finish it because

214

you're working for *him*.' He glared. 'Oh, it's a great bargain, isn't it? For the cost of buying up your debts he gets your airship, both the Cardington hangars, *my* unfinished ship, and *you*.'

Malcolm said huskily, 'And? Are you going to sell?'

Mahoney looked at the man as if he was out of his mind. '*Sell? Hell, no!* Nor are *you* going to sell yourself to that vulture!'

Malcolm's chin trembled. His face was going to crumple again. He whispered, 'Oh, God, what about Anne?'

'Anne?' Mahoney cried. 'You've got a roof over your heads, haven't you? That cottage is still yours. You've got a hangar – *my* hangar – the most indispensable item! You've got an airship half-built already! And you have the money to finish her. My bank's got to keep financing me. They don't want to lose their loan.' He looked at him: 'You're *years* ahead of any competitor!' He spread his arms theatrically. 'What more do you want?'

Malcolm gave a haggard smirk. 'God, you're a smooth talker.' Then he closed his eyes. 'Where am I going to get the staff – the equipment?' . . . He shook his head.

Mahoney cried, 'You've still *got* all your tools and presses because you leased them to me! Weston can't take them back until we've finished with them. And it's going to take him a *long* time to get new ones.'

Malcolm sniffed. 'What do we do now?'

'Right now we get your arse into gear, Malcolm!' He pointed outside. 'That airship isn't yours anymore, but until notice is served, you don't know it. You're not going to sit like a condemned man. We're going to demonstrate that ship, *today*, Malcolm – all over Sydney! And not for Weston. *We'll* get the benefit. Now, the first thing is a pot of red paint.'

Malcolm stared. 'What the hell for?'

Mahoney said maliciously: 'As your last decision as managing director you're going to paint "Redcoat" on that airship in red letters. When Weston arrives, he'll scrub it off; but it'll take him days and meantime he's going to fly it with our name on it – *if* he can find a pilot . . .'

215

CHAPTER 35

The paint was still wet, but there it was in blazing red: *Redcoat Airshiplines*.

There were hundreds of airport personnel watching. The first official demonstration was scheduled for the next day, but there were press men and television crews, and a buzz of expectancy. Lovelock, Mahoney, Malcolm and a Navy engineer were in the gondola.

Lovelock sat in the left-hand seat, pink and blond and cool as a cucumber. Mahoney was in the right-hand seat, tense as a guitar string. Both wore uniforms, and sunglasses. All the buoyancy tests had been redone. They were going through the checklist, flicking switches, Lovelock explaining them to Mahoney for the last time. 'O.K.?' he said. 'Nothing to it.' Then he turned over the engines.

They roared sweetly to life, screamed slowly to a crescendo in neutral pitch, then down. Mahoney said over his shoulder, 'O.K., Malcolm, this is it!'

Lovelock spoke into his radio. 'This is Airship, ready for weigh-off.'

'Airship, you are cleared for weigh-off.'

Mahoney's heart was pounding. Lovelock eased the lever that released the ship from her mast.

There was a gentle lurch, the coupling was gone, and the ship was free. Lovelock vectored the engines, and up, up she sedately rose, and a cheer went up from the crowd.

She rose slowly, shining in the sun, the earth and upturned faces dropping away. Mahoney's heart was pounding with excitement. Lovelock manoeuvred the engines, gently opened the throttle, and the ship began to ease forward.

A hundred yards ahead, Mahoney had lined up two of the crates that held Mrs Hutton's prize cattle, which he had flown into Sydney that morning. Ed was waiting there. Lovelock eased the airship towards them, then hovered. He pulled a lever, and down came the cargo cable. Ed hooked it on to the crates' harness. And Mrs Tana Hutton's cattle were ready to fly over Sydney.

Mahoney yelled out the window: 'Get your ass over there, Ed! And that water-bowzer!'

They rose, two big crates containing two big bulls rising slowly, up, up, up, fifty feet, sixty, eighty, a hundred, while down on the tarmac all faces were upturned. The airship rose swifter and swifter, to five hundred feet. Then Lovelock began Mahoney's publicity stunt.

'Do you want to take her?' Lovelock grinned.

'Yes – but don't let go yourself!'

'She handles like a dream!'

'Like a dream, Malcolm!' Mahoney shouted. It was a wonderful feeling, to be as light as the air and working with it, not against it, floating over the housetops like a sailboat on the sea. 'Like a dream, old Malcolm!' And Malcolm had tears running down his face, and Mahoney cried:

'This is only the beginning, Malcolm!'

The airship flew over Sydney, the cattle suspended. Down in the streets traffic stopped and people leant out of windows. It circled low over the commercial centre, engines purring, then down Macquarie Street towards the Opera House. Lovelock circled slowly over the Opera House, then out over the Harbour Bridge, and the hooting started.

First one cheery blast from a freighter, then others started up in a ragged chorus. Then cars, and the cacophony of honking rose up over Sydney. The ship was sailing magnificently over the harbour when the first helicopter appeared.

It was rented by Australian Broadcasting Commission and Lovelock went into another circle to allow it to catch up. The helicopter came chopping up alongside, filming into the gondola and they all gave their most dashing smiles. Another television helicopter came roaring across the harbour and Lovelock let it catch up also: then he began to put the airship through her paces.

217

He eased the throttle open and she surged, through forty knots, to fifty, to sixty, up to seventy, the two helicopters racing after him. Then he worked the elevators and the ship started down.

Lovelock sent her down towards the harbour mouth, down, down, and the blue sea was looming up, up. He levelled off when the cattle crates were twenty feet above the sea, the helicopters roaring alongside filming; Lovelock sent the gleaming ship purring out to sea for a mile while the television crews filmed the cattle skimming the waves. Then he began to climb.

She climbed up, in a long graceful curve, to two thousand feet, then he turned her towards Bondi Beach. Malcolm was moist-eyed with pride. The airship went purring along Sydney's coastline, the helicopters chopping furiously after them; then ahead was Bondi, packed with people. Lovelock slowed down to twenty knots, and they came in over the beach at two hundred feet, casting a huge shadow. Bikini-ed girls were waving. Lovelock circled the beach slowly, grinning.

'Now here we go, Malcolm.' And the airship rose, up, up, into the sun; then he turned her, over the suburbs, heading for the agricultural showgrounds.

There seemed to be miles of cars, stalls, grandstands, pavilions, funfairs, bars. People were thronging, gay hats and colour everywhere midst loudspeakers and music.

Mahoney felt marvellous. Lovelock had given him the controls again and he had the feel of the thing, just naturally knew it. He came over the car parks with Tana Hutton's prize cattle, and below people stared upwards and pointed. The airship flew low, casting its big shadow, then came sailing over the main grandstand roof. He went into a slow circle over the main enclosure, showing off the airship with his company name emblazoned on it, and now the loudspeakers were commenting on the spectacle and people were pouring out of the bars. Mahoney circled the paddock, then he flew her out over the rest of the showgrounds. First sedately, then at a cruising speed, then almost flat out. The airship went purring round the showgrounds at eighty miles an hour: then it was time to descend.

'O.K., Lovelock, she's yours.'

Ed had managed to drive the water-truck right into a paddock; he was waving his handkerchief. Lovelock circled slowly, then manoeuvred to the centre. He vectored the engines, and the ship began to come down vertically.

She came down as steadily as a helicopter, while Ed gave hand-signals; then the cattle crates gently touched the ground. Out of the airship came the ballast pipe. Ed grabbed the end and immersed it into the water-bowzer. Lovelock threw a switch and water began to pump up into the ballast tanks, to compensate for the cattle they were about to unload. Then Ed clambered on top of the crates, and unshackled them.

'*And away!*' he bellowed.

The airship rose and Ed jumped down and started jogging puffily for the car park.

The Admiral had parked the Navy truck in the middle of the car park. Lovelock hovered over it, then edged the ship towards the mast. The mooring line came down. Ed made it fast to the mast's line. Lovelock cranked in the slack; and the ship was moored, floating above the cars.

Crowds were surging from all directions. The gondola door opened and a folding ladder came out. Mahoney began to climb down.

'*Mr Mahoney.*'

He jumped to the ground and turned. Mrs Hutton was hurriedly wending through the cars, a grin all over her beautiful face.

'Of all the bloody cheek!' she yelled. '*My* cattle! . . .'

He had never felt better in his life.

The pressmen jostled beside them, Mahoney holding Tana Hutton's elbow firmly in case she should escape, as she led them to the Members' Pavilion. A reporter said, 'Did you have permission to carry the cattle over the rooftops of Sydney?'

'We had permission to test-fly the airship. That's a good test.'

'Aren't you worried you'll be prosecuted?'

'For showing the Australian farmers there are cheaper ways to get their cattle to market than driving them thousands of miles across the outback?'

'But what if your engines had failed?'

'I would simply have stayed up there. Like a balloon, and my engineer would have had all the time in the world to fix the engines.'

'But you might have been blown right out to sea.'

'Which is a hell of a lot better than crashing *into* the sea like an ordinary aeroplane!' He added, 'Once the *Graf Zeppelin* got as far as Gibraltar, when it developed engine trouble and had to turn back to Germany. It got into bad gales and finally it was flying on only one engine. There were no airfields and it was pitch dark and stormy. So the captain circled over a valley in France all night. When daylight came he put his ship down in a nice meadow, disembarked his passengers and sent them all home by train. Show me the jumbo jet that can do *that!*'

CHAPTER 36

It was holiday time for the farmers of Australia, and the Members' Stand was jumping with jolly, beery farmers who had never seen an airship before and who thought it all a beaut stunt; then one huge farmer was thumping on the bar and booming:

'How d'you reckon for some silence for this beaut bloke with his flying machine who is trying to say something significant to you beer-swigging dunderheads who wouldn't know dung from date-pudding' – and in one movement he picked up Mahoney, who weighed almost two hundred pounds, by his armpits and plonked him on the bar, followed by a startled Malcolm, an even more startled Ed, then an amiable Lovelock who felt perfectly at home on bars, and there were cries of 'Speech'. It was all going better than Mahoney had dared hope and he got to his feet on the bar. And maybe it was the shock of this awful morning, the adrenalin still pumping through his veins, and maybe it was the beer that was delightfully flooding his system, and maybe it was Mrs Tana Hutton standing down there grinning up at him, but Mahoney proceeded to make the wittiest speech of his life, which had the jolly Australian gentry in uproar and which somehow got his message across, and when he finally jumped down Tana Hutton laughed at him, 'God, you're a funny man, aren't you?' Then the barman was shouting: 'International call for Major Malcolm Todd! . . .'

Malcolm hunched over the bar and listened above the hubbub to Tex Weston saying:

'Thank God, I've been trying to get you for four hours, why aren't you at the airport? Is the ship all right?'

'Fine.'

'Great! Now, I've got good news for you! Listen to this: you are no longer broke, old man! You hear that? . . . You now have all the financial backing you need! Because your company has been taken over by a new one with all the money in the world. Now, it's still exactly the same outfit, same hangar, same workmen, same plans, only the name has changed. And you're the master-mind in charge! But instead of the breadline you've now got a whopping salary – plus a bonus on each ship!'

Malcolm rasped, 'Who are these guys?'

'I'll tell you more when I see you, but they're very big money indeed. And there are a number of contracts for the big rigids you want to build!'

'Who for?'

'That must wait. In the meantime, I just want you to —'

'And what about my shares in Todd Airships?'

'Well, they're valueless, because the company was bank-

221

rupt, but you can buy shares in the new company, as part of your bonus.'

'But I'll never be a majority shareholder.'

'My dear fellow, in Todd Airships you were a one-man band. That's why you went bust. But now there are no debts for you to worry about! You're at the top of our management team! Heavens, you're the only one who knows about building airships. Now relax on all these points until you get back. Meanwhile, I'm told you've got the ship at the showgrounds?'

'Correct.'

'Good idea to show her off! Was the test-flight A-O.K.?'

'I built her, didn't I?'

'Congratulations! Now, all you've got to do is get her back to the airport, then have a good rest so you're in good shape for tomorrow.'

'Weston?' Malcolm rasped.

'Yes?'

Malcolm's face was red and he took a big gulp of his brandy.

'You can stick your job right up your gaping ass! . . . And there won't be a pilot to fly her tomorrow for you, either, because Lovelock also says you can stick your job right up your gaping ass!'

Afterwards, when Mahoney tried to reconstruct that day, it got rather confused. He remembered Malcolm starting to get drunk, becoming puffier and redder in the face, looking as if he was about to burst into tears or burst into gleeful laughter. He would remember the feeling of reckless relief that his decisions were made, for better or worse, and Malcolm's too, but what he would remember best was looking at the beautiful Tana Hutton in the midst of the other people clustered round them and feeling absolutely on top of the world, the absolute certainty that before the day was out he would make mad passionate love to her, the complete confidence as he grabbed a new bottle of champagne and took her purposefully by the hand and pulled her out of the crowded, noisy bar. 'Where are you going?' she laughed.

'To the merry-go-rounds!'

222

'What makes you think I haven't got a lunch-date?'

'You have! With me! That's where I'm going to commence my irresistible courtship!'

They had a lovely time, that big, bright, Australian day.

Hurtling along in the roller-coaster, her long hair flying, terrified laughter all over her lovely face, clutching the safety-bar with one hand and her champagne with the other, screaming down into the dips and hurtling up the other side – *'Oh what a silly way to spend a dollar!'* And whipping around on the octopus, the long steel arms hurtling the spinning seats high and swooping low and then hurling them skywards again and around and round, and she had to clutch him tight with her hair lashing about her laughing face.

'Is this the way you commence all your courtships?'

'Never fails!'

It was an open Mercedes sports car, gun-metal blue. She drove fast, her hair flying, her dress hitched just above her knees. *'So you're going to seduce me, are you, Mr Mahoney?'* she shouted above the wind.

'Can we please drop the Mr?'

'So you're going to seduce me, are you, Mahoney?'

'Perish the thought! I have commenced to court you! Haven't you noticed my blandishments?'

It all seemed terribly funny.

The restaurant was a Victorian house cut into a hillside on a bay of Sydney Harbour. Painted boats were moored below, and there was a jetty for the Mosman ferry. He took her pretty hand across the table.

'You don't listen, do you? I am presently only bent on *courting* you.'

'Very well. Why are you busy courting me?'

'Because', he said, 'I want to see your long blonde hair flamed out across my pillow . . . Because I want to hold you in my arms and feel your lovely breasts pressed against me, feel your whole loveliness underneath me . . .'

223

'You do? How unusual.'

'Because', he said, 'I have been besotted by you for the last five weeks, quite irrationally thinking about you all the time, conspiring against the slings and arrows of outrageous geography to find a cargo coming down here, harassing my unfortunate staff of one—'

'Three.' She held up her fingers.

'How do you know I've got a staff of three?'

'I have my sources. Go on.'

He brought her fingertips to his lips, then leant across the table and gently pulled her towards him, and brushed her lips. 'Because', he murmured into her mouth, 'I desperately want to kiss you.'

She sat back slowly, smiling. He held on to her hand, and smiled happily.

'In short, because I'm madly in love with you and *madly* want to make love to you.'

The Mercedes sped along the winding beach road, deserted in the sunset, spacious gardens flashing by. She swung through a big isolated gateway at the end, into a big garden, swept up the drive, lawns and hibiscus flying past, then rocked to a halt in front of a large house with columns.

She looked at him, a laugh in her eyes; then she flung open the car door and kicked off her shoes. She started running for the beach, tearing off her blouse. Mahoney stared after her a moment, a smile on his face; then he pulled off his shoes and socks, and shirt, and ran after her. She unhitched her skirt as she ran across the sand, and flung it, whipped off her panties, and dived into the surf. Mahoney struggled out of his trousers and ran into the waves after her, and dived into the crashing sea. He came up beyond the breaker, and there she was, her golden hair streaming, thrashing away out to sea, her arms flailing. He thrashed after her, and for a glorious moment his arms clasped her slippery body and they struggled, gasping, grinning before she broke away. Then another big wave was rearing up, up, her head went down and her beautiful bottom came up, and she was gone. The wave came crashing with a thud like cannon and he dived deep under it and heard it roaring and wrenching, and when he broke surface she was still swimming out to sea. Then she twisted around to catch the swell that was coming. It was looming up, seething towards them, and Mahoney trod water, waiting for it. It came swelling higher and steeper towards them, towering, and now they were both riding up its slope, waiting for that vital moment to kick and strike out with the rushing swell. Then it *came*, and they both struck with it. And the wave took them skidding down its slope for a long thrilling moment, then with a roar it curled over their shoulders, and they were part of the wave, bodies rigid and heads just clear of the crashing foam. They went crashing in towards the beach, then it dumped them, skidding up the sand.

They lay on their stomachs, the wave seething backwards, grinning at each other.

It was dreamlike, yet afterwards he remembered every detail with crystal clarity, every sensation: the salty glow of sea, the glorious feeling of nakedness, the sand under their feet. The solemn wordlessness with which they got up off the wet sand, and just naturally took each other's hand, a little trembly, and started up the beach, stooping to pick up clothes, walking solemnly on. And all the time not daring to look at each other. Only once in that brief, important walk up the beach did he sense she was about to say something, then she closed her eyes and shook her head. They walked up the drive, up the steps to the big front door, and, without looking at him, led him in. On up the marble staircase, to the top, and then into her bedroom. There was a big double bed. She led him straight to it, and only then did she turn, and look at him, her arms hanging. On her face was a nervous smile, and nervous laughter in her eyes, and Mahoney felt shaky with desire, and with anxiety. He put his hands on her shoulders and gently, shakily pulled her towards him, and kissed her. Oh, the bliss of her against him at last, her lips, the sweet taste of her, and her breasts pressed fleetingly against him, her belly, her thighs. He felt a groan in his chest and he slid his arms around her. For a moment she stood there, rigid, and let him kiss her; then she turned out of his arms. She walked to the double bed, laid herself slowly down; then she lifted her head, with a twinkle in her eye. She buried her fingers into her long wet hair and held it out, then lay back, her damp tresses spread out across the pillow and a smile all over her lovely face.

CHAPTER 37

It was a magical night.

Afterwards, in those happy hours of new lovers after love, they talked. The moon was coming up. She got up and went downstairs, returning with a bottle of champagne, and she led him into her bathroom. And what a bathroom! It was really an indoor patio, with a glass roof, hanging plants, and glass doors which opened on to the treetops of the garden and the Pacific beyond. In the middle of this spacious place was a jaccuzi bath, a big hot tub of churning water; into this they lowered themselves, champagne on high, happy, still excited, half jokey, half serious, and they talked. Afterwards, in the long nights when they were far apart, in his cottage in the rainy woods or flying through the moonlight in his lonely aeroplanes, he would try to remember all the details of that magical night. He would remember her clasping one golden knee above the swirling water, tilting back her head and saying:

'Because I observed you with my animals. Because I've read a verbatim transcript of your Dorchester Hotel speech, where you told the world off about the environmental mess it's in – it made me want to rush out and buy your shares in airships.' She smiled. 'Because I have dug out transcripts of some of your political speeches, where you really mixed emotions – it made me wish I could vote for you. Because I heard you speaking at the debate at our Inn of Court – you made me wish I could do that. Because – she suddenly laughed at him – 'you make me *laugh* . . .'

She lay back in the frothing tub and locked her hands behind her lovely head and said: 'Because I wanted to create something important that wasn't there before. When I was a girl I thought I wanted to be a journalist. "Sure," my father said, "work on my newspapers during your holidays, but anybody can write up weddings, you must be an *opinion-maker*, and that is a twenty-year apprenticeship. But as you've been my daughter for fourteen years we'll count that as four, so I'll apprentice you to my editor-in-chief for the next sixteen years. Don't worry, they'll go by all too quickly."' She smiled. 'So every school holiday I had to report to his editor. And God help me if I let an error pass or didn't have an opinion of some sort afterwards, even if it was the wrong one. After a year, he said: "Now you must learn about economics. I give you one good acre. Take this hoe and go and grow some food. That is what the world needs. Learn about poor people." I said, "But I already know about vegetable gardening, Vader." He said, "Yes, but now you're going to *sell* them."'

'And did you?'

'My word. I found out how many cauliflowers you can cram on one acre. I also found out how much labour costs. He sent a truck to drive them to the market but he charged me for the petrol. After a year he said, "Now, what do you want to be?" I said: "An architect." "Why?" I said, "Because I want to look at a building and say: I built that." He said, "Very good, but you must know about real-estate. Find some land and then go to the bank manager and tell him you want to borrow lots of money." So I did. Of course, he set it up with the bank manager, guaranteeing my overdraft, though to this day he denies it. The manager was very stern. I found a semi-detached cottage near the railway. Vader said: "It is a ruin! Now you will find out what labour costs!"' She smiled. 'I sure did. But I re-sold it at a profit. Then he made me go to the Income Tax and

227

report every penny I had ever made. When I came back I was almost crying, and he laughed and laughed. He took me to a splendid dinner and said, "What did you learn today?" I said: "Never go to the tax man." And he laughed. "No, no, you are a citizen and you must plough back something of what you reaped." He wagged his finger under my nose. "But you must *prepare* yourself *before* you go to the tax man! Tomorrow you look for another house to buy. Then you start work in my accounts department . . . ' "

She said, 'Tell me about your wife?'

He smiled. 'I was about to ask you about your husband.'

She said, 'I divorced him. A couple of years ago.'

'Why?'

'Because he left me.'

'Why? Was he insane?'

She smiled. 'Because he was an old-fashioned Victorian who thought a woman's place was in the home. We didn't see eye to eye on that.'

'Did you love him?'

'Of course. But not enough, I suppose. And what happened to your wife?'

'She left me.'

'Why?'

He smiled. 'Because she thought I was an old-fashioned Victorian who thought a woman's place was in the home. We didn't see eye to eye on that.'

She smiled. 'And did you love her?'

'Of course. But not enough, I guess.'

'And? *Are* you an old-fashioned Victorian?'

'Oh yes.'

She smiled 'I'm going to a rather old-fashioned ball with my rather Victorian father tonight. Would you like to be our old-fashioned guest?'

Mahoney did not go a bundle on dancing, but he danced every number: he wanted nothing but to dance with her but he did so only once. She seemed to be everywhere, flitting off in the arms of an endless succession of big, beaming, clod-hopping, sunburned Australian farmers squeezed into dinner jackets. Old Erling Thoren took him by the elbow from table to table with an air of proprietorship. 'This is the dashing young man with that flying machine, one day he's going to be flying your beef.' Everybody seemed to think it was a very good stunt. 'Dance with the wives,' old Erling muttered, 'they'll love you for it, and they *talk*. There's a lot of beef here tonight, and not just on the wives, a lot of big beef . . .'

Each time he came off the floor, there was old Erling, ready to shuffle him on to the next party. 'You can dance with my daughter later, now you dance with the wives while they're still sober. Besides, then I haven't got to dance with them.'

Only once did he manage to grab her as they crossed paths. 'May I?'

'Oh, very well then,' the old man twinkled, 'but don't waste your time.' He said to his daughter: 'Next, he must dance with the Deputy P.M.'s wife. Don't exhaust him.'

She held herself well back in his arms as they danced. 'Can you bear with it? He can do you a lot of good.'

He walked beside the old man through the gardens in the starlight. Erling said in his slow Norwegian voice: 'What I want to say is partly based on intelligent theory, partly on flimsy evidence. Don't ask me the evidence; I can't tell you yet. If you wonder why I am telling you this, the obvious answer is that it concerns every intelligent person who is worried about where the world is going. Another possible conclusion is that old Erling Thoren is losing his marbles and enjoys letting the big Red cat loose amongst the pigeons. Very well, but please remember that the pigeons are fat and stupid and fast forgetting how to *fly* in the soft life of their suburban coops.' He pulled out a silver flask, took a swig and passed it absently to Mahoney. 'Now try not to ask foolish questions.

'The Russians want the Cape sea route. Already they can control Suez, through their puppets in Ethiopia and Aden.

229

Eventually, Castro will do their dirty work for them in Central America and they'll get the Panama Canal. In North Africa, Kaddafi eventually will do their dirty work for them, and also turn the Mediterranean into a Russian lake. Meanwhile, they dominate Angola, having won the war for the rebels over the Portuguese. They're helping the South West African People's Organization fight the South Africans in Namibia. And now that Rhodesia is gone, South Africa is surrounded.

'But' – he held up a finger – 'the Russians aren't too strong in Rhodesia, are they? They lost out to the Chinese. Russia backed the wrong horse in Joshua Nkomo. And the Chinese don't want the Russians to control the Cape sea route.' He paused. 'In those circumstances, the usual Russian tactic of supporting a long guerilla war may not work against South Africa. They may be contending with Mugabe's Chinese pals as well as the South Africans, so maybe a different sort of war is necessary – a quicker war. And if they're thinking of *that* . . .' He paused, and looked at him, his old eyes serious. 'What better way of moving large numbers of troops, very quickly, to strategic parts of Africa, where there are no airfields, than the airship? Especially if Kaddafi is rearing to start the ball rolling for them and send his troops en masse to take over the whole of north Africa.'

Mahoney stared at him. Maybe the old boy *was* losing his marbles.

'You mean Kaddafi is behind Tex Weston's take-over of Malcolm's company?'

The old man ignored the interruption. 'Imagine Kaddafi's difficulties in pulling off such a coup without airships? How could he get his troops to all the right places over such a vast area, keep them *supplied*, without your airships that can stay aloft for days? With airships he can move huge numbers of men huge distances quickly. How attractive for the Russians to encourage Kaddafi to pull off such a trick: it would give them a safe corridor right down central Africa . . .'

Mahoney looked at him in wonder.

'I'm sorry, but why are you telling me this?'

The old man paced beside him.

'It is nearly midnight and I'm worried about my daughter

230

strangling me.' Mahoney chuckled. The old man took his time, then continued: 'The capitalist system has one great strength and one great weakness – private initiative. It enables a crazy genius like Malcolm Todd to bring back the airship. It enables a man with balls like you to risk his neck to borrow money and buy one. And it enables Russia or Kaddafi to step in and take you over – quite legally. And use your airships to destroy us. Isn't it amazing how weak we are?'

Maybe, Mahoney thought, this whole, marvellous Thoren family was whacky. 'So Tex Weston is going to build airships for Kaddafi?' He shook his head. 'I didn't know you even knew Tex Weston.'

Erling snorted. 'Oh yes. I have sixty-one companies in different parts of Africa, and they all export, and I know Mr Weston, believe me.' He paused. 'Did you know that he used to be a C.I.A. agent?'

'No?' Mahoney said, surprised.

'And that he dares not set foot in America because he will be arrested? Some years ago Mr Weston's arms-dealing company managed to smuggle some new, hot-shot American weaponry to Libya, in defiance of U.S. embargoes. The F.B.I. want to talk to him about that. I think Mr Weston rather regrets that little episode.'

Mahoney shook his head. 'I had no idea . . . But if he regrets his Libyan connection, why would he build airships for Kaddafi? Weston's a capitalist, if ever I saw one. He even helped Rhodesia.'

'He's a big-time soldier of fortune. To those gentlemen money is all that matters. And power – he likes to control things. The morals of it mean nothing. He'll work for Rhodesia today, Russia tomorrow. If he does regret his Libyan connection, it's only because he's in trouble with America. Maybe Mr Kaddafi has him over a barrel, and that's why he's now got to front for him. But I suspect the reason is money.'

Mahoney sighed. 'Well, this is all theory.'

The old man said, 'Think about it. Weston flies to Libya a lot anyway. He's smuggled American arms to Libya, so he's in trouble in America, can't go back there, which must cost him a lot of business. So he's tied to Kaddafi. What does

231

Kaddafi want? He wants a united Muslim world, under his messianic leadership. He wants Chad. The Sudan. Uganda. The whole West Africa bulge: Nigeria, Ghana. And what do the Russians want? Revolution all over Africa, as part of their plans for world domination. They're supporting Kaddafi; he is their cat's paw in Africa.'

Mahoney paced, head down. He did not know what to believe.

'What can we do about it?' the old man asked. 'I don't know yet. But I know one thing you can do.'

Mahoney nodded. 'Information?'

'Exactly,' the old man said. 'Your Cardington hangar is next door to Weston's. You can be my eyes and ears. And there *is* something I can do.'

'What?'

'Helium,' the old man said. 'America supplies most of the world's helium. Did you know that before World War Two, about 1930, the Germans asked President Roosevelt for helium for the *Hindenburg*, and eventually Roosevelt refused because the zeppelins may be used as bombers? So they had to use hydrogen, and so the *Hindenburg* blew up in New Jersey.'

'Yes,' Mahoney said. 'But Libya itself has helium deposits.'

'But it would take a long time to set up the plant to extract it. I think Mr Kaddafi is in a hurry. And I think I have enough friends in Washington and London to stop him getting helium in a hurry.'

Mahoney was impressed with the theory, despite himself. 'He could still fly his airships on hydrogen.'

'Very dangerous. We will see . . . And now' – he looked at his watch – 'it's after midnight.'

And then, alone with her again at last, he felt strangely nervous. There was plenty to talk about, the people he had met, what her father had had to say, but they hardly talked at all. He did not want to talk about airships and Tex Weston, all he wanted was to make love to her again. He glanced at her, wondering why she was driving slowly. She

232

turned the Mercedes into the drive and rolled slowly to a halt.

She smiled at him. But they were both tense. He opened her door for her. They walked solemnly across the gravel, up the marble steps. She put the key in the lock. Then he took her in his arms.

He was shaky with desire. She stood still, the key in her hand. Then her arm went slowly around his neck. He felt her breath quaver: then her hand slowly turned the key.

She did not switch on any lights. The moon, shining through the windows, was light enough.

PART 6

CHAPTER 38

It rained all that English springtime.

Mahoney looked out from his hangar at Cardington on to the grey rain sweeping across the bleak fields: inwards he looked on to the vast iron cathedral that stretched on and on, shadowed in patchy lights, echoing, the rain drumming on it, the steam of workmen's breath sometimes weeping down from the cold high ceiling as rain. And looming up into this shadowed vastness was the massive, forbidding frame of his airship, yellowy silver, enormous ribs held together by great longitudinal girders that swept down, down the hanger; here lay millions of pounds borrowed at crippling interest rates. Mahoney had never dreamed that he would ever have a million pounds, yet here lay many times that staggering sum, in this huge construction that almost nobody believed in, that scores of tiny figures way up there on the scaffolding were so slowly, slowly working on; and Malcolm, fussing about, giving incomprehensible orders, his office a disaster area of papers and full ashtrays: and all the time the borrowed millions pouring steadily away. Sometimes Mahoney woke in the night, sweating, overwhelmed by the sheer enormity of his undertaking, the never-endingess of it: oh, yes, sometimes in the long nights he feverishly wondered if even he truly believed in airships. . . .

But, for all that, Mahoney had a wonderful spring, and mostly he did not care about the rain and the cold sweats that sometimes came in the night. Because Redcoat Cargo Airlines had never had so much work, and because he was in love.

Every time he came back from a flight, he demanded, 'What have we got for Australia, ladies?'

'Nothing so far.'

'Australia's a big country, England's a nation of shopkeepers, it must export to survive! Get on to the freight-agents and hustle up a cargo for Australia, ladies!'

At least twice a week he telephoned her. At least twice a week she telephoned him, in England or in the air.

'Where the hell are you, lover?'

'Hullo! I'm heading for Sierra Leone. How are you, lover?'

'This is a hell of a way to run a love affair, Mahoney. When're you coming Down Under again?'

'I'm working on it, believe me. Where are you?'

'I'm at ten thousand feet, going up to the station.'

He could picture her. 'Keep going and fly to England.'

'I'm thinking about it, believe me. Hey, Joe? . . .' She sighed. 'Isn't this a dumb way to live? Or would you get sick of me if we lived in the same town?'

He smiled. He saw her strong, lovely body, satiny skin glistening golden in the sun, her heavy, perfect breasts. 'Not in a thousand years.'

'O.K., Mahoney, that's it, I'm coming to England when I can swing it. And I'm going to fly with you. Or have you got a girl in every airport?'

'I've got a humdinger in Sydney.'

'Well, when are you coming down to her?'

'Just as soon as I've got a load.'

'I've got a load on my mind for you. Hey, Mahoney? . . . Do you think I'm falling in love? Or have I just got a severe case of the hots? Let's talk about something else. How's the airship?'

'Let's talk about something else.'

'Is it going *badly*?' she cried.

'That airship is going beautifully. Malcolm and my bank managers are driving me up the wall, but I've never felt better in my life!'

'Thank God . . . It's going to work, sport. Mahoney?'

He wanted to laugh. She didn't used to believe in it. 'Yes?'

She sighed. 'Nothing. I think I'm falling in love, that's all.'

*

She decorously watched his plane come into Mascot airport, dressed to kill, her hand shielding her eyes. Then she could contain herself no longer and she jumped and waved. She dashed through the terminal, a tall, svelte, happy woman with shiny blonde hair and a broad smile.

As he came striding across the tarmac she ran to him.

'Hullo, Beauty!'

'Oh,' she cried, 'it's been two whole weeks! This is going to be a record-breaking drive home! . . .'

The Mercedes swung into the garden, churned up the gravel, slammed to a stop. As she flung open the front door, she already had her blouse undone. She flung it on the floor, grinning, and unhitched her skirt. It landed in a heap and she kicked it and it flew through the air and landed on the bottom of the staircase. She started up, in her stockings and suspender belt, her high heels clicking, Mahoney hurrying behind her, his jacket flung on the steps, then his tie, then his shirt. Her frilly bra landed half way up: at the top stood an icebucket and champagne. She wriggled and kicked again and her panties flew silkily through the air; then she threw herself, laughing, into his arms. The jaccuzzi bath was swirling and steaming. 'That's to refresh you *after*wards,' she said into his mouth, 'I'm not going to waste this loud smell of my man . . .'

The bell on the flight-deck went *bing*-bong. A sultry, female voice intoned: 'I'm looking for a fly-by-night, Romeo Yankee.'

He shouted: 'Hullo, lover!'

He could hear her grinning. 'Where're you at, Romeo?'

'Over the Mediterranean, heading for Valencia. Where're you?'

'I'm flying up to the station. What time is it up there?'

'Eight-thirty at night.'

'The sun's just rising here. And it's so beautiful I just had to call you. The whole east's flaming red. Mahoney, let's collect sunrises.'

'And sunsets.'

239

'Oh yes, sunsets too.' She laughed. 'And moonlight over the African bush . . . And hear lions roar . . .'

'Yes.'

She sighed. 'Work, work, work. When are we going to do all these things, Mahoney? I could scream. When are you coming down again?'

'I'm always working on it, believe me.'

'You sure this isn't a sad case of unrequited lust?'

'Quite sure,' he grinned.

She smiled. 'I've been descending all the time, I'm going to circle around a bit and look for the animals.'

'I'm with you.' And oh, how he wished he were. He could picture her, headphones on, the sunrise glinting on her hair.

'Oh, it's so beautiful, Mahoney . . . I'm looking for the elephants. It could for all the world be Africa . . . Oh, why don't we just chuck up everything and come and live here?'

Mahoney sat wistfully in his battered Britannia over the dark Mediterranean heading for Valencia to buy eighteen tons of lemons to sell to wintry England where the rain was lashing down on his nightmare hangar. . . .

And yet he also loved the bloody place, and sweating, flustered Malcolm Todd, that rare breed of men who invented things, for whom bank managers were the mere buzzing of flies. And he loved his terrifying airship, the notion of it flying by its own weightlessness, in harmony with Nature instead of defying it. But that long, cold English spring the echoing hangar got badly on his nerves.

'For God's sake, you haven't done a thing since last time!'

'We have, we have. Don't worry.'

'Don't *worry*? I'm bankrupt if this thing doesn't start working for me soon!'

'Go fly your aeroplanes and leave the worrying to me.'

'Are these new men working out all right?'

'It would be better if we had the old ones.'

But Tex Weston had the old ones, and much more, in the bleak hangar next door. Where all the power was. All the organization. All the accountants, credits, lines of supply. All the money.

240

He never saw Weston at the Cardington hangars. He was amazed at the speed things were getting done. No building had yet commenced, but within weeks Weston's hangar appeared ready to roll. There were crates of tooling and rubber presses, gantries were in position, blocks-and-tackle, the cold air alive with hammerings. 'How's he managing it?' Mahoney demanded: 'It took you *months*!'

'Unlimited funds,' Malcolm said bitterly. 'They're working three shifts. Twenty-four hours a day.'

'But how did they get the tooling so fast, and the presses?'

'Italy. The Eye-ties can work when they're paid over the odds. Aeronautical team is Eye-tie too.'

'*Italian?*'

'Professor from some university. Went over to see him and got shown the door. But it's not exactly hard for him, is it, seeing he's got all my drawings and calculations. But you'll be in the air before him.'

'I should bloody *hope* so!'

Mahoney waited for Weston to contact him. Weston did not. But Erling Thoren did, by telephone from Canberra, several times.

'Have you any information for me?' the old Norwegian voice said.

'Nothing new. Their management has orders not to fraternize with the enemy.'

'He will contact you soon.'

Mahoney did not know whether the old boy was just enjoying playing cloaks and daggers. Erling said, 'And how is my daughter? You see more of her than I do.'

'She's keeping pretty busy,' Mahoney smiled.

'Yes, and now busier sleeping with you.'

Mahoney grinned. 'Please give her my love.'

'Ah yes, love is what makes the world go round.'

The old man had told him that the blimp had disappeared

from Sydney airport. Weston had made no effort to sell it to the Australian Navy: it had been deflated and air-freighted away. But it did not reappear at Cardington. Mahoney was unable to find out where it was. He asked Malcolm's lawyer, Roger, if he could check out the old man's theory.

'Well, there's no evidence to support it. It's a private company, but there's nothing sinister about the shareholders. Weston Corporation hold ten per cent, Weston is on the board. The other shareholder is an Italian trust company. Nothing remarkable about any of that.'

'But who are these Italians fronting for?'

'We'd never find out. Really, why would Kaddafi, with all his money, go to all this trouble just to get the Cardington hangars when he could build his own in Libya?'

'He expected to get Malcolm Todd, remember. The only expert. And in Libya he'd have to import all the materials and technology. It would take a long time. He's in a hurry. This way he takes over an existing organization.'

'Furthermore,' the lawyer said, 'there's the improbability that he would use airships for military purposes, they're too vulnerable.'

'On the contrary, they're ideal military vehicles for Africa.'

'You're paying too much attention to this Australian politician. I've made some enquiries, and he's regarded as an old prophet of doom. They call him Old Thoren-in-the-flesh.'

'Well, *I've* made some enquiries,' Admiral Pike said, 'and he's very much regarded as an elder statesmen!'

'Maybe. I'm not belittling a man who's built up the empire he has. But he seems one of those odd-balls who considers himself the sole voice of reason in a world of blabbering incompetents and he sees a red under every bed.'

'And he's dead right,' the Admiral glowered.

What Mahoney wanted to do was walk into the bastard's plush offices, twist his arm up behind his back until he cried out all the answers. Then one day he received a hand-written letter.

Dear Joe, Would you have lunch with me to discuss some business which is very much to our mutual advantage? My secretary will give yours a buzz. Sincerely, Tex.

Mahoney said to Dolores: 'When his secretary calls, tell her I haven't got a secretary. When Weston himself calls, tell him to meet me in the lavatory of The Rabbit at one tomorrow.'

Mahoney was deliberately twenty minutes late. Weston's Rolls Royce was parked at The Rabbit. Weston was leaning elegantly against the bar. His handsome face lit up. 'Joe, how nice to see you.'

'It's not nice to see me, Weston.'

Tex smiled. He said, 'I've always liked you. You've got guts. And imagination. Your only trouble is you have precious little business acumen. What'll you have to drink?'

'When I have a drink, I like to enjoy it.'

'Very well.' He went on: 'You're a babe in the woods of business, Joe. Sure, you've built a successful airline, but only by unconventional methods, buying your own cargo when you haven't got one. But now you're near bankruptcy because you've borrowed millions to build an airship you can't afford. If you fail to pay one single debt, any creditor could send you to the bankruptcy court – even the milkman.'

Mahoney's hands were thrust in his pockets. 'I understand the law of insolvency, and I'll make sure you're never a creditor of mine.'

Weston shook his head patiently. 'I don't want you to lose everything, Joe. You may be a babe in the woods, but you're a winner. That's why you've thrown yourself into airships. Your instinct told you they were winners, and you're right. That's why I've gone in for them too, because I'm also a winner.'

Mahoney's face was wooden.

Tex said, 'But the difference between us, Joe, is that I do not surround myself with losers. Malcolm is a genius, but he's the absent-minded professor type. He'd have got nowhere if you hadn't taken him in off the street. You did his talking for him. But then you let him run his own company, and he

243

shouldn't touch anything other than drawing boards – he's an engineer, not a chairman. So he sent his company broke. I know you're bitter with me, but he'd bankrupted a good industry, and what I did was perfectly legal, businesslike and inevitable.'

Mahoney just glared at him in judicial silence.

'In fact, I did you a favour, Joe. He'd have had to build those blimps – if he got the contracts – just to pay his debts and you'd still be waiting two years hence for your ship.'

'How very kind of you.' What does he want? Just my hangar? And Malcolm? 'Well, he's still chugging along. And all you got out of your vulturous coup was one hangar. And all his plans,' he added bitterly.

'It's a flying start,' Weston smiled calmly, 'if you'll pardon the pun. Will you have that drink now?'

'What is it you want, Weston?'

Weston turned and strolled for the corner. 'Shall we sit here?'

Mahoney leant against the bar. 'Provided you can shout loud enough.'

Weston smiled resignedly and strolled back. Mahoney was grimly pleased with his petty victory. Weston looked at him seriously.

'I want your goodwill,' he said.

Mahoney could not believe he had heard right. 'My goodwill?'

'And Malcolm's.' Weston shook his head. 'I really haven't done either of you any harm. It was inevitable you two would fail, from lack of finance. But you're both the midwives of the airship, and we want you on our side. You won't make it alone. As you said, you and Todd are only chugging along. We'd like to make you both an attractive offer.'

Mahoney almost burst out laughing. 'Bullshit, Weston! Todd you want, certainly, he's the world expert. My hangar you want, sure. My half-built airship. But *me*? Me, you don't need.'

Weston said quietly, 'After the publicity stunts you pulled at the Dorchester and in Australia, Redcoat's name is synonymous with airships. You've been pasted all over the world. Ask people who's building airships, they'll say "Redcoat". The C.A.A., the airlines, they respect you. You're a name. And you're one of the few licensed airship pilots at the moment. You're years ahead of any competition.'

Mahoney thought, More bullshit, Weston! You only want me because that's the only way you'll get Todd and my hangar. Once you've got them, you'll get rid of me. He said sarcastically: 'You want me to *fly* for you?'

Weston smiled. 'I want you to head the company.' Mahoney was genuinely amazed. 'With Malcolm in charge of technology. I haven't got the time, nor your expertise in airships.'

Mahoney almost laughed. *Head the company? – For five minutes, till you've got my hangar, then you'll fire me!* He said woodenly: 'What's your offer?'

'If we're getting down to business, I'd prefer somewhere more private.'

'It beats the lavatory,' Mahoney said grimly.

If Weston felt annoyed he didn't show it.

'Think well about how you're going to finish your airship, Joe. It's a staggering financial burden. One small delay, and you're bankrupt. And think about your friend, Todd. What's his future? He makes no profit on your ship until it's working. What does he do while he's waiting for you to pay him? He's got no capital. All he's got is your empty hangar, leased in *your* name. You're his whole future, and you've got no money . . .' He shook his head. 'You've got Malcolm over a barrel. You say I'm a vulture – but consider yourself. Sure, you helped him like a Samaritan. But when the time came to launch himself, you made sure he was hog-tied to you. You wanted the world's expert in your pocket – because that was the only way you could ever afford an airship. And you got him. You made a deal that he'd build you one at cost, to get him started; then you make your announcement in a blaze of publicity that launches his company on the stock market, gets him some public capital on the strength of the fact that he's building an airship for Redcoat. Nice work, Joe. Handsome dividends for Redcoat in the form of publicity, and Todd appears to be on his feet at last. Aha!' He held up a finger. 'But Todd was really your unpaid employee.'.

Mahoney's face was set with anger. 'Todd was his own boss, chairman of his own company. So much so that he broke himself building blimps against my advice. And he still would have succeeded if you hadn't pushed him under.'

Weston raised his hand. 'I genuinely admire your cleverness. And it took guts. And now Todd's *still* working exclusively for you – unpaid. Now the poor man is absolutely dependent on you because if you abandon him he hasn't even got that hangar.'

'Dry your eyes and make him another offer.'

'I also need you. And Todd wouldn't go without you. He wouldn't leave you in the lurch with an unfinished ship. You deserve better than that. What you both deserve – *and* the airship – is the kind of money my company can offer.'

'What's your offer?' Mahoney repeated grimly.

'We can do it in two ways. One is a package. A merger of Redcoat Cargo and Redcoat Airshiplines with my company. You transfer the whole lot to us, in exchange for cash and shares. You become chairman of the new company. A salary something like eighty thousand pounds a year. With your dividends, and perks, you'll be extremely well-off.'

Mahoney's eyes flickered involuntarily. *Eighty thousand a year!* No way could his services be worth that much to any industry. 'And the other way?' he said coldly.

Weston nodded. 'Maybe you don't want to give up your actual airline. We'd be sorry, because it's a little success story, but we'd understand. However, remember that you've all worked like slaves, and maybe now's the time to reap the rewards. You would still be in charge, but you'd have the benefit of our bigger organization – and our fuel prices.' He raised his eyebrows. 'As you know, we do a lot of work for the Arabs and they give us special fuel prices, which have been a godsend.'

Mahoney's pulse quickened. 'Which Arabs in particular?'

Weston shrugged. 'Libya. We do a lot of work for Kaddafi, and he's grateful because he's none too popular in some quarters.'

Mahoney was almost disarmed by the frankness. Erling's theory took another step towards the window. 'Go on,' he said tersely.

'Well, if you keep your airline, we still want your hangar – and you, of course. In which case, we'll have to buy your unfinished airship as well. It's no good to you without the hangar, is it? You can hardly drag it outside and finish it in the open.'

'And how much are you prepared to pay for both?'

Weston shrugged. 'In principle, what you've got invested in it – plus, of course, a reasonable amount identifiable with your effort.'

'How much?' Mahoney repeated.

'Without commitment, possibly as high as a million dollars *profit* for you.'

A million? . . . Mahoney wanted to throw back his head and laugh in glee. He could be rich at last! If Weston was saying that much he was prepared to pay two million! And what struck Mahoney as perversely hilarious was that he was going to turn it down! *Joe Mahoney was going to decline two million dollars!* . . .

He said icily, 'Weston, your profit on one airship alone will be several million *pounds*. But – no hangar, no airship, no profit. However, I'm not going to haggle with you now.' He paused. 'But what if I don't want to work for you but do want to sell you the whole lot?'

Weston shook his head. 'I need you to run a big organization like that, two hangars both building airships.'

Liar, Mahoney thought. You need me for a different reason. 'I'm flattered. Perhaps we should have that drink now. While you tell me absolutely everything about my job. What contracts you've got to build ships. Who for. What for. Terms. Everything.'

'I can't disclose all that until you've started the job. Those are business secrets.'

Mahoney straightened up. 'Very well. Goodbye.'

He turned for the door. Weston caught up with him just outside.

'All right. Come to the car. We can have a drink there.'

The Rolls Royce purred down the country road, the chauffeur separated by a panel. The liquor cabinet was open.

'The Russians,' Weston said simply.

Mahoney tried not to stare. So old Erling Thoren was almost right. 'How many ships?'

'Only six. But they'll soon be wanting more. And', he said, 'so will the Americans.'

Mahoney was taken aback by his disarming manner. 'And what do the Russians want airships for?'

Weston looked at him, then smiled widely.

'You're an alarmist, Joe – you spent too long fighting the communists. For the same reason you do. Cargo. For example, the Siberian route. Russia has mind-blowing communication problems. The airship is ideal for them.' He smiled patiently. 'They do not want them for military purposes, Joe.'

'How do you know that?'

'Because', Weston said, 'I don't believe in the military role of the airship. They're simply too big a target. Malcolm is whacky on that one.'

'But why're they buying from us? What's their hurry?'

'They simply haven't got the technology yet. Nor the hangars.' He looked at him. 'In America they can buy all the 747s they want. Mr Boeing – and the president – will be only too happy to take their money. And so am I.'

'But how do you know the Russian Army doesn't want them?'

Tex Weston said: 'Because they told me.' He smiled. 'Joe, it's no secret that I trade with Russia. Thousands of other companies do too, you know. The Russians are hungry. Communism is so inefficient that they cannot even feed themselves properly, and have to buy wheat from America and Australia just to put bread in the shops. Meat. Eggs. Milk. Butter. You name it, they can't produce enough of it. Every year the Kremlin panics about food riots. And that's politically dangerous. On the other hand, capitalism is so efficient that every year we over-produce. Butter mountains. Fruit mountains. Sometimes we even destroy it. And the Russians want it –

usually in a hurry.' He shrugged. 'People like me supply them with some of what they need.'

'Personally,' Mahoney said coldly, 'if I were the President of the United States, I would not sell the Russians the wheat. I'd let them have their food riots and show communism up for the inefficient bully it is.'

'Not very humane of you, Joe.'

'The Kremlin is not very humane either and it irks me to help them. However, I asked you about the army.'

Weston draped his arm across the back of the seat. 'Joe, the Russians I deal with are just like officials the world over. They've also got mothers-in-law, kids with pimples to worry about. They take me to their clubs, their theatres. The army bureaucracy I know particularly well because an army marches on its stomach, and they drink like fish. Their military expenditure already impoverishes them, without adding airships to the bill. We talk about recession? To them, our recession is a boom.' He looked at him. 'Furthermore, I have a company which deals in arms. In that business, we have our ear very close to the ground. I happen to know that nobody believes the airship is a military vehicle.'

'All right,' Mahoney sighed, 'so you've got both ears to the ground, simultaneously. What *do* the Russians want these airships for?'

Weston took a breath.

'The Russians are scared of us, Joe. The only thing that's efficient is their internal security. Sure, they out-gun us in Europe, but that's all. Three years ago they could have taken West Germany overnight, literally, and neither NATO nor America would have retaliated, particularly under Jimmy Carter. A few weeks later Russian tanks would have been at the Pyrenees, before we held them – with the help of the mountains. Now, the Americans are re-arming and the Russians know we will retaliate. What do they want more problems in Europe for? They're having enough trouble with their eastern-bloc countries.' He shook his head. 'Russia has lost its chance.'

Mahoney said tersely, 'What's this got to do with our airships?'

249

'Evolution,' Weston said simply. 'The two strongest animals in the international jungle cannot fight each other any more because of MAD – Mutually Assured Destruction. Bigtime warfare is out. So, the battle now will be an economic one – and for the hearts and minds of the Third World, and their raw materials. Trade and aid in exchange for cheap raw materials. Survival of the fittest has now gone full circle – we're back to polite barter. And that's where the airship comes in.'

'So the Russians want airships so they can open up the Third World to their influences more easily?'

'*Trade* with the Third World. *Aid*. It's a hell of a lot easier to trade and give aid if they haven't got to build roads and airports first. And for the same reasons the Americans will soon be wanting airships.'

'And we're going to help the Russians? What about freedom of speech? The pursuit of happiness?'

Weston tilted back his head and laughed shortly. 'Really, Joe, you sound like an American undergraduate. You know perfectly well that a poverty-stricken man cannot pursue happiness. A hungry man who thinks the world is flat wants food, not freedom of the press. Democracy works fine in Troutsville, Virginia, but not in Africa and the Amazon basin.' He nodded at him. 'There are only *private* capitalists and *state* capitalists, Joe, but Man is over-populating the earth and soon the world's resources will have to be distributed by governments, like the dole.'

'And why do you want to employ me so badly?'

Weston sighed. 'Because, after Todd, you know more about airships than anyone else. Because everyone respects you. Because you're a trained lawyer who can present arguments persuasively.'

Liar, Mahoney thought. He said, as if it were a passing thought, 'Tex, I believe you're in a bit of trouble with the F.B.I. about an illegal arms deal with Libya?'

Weston smiled sadly. 'So you know about that?' He shrugged resignedly. 'O.K. But *don't*' – he looked at him sincerely – 'let it worry you, about being associated with me.' He shook his head. 'I cannot tell you how much I regret that little indiscretion – how much business it has cost me. I myself am quite innocent, Joe. But, yes, my company – some over-enthusiastic underlings – were involved, so I must take the rap."

'Why don't you go back to America and clear your name?'

Weston sighed. 'Would you? You know how the U.S. regards Kaddafi. My company did it. And yes, it was profitable. And *yes*, we are in Kadaffi's good books. Once the deal was done I could hardly get the goods back. But *no*, I am not personally guilty. And I have been trying to shake off the stigma for some time. Would *you* – if a similar cloud hung over you – would you go back to Zimbabwe nowadays to face the music?'

Mahoney sighed wearily. The man was very convincing. A superb con-man. Weston said, 'Forget that, Joe.' He looked at his watch. 'You have to give me your answer now.'

'I have', Mahoney said, 'to do nothing of the kind. We haven't even begun to discuss money yet.'

And he wanted to throw back his head and laugh. Because he was going to turn down two million dollars! And it felt marvellous! He was either going to go bankrupt or make umpteen millions!

'Is it me or my breathless daughter you want to speak to?' the old man said. 'Because she is in Sydney, you know.'

'It's you,' Mahoney smiled.

'Well, for God's sake telephone her because she is getting very short of breath, she hasn't spoken to you since yesterday.'

Ten minutes later he had given Erling Thoren the story. And the old man laughed gleefully. 'You know why?'

Mahoney grinned. 'Helium?'

The old man laughed. 'You are as light-headed as my daughter!'

'You said you had enough friends in Washington to stop him getting it. But I still don't understand, because Poland exports helium.'

251

'Yes, but Britain is not yet a Russian satellite, and if somebody whispers in the prime minister's ear Poland would suddenly find it very difficult to export helium into England for Mr Weston. Britain cannot arrest him for the F.B.I. but they can make life very difficult for him. Don't be fooled, it's not the Moscovites he's working for, it's the Arab gentleman! Now, please telephone my daughter because she will strangle me if I spoke to you and she didn't. Did you say one million?'

'Yes. But I have neither refused nor accepted.'

'Good, let him wait! A million is nothing, anyway. All right, please phone my daughter, but a wise man never tells a woman too much. My daughter is a genius but all women in love are stupid – it is something to do with their ovaries, you know.'

Ten minutes later he was talking to her. She said, 'He phoned me a moment ago and said I'm not to ask you any questions; apparently it's something to do with my ovaries.'

Mahoney lay on the bed and laughed. And oh, he was in love.

For the next three weeks Mahoney stalled Tex Weston. Every few days Erling Thoren telephoned him, to find out what was happening. Sometimes Mahoney was convinced the old man was just hugely enjoying himself. 'Never be tempted,' Erling intoned from twelve thousand miles away. 'All he wants is your respectability, so that he can get helium. You are a very respectable young man, now, you know, and not just because you are sleeping with my daughter.'

'But how do you actually *know* that helium is his problem?'

'Wheels within wheels,' the old man said happily. 'Today I bought a match factory,' he added.

Mahoney blinked. 'You're going to make matches now?'

'In Malaysia. My daughter will not talk to me because she hates cutting down trees, but Malaysia needs matches and it is a good little company going bankrupt. It happens all the

252

time, like Mr Todd and Mr Weston, except I can get phosphorus for my matches anywhere and Mr Weston cannot get helium because there are people in Washington and London who do not like Mr Kadaffi. And the British will never permit an airship to fly on hydrogen. Mr Weston is in trouble. Now, please put in a good word for me with my daughter . . .'

The next week, Dolores gleefully telephoned him in the Canadair.

'Thought you'd like to know – I've just heard from Malcolm that Weston is closing down his Cardington hangar! He's moving all his gear out, we don't know where to yet! . . .'

CHAPTER 40

She landed the plane in Cooma, and they piled into a taxi and she pulled the champagne from her bag and the cork popped. They were laughy, deliciously happy to be together again. The taxi wound up into the mountains, the trees laden with snow. They pulled into Threadbo, and the passenger-snowcats were waiting. Mahoney had never seen such a conveyance before. The big red vehicle went chomping up the mountain like a tank, the snow banked fifteen feet high. Everybody was in a holiday mood. Then in the snowing twilight, they saw the twinkling of the lodge.

The place had roaring log fires, two bars with sawdust on the floor, a cosy dining-room with red-check tablecloths, a cafeteria with wooden tables and steaming tureens: the lodge was full of people, faces flushed and healthy. Somewhere a juke-box was playing dancing music. It was a jolly place. Theirs was a room at the very top, with a verandah overlooking the snowy mountains. Standing in an icebucket was another bottle of champagne, compliments of the management. 'How do you like the lodge?' she asked anxiously.

'It's lovely!'

'You sure?'

253

'Of course,' he laughed. 'Why?'

She said with a delighted grin: 'Because I've just bought it.'

And the champagne cork popped and she hugged him in delight. And oh, the wonderful feel of her in his arms, her wide mouth crushed against his, and the delicious smell and taste of her. They collapsed back on to the bed so the champagne spewed, laughing as they tore off each other's clothes.

And hurtling down the snowy slopes, the trees flashing by, the lovely shape and style of her, her red ski-suit clinging and her hair flying; shussing flat out beside him, eyes sparkling behind her sexy goggles, sticks flicking, the glorious feeling of complete control over the snow, of dancing with it, of showing off, the joy of sharing such thrills. And crunching back to the lodge in the sunset, good and tired and aching, and climbing into the steaming bath together, squashed up and slippery. She smiled at him sadly and said: 'Two nights together in two weeks is a very dumb way to live, Mahoney.'

'So what are we going to do about it?'

She sighed. 'That's why I didn't want to fall in love with a fly-by-night.'

'Don't think I haven't been pondering.' She sighed. 'I'm a career woman and my career is here . . . What would I do in England? Don't answer that, I'm just pondering out loud.'

'You'd live with me,' he said. '"And be my love."'

She smiled. 'Ah . . . And when we finally make it out of bed, what would I do?'

'Thorens have a big office in London, you could run that.'

'I've thought about it, believe me. But it's got its own competent manager. They don't need the boss's daughter.'

'You could run Redcoat Cargo Airlines,' he said.

She smiled. 'And tell you and the dreaded Dolores how to do the job? I want to stay your *lover*, Mahoney.' She sighed.

'I can only run anything as the boss. That's my trouble, as my father says.'

'What does your father say?'

She dropped her voice a few octaves, into the slow Norwegian accent: '"So you are in love with that crazy young man with the flying machines. Well, you must do your fokking, I suppose, but you will find out you're not the boss anymore, ho-ho-ho."'

'He thinks I'm crazy?'

'He thinks you're wonderful – he thinks *I'm* crazy to be head over heels in love with somebody twelve thousand miles away, he doesn't think it'll last but he's worried I may leave him.' She spread her arms in despair. 'I knew it was fatal to send you those mushrooms . . .'

'I told her she should never have sent you those bladdy mushrooms,' the old man twinkled. '"Fatal," I said.' He poured more port. 'Now, if I want to see my daughter I will have to offer you a job.'

'Vader, we're not exactly getting married, you know.'

'I am very glad to hear it,' the old man twinkled, 'because this crazy young man would never accept a job from me, would you?'

'No,' Mahoney grinned.

'No, and I am very glad to hear that too because you are a dreamer. I like dreamers very much but they risk everything on crazy dreams.'

'You don't consider airships crazy!' Tana said.

'They are absolutely crazy for commercial purposes,' Erling said. 'For military purposes they are ideal for certain places. But they will not be commercial vehicles because of the expense of new special airports. Crazy. You will find out. I am never wrong, you know.'

'That's a terrible thing to say!' she protested.

'I am very seldom wrong,' the old man said, 'but I am not worried because I am sure you will sell it as a military vehicle, you will even build more. That is why I invited you to dinner tonight.' He reached for his briefcase.

255

'I thought so,' Tana said. 'Flying from Canberra just to see me, my poor achin' ass.'

'I am very sorry about your ass,' he twinkled, 'but I warned you it was fatal . . .' Mahoney laughed and the old man opened his briefcase, very pleased with his joke. He pulled out the brochure Mahoney had sent him years ago, turned to the diagram of the big rigid. 'That's your size, no?' He unfolded a photostat enlargement of it. He tapped the cargo-hatch in the belly. 'Somewhere above that hatch you have a winch for hauling up the cargo?' He unfolded another paper. It was a draughtsman's drawing of two telescopic steel arms. Mahoney identified it immediately.

'That's the trapeze the Americans used on their old aircraft-carrier airships,' he said.

'Correct. Very simple. You just fix it somewhere near the winch. Then you can lower it down through the hatch. The aeroplane flies up, hooks on, and you haul him up on board.' He looked at Mahoney soberly. 'You must install that trapeze on your airship, young man. To give it a better military capability.'

Mahoney was touched by his concern. 'It's a very good idea.'

'It's an essential idea, to sell it to the military. And it can also be used for cargo.'

'What will it cost?' Tana demanded.

'Nothing,' the old man said. 'I am making you one in my shipyard, it is nearly finished already. Next time you come to see my daughter you can take it back in your aeroplane.'

Mahoney was overwhelmed. 'Well, thank you very much, Mr Thoren.'

'As long as you never have to call me Vader it is a pleasure. And you still don't know where Mr Weston has gone with his fancy equipment?'

'No.'

The old man smiled maliciously. 'I think I do.'

'Where?' Mahoney and Tana demanded simultaneously.

'To some place where they will let him fly on hydrogen for the time being. Where do you think that is?'

Mahoney didn't know how much credence to give to the old boy. 'Libya?'

Erling grunted. 'I am trying to find out. But if it *is*, why does Mr Kaddafi want airships so badly he will fly them on hydrogen?'

He began to fold his diagrams. Tana touched Mahoney's foot under the table and nodded surreptitiously at the door but the old man caught it. 'Well, I know you have urgent things to do, so I will make myself scarce at last.'

'I'm only taking him to see my offices, Vader,' Tana grinned.

'Oh, I am sure.' He turned to Mahoney. 'I offered her space in my building, but she is very independent, you know. Myself, I cannot stand career women.'

It was a four-storeyed Victorian building near the railway station. 'Not the flashiest part of town,' she said.

'You should see Redcoat House.'

'I intend to.' She unlocked the front door. 'These are only the administrative offices. All the hard clerical work's done at the actual canning plants.' She switched on lights.

The ground floor had a large wooden counter, like an old-fashioned grocery store, a dozen desks behind. The walls were lined with shelves, displaying rows of cans, all Fairwinds' products.

'We try to put across the image of good, old-fashioned wholesomeness. We also do our seed and health-food business from here, though our warehouse is across town.'

He was very impressed. He followed her into a creaky elevator. He took her in his arms as they went upwards. 'Hey,' she murmured into his mouth – 'standing up in an elevator? . . .'

They got out in slight disarray. 'This is – phew . . .'

It was an old-fashioned office, and the centre was dramatically dominated by a small plough. The walls were crammed with photographs of farmlands in old, ornate frames.

'The plough is our symbol,' she said. "*The old values are best,*" we say. Here we co-ordinate all farm management: maintenance, transport, accounts. And the canning plants.

The seed nurseries. We also manage Vader's vineyards. And these are pictures of the various farms . . .'

She led him to the nearest one. It showed a harvester in a vast field. The next photograph was a vista of fruit trees, forklifts loading crates on to trucks.

'All the same farm?' he asked in wonder.

'No. I'll show you them all one day. And it all ends here, or here.' She showed him photographs of two big canning factories, glaring in the sun. 'Rather sad, isn't it? What happened to the old-fashioned market? I prefer this . . .'

It was an aerial shot of a herd of cattle crossing a plain, the dust rising up. 'And this . . .' Two jackaroos smiling into the camera, their faces puckered by the sun, cattle milling behind them. 'And this.' A muddy girl was standing in a patch of cauliflowers, a hoe over shoulder, grinning jauntily at the camera. In the background was a battered utility truck.

'I'm most impressed,' he said.

She smiled: 'You're meant to be, darling. But it's all thanks to the banks. It's amazing what they'll do once you've got some equity.'

She led him up the stairs, to the next floor. There were drawing boards. The walls had dozens of photographs, street plans sprinkled with red flags. In the centre stood a wheelbarrow, a pile of bricks in it. There was some lounge furniture around a coffee table which held brochures.

'The Real Estate Department. I have as little as possible to do with it now. Never a landlord be, Mahoney. But here we do our building and restoration plans, general management, letting, buying and selling. "*Buy land*," Vader said, "they aren't making any more of it." But one of our most profitable buildings is this.'

The photograph showed a tall office block on a waterfront, a forest of buildings behind. In the sea in front, a junk sailed by.

'Hong Kong. And that building stands on reclaimed land.'

Mahoney had had no idea of her wealth. 'And it's yours?'

'When it's paid for.' She put on a Norwegian accent: '"Never build with your own money, use the bank's, that's what they're for." And it all started like this.'

258

It was a photograph of a semi-detached cottage in a bleak street. A pile of mortar was being mixed by a workman and a teenage girl in gumboots.

'The nymph from the cauliflower patch?'

'With tits.' She added, 'It helps if a rich daddy's bullying you.'

'Is he a bully?'

She rolled her eyes. '*Is* he? Now I'll show you *my* office.'

She led the way, switching off lights. Up the last flight of stairs.

It had been the loft. The beams were black, the windows small. There was lounge furniture, a wooden kitchen table surrounded by quaint chairs, a desk, a refrigerator with a kettle on top. On the walls were posters of African wildlife, the Great Barrier Reef, Save-the-Whale, Greenpeace, Friends-of-the-Earth, skiing slopes, the Antarctic.

'This is also the board room. Our table, solid oak. This is also the new Fairwinds Travel office. Right now I'm trying to set up deals with agents, but we're going to be a very specialized outfit. Travel to unusual and rugged places. Like African safaris. Asia. Nature trails. Even the Amazon. The Antarctic—'

'The Antarctic?'

'Yes, low-flying day drips down to the South Pole and back. We'll charter DC 10s off Vader. I hope we'll do our first Antarctic flight this December. And this you'll recognize.'

It was an aerial photograph of her station, the row of huts along the river, the airstrip over there, the stockade. She gave a happy sigh, 'It looks like nothing now, but it's going to be wonderful.'

'It's pretty wonderful now,' he said. 'And what does your father think of Fairwinds Travel?'

She smiled, 'He thinks it's crazy.' She put on her Norwegian voice: '"I've always taught you to invest in fundamental things that people need: land, food, houses."' She wagged her finger, '"It is your duty to contribute to the economy."' She smiled wearily. 'So travel services to outlandish places is parasitical. For rich people only. Bound to fail.'

Mahoney smiled. He suspected the old boy was right. 'Is he on your board of directors?'

'Hell no, I wouldn't have him.'

Mahoney grinned. 'But he'll charter you his aeroplanes?'

'Oh yes, says he might as well make some money while I lose mine, teach me a good lesson.' She smiled. 'I'm convinced there's a market. The old man forgets about the *soul* – making people *aware*, before the beauty's all gone.' She looked at him. 'Am I just going to smother the world in mushrooms all my life?'

Afterwards, lying amongst her telephones, the in-basket scattered on the floor, her dress over her hips, her panties dangling from an elegant ankle, she sighed, 'If they could see me now . . .'

And riding back to the camp in the sunset, the sweat staining their shirts, the dust puffing up from the cantering hooves, the friendly feeling of the horse beneath you that makes you badly want to own a horse again. They dismounted, good and tired and smelling of horses, grabbed towels and soap and walked downstream and peeled off their clothes and dived into the deep pool. The bliss of the cool water, the glorious satiny feeling of swimming naked with your woman. He dived under and she shrieked as he broke surface with his arms upstretched, jaws agape, and seized her lovely slipperiness in his arms.

Afterwards, when they lay on a blanket by the fire in the moonlight, in the hour after love, they heard their first elephant squeal. It was a distant, old, atavistic sound. She sat up, eyes shining. Then she spread her arms and collapsed back.

'Oh God, I'm so happy . . .'

Later, lying in his arms in their hut, the moon shining silver out there, she said: 'When you've got your airship flying, and earning its living, what are you going to do with your wonderful life?'

He lay there. He was in love, and he did not care as long as it was with her. 'Build another airship?' he said. 'What do you think I should do?'

He thought she was going to say, 'Come and live in Australia.'

She was silent a moment. Then she said: 'Go back to live in Rhodesia. Where you belong. And go back to politics. And even if they don't want a white man, you can still exert great influence . . .' She smiled, and turned her head to him. 'You're going to be a very wealthy man, Mahoney. A wealthy *international* man. And rich men are powerful . . .' She shook her head. 'And what about the animals? And the poor people?' She smiled at him. 'You'll be a voice to be reckoned with. Like my father. *That*'s what a man like you should do.'

CHAPTER 41

She looked at herself in the mirror, from all angles. Oh, the beautiful clothes in this town! She was in new black boots, a swirling tweed skirt and jacket, a high-ruffled blouse: her hair was perfectly coiffured. She knew she looked great. Sophisticated. Elegant. And she felt as nervous as a schoolgirl.

She paid by credit card, went out into the dismal rain. She stuck up her new umbrella, and impatiently tried to flag a taxi. Finally an empty one came along. 'Fortnum and Masons, please.' My word, she loved London town, rain and all . . .

She hurried through the magnificent food hall. It smelt of spices, exotic cheeses, hams. At the tangy fish department she bought four lobsters, trout, Sydney oysters. At the poultry counter she bought two pheasants. At the meat section, a leg of lamb, a rack of spare ribs, two steaks. She surveyed her purchases anxiously, then bought all the herbs to go with all this provender. Then butter, cheese, yoghurt. To the Health Food section. Wheat-germ, whole-wheat bread, brown sugar. To the odiferous fruit section. English strawberries, South African oranges, avocado pears. She went in search of the liquor department. Six bottles of Dom Perignon champagne.

Then she telephoned Hertz and asked them to deliver her

car to the front of the store. The nice man helped her load her purchases. She got behind the wheel, unfolded the map. Her heart was beating like a girl's.

She drove slowly up the lane, peering through the rain. Then, there was the thatched house, through the trees. She parked, and got out. She put up her umbrella, and stood there, looking around her.

It was absolutely charming – but, oh, what a mess. The garden was overgrown, the plaster crumbling in places, the thatch coming down in places, the woodwork peeling; there was a tumble-down cowshed that looked as if he had intended converting it into a garage. But the *potential* of this place . . .

She walked slowly around it, inspecting, peering in windows. It would be a dark house – a little eerie, perhaps. It was completely silent. Only the dripping of the rain off the eaves, the swish of her feet through the weeds. She tried the back door. Locked, of course. She turned back to the bathroom window.

The glass shattered with the first smack of her umbrella. She lifted the catch. She hitched up her new tweed skirt.

She lowered herself into the bathtub, and climbed out. She opened the door, and found herself in a short hall to the front door. A room to one side. She looked in. His study. Books and papers piled everywhere. Opposite, a door led to the rest of the house. She opened the front door, hurried to the car and began to unload it. She carried everything inside. She parked the car behind the cowshed, out of sight.

He had obviously built the table himself: planks nailed together and varnished. But it was good and strong. There was a gas-oven, but also an old hearth, cobble stones around it. The ceiling beams were low. It was a cheerful kitchen.

She went into the living-room. It had an old fireplace which you could walk into. The furniture was threadbare – he'd obviously picked it up for nothing. There were no ornaments. A worn blue carpet on the stone floor. It could be a lovely room. In the corner was a narrow staircase.

She climbed the dark, worn steps. They curved. At the

top was the door into the main bedroom. She smiled. It was a goddamn mess. Clothes strewn, drawers open, wardrobe agape. There were books and magazines everywhere, on homemade shelves and on the floor. The bed was unmade, the duvet in a heap. But the bed! It was a big, brass four-poster. Where had he got *that*? She sat on it experimentally, and sank into a feather mattress.

She got up and walked to a female dressing-table in appalling taste. It had little pink frills, a chintzy stool to match. *How could the woman have put that piece of furniture in a two-hundred-year-old house like this?*

She could not resist it. She opened the top drawer. It held a miscellany of foreign coins and banknotes. The second was empty. She pulled out the bottom drawer. And yes, here she was. Upside down, but she knew it was her.

She lifted out the portrait.

She looked at her. With dislike. But, regrettably, she had to admit that she was beautiful. Shelagh looked out of the frame, smiling. Blonde hair shoulder length, eyes big, mouth sensual over perfect teeth. It was a handsome face, almost mannish in its good looks.

And hard? . . . She stared at it, then put it aside.

She picked up the photograph underneath. It was also face-down. Shelagh again. This time she was in a bikini, standing by a pool, about to dive in, grinning sideways at the camera. Tana looked at her critically. And she had to admit that she had a lovely body. Long legs, well shaped. A very good bust. She could see the sex appeal of the woman.

She turned the next frame. She stared.

The woman was naked. Standing in front of this very dressing table, looking as if the photographer had caught her by surprise. Her hair was awry and she had one hand on one jutting hip indignantly, her eyes half-closed in a cuss. Tana breathed. Yes, she did have a lovely body. But . . . there was something else about her.

Then she realized. The woman could almost be her.

Almost . . . If the hair was longer. She crooked her finger over Shelagh's hair. And, yes . . . Though she hated to admit it, there were similarities. In the line of the jaw, the shape of the mouth. The eyes? . . . But no. She could see a hardness in that face that wasn't there in hers.

She put her finger over the head entirely and looked at the body. And was she looking at the famous Tana Thoren legs? . . .

No, she was not. Good legs are simply good legs!

She picked up the last photograph, with misgiving, and turned it over. And stared.

It was an old photograph, but it was not of Shelagh.

Another woman was looking at her, smiling. She had a gentle, handsome face. Large eyes, and a wide, sensuous mouth. And what struck Tana, immediately, was that she, too, had long blonde hair. She knew immediately who she was. Mahoney had only mentioned her once, when she had asked him about his past: this was Suzie, the girl from South Africa. The one that died. Tana stared at her. For a moment she didn't know how she felt. Then she knew. She felt an accord with that lovely woman. No pang of jealousy, as she did with Shelagh. And it had nothing to do with the fact that she was dead. She felt she would have liked her . . .

Enough! She packed the photographs away. And hurried down the stairs.

The groceries were packed away. She had given the floor a quick sweep, tidied around, picked some wild flowers, put them in a beer-mug of water.

She went to the living-room, screwed up a newspaper, threw it in the hearth on top of old ashes, laid kindling on top, then logs. She put a match to it. The flames began to crackle up. She hurried upstairs. She pulled the duvet straight on the bed, closed drawers and wardrobes. She switched on the electric blanket.

She went down to the kitchen again, swilled out the mop bucket, filled it with ice, buried a bottle of champagne in it. She carried it upstairs to the bed, and went back downstairs.

She looked at her watch, pulled up her skirt and unhitched a stocking. She took off her boots, peeled the stocking off, and dropped it inside the front door. She went into the living-room, peeled off the other stocking, and dropped it. She was grinning. At the foot of the staircase she pulled off her panties, and dropped them. Then she heard his car coming.

She fled up the steps, breathlessly unhitching her skirt. She dropped it halfway. She flung down her bra at the top, as she heard his key in the latch. She jammed her feet back in her boots, then draped one arm up the brass bed-post. She put her other hand on her hip and jutted it seductively.

She heard him stop inside the front door. She heard an uncertain step into the living-room. Then:

'Tana!' he yelled.

He came bounding up the staircase, two at a time. And oh, the laughing, and the clutching, and the joy.

CHAPTER 42

They had a wonderful time, that long month of June. It seemed that England had decided to put her best foot forward for them and wheel on a beautiful summer. The sun shone, the fields were in bloom and the birds sang.

The first few days they spent entirely at home and almost entirely in bed. But they did little sleeping. She said: 'Do you want to go out?'

'Is there a man alive who'd want to go out? Do you?'

She said happily, 'I want to see everything. Redcoat House. Your hangars. Your airship. Even the dreaded Dolores. The only thing I don't want to do is get out of your bed.'

They did get up from time to time, of course, to get more beer and wine, to bathe, to make a sandwich. 'It's a good house, Mahoney.'

'It's going to be, when I finish restoring it.'

'You only need a good woman – Australian, mate.'

She examined the plumbing. He said: 'It needs a bit of work.'

'Yes, I'll have a go at it. When we make it out of bed.'

They wandered around the garden, in their dressing gowns, picking wild flowers. 'One day, this will all be lawns,' he said.

'And tulips and roses,' she said. 'Why not this summer Mahoney?'

'When we finally make it out of bed,' he said, 'it'll be winter.'

Seeing his enormous hangar standing in the sunshine filled him with pride all over again. And he saw it through her wide eyes.

'My *word*, Mahoney! *That* big?'

She stood in the doorway, in awe, staring up at the huge silver structure towering above her, the scaffolding, workmen way up *there*, riveting the aluminium skin on to the huge frames.

'Oh, *my* . . .' she breathed in wonder.

They walked slowly down the huge hangar, heads tilted back, under the ship's massive belly that curved up above them in all directions. Malcolm had appeared, on his best behaviour, looking pink and flustered. Tana stopped and pointed up at a circular opening in the bows. 'What's that?'

'That's the "thruster". There's an engine and propellor inside. It can thrust the bows to left and to right. Very important, used in manoeuvres like docking. There's another in the stern.'

He led the way up a ladder, through a hatch, into the dark belly.

'This is the lower cargo hold.'

It was like being in a wide tunnel. Naked electric lights stretched away into darkness, lighting up patches of aluminium bulkhead. Far away, workmen were busy, like ghosts.

'It's a warehouse . . .'

'And it can be converted very fast to a liner-in-the-sky.'

'It's called "Quick Change",' Malcolm said busily. 'Most aircraft can do the same. All the seats and kitchens? – they can be taken out in a few hours so the plane can carry cargo.'

'Windows,' Mahoney said. He walked to the bulkhead and tapped a panel. 'We can unscrew these and put windows in their place. This area can be the saloon, restaurant, bar – even a dance floor. Plus a promenade deck, so passengers can stroll and look down at the landscape – even sit in deck chairs. Further aft', he pointed 'will be cabins. Just like a ship.'

'Altogether,' Malcolm said proudly, 'we can carry four hundred passengers, in ocean-liner conditions.'

'I'm overwhelmed. The *size* of it . . .'

Malcolm led the way on, down the belly, to a ladder. He climbed up it like a young man. Tana followed. Mahoney looked up her perfect legs as she climbed, and oh dear he was in love. She passed through a manhole, into another hold. 'Keep climbing,' Malcolm called. She followed him, up through another hatch, into a standing-place the size of a telephone booth. The ladder went on upwards, encased in a cylinder. It got smaller and finer, disappearing into a pinprick of light at the top. 'My God!' The booth had an airtight door. Malcolm opened it and flicked a switch. She entered, and stared.

They were standing inside the eliptical hull itself: pinpricks of electric bulbs showed giant girders curving upwards. It was like being in a cathedral. Pipes and cables ran forwards and aft, disappearing into blackness. Malcolm's voice echoed.

'All this space will be filled with helium. Not contained in a bag – the hull itself *is* the container. Once it is filled, a man who has to come in here, to do repairs, will have to wear a breathing apparatus.' He pointed upwards, at the tubular ladderway. 'In flight, he can climb up to the very top, out of a hatch, on to the top, if he wants to.'

'Why would he want to do that in flight?' It echoed.

'To repair something out there. A leak, for example. We also have television cameras up there, so we can see what's above us, and they might malfunction. He'd use a life-line, in case he slipped.'

Mahoney said: 'The German riggers aboard the old Zeppelins had to go up top regularly in flight to sew up tears in the canvas. They used to scorn life-lines, as a matter of principle.'

Malcolm shone his flashlight. A mass of machinery was fitted against the faraway bulkhead. 'Part of the four engines. Allisons. They can be vectored to drive the ship upwards or downwards vertically, or to make her hover.' He pointed.

267

'Fuel tanks are in the centre, to give correct balance. The water-ballast tanks are fore and aft. So are additional fuel tanks – we can pump fuel from one to the other to shift weight, as ballast.' He explained: 'The amount of ballast depends on the weight of the cargo. The more cargo, the less ballast. As the ship loads each ton of cargo, she pumps out a ton of ballast. When she unloads the cargo, she pumps water on, to compensate for the loss of weight. If she suddenly needs to fly high, say to cross a mountain, she may have to discharge some ballast to make her lighter. But as she's flying along happily, she's burning fuel, so she's getting lighter. On shorter runs this is no problem – we take off with plenty of ballast, a little heavy, and reckon to arrive at about equilibrium. On longer runs, as we get lighter by burning fuel, we may have to stop over lakes or the sea, and pump some water up on board to compensate. You work out your requirements in advance. If she has to discharge ballast unexpectedly to get over a mountain, you get down the other side aerodynamically – fly her nose downward, like an aeroplane. No problem. Now, this way.'

He led them along a man-way, heading for the distant bows. They walked about a hundred yards. Malcolm pointed with his flashlight.

She was looking at a mass of white fabric, like a deflated balloon. It seemed the size of half a tennis court.

'The ballonet,' Malcolm said. 'Rubber. There's another at the stern. In flight, these ballonets are inflated with outside air, to a predetermined extent, with electric pumps. Now, as the airship rises, the helium in this hull expands. It must have somewhere to go. So air valves *out* of the ballonets, shrinking them, to give the helium more space. As the ship descends, the helium contracts, so we pump air *into* the ballonets, to fill up the excess space. Got it?'

'Got it.' Mahoney had explained the principles; she just didn't yet believe they really worked. 'The air also acts as ballast?'

'Correct. Air has a positive weight. Now, when an airship flies into bright sunshine, the helium heats up – "superheat" it's called – and it expands, doesn't it? When helium expands, it gains lifting power, so the ship will tend to rise. Now, an airship is inflated with a predetermined amount of helium to fly her at a predetermined maximum height, usually about seven thousand feet – called her "pressure ceiling". If she goes higher, the helium will expand so much that it will burst the hull unless we control it. So we have automatic valves, on top of the hull, and on the sides, to vent off the excess helium. Or the captain can do it usually, to make his ship go higher. But venting helium is expensive, so normally he will keep her lower aerodynamically. Simple.'

'Oh, simple,' she echoed.

They were in the belly of the ship again. Mahoney pointed. 'There are cargo doors all the way down. But look at this.'

He pressed a switch. There was a whirring, and two big flaps opened in the floor, swinging slowly upwards. She could see the concrete.

'The main cargo door. But look.' He pointed at the ceiling. Against it hung the trapeze which her father had made. Mahoney pressed another switch, and the trapeze slowly descended through the opening.

'It can be used as a cargo hoist. But its real purpose is the launching and retrieval of small aeroplanes in flight.'

Malcolm was beaming. 'Splendid of your father! Makes it an attractive military vehicle – a flying aircraft carrier.'

She looked at the trapeze distrustfully. 'It sounds damn dangerous to me.'

'Oh no,' Malcolm said. 'The Yanks got it down to a fine art before World War Two. They could even do it during storms. They maintained it was easier than landing on an aircraft carrier. Because a plane touches down at a high speed. But when they hooked up to the trapeze they were only doing about one mile an hour, because the airship was doing the same speed they were.'

She turned to Mahoney. 'Now listen, sport, I've only just fallen in lust with you. You're not going to do any damn-fool thing like that!'

'No *way*,' Mahoney grinned at her.

Malcolm had to leave them. Mahoney led her towards the nose. They came to a door. 'Crews' quarters,' he said.

She entered. Carpeted steps led to the first floor. On either side of the landing were panelled doors.

Mahoney opened the first. She walked into a large cabin with a bed against a window that looked out on to the hangar below. There were lockers and chests of drawers. Every bulkhead was panelled in oak veneer.

'It's beautiful, Mahoney!'

'This is the second officer's. The first officer and engineer have their own cabins across the landing.' He led her out, and up the next flight of stairs. It opened on to a large saloon. Off it was the galley.

She walked slowly around the crew's saloon.

'The *space* . . . And what a view you're going to have!' She stared through the sweeping window: sat experimentally on a sofa. She pointed to another door. 'What's through there?'

'In a moment,' Mahoney said. 'This way.'

A curved staircase led upwards out of the saloon. 'The bridge.'

She looked around, enthralled. Windows swept around, in a crescent, giving a panoramic view. On one side of this crescent was the computer and navigation station. On a dais in the centre were two seats for the captain and co-pilot, in front of a bank of instruments, from which protruded two steering yokes, like a conventional aircraft.

'The officer on watch can sit, like a pilot. But he can also walk around his bridge like a sea captain.'

'Oh, *wow*, Mahoney.' A bank of television screens showed the air space around the ship. She could imagine the fields and towns gliding by below, so close she could see the upturned faces, and she could *feel* the thrill of this wonderful way to fly, surging serenely out over the oceans . . .

And he took her in his arms, and she whispered. 'But right now I want you to take me to the owner's suite.'

He took her by the hand, and they clattered back down the steps, grinning, into the saloon. To the last unopened door.

He threw it open. There stood a magnificent stateroom, with a double bed and a huge window, with its own lounging area. There was a bathroom with a real bath. She kicked off her shoes, and her fingers were plucking at her blouse as he toppled her, laughing, on to the bed,

After that week he simply had to start earning a living again. 'But you're coming with me,' he said.

'Wherever thou goest, sport, there go I also.'

It was like a honeymoon on wings. 'Where do you want to go?' he said. 'We've got a cargo for Athens, another for Khartoum, another for Nairobi . . .'

He made sure he flew with Ed, so he would work as little as possible. Sometimes she sat in Ed's seat. It was fun droning through the night with her, in the glow of the instrument panel, the stars outside; it was even fun taking the infernal machine off automatic and flying it manually for a bit, showing her what a pain-in-the-arse heavy-duty planes were after her dinky Cessna: it was beautiful watching the first light come into the sky, pearly pink, then riotous red, and down there Africa being reborn, vast and misty mauve. Then they were descending, and Africa was growing before their eyes, hot and earthy, the bush and the palms and the tall green grass; and even landing, the part he hated most about flying, bringing fifty tons of machinery down through thin air on to that tiny strip of killer concrete at a hundred miles an hour, the mind-blowing lunacy of such a manoeuvre – even that was almost fun with her watching him do it. They opened the cargo doors and let the warm African morning flood in, broke out the cold beers, and went happily down the ladder with their overnight bags, on to the soil of Africa again.

The month went that way. They hardly knew or cared what was happening in the rest of the world. Zimbabwe was in the news: a visiting Swiss banker was tortured by the Fifth Brigade, the prime minister's 'private army', when he was sight-seeing too near their encampment; two white farmers were acquitted by the High Court for illegal possession of

271

firearms and were promptly re-arrested and detained without trial; three English tourists were found murdered in the mountains; thirteen brand-new Zimbabwe Air Force aeroplanes were blown up and six Air Force officers were tortured into confessing, were acquitted by the High Court and promptly re-arrested. But the news was days old by the time Mahoney and Tana heard it, and he hardly thought about it beyond cursing and shaking his head and saying I told you so, because he had never been in love like this, and he was on his honeymoon.

Then that lovely June began to draw to its end.

She lay beside him in the double bed, her hair flamed across the pillow, and sighed at the ceiling.

'I've got to go home on Saturday.'

He held her. 'Don't even think about it,' he said. 'You're coming back.'

'Ah, yes . . . I'm coming back . . .' She sighed cheerfully. 'I have to, you bastard. You can't have a chance of such happiness and not see it through . . . And that's why you're a bastard. Because you knew full well I didn't want to fall in love.'

He kissed her neck. 'You sent me the mushrooms.'

'*You* telephoned me with that honey-talk. After I'd sent you a telex saying Mrs Hutton emphatically regrets.'

'Ah, but you sent me the mushrooms.'

'But you sent me the roses. *Eleven* roses. "The twelfth one is you." God, how corny can you get? . . .' She laughed, then sighed. 'You're so confident of me. You know I'll come back.'

He held her tight. 'Of course I'm confident of you. I've never felt stronger and happier in my life. Because I love you.'

'Do you?' she said. 'Love me?'

'You know I do! Aren't *you* confident?'

She said: 'I know that we are right for each other.' She paused. 'But I'm not entirely confident in you. I think you still love *her* a little.'

He said quietly: 'I don't even think about her any more.'

She smiled in the dark. 'I'm not asking you to reassure me.'
She half laughed: 'Of course I am, but what I really mean is
. . . Of course you think about her. And of course you love
your child and think about her. You're only *in* love with
me.' She held him. He started to speak and she interrupted
resolutely: 'Maybe I shouldn't say this. But I'm going to . . .'
She thought, then took a breath: 'I'm going to reorganize my
whole life to come back here. If you have any doubts . . .' She
stopped. 'I'll rephrase that. *Shouldn't* you – to make absolutely
sure you're doing the right thing – go and see Shelagh, just to
lay any ghosts?'

Mahoney lay there in surprised silence. She squeezed him.
'Don't answer that.' She sat up. 'We've got two whole nights!
Let's be happy! Do you want to make love? Do you want to
fetch more champagne?'

PART 7

PART 7

CHAPTER 43

It was one of those bucket-shop deals on Air Zambia, and he was going to have to spend Sunday in Lusaka, awaiting his connection. After he paid the fare in cold hard cash, standing in the check-in queue with a row of Africans with their overnight bundles, he wondered what the hell he was doing spending all this time and money, going back to see Shelagh. Later, sitting in the crowded aeroplane, drinking the duty-free whisky he had bought for her because the air hostesses had no more, staring out the window at the night, it turned over and over in his mind. What the hell am I doing? Just to find out whether Tana was right, that maybe you still love Shelagh although you're *in* love with Tana? . . . You're wasting your time, because simply *being* on this aeroplane you know it's not true . . . You don't *want* to go. So, O.K., he said to the moonlit night, that's good, because the experiment is a success, you know already what the proof is – you've done the right thing.

The responsible thing. Because right now Tana is reorganizing her whole life, and it's right that you go to see your wife to make sure you lay any ghosts. Because the hard fact is that until recently there *were* moments when you yearned for her, and for your child . . . Not last month, when Tana was in your arms; but when you sometimes woke up in the middle of the night and the rain was dripping off the eaves, and ah, yes, you wanted to lie there and know that your darling daughter was asleep next door and tomorrow she would come pattering down the passage and you were all together as a warm family . . . And that was natural enough, but now he also knew that it was just a dream, and that was a tremendous relief. And he was glad he was doing what should be done. It was early morning when they got near Lusaka. When the captain told them to fasten their seatbelts, in an African accent, Mahoney strapped himself in so tight he almost gave himself cramp. But the captain touched down very nicely, and then the whole plane broke into spontaneous applause. Suddenly everybody was laughing and clapping, white teeth flashing in black happy faces. And Mahoney laughed and clapped too, and he loved every one of them.

He didn't love them by the time he got his luggage. It took an hour to get through Immigration and the officer looked at his passport as if he had made it himself, then asked for a cigarette, then took the whole packet. It took another hour to get his luggage out of the customs bun-fight. He had checked it through all the way from London to Zimbabwe, but the luggage man felt he had to tear off the label and replace it with an identical one. Then he went to the information desk to ask when the buses went into town.

'I don't know,' the information girl said.

'But there *are* buses?'

'I don't know, sometimes, sah.'

'Well,' Mahoney said, 'have you *seen* any buses today?'

'You must look outside-i, sah.'

So he went outside and had a look. The car park was big, built by the British. But only one battered taxi stood there, and hundreds of passengers with their bundles, under the African sun. He went back to the information girl. 'No buses,' he said.

'Yes, sah,' she said.

'But how are all those people going to get to the town?'

'By bus, sah.'

Mahoney said to hell with it and went up to the bar.

It was almost empty. One elderly white man sat morosely at the bar, a few whites off his plane were at tables. There was a solitary black barmaid. The long shelves behind her held three bottles. 'What kind of beer do you have, please.'

The morose man said, staring in front of him: 'Only one kind of beer. Only one bottle left.'

The girl heaved herself off her stool. She plonked the beer on the counter and sat down in a lump again.

'Fun joint,' Mahoney said to the morose man.

'Swinging,' he said, staring in front of him.

'No buses,' Mahoney said.

'Depends whether they can get one started. And this is an

278

international airport?' He waved his hand tiredly. 'I remember the days when this bar was full. Look at the size of it. Look at those shelves.'

'How long have you lived here?'

'Twenty-odd years.' The sad man sighed. 'Mining engineer, me. Remember the days of the copper boom, everybody rich and happy and the saying was "Go north, young man"? We were going to have "partnership", remember, equal rights for all civilized men? Now look at it.' He waved his hand at the shelves.

'But you stayed,' Mahoney said.

'They still need mining engineers, don't they? I'll give you a lift into town when my car comes.'

A white woman sitting at a table exclaimed: 'Eight dollars!'

Mahoney turned. She was tired and fat, with two children. A waiter was holding a sandwich, looking bewildered. 'Take it back! It doesn't cost half that at the Ritz! And not' – she lifted a corner of the sandwich – 'even any butter! We'll go hungry!'

The waiter stood there, holding the offensive sandwich; then clicked his tongue. He sauntered to the bar, leant against it, and began to eat the sandwich. The morose man nodded at the window. 'There's the car.'

When they got into town he said, 'Only hotel that's any good is the Pondoroso. All the other good old hotels – ruined.' As he dropped Mahoney off at the hotel he said: 'Keep going. Right south. Or right north.' He jerked his head. 'Like England.'

Mahoney walked down avenues of jacarandas with storm-water ditches six feet wide. The houses were single-storeyed, in large, dry gardens. They used to belong to whites in the brave old days of Partnership, when there were garden parties, servants in starched white uniforms. Now they all had bars on the windows and there were old, battered cars, the gardens were overgrown, and he did not see one white person. He walked to the railway bridge, into the hot, dry main street.

It was lined with single-storeyed Victorian shops selling

trinkets and clothes. Hot and dusty and paint-peeling. Africans were staring in windows, squatting in the sun. He looked in the windows at locally made shirts and trousers, and they were more expensive than London. How come? he thought. The country's bankrupt, massive unemployment, vast cheap labour, and their inferior products are more expensive than London? There was a big supermarket. He looked in the windows. The shelves were more than half empty. He thought. And the cupboard was bare. And this is the main street, of the capital? What is it like in the bush?

Next door was the Russian Cultural Mission. And, ah, yes, it was wonderful in Russia . . . All was sunshine and flowers in the People's Paradise where cups runneth over. There were splendid photographs of rosy-cheeked Russian girls harvesting crops with wide smiles, stalwart Russian lads in love with their tractors, bikini-ed beauties besporting themselves on the Black Sea, supermarkets overflowing and tables groaning. There were happy Zambians shaking hands with beaming Russians, philosophical Zambians studying Marxism, athletic Zambians racing comradely comrades, no-nonsense Zambians learning about machine-guns, joyful Zambians cheering Moscow May Day parades. . . .

Mahoney walked slowly back up the main street, which, he learnt, was called Kenneth Kaunda Way. He thought, The whites pull out so the Reds can move in. Isn't it marvellous how we democratically let them seal their own fate, and our own in the process? Now we've got Marxists all the way to the Limpopo, and the West won't rest until the comrades control Cape Town.

He walked back over the railway bridge, and looked down at the tracks. This was the railway that was going to run from Cape Town to Cairo. However, Zambia was as far as it got before the British began to hand over their empire. Now the railway hardly ran at all. But now there *was* a brand-new line, oh yes, going from here to Tanzania, the fabled Tan-Zam railroad built by the communist Chinese. But did it work? Did it hell. It was a shambles, now the Chinese had left. And it was a shambles in the port of Dar es Salaam now the British had left, a shambles in the ports of Benguela and Beira now the Portuguese had left. The only ports the Zambians had were the South African, and that was anathema. They would have to ask the Chinese to come back to get the Tan-Zam railroad cranked up again – for a while.

He shook his head. If ever a country needed airships it was land-locked Zambia . . .

He suddenly stopped walking. How ironic! . . . *This* is what he had been talking about, the importance of the airship to the Third World, yet it seemed he had just thought of it! Instead of that shambolic railway and those shambolic ports he saw his fleets of airships flying from Cape to Cairo; the vast reservoirs of African man-power working to produce the cargoes instead of sitting on their asses in the sun bogged down by poverty . . . And he wanted to laugh, because the real struggle for Africa had only just begun! But not a struggle to divide her up, this time – but to save her life; to save her from bankruptcy and famine and communism. And only his airships could do it! His airships were as important to Africa today as the steamship had been one hundred years ago! . . .

Joe Mahoney stood on that railway bridge, and he wanted to throw his arms wide and praise the Lord for casting him in an historic role. *Because he was truly going to save Africa!* He walked up the dusty avenues to the hotel with a spring in his step, past African women sitting under the trees suckling their babies, and he smiled and waved and they laughed and waved back, and he loved every one of them.

CHAPTER 44

He felt even better with half a dozen beers sloshing around inside him, as the plane came over Salisbury in the late afternoon.

He looked down at the spreadeagled city, the highways well-paved swathes through the green, and the suburbs with their swimming pools and tennis courts, the hotels and office blocks rising up; and for a moment he felt like he always had, once upon a time a hundred years ago, the lovely feeling of coming home. He did not care that somewhere down there was her new lover, he was simply looking forward to seeing her for old time's sake, and he was tremendously excited about seeing his Cathy. When the plane touched down he was smiling all over his face.

The immigration officers were black – and unsmiling to boot, because if you're an official you must be severe-looking. 'You were born in Zimbabwe?' the man said with grim suspicion. 'Yes.' The man looked something up in a book, but decided there was nothing to be done about it. The customs officer was also magisterial, particularly about the half bottle of whisky. 'Why you bring this bottle?' 'I'm going to drink the other half,' Mahoney said. He did not like being treated like a petitioner in his own country, and it was a shock that all the officials were black, but he thought, Why not, this is what you recommended years ago. He went to the Hertz desk and rented a car.

He drove slowly into town. It was all much drier and drabber than he remembered. There were many more Africans about, and fewer cars. He drove slowly up Jamieson Avenue, where the statue of Cecil John Rhodes had stood. It was now Samora Machel Avenue. He thought: Lord, Samora Machel, the communist dictator of Mozambique, the guy who's reduced Mozambique to an economic ruin, and we name our principal street after him? He drove up past the High Court, where he used to make his money, and all the way up were huge portraits of the prime minister. He thought, *God – the guy's been boss for several years, and he still needs his picture everywhere?* It was eerie. It was the Big Brother number. He drove on up the avenue, towards the suburbs, and pulled into the Red Fox Hotel.

He had a beer in his room while he bathed and shaved. The sun was going down in a blaze behind the trees. He was very excited again. It was wonderful to be going to see his child.

He drove down the jacaranda-lined avenues, his excitement about Cathy mounting. It all looked the *same* . . . The apartment blocks were spacious. But no, not the same: there weren't many cars parked under the trees. Less than half the dwellings shone lights. There was a half-empty atmosphere. It was completely quiet. He thought, Maybe it's because it's Sunday. But no, nearly half the whites had left the country.

He walked up the strange-familiar, red-cement staircase. It seemed unreal. Yet exactly as he remembered it. Down the corridor, to the end. And there was her apartment . . . How many times had he opened and closed this door; half the time in joy, half in hurt and anger. He selected his old key off his key-ring. He knew she was not home yet. He was going back in time. He walked slowly in.

It was a big apartment. A wide passage led past the kitchen, into the living-room. He stood, looking around him. It was heart-stabbingly familiar, and strange. So this was where his wife and child lived . . . Possibly where Cathy had been conceived.

There was an elegant chaise-longue, a dining table. So this was where she entertained her lovers . . . He turned away from the thought, to the first room. And yes, this was his Cathy's room.

And his heart squeezed. Because it was a little girl's room – not a toddler's anymore. Instead of teddy-bears there were dolls. Stuck on to the walls were her drawings, of princesses in spiky crowns, and houses with smoke ballooning out the chimneys and big flowers in the garden. There was a dressing-table with a real hairbrush and hairclips and ribbons. His baby wasn't just a baby any more, and she had grown up without him . . . He turned away abruptly. He went into the kitchen, got a glass and poured a big shot of the duty-free whisky. He took a gulp, to stop himself thinking.

He walked down the corridor, to the other bedroom.

The door was closed. As if saying Private. For a moment he hesitated. What did he want to go in there for? To hurt himself? But she could not hurt him any more. He opened the door.

The bed was six feet square. It was so obviously a bed to make love on, enormous and frilly. In a flash he saw her spreadeagled on it, her eyes closed in ecstasy. For a moment he felt a little rage of emotion. He turned back to the door.

Then he stopped. What was he afraid of? She couldn't hurt him.

He made himself turn, and looked about the room.

It was so neat and feminine. So organized, the complete opposite of the rough and ready room he had given her in the unfinished cottage in the woods. The opposite of Tana's sprawling, untidy room. Her brushes and cosmetics; he recognized the brush, the alarm clock, the nail set. He turned slowly to the wardrobe, and reluctantly slid back the door. There were some dresses he recognized. Her shoes racked neatly underneath, her sexy high-heels, her boots, her no-nonsense walking shoes. And the faint, familiar scent of her.

He slid the door closed with a small bang. He made himself walk into the bathroom.

Only the standard female gear. Nothing male. Behind the door hung the gown she had bought in Marks and Spencer, a filmy negligée he had never seen. He turned away. This was foolish. What was he looking for? Just a memory, or some hard evidence to hurt himself with? Then he saw it.

It was only in one corner of the basin, as if she had carelessly rinsed it out: a thin line of male bristles, left behind after a shave.

He walked slowly back into the bedroom. He did not like himself. He went to the bedside table, and opened the little drawer.

There it was. The little plastic card of contraceptive pills. He slid the drawer closed. He walked back to the living-room.

He sat down in the armchair in the half-darkness. By the time he had lit a cigarette the throbbing had gone out of his face. Then he heard her at the door.

She flung open the door and called, 'Anybody home? Oh, hi! Half a minute, I've just got to tell them I won't be having dinner . . .' She disappeared.

He thought, I've sent her a telegram, and she might be having dinner out? He turned to the window. He saw Shelagh come out of the building, and go to a car parked under the trees. He could not see inside it. She bent, then stood back, smiled and waved. The car reversed out. She turned and walked back, her arms folded. Half a minute later she came in the front door, smiling. 'Hullo!'

He put his hands on her shoulders and kissed her cheek. 'You're looking beautiful. Where's Cathy?'

She held up a palm. 'She's spending the weekend with her friend, you'll see her tomorrow.'

He was astonished, and bitterly disappointed. 'What time tomorrow?'

'After school. You can have her to yourself because I've got a dinner party, I'm afraid.' She straightened a cushion. 'I couldn't remake all my arrangements. And besides, if there're going to be any scenes, I'd rather she didn't witness them.'

He was disappointed. But resigned. 'No scenes, Shelagh.'

'Good.' She turned to him brightly. 'Well, got a drink, I see. I'll get wine.'

He watched her walk to the kitchen. She called: 'So – how long are you here for?'

'A couple of days. I have to go to South Africa,' he lied, 'chasing a cargo deal.'

'Oh?' She reappeared, with a glass. She sat down elegantly on the sofa. 'So . . . What brings you to darkest Zimbabwe at last?'

He had stopped shaking inside.

'Just a sentimental journey.' He added, for something to say, 'And to check out the political scene.'

She nodded. 'I've wondered how you could resist it so long.' She shook her head. 'You've really changed, haven't you?'

'Why?'

She looked at him. 'African politics used to be your big thing. Then you got hooked on aeroplanes, and just cut yourself off.'

He smiled. 'The other way round. I cut myself off first. Because nobody followed my advice. So the guerrillas won, and so you've got a communist government now, exactly as I said.'

She opened her mouth as if to argue, then closed her eyes briefly and shook her head. Suddenly she seemed more relaxed. And suddenly Mahoney just wanted to be happy. That nonsense in her bathroom and bedroom was all over. She was the woman he had married, and yes, he still kind of loved her, for all the good times, and she was the mother of his beautiful child; but it was over and all he wanted now was peace with her.

'I came to see you. And Cathy,' he smiled.

She looked at him over the rim of her glass, with a twinkle in her eye.

'I thought you'd never say it.' Then she smiled, maybe a little embarrassed. 'Well – you'll want to eat something, having come all this way on a sentimental journey. Would you like a bath?'

'I had one at the hotel.'

Surprise crossed her face.'Oh? But I'd have put you up, I presumed that if you were coming this way . . .' She shrugged. 'Things must be looking up in Redcoat. Well,' she said with finality, 'I need a bath, I look a fright. Can you amuse yourself?'

'Of course.'

She got up. She turned for the bedroom, then stopped at the doorway and smiled. 'Welcome to Zimbabwe. It's nice to see you, Joe.'

He went to the kitchen for another drink. He stood, the bottle poised, examining how he felt. He was sober and a little drunk. And he was happy. Because it was harmonious. Because his decisions were made. He was glad he had come to confirm them, and it *was* good to see her, too, despite all the bad things that had happened. Of course there was still feeling – even love. Old love, wise love, with the knowledge that it was no good for living together, entirely different from the other kind of happy, Tana-love. But love nonetheless. It was entirely natural that he should feel a pang. She had been his lover, his wife, the mother of his child, and she was beautiful.

She sat opposite him at the table, groomed, the plates pushed aside, the third bottle of wine started. She said, 'Her teacher says she really is a gifted child. You're going to be very proud of her.'

286

'I'm purring. And why shouldn't she be gifted, with parents like hers?'

She smiled. 'But don't let's talk about Cathy. I'd like you to myself for a change. How's the airship? Is she on schedule?'

'More or less.'

'And the cost?'

'More or less, too.'

She shook her head. She was feeling mellow. 'I still can't believe you've done it. But then you always were a loner . . . I really am most impressed.' She added: 'So are my friends.'

He smiled, 'You just don't believe it will work.'

'Oh, I guess anything you set your mind to will work.' She added, 'Until it flounders in a storm. But there's no stopping you, is there?' She sighed. 'I just pray you're not in it at the time.' She sat up. 'But Redcoat is doing well?'

'We're about the only airline that is.'

'Marvellous! . . .' She smiled. 'What do you know about aeroplanes? . . . However, can you afford to pay me for my shares yet?'

He said: 'Not in full. '

'I was about to write to you about it. I'm sorry you didn't get much for the farm. But what can you expect, as an absentee landlord? Never mind, the share money can wait. That isn't why you came to see me, I hope?'

'No,' he smiled.

'You had no trouble with Tex about the shares?'

He wasn't going to tell her about Weston. 'Not really, thanks to you.'

She said, 'He's a very nice guy actually, rather misunderstood I think.' She added, 'You haven't registered the shares in your name yet, have you?'

'No. I can't until I have a letter from you, anyway, saying the price is paid.'

'So.' She stared at the ceiling. 'Redcoat's a success story. Soon your airship will fly sucessfully. *Then* will you be satisfied – and come back to Rhodesia where you belong, and practise law?'

He was taken by surprise. 'To Zimbabwe.' He shook his head. 'No.'

She said, 'O.K., Zimbabwe. But it's still a *marvellous* country. You would be Leader of the Bar now, or maybe even a judge, with your liberal political record. So it's got a black government now. That's what you yourself wanted!'

He said, 'I never *wanted* a black government, any more than a Tory wants a Labour government. I wanted to be fair to the blacks, unite the people and get external recognition, so we could win the war against the communists. And a communist government is what you've got.'

She said, 'It's their choice, Joe!'

He thought, Oh dear long-haired Shelagh with her English complexion and her Labour Party politics.

'Communism wasn't the people's choice, Shelagh. The communists won the war, and they made bloody sure they won the election. The people did not *choose* communism – they're primitive people who were bullied into taking the line of least resistance. The communists told them the war would go on if they didn't vote for them and the skies would rain transistor radios and bicycles if they did.'

She said slowly: 'For somebody who couldn't tear himself away from his money-making to come back to his own country and see for himself, you know a hell of a lot, don't you?' She glared at him. 'Joe, they're not *communist*! The African is not a communist at heart – he's a *capitalist*, with all his goats and cattle, he wants them for himself.' She shook her head earnestly: 'They're only *socialists* – and Africa *needs* socialism. It's a developing continent, it *needs* free Health and free Justice—'

'They had all that under the white man, and more.'

She cried, 'But what about Industry? Why *shouldn't* the profits of the fat shareholders in London and Johannesburg belong to the workers? Why *shouldn't* the workers have the benefit?'

He said flatly, 'Because the fat shareholders provide efficient management and if they don't get their profit they won't invest and there'll *be* no industry. That's why.'

She cried, '*Why* must it be like that? With aid from Britain and America and Russia and China, why *can't* the workers be the shareholders in their own factories and take their dividend home?'

He said, 'Ask the Kremlin why they haven't managed to pull off that trick in sixty-five years. Ask any first-year economics student.'

'But it *can* be done! It just takes reorganization!'

'Like getting rid of the fat shareholders? Making a one-party state—'

She cried, 'Oh nonsense, it *won't* be a one-party state! The Africans are a very democratic people! We've got a Westminster-style constitution, which the British gave us! The whites are guaranteed twenty percent of the seats in Parliament. It's *nothing* like you think! I've still got my job, haven't I? They're doing damn well, and I'm proud to be part of the team.'

He said, 'What about this Fifth Brigade, the prime minister's private army under nice North Korean officers? What about that Swiss banker?'

'But soldiers are soldiers everywhere – a bit rough and ready! You're so arrogantly paternalistic – like a schoolmaster!'

'Africa needs paternalism, Shelagh.'

'But why can't this country have its own black father-figure? Mugabe's a good man!'

He sighed: 'Darling, he's got an excellent brain. But he's a communist. You can never trust a communist.'

She sat back and smiled. 'You called me darling. I thought you never would.' She waved her hand. 'Carry on. Darling.'

He smiled. But his pulse fluttered.

'Shelagh, a Marxist is dedicated to "liberating" the world from the capitalist "yoke", like an evangelist is dedicated to saving souls. It's absolutely basic to their principles, and the ends justify the means. *Any* means. It's only a question of waiting for the best opportunity, and the prime minister will get rid of his political opposition, set up a one-party state, you mark my words. He'll put an end to democracy, because Marxists won't tolerate any opposition. It's fundamental, Marxists want a "dictatorship by the proletariat". Which means a dictatorship by the Party bosses. For ever. By definition, there can be no real democracy in a Marxist state.'

289

She shook her head, and began to pick up the plates, wearily. 'Very well, that's enough of politics. I'll get rid of these.'

He had it all figured out. His decisions had been made; he was going to do nothing to rock the boat. Nothing to provoke any emotional stress, distress, recriminations. He was not going to tell her about Tana; he was not going to talk about divorce and settlements. All that would come naturally, when they were far apart again. Shelagh had made her decisions long ago, and at last his acceptance was complete. Nonetheless she took him by surprise when she came back from the kitchen and said:

'Now tell me why you've come to see me.' Then she smiled. 'No, don't. I don't want any confessions. I don't expect you to have been exactly celibate.'

He smiled. 'No confessions, no confrontations.'

'And no decisions?' she said. 'Please.'

'No.' It was the truth; but it was also a lie. Because maybe it led her to believe that no decisions had been made. And, oh God, he was to live to regret that lie.

·She smiled: 'I'm glad you came. I was about ready to see you again too.'

He wondered what that meant. Big deal, the deserting wife is about ready to see her husband again! Then she got up and kissed him lightly on the mouth.

'And now, it's my bedtime. I've got school tomorrow.'

He stood up. 'O.K. What time must I be back to get Cathy?'

She looked at him. 'You are *not*', she said firmly, 'going to drive to your hotel after all you've drunk. Do you want to end up in jail? You can sleep in Cathy's bed if you're determined to show your independence, but *please* don't drive!' She paused. 'Or are you punishing me?'

He shook his head. 'No, I'm not punishing you, Shelagh. You're right, I shouldn't drive. But I'll sleep in Cathy's bed.'

She was relieved. 'Very well. But please don't punish me for coming back here, Joe. I did what I had to. Not all marriages are straight-forward. Can't we just enjoy each other's company, without tension?'

He smiled. 'Of course.'

She stretched and kissed him briskly. 'Then after you with the toothbrush.'

He heard her undress as he brushed his teeth, heard the wardrobe door slide. He thought, Maybe this is unwise. But he did not care. He was not misleading her. She had made it clear she wanted no confrontation, no discussion, just peace, as he did. His heart was hard, and he was happy to be happy. He heard her winding her alarm clock. He walked into the bedroom.

She was getting into bed, wearing a long red nightgown he had never seen. She grinned, 'I sleep in them these days.'

'Pretty.' It seemed she had never looked lovelier. He bent and kissed her forehead. 'Goodnight.'

'Goodnight.'

He went to Cathy's room, got undressed and climbed into bed. He lay there, eyes closed, trying to cut out the thought of his child, smelling her little-girl scent on the sheets. He ached to feel her skinny little frame in his arms, his very own child, to hug and squeeze. Tomorrow he would . . .

'Joe?'

He opened his eyes with a start. Shelagh was standing there, the moonlight streaming through the window on her hair. She smiled down at him.

'Isn't this rather silly? Why not the big bed?'

His heart was hammering.

'No, Shelagh.'

She smiled. 'You're afraid of getting hurt. You needn't be, if you just accept me as I am, darling.'

He wanted to say, 'That so?' He said, 'I cannot accept that, Shelagh.'

She looked at him, half a smile on her face: then she stooped and got the hem of her nightgown and swept it off over her head. For an instant he saw her loveliness in the moonlight, then she swept the blanket off him, and she was astride him. She crouched over him, her breasts right in front of him, her arms tight around his shoulders, her soft thighs gripping his. He began to struggle up, but she

291

snuggle-pinned him down, grinning, and she plunged her mouth on to his. He struggled again, and she laughed and he thought, *All right you bitch*, and his heart was pounding.

And, God forgive him, the bliss of her crushed against him again, the feel and taste and smell of her, her breasts and loins pressed hard against him, the bliss of the hot depths of her again, the look on her face, and he hated her and when she cried out in her orgasm it seemed the sweetest sound he had ever heard, and he hated himself even more.

CHAPTER 45

In the morning it was worse.

At first, when he woke up, at his lowest ebb, with a hangover, he did not know where he was: then he remembered. She was getting dressed in her bedroom. He lay in Cathy's bed, racked with guilt, pretending to be asleep, desperately thinking, *What have I done?* . . . A minute later she tip-toed into the room, put a cup of tea down by his bedside, and tip-toed out. He heard the front door close.

He swung out of bed. He took a gulp of tea, trying not to think, strode to the bathroom. He slammed on the shower and let it beat down on his thudding head.

He got dressed hurriedly. He just wanted to get out of the place, feeling as if he had committed adultery. There was a note on the dining table: '*Good morning! Eggs, bacon, in the fridge. Have a nice day! See you at four.*'

He turned for the front door, opened it; then stopped. And oh God he loved Tana.

He stood there, trying to assuage his guilt. Racked. Then he took a deep breath. *Nothing is so useless as guilt.* It was done and could not be undone. He had come back to straighten Shelagh out in his mind, and sleeping with her had done that! Without hurting Tana, thank God, because she would not know. And *certainly* without hurting Shelagh! Whatever was going on in her mind, it was not coming home.

He turned grimly, and left the apartment.

It was a glorious morning. And for a moment he was leaving her apartment to go to work. He drove up the avenues. Or it was seven years ago, and he was leaving some girl's apartment between bust-ups with Shelagh, driving to work. And thank God those days were over . . . It was both sad and happy to feel as if he was driving to chambers to put on his wig and gown to do battle with all those smart guys who knew more law than he. Thank *God* that he was not driving to work in this beautiful, landlocked, Marxist country, that he had made a new life, and got out with some loot. By the time he had gone six blocks he had sorted it all out. He had come back to see his wife for the sake of Tana Hutton, and he had had his last fling with her, and no harm had been done, and he loved Tana Hutton. And maybe he did still have a kind of love for his wife, but it was *old* love, a natural love, and he *knew* he loved Tana, and he was glad that he had come back. And tonight he was going to see his beautiful child . . .

He turned out of the avenues, into the traffic, heading for the city centre. Then he heard the sirens.

He thought it was an ambulance; but in his rear-view mirror he saw two police motorcycles coming screaming down the highway abreast, scattering cars, and behind them was a black ministerial car. Mahoney pulled into the kerbside lane, but kept driving, watching the mirror. The motorcade came screaming down the road at sixty miles an hour, cars swerving out of the way, the morning shattered by the sirens. A hundred yards ahead the traffic lights were changing from green to amber, and Mahoney slowed. He coasted towards the intersection, watching his mirror. The traffic lights turned to red. Mahoney pulled up at the intersection. The motorcade came screaming on. To the left, the lights had turned green for traffic crossing the intersection. There was only one car entering. It was driven by a white woman, a man sitting beside her. Mahoney stared, horrified.

Evidently she had not heard the sirens. The woman accelerated into the intersection, oblivious of the motorcade coming on through the red lights, and Mahoney flinched. There was a furious screech of tyres and the motorcyclists swerved and the wailing ministerial car screeched and the woman swerved frantically, confused. The police motorcyclists swung past her, the ministerial car swung around her, blasting, forcing her to the kerb, and both cars screeched to a halt. The doors burst open and the minister and his bodyguard scrambled out.

The black minister advanced furiously on the white woman's car, shouting. He wrenched the door open, and seized her wrist and wrenched her out. The woman was screaming and the minister's hand came back and he swiped her across her face. She cried out, and he swiped her again. The white passenger was scrambling to her assistance. The bodyguard grabbed his arms and the minister hit the woman again. Mahoney began to get out of his car, shocked, to do something, then the black chauffeur was pulling the minister off the woman, pleading. The minister shoved her back into the car, and slammed the door. He strode furiously back to his vehicle. The bodyguard and chauffeur scrambled in after him. The police cyclists hastily got into formation, and the motorcade roared away down the road, sirens wailing, heading for parliament.

Mahoney drove into town, shaken, angry. He could hardly believe what he had seen. *God, what has this country come to?* . . .

He parked behind the High Court. He grimly crossed Samora Machal Avenue, where the statue of Cecil John Rhodes had stood, where the big portraits of the prime minister now hung from the lamp-posts. Ahead was the red-brick office of the big man himself. Mahoney walked towards it, heading for his old chambers in the block beyond. Six blacks suddenly barred his way. He looked at them, surprised. One pointed imperiously.

'You cannot walk past the Prime Minister's office!'

Mahoney was taken aback.

'I'm sorry. You used to be able to walk here.'

'It is a pity you do not know this!'

'O.K. . . .' Mahoney walked grimly around the block, up

past the Appeal Court, crossed the street to Bude House. Oh God, it was a different land, now . . . He rode up in the elevator, got out, and there were the familiar doors. He opened them. A black clerk was sitting at Dolores' old desk, talking in Shona on the telephone. Mahoney waited impatiently.

'Good Lord!' cried a familiar voice.

Mahoney turned, smiling. 'Hullo, Dave!'

'Well, *look* who's here!'

Dave Robinson sat behind his desk, eyes closed, listening grimly to the tale of the minister's motorcade. 'Oh God,' he muttered. 'Typical. This is what has become of us? . . .'

'*Typical?*' Mahoney said incredulously. '*This* is what life's like in Rhodesia these days?'

And Dave shook his head, and proceeded to tell him how life was in Rhodesia these days: 'See these?' – Dave indicated the creases on his forehead - 'And these' – the piles of briefs upon his desk – 'they're bankruptcies . . .' He indicated the room next door. 'Remember our liberal common-room where we bitched about Ian Smith and his cowboys? Well, it ain't such a liberal common-room anymore.'

Lawlessness, Dave said. And misgovernment. And incompetence.

Take lawlessness. Gangs of armed thugs roaming the bush, holding up cars, shooting up farms, murdering whites, murdering blacks. And now it's political dissidents, the Matabele guerrilla-boys who lost the election, roaming the bush and banding together and plotting to overthrow the government – there's going to be civil war here all over again, you mark my words. And now the Prime Minister's got his own private army, just waiting to be let loose upon the land; and when he unleashes them, oh dear . . .

'Did you hear about the Swiss banker they tortured? – made him kneel naked for twenty-four hours while they beat him and pissed on him? And the three young English tourists found murdered nearby? And the two white farmers who were acquitted by the High Court and promptly rearrested? And the six Air Force guys who were tortured into confessing to the sabotage of the aeroplanes – they were acquitted and also promptly rearrested and the poor bastards are still inside . . . And the minister responsible is yelling in Parliament about the disgusting inherited Judiciary! . . .

'See there?' Dave indicated his greying temples. 'This is the country I'm bringing my children up in? A future one-party state where even cabinet ministers simply don't understand about the independence of the Judiciary and the Rule of Law? And now the government has started a one year crash course for black magistrates – *one year and they're on the bench!*' He spread his hands. 'Now I ask you, with tears in my eyes – *why?* Why must they take an efficient system like we had and screw it up? *Why* must they make a sow's ear out of a silk purse? . . .'

'Teething problems,' Peter Hetherington said worriedly. 'It'll get better when they get used to their own importance and settle down to the responsibilities of government, you'll see. You said so yourself in your election campaign.'

'I said', Mahoney reminded him, 'that there may be a lowering of standards but that was better than losing the war. If we'd done it my way we could have *controlled* the transition, *groomed* the right blacks to take over, *groomed* a new black civil service.'

'The standards will be acceptable,' Peter promised.

'You mean there'll be a tolerable level of incompetence? And what about this Fifth Brigade? How acceptable is that?'

Pete rubbed his brow. 'Yes,' he admitted. 'But maybe that too must be seen in context. The Matabele have been behaving very badly since they lost the election. Arms caches have been found. Rebellion is in the air down there. So maybe the prime minister needs a special brigade of loyal Shona soldiers up his sleeve, if they get out of hand – like the British use the Gurkhas.'

'Bullshit, Pete! It's his private army to crush political opposition – the Shona hate the Matabele. And what about all these people who've been tortured and who're being kept in jail even though they've been acquitted by the High Court? And what about these one-year-wonder magistrates?'

'They'll learn,' Peter said.

'You don't put a magistrate on the bench to *learn*, Peter! And any police force is only as good as the officers who lead it! And where are the officers?'

'The new ones will learn . . .' He sat forward earnestly. 'As long as the whites stay, as watch-dogs. That's why I'm staying.' He looked at him. 'And that's why you should come back, Joe.' He nodded. 'We're needed even more now. We could have a big influence on the government, and the prime minister is a very sensible man.'

'And how long will there be an opposition?' Mahoney sighed. And suddenly he was sick of politics. What the hell, it wasn't his problem anymore, he didn't live here anymore – his problem was to sell airships now. 'Peter, the prime minister may be a genius, but he's also an African politician *and* a communist. And neither of those two can tolerate opposition. Power to an African means undisputed power. Power to a communist means undisputed dictatorship by the communist party. End of story.' He shook his head. 'However, can we talk business?'

Pete smiled. 'I thought this was an historic social visit. What do I know about the freight business?'

Mahoney sat back. He said: 'You're one of the best lawyers I know. I want to engage you as my lawyer.' He smiled. 'But I'll only pay you if you get results.'

Pete looked surprised, then amused. 'What have you done now, Mahoney?'

Mahoney reached into his briefcase, pulled out his airship brochures.

'You must know the prime minister – you often represented members of his party in the good old days.'

Pete grinned. 'What's this I hear? Joe Mahoney seeking political favours from the *communists*?'

Mahoney said: 'I want you to see the prime minister for me. I want you to be my advocate. I want you to beat his door down until he listens to you . . .' He smiled at him: 'I want you to be my salesman.'

'Your *salesman*?' Peter echoed.

Mahoney smiled. 'There's one percent commission in it for you. On fifteen million pounds, that's a hell of a lot of money. Payable in Switzerland . . .'

CHAPTER 46

It was a beautiful day!

Mahoney felt he had done a beautiful morning's work. Pete had gone for it hook, line and sinker. He could have had no better man working for him! Pete could marshall all the facts and argue his case superbly – and Pete was sold on airships. Within an hour Mahoney had convinced him. It was mid afternoon when he left Meikles Hotel, with a spring in his step. He did not care about the things he had seen and heard about this country – it wasn't his problem anymore, thank God. He was a businessman now. And his airships were going to make him a fortune ferrying this country's goods to the world – *that* was going to be his contribution.

He was grinning with excitement as he parked outside Shelagh's apartment. He climbed the steps two at a time. The front door was unlocked. He knocked, and flung it open.

And there stood Cathy, in the passage, all dressed up for her daddy, smiling uncertainly, her mother behind her, beaming.

'Cathy!'

'Hullo, Daddy,' she smiled, rehearsed.

He strode to her, and picked her up, and hugged her, laughing – and, oh God, there was no grander feeling than his child in his arms, his very own child.

She sat in the car, very formal, very shy, her little legs stuck out, being very polite; and he loved every hair on her golden head.

'Do you remember me, darling?'

'Yes. You're my daddy.' His eyes burned, because her mother had coached her.

298

'What else? Do you remember England? How I used to take you on the swings and roundabouts?'

'Did you?' she asked earnestly. 'Can we go there now?'

He smiled. 'Another time, darling. Do you remember our house in England? In the trees?'

'It rained lots,' she said.

'It certainly did!' He was delighted with her for remembering something. 'And do you remember our house?'

'Yes!' she said, pleased. 'It was big.' She made a circle over her head. 'As big as that. And it was spooky!'

So she really did remember something about it! 'Do you remember my aeroplanes? I used to take you to see them.'

'Yes!' she declared. 'Mommy and I went in an aeroplane.'

'That's right,' he said. 'But that wasn't mine.'

'Have you *really* got an aeroplane?' she demanded.

'Yes.'

'A real big, *big* one?'

'A big, *big* one.'

'*Wow!*' Cathy said with big beautiful eyes, and he wanted to stop the car and hug her. 'Daddy, will you take me for a ride in your aeroplane?'

Oh, he wanted to take her for a ride in his aeroplane, he wanted to take her everywhere with him, he didn't want her out of his sight ever again.

The countryside was dry, but beautiful in the late afternoon. His old farm was not, however. He stopped at the main gate, and stared.

Maybe it had been a mistake to come here . . .

The fences he had put up at great expense? They were all gone. In some places the wire hung from the uprights, but most of it had been cut and taken away. And the fields that should by now be ploughed? They were hard and dusty. Scattered across them were scrawny goats and cattle, and a string of mud huts with cattle pens made of brushwood. Mahoney stared, appalled. This used to be his *arable* land! Now it was a dustbowl . . .

He knew it was a mistake to drive on to see the house, but he had to. As he came over the rise, he stopped again.

For a moment he could not grasp what he was looking at. There was the house, exactly where it should be; but yet it was not. Then he realized. There were no trees . . .

'Oh, *no* . . .'

All the lovely trees there had been – the frangipanis and the great msasa, and the eucalyptus forest? All gone . . . The beautiful fruit orchards he had planted all around? Gone . . . *Oh, God, why? . . . Fruit is money . . .*

Mahoney could not believe it. His once-beautiful farm looked appalling, naked, dry under the afternoon sun. His pretty house now had half a dozen mud huts sprinkled around it. Where the lawns used to be, more cattle and goats: the security fence was still there, but it was now a cattle pen. The hedges all gone, the flowerbeds. 'Oh, *Lord* . . .'

He drove slowly on, to the gates. He got out sadly, and took Cathy's hand. He opened the gate and started walking up to the house. There was no drive any more; it was trampled cattle dung. He came to the swimming pool, and stopped.

The tiles were cracked. The pool was half-filled, with refuse. A child squatted in the shallow end, back to him, defecating. Flies swarmed, and there was a stench. Mahoney turned away. He walked grimly on, past the stump of the frangipani tree. An African man appeared. Mahoney greeted him in Shona and mounted the steps. A cooking fire was smouldering on the verandah between three blackened stones.

'I'm looking for an old man called Elijah,' Mahoney said.

He waited on the verandah while the man cycled off to fetch him. The living-room had cooking pots around the hearth, and blankets. His old furniture was still there, but it was torn and sweat-stained. Electric wires hung out of the walls. A shyly smiling African woman brought him a mug of sweet tea. Black children came to peep at him round the doorway. Mahoney sat on the verandah wall with Cathy, doggedly drinking the tea, to be polite. He could not bear to see the rest of the house.

*

The ritual was over, the handclapping, the lengthy questions about the health of wives and children, and childrens' children, and the cattle and goats and the rains. Mahoney did not want to walk around his old farm with Elijah; he did not want to talk sitting on his haunches, as men should, where there was no frangipani tree anymore, no lawns, only dung. He walked slowly beside Elijah towards his car. He said, 'Which of your sons bought it?'

'Pakitcheni,' Elijah said. 'The one who owns the store.'

Mahoney remembered him. He was dumbfounded. Pakitcheni was the eldest son, the bright one, the prosperous one. 'But didn't he ask your advice?'

'Yes, Mambo,' Elijah said. 'I am his father.'

And then Mahoney realized. The penny dropped. Elijah was only pleased to see him; he was in no way embarrassed about the state of the land. It had not occurred to him that the place was hardly recognizable. Mahoney shook his head. He had to watch his tone: he wasn't the boss here any more.

'Why did he chop down the fruit trees, old man?'

'Ah,' said Elijah, 'for firewood.'

'But the fruit,' Mahoney said. 'The fruit was worth a lot of money.'

'Ah,' Elijah said, 'the fruit was small, and the insects ate it.'

'But did you not prune the trees, as we used to? And spray them?'

'Ah,' Elijah said, 'the medicine was finished.'

'But Pakitcheni had a car to fetch more from town.'

It dawned on Elijah that he was being criticized. He mumbled: 'I did not know which shop has the medicine . . .'

Mahoney wanted to cry out: *Over a thousand fruit trees, Elijah! – and you helped me plant them!* . . . He shook his head. He did not have the heart to ask about the eucalyptus forest. He did not want to remind the old man how eucalyptus grows again if you cut it at the right time. He did not want to mention the garden, the beautiful garden Elijah himself had helped to build. He did not want to embarrass the old man. But the swimming pool? He had to say something about that. 'What happened to the pool, old man? Does not your son like it?'

'Ah,' Elijah said. 'The pump is broken.'

Mahoney sighed. The pump breaks down so the pool gets turned into a garbage hole. The septic tank gets full so they crap in the swimming pool. He could not bear to ask about the bore-holes, the fences, how many cattle they were trying to support on the land. He just wanted to get out of here.

'My heart is glad to have seen you, old man. Stay well.'

'Go well, Nkosi.' The old man looked genuinely sad.

Mahoney and Cathy got into the car. He hesitated, then said out the window: 'Tell me, old man, how were the elections in your area? Did the people vote freely?'

'Ah,' Elijah said, 'they voted freely, Nkosi.'

'There was no intimidation?'

Elijah shook his head. 'There was no intimidation.'

'Are you pleased with the government?'

'Yes,' Elijah said.

'Why?' Mahoney said. 'You are not a communist, old man.'

'I am pleased', Elijah said, 'because the war is ended.'

The sun was beginning to go down. They sat by the stream and had the picnic supper which Shelagh had packed for them. She had included a bottle of wine. Cathy rummaged through the sandwiches, prattling away; Mahoney sat, trying not to think, wanting her to talk. She was happy with her picnic with her daddy. She did not remember him, although she pretended, to please him.

But he was a stranger to her, just a pleasant curiosity. His tears were burning, and he could see the farm as it might have been, with sunshine and flowers, the splash of the pool and the shrieks of laughter, his beautiful child riding her pony, the puppy gambolling on the lawn . . . And he wanted to pick up his child and hug her and somehow get it into her little head that she could always turn to him, for the rest of her life, *always*, somehow explain that although tomorrow he was saying goodbye it was never really goodbye until the day he died, and she would come to England to stay with him for holidays often, *often*, and he would take her for rides in his aeroplane, and his airship, she could fly all over the world with him, and anyway in a few years time she would be coming to school in England and come to stay with him every weekend . . . And he wanted to make her understand that he did still love her mommy, in a special grown-up way, that one day she would understand; and he wanted to tell her about Tana, how lovely she was, how much she was going to love Tana – that they were all going to be happy together . . .

Cathy was asleep by the time they got home. He carried her upstairs. Alice, the nanny, was sitting on the carpet in the living-room, watching television. 'I'll put her to bed,' Mahoney said. He undressed her, careful not to wake her. She looked so beautiful, lying there. He put her pyjamas on, and pulled up the covers.

He looked down at her. Tears were glistening in his eyes. 'Good night, my baby,' he whispered. Then he could not resist it, and he lay carefully down on top of the bed and gently took her little sleeping body in his arms, and rocked her. For a minute he held her, then he carefully got up.

Alice gave him a letter. It was from Shelagh, inviting him to make himself at home until she came back about midnight. Beer and wine were in the fridge. He could go to bed in her room if he wanted to. 'Fear not, I will not molest you! Love.'

He scribbled a note saying that he was leaving Alice as babysitter, that he had to go back to his hotel to receive some telephone calls, that he would come back for breakfast, to say goodbye.

He was awake before dawn with a heavy heart. Today he was saying goodbye to his child. He got up straight away, to stop himself thinking. At seven o'clock he parked outside the apartment.

Alice was in the kitchen. He looked into Cathy's room. She was still asleep. Shelagh's door opened and she came out in her dressing gown, damp from the shower.

'Oh, hi! she smiled. 'Alice,' she called, 'bring two coffees please, then get Cathy up. Come into my *boudoir*,' she leered jovially.

Alice brought in the coffee on a tray. Mahoney sat on the

303

bed while Shelagh sat at her dressing table, brushing her hair. The door was open. Mahoney had never seen her so cheerful in the morning. While she put on her face she prattled away about what an amusing dinner party it had been. Mahoney watched, restlessly. She looked ravishing, but it was his child he was thinking about. 'I'll go and get Cathy dressed,' he said.

She held up a hand to the mirror. 'Please . . . It takes her an age in the morning, even with me yelling. If you go in she'll never get dressed. Don't I deserve *some* of your time?'

'O.K.' He smiled.

'Do you really have to leave today?'

'I must.'

'Oh well!' She leant to the mirror, began to put on mascara. She half-smiled: 'Why didn't you accept my invitation to sleep here last night?'

He said quietly: 'You know why, Shelagh.'

'I wouldn't have raped you again,' she smiled widely at the mirror. 'Honest.'

Mahoney just smiled. Shelagh concentrated on the mascara, head tilted back, lovely eyelashes down. She finished, then smiled at him in the mirror; then got up. She pushed the door closed with her foot, and slipped the lock. Her robe fell from her shoulders. Mahoney stared at her, taken off-guard. She sauntered towards him, smiling widely: 'We've got twenty minutes. I can be a little late for school . . .'

Mahoney got to his feet, his heart pounding, and moved back. 'No, Shelagh,' he said.

She advanced and slid her arms around his neck. 'I refuse to let you off so easily. I was thinking about you all through dinner.'

With all his guilty heart he did not want to make love to her again. He gently pulled her hands off his neck. 'No, Shelagh.'

Her hands froze. She stared at him a moment then turned away.

'I understand.'

He took a breath. 'Shelagh —' he began.

She sat down on the bed and put her hands on her ears. '*Please*,' she said, 'I understand!' She sat there, eyes closed;

then shook her head fiercely: 'I did what I had to do – for *me*. Don't think I haven't suffered too!'

She burst into racking sobs. Mahoney stood there; then put his hand on her shoulder and she cried:

'*Please don't say anything! Just go to Cathy and leave me alone.*'

She emerged from the bedroom fifteen minutes later, smiling and looking as if she had stepped from a bandbox. Cathy was prodding at a boiled egg, staring into space. Mahoney looked up at Shelagh with a gaunt smile. 'Eat up!' she cried at Cathy. 'What about breakfast for you?' she said to him.

'Just coffee is enough, thanks.'

'Alice,' she called, 'bring the Nkosi more coffee. And get this lazybones to school!'

'I'll take her to school,' Mahoney said.

Shelagh took a gulp of half-warm coffee. 'Alice, the Nkosi will take Cathy to school. And now,' she smiled down at him, 'I really must dash, or I'll miss the drum.'

Mahoney stood up. 'The drum?'

'Yes, we don't have school bells these days, we have a drum. Rather quaint, don't you think?' She bent and kissed Cathy. 'Goodbye, darling – and hurry *up!*' She turned to Mahoney brightly: 'See me to the stairs ... .'

He walked with her to the front door. He closed it behind them. She turned to him brightly. He had never seen her so beautiful.

'Well . . .' she said, 'so long. It's been lovely seeing you again.' She kissed him briskly on the mouth.

'Goodbye, Shelagh.'

'Au revoir. I refuse to discuss goodbyes!' Then she fluttered her eyes tizzily. 'Why didn't we make love like that in England? You see, separations aren't such a dumb idea! All right . . .' She kissed her finger and put it on his mouth.

She turned and walked quickly down the open corridor. He stood watching her, his eyes burning. She was a beautiful woman. At the stairs she looked back and flashed him a smile. Then she was gone, in a swirl of skirt.

Mahoney leant against the doorway, eyes closed. He heard her car start. He dropped his head and felt the sob come up his throat.

But afterwards, when he had walked Cathy to school, and knelt, and hugged her and kissed her, and she turned out of his arms and run happily into the playground, and he had broken down and wept, he knew loud and clear that it was his baby that he was weeping for.

And, oh, he longed for Tana, to hold him and to tell him that she loved him.

CHAPTER 47

When you've been running around the bush for a few years like a dog on a tennis court getting your arse shot off by communists who chop the legs off old men and bayonet babies, and for years you've been working the rest of your arse off earning money you couldn't spend because your cowboy government you're getting shot up for won't let you take it out the country, and in the end you say to hell with the lot of you, a plague on both your houses, and you go to live in sunny England and you work your whole arse off and finally you're making money which no communist junglebum is going to take away, and everything's civilized, even if it is pissing with rain, and you settle down in the pub and read about how the war's going badly in Rhodesia, it's easy to say: I told you so, thank God I left. When you're flying around Africa and you're holed-up in some beat-up hotel and the streets are breaking up and nothing works any more, it's easy to say: see, this is what Rhodesia is going to be like after the Comrades win the war, and all because people didn't listen to me. And it's easy to wash your hands of Africa. When you're way down under in sunny Australia, with your beautiful woman you are head over heels in love with, and you know that nobody is going to slash back the forests, and when you're lying together in the big hot jaccuzzi bath, drinking champagne, and at last the

306

world is paying attention to your huge flying machine and getting excited, it's easy to say: home was never like this . . . And, by Christ, when you come back to your old home town, and now the blacks are boss and the shops are half empty and the newspapers are full of communist propaganda, and you daren't drive in the country at night because Enemies of the Masses are whooping it up, your old model farm has turned into a dustbowl and a cabinet minister starts punching a woman – then, by God, it's easy to say, to hell with Africa.

But when you're back in your old Africa, on a sentimental journey, and you've said goodbye to your child and you're driving through the bush in the early morning, the yellow grass tall and the mist hanging in the trees, and the sky so blue, and the road signs warn of elephant and the picannins wave to you like they always did, and the long afternoon shadows come, and the flaming sunsets, and there're the cricking of the insects and the smell of woodsmoke and the sound of the drums and you find yourself speaking in Chilapalapa and Shona again, without even thinking, then Africa gets you right here, right here in the heart, like it always did, and it's not so easy to say to hell with Africa any more. And Mahoney wanted to throw up his arms and shout to the people:

'Hey! – what the hell is this! How can you ruin a good country like this? Now just you listen to me!'

And although he had washed his hands of Africa, he had not, really, and maybe you never do, and somehow he just naturally felt he could shout and bully some sense back into these people, because he *knew* them – they were *his* people and they were *good* people, all they needed was enough people like him bullying some sense into them . . .

Every fifty miles he saw the sign, POLICE, in the middle of the bush, and he slowed down, pulse quickening. Sometimes there was a tank. There was usually a bus, African passengers milling everywhere, police searching through their bundles. But the black officers who came to his car were always polite. 'Good day, sir. We must search your car, please.' He thought, See what pleasant people they are? Then he looked at the soldiers, their machine-guns ready, inscrutable, and he felt his

307

flesh creep and he thought, Thank God I'm not ruled by you. But I warned them – these are the wages of losing a war . . .

And black . . . Driving through the little towns, eighty miles apart in the bush, which used to be white towns, prosperous: he did not see another white face. He stopped in Gweru for a beer. He used to come here on High Court Circuit in the old days, when it was called Gwelo. He walked slowly up the Main Street. It used to be a thriving town, the Victorian shops full and busy. He did not see one white face. There were posters of the new mayor, his mouth open, teeth crunching on an iron bar, with the caption 'I BITE'. Mahoney walked down to the Midlands Hotel for his beer. He stopped, and stared. The Midlands used to be a grand old hotel, half a block long, great pillars, a huge old dining-room with potted palms and ceiling fans and crisp-uniformed waiters: now it was all closed up, the windows dirty, and the entire street-level converted into bars with handpainted signs, each blaring out different music. He thought, How bloody sad . . . That Midlands Hotel summed it all up, what was going to happen to the whole country. And he just wanted to get the hell out of Rhodesia. Out of *Zimbabwe*.

He drove grimly out of town, and entered the vast flat dryness of Matabeleland, heading for Bulawayo, which means Place of Slaughter.

Politics, politics, everybody talking politics.

But it used to be politics with freedom of speech, politics yelled down the bar if you wanted to, *'Ian Smith and his cabinet are a bunch of cowboys!* if you wanted to. Now it was muttered politics, whispered with a glance over the shoulder to make sure the black barman could not hear.

'Trust nobody. There're spies everywhere.'

So my factory's got two big latrine blocks, both in good condition. One day I get to the factory and there's a strike. The Workers' Committee's yelling that they want drinking taps outside the latrine blocks. But the taps are perfectly hygienic, I said. Shut up, yells the Labour Officer, you are not allowed to speak! O.K., I said, so I'll give you taps elsewhere. So they yell at me they want it today! But it'll take a plumber a few days, I said. So they all start yelling, To*day*! – To*day*! . . . And the Labour Officer writes in his notebook, 'The Management forces us to drink from the toilets.' And the strike lasts two days. Now – how can I run a business like that? . . .

'Fools,' Mahoney sighed.

'Drop your voice,' he said.

So I had to see my bank manager and he says, I've got something to show you. He points and there's this black sitting, feet up, reading a newspaper. He's one of my tellers, he whispers. Why isn't he working? I said. Because, says the bank manager, that guy stole money from the till and he's just finished his jail sentence. But I'm not allowed to fire him. Now, can you imagine? Having a convicted thief working in a bank? But there's only one guy in the whole country who can fire anybody and that's the minister . . .

And look at our newspapers – and listen to our radio . . . Comrade This and Comrade That. The radio headlines read, Comrade Betty Chitimoyo won-i the Good Housekeeping Award-i today, the British won-i the Falklands war . . . In that order. Now, that's Zimbabwe culture for you. 'It isi six o'clock-i, Greenwich. Meantime, here isi the news . . .' And look at health. Now we have state-registered witchdoctors legally practising medicine! Wandering the hospital wards in all their gear, throwing the bones to find out what's wrong with you. Now, that's progress . . .

'You're kidding?' Mahoney said.

I am not. The whole country going to rat-shit, misgovernment at every turn. I used to think like you, that we should give the blacks the vote and accept a lowering of standards, but I can't accept downright misgovernment. Here's one instance: the country needs foreign exchange. To earn foreign exchange we must export. To export, our industrialists must import raw materials. To import they must pay with foreign exchange. Ah! says our government, but we're *short-i* of foreign exchange. But, says the industrialist, if you don't allow me foreign exchange then I can't manufacture enough, and I'll have to fire half my black workers! But, oh no, he's not allowed to do that either. But, says the manufacturer, I'll go bankrupt, then they'll *all* be out of a job! But, oh no, he can't fire anybody! The only person who can fire anybody is the Minister of Labour himself.

'Now, I ask you, with tears in my eyes . . .'

And look at education. Everybody reduced to the lowest common denominator. Sixteen-year-old black kids in the same class as nine-year-old whites. Look at the university. The government's decided the high failure rate amongst black students is because of 'cultural differences', so we must make university courses 'more relevant to Zimbabwe . . .'

More relevant? . . . My poor achin' ass!

So what's it going to be like in five years' time when even more whites have left and nothing works any more? How can I let my children grow up in a country like this?

'So what are you going to do?' Mahoney said.

What the bloody hell can I do? I can't get another job. I couldn't sell the business – just you go through the suburbs and see the empty houses, with swimming pools and tennis courts, and you can't sell them for a song! And I'm not allowed to take my money out, so how the hell *can* I go? But the kids *must* go. They can't grow up with a 'more relevant' Zimbabwe education, can they?

Politics, politics, the wages of sins.

'What about this Fifth Brigade?'

Oh Jesus, the Fifth Brigade. Talk in whispers about the Fifth Brigade. The Prime Minister's answer to the Matabele. And when he lets them loose, oh God . . .

Oh God, when will the world ever learn? *When* will they ever learn that democracy in Africa does not mean Democracy, that One Man One Vote means only One Man One Vote Once? *When* will the world ever learn that Africans cannot tolerate disagreement, that they don't understand about the Independence of the Judiciary, about the Rule of Law, about a Loyal Opposition – *that they simply don't understand*? . . .

Never? Not until the whole of Africa is a shambles, starving and bankrupt and diseased? Not until South Africa is overrun too, and the Russians patrol the Cape? Not until Suez is gone, Panama gone, the Cape route gone . . .

And Mahoney wanted to bellow to the skies:

And why did the white man never learn to give his black fellows their share of the sun and maybe all this would never have happened? . . .

CHAPTER 48

Two days later he stopped at the top of the great Zambesi escarpment. Way down there the mighty valley began, hot hard hills descending, in an endless jumble, going on for ever, mauve turning to mistiness, so vast you could not even see the mighty inland sea. Mahoney looked down over his valley, and, oh, it was his Africa, *his* valley, where it all began, and where it had ended.

'Hullo, Suzie,' he whispered. 'I'm back.'

His car wound down the escarpment, the hilltops lit by the setting sun, casting big shadows, the tall grass golden; there was elephant dung on the road, and then he saw elephants feeding, first a solitary bull, trunk stretching, then more, and more; and warthog, tails up, fleeing, and antelope leaping across the road in dozens, bounding, graceful bodies stretched out, and baboons scampering. The last sun was going, turning the sky riotously red, when he got the first glimpse of the great lake, dark blue between the hills.

It was dark when he got on to the familiar roads cut along the jagged lake-shore of frangipani and baobab and mopani trees, and the lake stretched on and on out there in the moonlight; then he glimpsed the lights of the fishing boats. It felt as if he was coming home. And he wished with all his heart that Tana was with him.

He did not immediately go to the *Noah's Ark*, nor to Suzie's grave. He drove to the Lakeview Hotel, to get a little drunk. That lovely Lakeview Hotel, where he used to hang out as a soldier when this country was still Rhodesia. Where the nurses used to come, and the girls who ran the casino tables and the secretaries and tourist guides and housewives and police wives and daughters, where they used to sing and dance and argue politics and hold post mortems on military tactics and cricket matches, and maybe did a little loving if you were lucky and just got a little drunker if you weren't because just thank God you were still alive. Mahoney walked into the hotel. The pretty receptionists were gone; there were black male receptionists. He walked into the bar.

It was all the same, the roof-beams and leaded windows; but the bar was almost empty. There were only two white men, talking quietly. And Mahoney felt like walking out again, for the sadness of it.

'Scotch, please.'

The black barman smiled apologetically. 'Ver' sorry, no Scotch today.'

'Why the hell not?'

'Foreign Exchange,' one white man said. 'No Scotch in the country.'

Mahoney sat drinking old tennis shoes brandy, waiting to get a little drunk. He said, 'Does it ever jump in here anymore?'

'No.' The man glanced over his shoulder. 'Those were the days.'

Mahoney said, 'Any army guys left up at the barracks?'

'All gone. Only blacks now.'

'Police?'

'All gone. Black, now.'

'Nurses?'

'All gone.'

It was so sad. A whole way of life gone. 'Do you remember Lofty Jackson?'

'Sure. Stopped a bullet.'

Mahoney stared. *Lofty dead?* . . . But Lofty was indestructible . . .

'And Monty Montgomery?'

'Dead.'

Oh, God! Both those guys had taught him all the soldiering he knew. They were marvellous soldiers . . .

'Do you remember Max Cummings the Selous Scout?'

'Sure. In South Africa, I believe.' The man looked over his shoulder. 'Better keep quiet about knowing Max.'

'Why?'

The man smiled. 'Who d'you think blew up the Air Force planes?'

Mahoney stared at him. Then shook his head in disbelief. 'Did you know Bomber Brown, the airman?'

'He's still in the Air Force.' He glanced over his shoulder. 'They still need white pilots, don't they? Any asshole can be a politician, even me, but aeroplanes crash.'

He smiled. 'Do you know the *Noah's Ark*?'

'Sure. Owned by some rich guy in England, why, want to buy her? The guy won't sell, a few people have tried. He used to be a Rhodesian, got smart, took the Chicken Run and got rich.'

The Chicken Run! The man said: 'You used to be stationed here?'

'For a while. Then I took the Chicken Run.'

He went out into the hot starry night. He did not want to go up to her grave yet. He drove slowly up to the dam-wall lookout.

It was completely quiet.

There it was, silvery in the moonlight: the mighty gorge, the home of Nyamayimini, the river god; the giant, curved wall stretching across it. High up on one side the great lake began, stretching on for hundreds of miles: and yawning below, on the other side, the river re-emerged from the turbines and swirled away, dark and invincible again, into the steep rock gorge.

He sat there, sipping brandy. This was where it all began . . . The big, brave days of Partnership, Equal Rights for all Civilized Men, partnership to beat the reckless Winds of Change; and we built this mighty dam, white hand clasped with black across the Zambesi . . . And, oh God, the heartbreak of the valley dying. Like all of Africa was dying. And now Rhodesia was dead and gone too, like that valley down there, a whole world gone, and now the Matabele were going to rise up against the Shona, and there was going to be yet another war, because not even black hand could be clasped with black

313

hand, and those big brave days of Partnership and this whole valley were in vain . . .

And maybe it was because he was beginning to get drunk, but the tears were running down his face.

The *Noah's Ark* lay fifty yards off the jetty, in the moonlight.

'Hullo, girl,' he whispered.

All the rowing boats were chained up. He took off his shirt, wrapped it round the brandy bottle, and tied the bundle round his neck. He left his shoes on the jetty. He lowered himself into the cool Zambesi water, and started swimming. Halfway there he remembered the danger of crocodiles. He reached and gripped the gunnel of the *Ark*. 'Hullo, baby,' he said. He swung up one leg, and heaved himself aboard, grunting.

He sat on the gunnel, getting his breath back. The night air was warm and the taste of the water on his lips was something he hadn't known for many years, real water.

'Suzie?' he said.

But Suzie did not answer.

He sat there, remembering the sun beating down out of the mercilessly blue sky, making this steel deck too hot to touch, the treetops sticking up above the water, the hundreds of islands being swallowed up, the starving animals retreating, retreating, eating even the drowning trees. And he tried to tell her what it was like, seeing Africa dying, the heartbreak of it; how they swam ashore and tried to drive the animals into the water to make them swim while they still had strength, and how they had to catch the ones that wouldn't . . . He tried to tell her about the dust and the terror and the toothclenched sweat, and the blood. And herding the swimming ones, trying to head them off from another drowning island and on, *on*, towards the misty horizon way, way over there; and trying to pull the drowning ones out of the water. He tried to tell her what it was like to herd a drowning elephant, so huge that there was no way you could help it except by goading it on, and on, like a submarine, just its trunk-tip sticking up like a periscope, gushing her exhausted breath like a whale, her hooves weakly churning . . .

'Who're you telling this to,' Suzie smiled, 'me or Tana?'

And he wanted to laugh, because she had come back! 'To both of you!'

She smiled, 'And why are you unhappy?'

He wanted to weep it: 'Because those were marvellous days, Suzie! Those were big brave days of Partnership when I was young and strong, and I did it, I helped save those animals, Samson and I, we helped save a little bit of Africa, Partnership has gone to hell but at least I did that! . . .'

'And what are you going to do now?' Suzie smiled. And he wanted to spread his arms to the African stars, but Suzie said: 'Tana's rich and can save the animals without you. What *else* are you going to do?'

'What do you mean?

She smiled.

'You're saying this, Joseph, not me. I don't exist. Why were you weeping when you looked down on the valley, at the dam wall? Because your Africa is dying? Because you have washed your hands of her, all over again? Isn't that why you were weeping? Are you truly glad with all your heart that you washed your hands of Africa long ago and made a new life for yourself? Oh, you'll ply your airships here and carry their communist cargo and make a fortune in the process, but you won't hold her hand any more. Is that what you were weeping about? Is that all you killed for? Is that all that's left, is that all you're good for now, making money? Is that all Samson died for, swinging with a broken neck at the end of a rope? Is that what all the blood was shed for, all those people out there in the bush? You wanted to help them, illiterate, superstitious people just scratching a living from the soil with no way out except to the hopeless squalor and poverty of the towns. Is that all that's left of the big brave days of this valley? The night before they hanged him, Samson said, "And think of the valley, Nkosi." Is that all he meant, Joseph? Can you simply wash your hands, of all that blood?'

And Mahoney dropped his head in his hands.

PART 8

PART 8

CHAPTER 49

There were no moons that autumn, no sunsets, just the weeping English rain, dripping off the cottage eaves, drumming on the cavernous roofs of Cardington. The only time Mahoney saw the sun was when he broke through ten thousand feet or so. But that autumn Mahoney did not mind the bloody English weather; he did not mind the worry about money for his airship that Malcolm Todd was building oh so slowly, because he was not only so busy hauling cargo to pay for it, he was also in love.

Twice a week they spoke by telephone; twice a week they received letters from each other. He wrote:

'I hear that a brand new airship construction company is being formed, called Airship Industries – a very reputable crowd this time. I am delighted that lighter than air flight is catching on at last – and not worried about the competition because we're so far ahead of the game. Dolores has so much cargo banked up for old Redcoat we have to do hand-writing exercises, lie through our teeth, we're even chartering extra planes. If it weren't for the airship we'd buy two more Canadairs. Meanwhile there are a thousand-and-one more things to work out for the airship: what routes for the airworthiness trials, what charts, what permissions to seek from which governments, what facilities en route. The C.A.A. want to see her perform through a range of climates, from European winter to equatorial sunshine, but nobody can tell me how many hours or miles will satisfy them. How many life-rafts in case we ditch at sea? Fire-fighting extinguishers. Medical equipment. Victualling. How many people can we carry on trials, and for what reason? I am dealing by telephone with a faceless wonder at the C.A.A. called Perry who sounds a real self-important Cockney. He has decreed that no press or television will be allowed aboard, which is a hell of a blow because it would have been marvellous publicity – only observers accredited from governments, and "serious potential customers". But,

319

fear not, I have insisted that one member of Redcoat staff accompany us as "chronicler and clerical factotum", which thankfully appealed to his bureaucratese. How does that grab you, my beautiful, diesel-driven Australian factotum? Please accept in triplicate.

'After much argument, we have arrived at a name. She is to be called *Rainbow*, and her colours are to be all those, painted in a curve, sweeping up from her bows down to her stern.'

She wrote:

'I accept, I accept, I accept, and what a wonderful name for her, and oh I'm so happy, Mahoney!

'Everything is going smoothly except for this severe case of the hots I've got. I am so sure that everything will be organized here by mid-November that even today I booked my plane seat. Better reschedule your life to allow a week in bed starting seven p.m. 15 November. The C.A.A. today verbally assured me that I'll get permission for the Antarctic flights; we're waiting for written confirmation from the Americans that their base down there at McMurdo will co-operate. The only sticking point is altitude: the C.A.A. officially wants us to stay at sixteen thousand feet all the way, even across the Ross Ice Shelf, which is ridiculously high for sightseeing, though they concede unofficially that two thousand feet would be perfectly safe. Bloody bureaucracy. Meanwhile, the travel agencies are cranked up, our advertising material all done. The inaugural flight is 17 December, but it'll have to go without me as I'll be otherwise employed as a clerical fucktotum. Vader is being his usual pain-in-the-arse. Boy, is he driving a hard bargain on chartering his miserable DC 10 to me, hoping I'll lose so much money I'll quit. He is very depressed about me going to England "just to sleep with that crazy young man". He morosely sends his regards. Actually, for all his hang-dog expression, he is doing sterling spadework for you amongst his cronies in Canberra. Don't be surprised if he turns up at Cardington one day with a delegation of beat-up beer-swigging Aussie politicians with corks dangling from their hats . . .'

*

320

The telephone ringing woke him. 'Hullo,' he muttered.

'Get that woman out of my bed!'

'*Hullo!*' he shouted.

'Have you kicked her out?'

'Yes! There she goes, limping. How *are* you?'

'Next time, break her leg. Oh, Mahoney, I miss you!'

'I miss you too. Where are you?'

'At the office, sorting things out for my imminent departure, hiring, firing, throwing my weight around. We expect a bumper carrot crop. How's that for a clerical factotum? Only five weeks to go, Mahoney . . .' She sighed. 'How's the *Rainbow*?'

'I was out there yesterday. He's driving me mad, but says he's on schedule. Roll-out of the hangar is 15 December.'

'Is that official?'

'The C.A.A. were there but nothing can be official until she's fully inflated and the engines fully tested inside the hangar. That's weeks away yet. It's mostly electrical now.' He added, 'I've heard from that big American, Tank O'Sullivan. He's coming on the trials as a customer! And the Ugandan Government is sending two people. Chinese Embassy say they're considering.'

'Great! Anything from the Zimbabwe Government yet?'

'No, only a letter from my lawyer pal, saying they're "considering".'

'They'll all come. And of course Vader will be there, boots and all, unofficially representing the entire goddamn Commonwealth of Australia. Oh darling, it's so exciting!' She added, 'But must Vader come on my honeymoon?'

He smiled, 'It won't be much of a honeymoon, I'm afraid.'

'Listen, the way I feel I can make a honeymoon on a short, crowded bus-ride. By the way, he bought a sewerage farm yesterday.'

'A *sewerage* farm?'

'Yep. And not just a farm, a *factory* that makes sewerage plant and equipment. He's going to smother Asia in sewerage plants.'

'But what does he know about sewerage?'

'He talks a lot of it and he can read a balance sheet. He says

321

to tell you he's got a surprise for you. And a funny story.'

'A surprise?'

'He's very pleased with himself about something. Don't be surprised if he shows up suddenly. *Just get rid of him before I arrive, Mahoney . . .*'

Then one day, just as they were boarding the Canadair, Dolores came running across the tarmac through the rain, grinning all over her wet face, waving a letter.

'Get a load of this!' she cried, clattering up the ladder.

It was a hand-written letter from his lawyer, Peter Hetherington. Mahoney read aloud: '"Dear Joe, I'll be writing at length when the decision is formalized, but meantime I want you to know that the Prime Minister today told me that he will send two observers on your forthcoming airworthiness trials. Furthermore he wants his lawyers to discuss with me the terms under which the Zimbabwe Govt might enter into a contract with your company, if the trials are satisfactory, to lease from you, with an option to buy –'

'*Yahoo!*' Pomeroy screamed.

'– up to *four airships*!' Mahoney shouted joyfully.

Two hours later, over the Mediterranean, the telephone chimed and the Berna operator said, 'We're calling your party in Australia now.'

'Hullo?' she said sleepily.

'Kick that man out of my bed and get an earful of this, beauty!'

'Hullo, darling!' she cried.

He said: 'The Zimbabwe Government is interested in leasing and or buying four airships! . . .'

'*Oh, Mahoney!*' she breathed.

'Provided we hold part of our trials in Zimbabwe, to demonstrate the ship's capability to work in her climate.'

'Oh, *Mahoney*! . . .'

*

'*Malcolm!*' Mahoney yelled. '*When will you be finished?*'

From somewhere in the cavernous gloom: '*When I am done! Go fly your aeroplanes.*'

'*But are you still on schedule?*'

'*How should I know, dammit! I've never built one of these before!*'

The next time he went to Cardington he heard a small aeroplane. He went out into the drizzle. A little bi-wing craft was buzzing round the airfield, coming in to land, followed by a helicopter. It touched down with a bump and came churning towards him. It had two men in it. One got out, wearing goggles and a leather helmet, and started striding lankily towards him. He had a long scarf wrapped dashingly around his neck and he was beaming.

'Hullo, young man, I have a surprise for you!'

'Erling Thoren!' Mahoney cried.

The old man slung an arm around his shoulder and led him briskly. 'Now, no arguments, because if you're sleeping with my crazy daughter I cannot afford to see you bankrupt, you know. So this' – he stopped and waved his hand like a show-man, immensely pleased with himself – 'is my insurance!'

Mahoney stared at the little aircraft.

'*This,*' the old man hugged his shoulder, 'is an old Curtiss XF9C-2 fighter, completely refurbished – the same as the Americans used in their old airship carriers! I had a hell of a job finding one. And look' – he pointed at a bar hooped over the cockpit – 'an identical copy of what the Americans used for hooking up to the airship in flight! And look!' He pointed proudly at the machine-guns.

Mahoney was overwhelmed. 'Mr Thoren . . .' he began.

'No arguments!' the old man grinned. 'You must present your airship as a military vehicle! This aeroplane is not a Harrier, but your ship can carry Harriers too. It's just a question of demonstrating something, you know!'

'Mr Thoren . . .'

'Yes, you are very grateful, but what else does an old man have to worry about except his crazy daughter?' He said earnestly: 'You must sell your ship as a military vehicle – I'm con*vinced* of it.'

323

'I will,' Mahoney grinned, and he loved the crazy old man.

'You think I am crazy, but I am not. And I will tell you something else.' He started striding towards the helicopter. 'Your friend Mr Weston is in Libya, building airships for Mr Kaddafi.'

Mahoney walked beside him, bemused. 'How do you know this? . . .'

The old man's eyes twinkled. He was delighted with himself. 'Ask no questions! Just make my daughter happy, young man!'

He strode away joyfully towards the helicopter.

CHAPTER 50

Mahoney was overwhelmed by the gift, Malcolm was over-joyed, the Admiral was over the moon.

'Young fella, you and Lovelock better start practising! I'll write to the Zimbabweans and tell 'em – this'll knock 'em dead.'

'Admiral.' Mahoney held up a hand. 'I'm not a stunt pilot, I don't even like flying. And Lovelock cannot leave the ship once she's airborne; he's our only experienced airshipman.'

'Then I'll get Air Marshal Thompson to send a couple of his crackerjack pilots over!'

'Admiral. That airship is worth millions of pounds. I'm not about to screw it up with tricky flying stunts we know nothing about.'

The Admiral glowered. 'Are you looking a gift-horse in the mouth?'

'No, dammit! Of course we're taking it with us to show them, but right now we haven't even flown the airship yet.'

'But Lovelock says it'll be dead easy!'

'And I know that Lovelock has not yet tumbled to the fact that he is mortal. Lovelock has solid bone between his ears, he hasn't even heard of the laws of gravity. He thinks he's an angel, and he certainly does not understand money and how much I'll lose if he knocks a hole in the hull.'

'Then I'll phone the American Navy, old Admiral Morely, and tell him to look smart and send one of his ace navy fliers along. I've even arranged ammo for the thing!'

'Ammu*nition*?'

'Of course, you can't demonstrate a warplane without having some of the real thing! Hell of a stunt, tickle 'em pink!'

'Admiral,' Mahoney sighed, 'I don't want to know from which of your military buddies you purloined ammunition; but we are a *civilian* aircraft.'

'You sound like the bloody C.A.A., young fella! A perfect pain in the rectum!' The Admiral stomped away. The Admiral stomped back. He held up a finger. '"There is a tide in the affairs of men, which, taken at the flood . . ."' He stomped away.

Two days later he telephoned, wreathed in smiles.

'Got a signal back from Admiral Morley! He's sending his crackerjack pilot, fella called Dwight J. Perkins the Third!'

Mahoney said, 'Excellent.'

'Is that *all*?' The Admiral glowered. What I want to know is . . .'

'The answer is, *when* we know what we're doing.'

Mahoney did not fly for the next ten days: he worked solidly on the arrangements for the trials. He had to seek permission from several countries to fly through their airspace, arrange emergency refuelling facilities and mooring space in each. The airship was to carry an emergency mooring mast, plus gear for anchoring it. Mahoney did not yet know his final route to Zimbabwe as he had not yet heard from a number of African governments, so he had to work plenty of alternatives, telex all the authorities in each. Half did not reply because they did not know what he was talking about. He sent more telexes.

The final number of observers was not yet known, so neither was the number of cabin units to be built, the number of sheets, towels, crockery sets, chairs, toilet rolls. The victualling was not yet known, so neither was the final take-off weight, optimum altitudes over which sectors of which alternative routes, fuel weights against ballast requirements. Mahoney worked out a large number of permutations, then checked them with Lovelock. He was vastly impressed, and relieved. Lovelock, who appeared not to have a brain in his head, juggled esoteric formulae as casually as a computer. Mahoney had delegated responsibility for the launching ceremony to the Admiral, to get the old sailor out of his hair; but the Admiral felt he was responsible for everything.

'I say, young fella, here's some letters I want you to sign! Telling these governments to buck up their ideas!'

'Which governments?' Mahoney said warily. He read the letters, while the Admiral stood over him.

'Admiral, you can't talk like that to cabinet ministers. Leave this to me.'

'Well, *when* will you do it, young fella? That mast for Zimbabwe must be sent in plenty of time. I've told Malcolm to get on with it but he's such an old gas-bag! Everything must be ship-shape!'

'Admiral, don't disturb Malcolm. I've written to my lawyer about the Zimbabwe army engineers helping erect the mast.'

'Oh very well. But I need to know how many chairs we need for the marquee on launching day.'

'We're having a *tent*?'

'Of course. It may be pissing with rain. Air Marshal Thompson has lent me his RAF band, though I'd prefer the Navy one. But can't look a gift-horse in the mouth, like *some* people I know! I've chosen "Red Sails in the Sunset" and "Speed Bonny Boat".'

Mahoney thought. 'What about "Rule Britannia"? And "When The Saints Come Marching In"?'

The Admiral suddenly smiled at this glimmer of intelligence. 'Excellent, young fella, good to have you aboard!'

The next day he telephoned, beaming smugly.

'I say, young fella, are you seated?'

'Sitting?' Mahoney queried.

'Better grab a pew, old man, while you hear this . . .' He puffed on his cigar. 'I', he said, 'unofficially approached an old chum of mine who's got a contact or two in Buck House . . .'

'Buckingham *Palace*? . . .' Mahoney echoed.

'And I have it on pretty lofty authority that . . . *Wait* for it! . . . *If* we write a nice letter – *through* the proper channels – old Liz her*self* may feel kindly disposed to launching the *Rainbow*!'

'The *Queen*?' Mahoney cried joyously.

And then at last the glorious count-down began.

'Ten days, Mahoney – start counting,' she sang.

'When I come back from Accra it'll be only seven,' he grinned.

'Better get fit. I've got an awful lot of hard work for you . . . Oh, Mahoney,' she swooned, 'I'm wet through for you.'

'The guys in Berna', he grinned, 'are all huddled round this hook-up.'

'Oh, let them have a good time, I'm so happy . . . Mahoney? I really love you.'

On the fifth day she called him: 'Mahoney, the piss-up's begun.'

'Hullo, beauty! What?'

'The office piss-up. My farewell. Can't you hear it? They're singing "For he's a jolly good fellow". That's you. For ridding them of me.'

He grinned. 'I thought Friday was your last office day.'

'I brought it forward, I couldn't bear the suspense. Mahoney, where are you?'

'We're on the way to Athens. We'll be home tomorrow.'

'For God's sake fly carefully.' She paused. 'Mahoney? . . . I'm scared.'

He laughed: 'Why?'

She puffed on her cigarette. 'I've made such a big deal of this. Appointing managers, and so on. Everybody knows. Supposing you don't love me?'

He laughed. 'But I do!'

She pulled on her cigarette. 'I'm being a girl about this, aren't I? . . . I'm flying up to the station tomorrow.'

He sighed. 'I don't like you flying that aeroplane alone.'

'Hark who's talking. I must see to the animals. Mahoney?'

'Yes?'

She hesitated. Then: 'You sure about Shelagh?'

He smiled. 'Quite sure.'

'But supposing she takes it into her head to come back?'

He said: 'She won't. If she does, it'll be to visit her parents.'

'*And* you?'

'She can't visit me with you in residence, can she?'

'Women can change their minds when they see another woman's taken over.'

He smiled. 'I know Shelagh. She won't.'

She said: 'But you haven't told her.'

'You know why.' He smiled. 'In five days you'll be living in England with me. Please be happy.'

'Oh I *am*! I'm just scared witless.'

He smiled, 'Well, here's something to cheer you up . . .' He told her.

'*The Queen!*' she shrieked.

Then, when he got back to the cottage the following afternoon, there was a letter waiting for him. It had been posted in London the day before, and the address was in Shelagh's handwriting.

CHAPTER 51

He stared at the envelope, his heart hammering. Posted in London? . . . *Oh God, no* . . . He tore it open feverishly, and his heart sank. It began 'Darling . . .' He speed-read the first lines. Then closed his eyes in relief. It had not been posted in London by Shelagh.

He frowned. It was a short, mysterious letter, as if he was meant to read between the lines. 'Sorry to put this on you, but this is to tell you that you can trust Jake Jefferson on my behalf, so please telephone him urgently at . . .'

Mahoney took a deep breath. Jake Jefferson? . . . He felt very uneasy about this. A voice from his guilty past. But of course he had to phone him. He couldn't just ignore the man.

He walked to the kitchen, and poured himself a whisky before dialling the number. He was not disappointed to be answered by an answer-machine. He left a message on it.

*

328

They both felt awkward. Mahoney had never felt comfortable in the man's company, though he liked and respected him; and Jefferson looked thoroughly uncomfortable too. He tried to look Mahoney in the eye, but kept speaking to the wall just above his head.

'I'm sorry to be troubling you with this – and if you can't help I'll quite understand. But . . . I believe you owe Shelagh quite a bit of money?'

Mahoney nodded warily. So this was what it was about. 'True. I'm buying her shares in Redcoat from her.'

Jefferson said, 'I didn't know that detail. However, what she and I suggest – *if* you're agreeable, of course – is that maybe you could pay me some of that money in pounds, and then I'll pay her the equivalent in Rhodesian dollars. That's what her letter meant. It's her authorization to you. She was scared it might fall into the wrong hands, because, of course, it's illegal.' He added hastily: 'I assure you, I've got money in Rhodesia, but I'm not allowed to take any out of the country.'

Mahoney sighed. He genuinely wanted to help the man – he was a nice guy and he felt hellish guilty about him. He shifted.

'Jake, I was in the same predicament myself once.' He massaged his brow. 'And as you probably know, I'm building this airship. So until that's working for me, I'm living on massive bank overdrafts.'

'I understand,' Jefferson murmured, embarrassed.

'No, no,' Mahoney said, 'I'll help you, I'm just explaining my position.' He said uncomfortably: 'How much would you need?'

'I'll give you an attractive rate of exchange – two Zimbabwe dollars fifty to the pound, that's almost double.'

'Jake, I don't want to make a profit out of you.'

The man said earnestly, 'But you'll be doing me such a kindness and you're strapped for cash yourself.' He added uneasily: 'I was hoping for something like ten thousand pounds – but of course . . .'

Mahoney groaned inwardly. He owed Shelagh over ten

times that amount, but right now ten thousand quid was a fortune.

'Jake, how urgent is this?'

Jefferson said, 'Of course, I'd be grateful for even a few hundred pounds, to tide me over whilst I'm in London.'

'Of course I could let you have, say, three hundred pounds, immediately. But . . . um . . . would you tell me what you need the rest for?'

Jefferson sat forward on the hard chair. 'Well, two things, really . . . The first is . . .' He stopped. 'I've retired early from the police. I just can't live in Zimbabwe any more.' He sighed. 'However, I have the opportunity to team up with a couple of ex-Rhodesian police and army chaps and start up a security firm in Switzerland. You know, security services, industrial investigation, and so on.' He smiled bleakly. 'What else is an ex-cop good for? And, of course, I need some capital for that venture.' He added, 'These chaps know their stuff after seven years of undercover war and we've got a lot of – er – international connections.'

Mahoney nodded. 'Interesting.'

'Very. We also believe it will be very lucrative. But the most important reason is my son.'

Mahoney felt his pulse trip. 'Sean?' he said.

Jefferson took a breath. 'He's got to get out of Zimbabwe, for his education, Joe. The standards now are just not good enough . . . Almost everybody is reduced to the pace of the African children. And Sean really has a first class brain.' Mahoney found himself glowing with pride. Jefferson smiled weakly: 'I know every father thinks his son is wonderful, but Sean really is extremely bright. And excellent at sport. So, I've brought him over here to look for a good school.'

'Sean's in *England*?' Mahoney exclaimed.

'As a matter of fact he's right outside now, in the car.'

'Sean's *here*?' Mahoney cried. 'Well, bring him in!'

'Shall I?' Jefferson said, pleased.

'Of course!' He added, trying to explain his pleasure, 'Good heavens, I always thought he was a fine boy!'

'Oh, he is,' Jefferson smiled proudly. 'I'll fetch him.'

Mahoney wanted to hurry outside with Jefferson, but he

made himself wait. His face felt flushed. Jefferson came back, smiling, Sean following. 'Sean, you remember Mr Mahoney, the lawyer?'

'*Hullo, Sean!*' Mahoney shook hands, beaming, trying not to stare. He felt overwhelmed, by emotion and pride. He was a strapping fourteen-year-old, already almost as tall as Mahoney, clean-cut and good-looking. And, God, Mahoney could see Suzie in that face – and himself. 'How nice to see you, Sean! The last time was at Kariba, six or seven years ago. You were going fishing, remember?'

'Yes, I think so, sir.'

Mahoney beamed. 'Your father tells me you're top of the class!'

'Well, yes,' the lad replied, a little embarrassed.

'And', Mahoney demanded happily, 'what'll you do when you finish school?'

'Well, either law, sir, or the Royal Air Force,' Sean smiled.

'The law!' Mahoney said enthusiastically. 'It's a grand profession, if you set your mind to it. Which I never did,' he added.

'But you're a Q.C., sir.'

Mahoney was taken aback that he knew. 'Well, that was a bit of an industrial accident.' He went on: 'Don't go into the Air Force.'

'But you're an airman too, sir,' the boy smiled.

'Another accident,' Mahoney grinned. Jefferson smiled.

'He's been avidly following the news of your airship – and he's got keen on aeroplanes recently.'

'Has he?' Mahoney grinned. He took a breath. He said: 'Well, Sean, when you're at boarding school here, and you get weekends out – if you can't get to your father – you'd be very welcome to come to me, and maybe you'd like a few trips in my 'planes, see how you like them – would you enjoy that?'

'Oh, *would* I! . . .' Sean said enthusiastically.

Jefferson smiled. 'That's very kind of you, Joe. It wouldn't be till next September, of course, when the new school year starts.'

He loved the lad and longed to talk and talk with him. Mahoney sat back, happy, and a little confused. He looked at

331

Jefferson, then said to the boy: 'Sean, would you leave your father and me alone a moment?'

'Of course.' He stood up, and offered his hand. 'Goodbye, sir.'

Mahoney stood. 'I hope to see a lot of you, Sean.'

He sat down again, in a confusion of happiness and relief. It was absolutely clear what he had to do. No way could he refuse to help with his wonderful son's education. He said, 'Yes, Jake. I can swing ten thousand pounds with my bank manager.'

'Joe, are you *sure*? I'd hate to see—'

'I'll be out of the woods as soon as the airship's flying.'

Jefferson said earnestly, 'Joe, if you're paying interest on an overdraft, I insist on giving you double the official exchange rate.'

Mahoney said: 'No. All I'm doing is paying my part of my debt to Shelagh through you.' He pulled open the drawer, took out the company cheque book. He began to write a cheque for ten thousand pounds, a little shakily.

Jefferson said, 'I'm deeply indebted to you, and I'll pay Shelagh the Zimbabwe dollars immediately.'

'O.K.' Mahoney signed, then pressed the office intercom. 'Dolores, please come in and countersign a cheque.'

'Joe?' Jefferson said. 'Will you come to lunch with Sean and me?'

Mahoney could not have borne it right now. 'No, thanks, I'm flying tonight, and you should save your money.'

Dolores came in. Her eyes flickered at the amount and she shot Mahoney a glance. He said, 'Mr Jefferson is doing some security work for us.'

'I see.' Dolores signed, smiled briskly, and left.

Jefferson said, 'If I ever *can* do any security work for you – free of charge, Joe.'

Mahoney smiled guiltily. 'You'll never get rich that way, Jake.' He added, 'I'll be solvent again soon. Then I'll be able to repay Shelagh much more – through you, if you still need it.'

'That would be wonderful!'

He heard himself say, 'And meanwhile, if there's a problem

with . . . school fees, for example – well, let me know, and maybe I can help . . .'

After Jefferson left, a very happy man, Dolores came in.

'What was all that about?'

He smiled. 'Exchange control problem. I owe money to Shelagh.'

Dolores said: 'Jake Jefferson? . . . Wasn't he your Suzie's husband?'

'Yes,' Mahoney smiled.

'Ten thousand quid? That's a lot of money for us right now, Joe.'

'Yes, I'll repay Redcoat.'

Dolores looked at him quizzically. 'Amazing,' she said. 'That son of his. I've never seen such a resemblance between two people in my life as between you and that boy.'

'Really?' And Mahoney wanted to laugh and spread his arms wide. *His son was coming to England! And next week Tana was coming to England!*

CHAPTER 52

At last the day dawned.

He was up till late, working on the latest arrangements for the airworthiness trials, to have it out of the way. At two a.m. he threw himself on his bed, very tired and very happy.

At dawn he was wide-awake. He showered, got dressed. He straightened the duvet, kicked his laundry into the wardrobe. He washed the week's dishes. He drove down the muddy lane to Redcoat House. But he could not work.

'For heaven's sake go and have a drink, Romeo!' Dolores said.

'And a valium sandwich,' Nancy said. 'And tie your kangaroo down, sport.'

At eleven o'clock he gave up and went to The Rabbit for the first time in weeks, and he was laughing inside.

'Hullo, stranger. Today's the big day your boomerang comes back,' Danish Erika said. 'I hope it hits you on the head!'

Mahoney grabbed the soda syphon and squirted it at her. She fled down the bar, laughing.

He got to Heathrow Airport two hours early, repaired to the bar, and just gave himself up to the excitement of waiting for her.

At four o'clock he stood at the windows, trying to listen to the mumbling of the tannoy, watching the grey eastern sky. Every minute a dot appeared.

'Qantas Airways announce the arrival . . .'

He hurried downstairs, got a place amongst the horde against the barrier. An interminable half-hour passed. There was a steady flow of passengers from all over the world. Forty minutes. Any minute now. Forty-five. A lot of black people were flooding through now. It was now fifty-five minutes since her plane had landed. Mahoney felt panic rise. One hour. He knew she had changed her mind. As he turned to hurry to the Qantas desk she yelled:

'*Mahoney!*'

She burst through the customs door, waving frantically, then disappeared back inside. He started towards her against the tide of passengers, grinning. She reappeared pushing a laden trolley, followed by a porter, a smile all over her lovely face. '*Tana!*' And she abandoned her trolley and came running, dodging, long hair bouncing, arms wide. He pushed his way towards her, laughing.

The car rocked to a stop outside the cottage, they flung open the doors. She left everything in the car, scrambled out, and dashed through the rain. He rammed the key into the lock, kicked the front door open, then scooped her up in his arms. She clung, her wide mouth laughing into his.

He carried her over the threshold, dripping, bumping into the doorway, down the passage, bumping into the next doorway, laughing with the joy of each other, across the living-room, tramping mud, her fingers tearing at his collar. He put her down at the staircase, and she ripped off his tie. She backed off, kicked one leg and her first high heel flew, then the other. She whipped her blouse over her head and it went sailing across the room. She began to walk backwards up the staircase, fingers plucking at her skirt, hair hanging rakishly over one eye. He tore off his shirt and advanced on her up the stairs. Her skirt fell in a heap, she retreated upwards in her stockings and suspenders, grinning; he peeled off his socks, hopping first on one leg, then the other – then she turned and ran for the bedroom. He bounded up the stairs after her, as she took a running dive at the bed. She landed in a wildly erotic crash of arms and legs outflung, her hair all over the pillow, and he dived on to the bed beside her, took her in his joyful arms, and she laughed:

'Oh I'm so happy . . .'

CHAPTER 53

He had used all his flying hours for November; legally he could not do any work whatsoever, and that was just fine. It rained all the time; that was fine too. 'Mahoney, I don't intend getting out of bed anyway.'

Occasionally Dolores telephoned for instructions, but there was nothing much for him to do. All his airship work he had in the cottage, and he had gone as far as he could on that. They got up late, and spent a long time in the bath together. They talked a great deal, laughed even more. After a long breakfast he'd do a little work, telephoning the bank, telephoning Malcolm. Then it was lovely to have nothing to do except be with each other.

Once they drove up to London for lunch. The shops were beautiful, tarted up for Christmas. 'Oh, the clothes in this town, Mahoney!' Normally he hated shopping, but it was great fun doing it with her; it was lovely to walk hand in hand down the crowded streets with his tall, beautiful woman, in love with the world, people envying them their happiness, lovely to sit in the salons while she disappeared into changing rooms and came swirling out in some creation, making her parade a

335

bit. It was sexy to be called into the cubicle, and there she was in her underwear, holding a dress up against herself, saying, 'How does this grab you?'

And he wanted to grab *her*, then and there. Oh, it was great to be Joe Mahoney, six million pounds in debt, the man to bring back the airship which was going to make him a multimillionaire. And oh, what he was going to do with it! Dress his woman in all the gear, from Dior to St Laurant to Fredericks of Hollywood – and he was going to dress himself decently too, for the first time in his life. Everything of the best, goddamnit – that's how she made him feel.

Twice they drove up to Cardington. He had been sick to death of Cardington, worried to death by Cardington, haunted by Cardington, but now he saw it through her shining eyes again, and he was in love with Cardington all over again. The gigantic beauty of his ship! The vast shininess of her sweeping up!

'Oh, *Mahoney* . . . And her *colours*! . . .'

All the colours of the rainbow swept in a crescent from her nose to her tail in a gleaming swathe: violet, indigo, blue, green, yellow, orange, red. Tana flung her arms wide, a tiny figure under the towering nose:

'*I've got a man who's not scared to build something this big!*'

And he was filled with pride at his creation. '*Mal-colm,*' he bellowed.

From somewhere faraway: 'Go away! . . .'

It was two weeks since he had seen it, and he was delighted. The foremost part of the upper hold had been transformed into the saloon. An ornate bar stood against the bulkhead, a carpenter still working on it. A blue fitted carpet was in place.

'All "quick-change",' Malcolm beamed. 'This can be dismantled in a few hours and converted back into cargo space.'

'It's beautiful!' she exclaimed. 'The *view* we're going to have!'

Panels of bulkhead had been replaced with big glass windows. Malcolm led them to the aft bulkhead, flung open a door. A wide alleyway led off to another doorway. A dozen doors led off each side. He opened the nearest.

It was a large cabin, with a big window. It had two wide

bunks, a sofa, dressing table, washbasin, wardrobe. The furniture was dark blue velvet, bulkheads were oak panelled, the lamps were ornately old fashioned. It was spacious, luxurious.

'It's *marvellous*, Malcolm!' Mahoney said, delighted.

She sat on the sofa in wonder. 'But the *cost*?'

'Not so much. All this is "quick-change" too.' Malcolm tapped the bulkhead. 'Fibre-glass panels, this oak is just a thin veneer. They can be disassembled for cargo purposes. Or, we can make the cabins larger or smaller by moving the bulkheads. We've made them large, to impress our customers.'

'I'm delighted, Malcolm,' Mahoney said.

Malcolm led them halfway down the corridor. 'Bathrooms.'

There was a row of shower cubicles, washbasins, two bathtubs, all in cream. 'Another bathroom opposite. Toilets next door. Also, the cabins could be fitted with their own bathroom if the passenger wants it. We're plumbed for it.'

'It all looks so permanent. What's through that end door?'

Malcolm led them down the corridor, opened the end door. On to blackness. He flicked a switch and it lit up. Emptiness. Only the hold going on and on, like a tunnel. 'We've only put in enough accommodation for these trials. But when necessary, all this can be quick-changed into cabins and promenade deck, all the way down to the end.'

'Amazing,' she breathed. Then, 'May I ask a favour?'

'Anything,' Malcolm beamed.

'Can you put Vader's cabin right down at the tail?'

One weekend they went up to London to see a show. Thorens owned an apartment for visiting firemen, in Lower Regent Street. It was a grand old building, with red-carpeted staircases, gilded elevator, high ceilings, within sight of St James's Palace. 'Very nice neighbours,' Mahoney mused. They spent two happy nights there, but on Sunday morning they just wanted to go back to their own cottage. Sometimes they went out for a drink, and that was lovely too, sitting in the pretty English pubs, the beams low and the fire in the grate, drinking wine and eating bangers and mash; the locals all fell in love with Tana because she was beautiful and laughed and joked with them. But it was even better coming back to the cottage, the smoke curling up the chimney.

'I want to look at that atlas again.'

She opened it on the rug in front of the fire. She traced her finger slowly across the Mediterranean.

'The Greek Islands . . . Oh, can you imagine it? Sailing along at one thousand feet? . . . Those turquoise waters and white coves?' She looked at him with shining eyes. 'Then the Holy Land . . . Galilee. Jerusalem . . .' She sighed happily. 'Then the Nile . . . Floating just above the Pyramids in the moonlight . . . Oh, you're a genius, Mahoney. To bring back this golden age of travel.'

He smiled, 'Malcolm's a genius.'

'Yes. But you're the man who had the *vision*. When nobody would believe in it. Even I thought you were crazy, even when I was absolutely cock-struck, as us Aussie-tarts say, and sending you mushrooms – even my insane father thought you were right up your gum tree! Now he's convinced you're the saviour of the whole world from the communist scourge . . .'

And lying in front of the fire, stroking, nibbling, un-urgent kisses that turned into longer, then urgent kisses, bodies twisted together, the feel of her satiny back and hips and legs, the soft smooth secret of her thighs: the joy of slowly pulling clothes off each other, the blissful feel of her breasts pressed against him, the taste and smell and texture of her, her long soft hair, her neck, her belly, and then the groaning happiness of the warm sweet depths of her, enveloping. And tomorrow and tomorrow and tomorrow, for ever.

On the first of December he had to go back to work. It was a routine flight to Accra. She went with him. When they were halfway across the Sahara, Dolores came on the air.

'Malcolm Todd's just called! He's started pumping the helium into her! She should be off the concrete within a week!'

'Oh *yes*!' Mahoney shouted.

'And', Dolores said, 'there's more good news! From Peter. Are you ready for it? . . . The Zimbabwe government accepts your terms! They'll sign a contract that, subject to satisfactory

338

trials, they'll lease two identical ships for two years with an option to buy!'

'*Oh yes!*'Mahoney yelled.

CHAPTER 54

Rain swept across Cardington. But inside the Redcoat hangar it was a beautiful day.

The *Rainbow* stood on the vast floor, a gigantic sweep of gleaming metal that tapered hugely away into the distance. Her scaffolding was gone, replaced with a network of ropes tied to the floor-bolts. There was anticipation in the air. All around her clustered the workmen who had built her, rivet by rivet. Attached to the valves in her belly were stout pipes that led to a big tanker of helium, the fourth to be used. There was a hissing noise.

Mahoney strode under the massive hull with Tana, greeting the workers by name, cracking a joke. 'How does it feel, Mr Mahoney?'

'Marvellous,' he grinned, 'thanks to you all!'

Somebody quipped, 'Do you think she'll fly, sir?'

Way down there, Malcolm was talking to the engineers. '*Mal-colm!*' Mahoney bellowed. '*When will you be done?*'

Malcolm yelled back: '*When I'm finished! Go'n fly your aeroplanes!* . . . '

Just then a shout went up: '*There she goes!*' Mahoney spun around, and Malcolm dropped to his knees, his eye to the floor. Mahoney dropped to his stomach, and peered. All through the hangar men were lying down. And – yes! He could see a chink of light under the main wheels! The great ship was just a fraction off the ground! He let out a yell: '*She flies!*' He scrambled up laughing, as if he had doubted all along that she would. '*She flies!*' And Tana was laughing, too, and all about men were grinning and shaking hands with each other. Mahoney grabbed Malcolm's hand: '*Congratulations!*' He grabbed Tana and hugged her: '*She flies!* . . . '

It seemed the happiest day of his life. Then through the noise and excitement a clerk was tapping him on the shoulder, saying, 'There's a call for you, Mr Mahoney.'

He grabbed the walkie-talkie telephone. 'Hullo!' he shouted happily.

'Hullo,' Dolores said.

'Dolores,' he shouted, 'she's off the floor!'

'*Wonderful!*' Dolores said. She hestitated. 'Then I'm sorry to be the harbinger of bad news.'

'What?' he demanded.

Dolores said: 'A cable has just arrived. From Shelagh.'

His heart sank. 'What does it say?'

Dolores said: 'She's arriving tomorrow. With Cathy. For the Christmas holidays . . .'

They drove slowly back through the rain. They were quiet. He was angry: with Shelagh, for descending on him, for spoiling today of all days – and with himself, for not having told her everything in Zimbabwe. He muttered, 'I should have goddamn *told* her!'

Tana sighed. 'Yes, you should have. This is what I was frightened of.'

He said, 'I was simply not emotionally *tough* enough. To turn the exercise into a – soulbearing *mess*.' He sighed angrily. 'I only went there to lay a ghost. And I didn't want to risk changing her mind.'

She smiled gently. 'There were no pangs?'

He looked at her, then back at the road. Oh God, why shouldn't he tell her the truth? 'There usually are in such circumstances. But they were tied up with her being Cathy's mother.'

She said gently: 'Not with her? She's very attractive.'

He said grimly: 'I had no difficulty.'

She said: 'Did you sleep with her?'

He was staring at the road, but he mentally closed his eyes. She said: 'Don't answer that. It's none of my business, and I don't want to know.'

He took a deep, tense breath. Oh God, what was the point

in telling her the truth? It would only hurt, and it was irrelevant now.

'No,' he said.

They stopped for a drink in a country pub. He stared at the fire and said, 'I'll phone her tonight.'

She shook her head. 'Lord, on the eve of her departure?'

He said, 'She's only coming for a holiday, dammit, not to resume conjugal rights! She always spent Christmas with her parents, anyway.'

She stared at the fire. 'It may change her attitude entirely.'

'You're assuming that she loves me. She doesn't.'

'Doesn't she?'

'Hell, no! She's chosen her course.'

She said: 'Has she? Or does she think she can have her cake and eat it?' She added: 'Nothing makes a woman think again quicker than to find out there's another woman.'

He kept getting the engaged signal. He slammed the telephone down and paced across the kitchen. She sat at the table, staring at nothing. He went back to the telephone and placed the call through the operator.

'I'm sorry,' the woman said, 'the phone has been disconnected.'

He put the phone down. Then punched his palm. '*Dammit!*'

'Why would she disconnect it?'

'Because she doesn't want the servant using it while she's away.'

She smiled bleakly. 'Well, at least that shows she intends going back.'

'Of course she's going back.'

She mused: 'Her telegram doesn't say what flight she's on, so you can't even meet her and tell her. She'll just arrive at the front door.'

He said grimly: 'I won't be here until evening. I fly to Rome tomorrow.'

She said quietly: 'Nor will I be here.'

341

'Sure. You're coming to Rome with me.'

She stood up, went to the counter and poured more wine.

'Joe, I'll be moving into Thoren's apartment in London tomorrow.'

He turned and stared at her. 'You are not!'

She turned to him with a rueful smile.

'Oh, Mahoney, I must. Until you've sorted this out. Can you imagine, if I'm in residence when your wife rolls up! Oh, no. I have no business here.'

'You have every business here! And if *you're* here, she can't move in!'

'She might.' She raised her eyebrows. 'Oh, she might. Leap to the defence of her hearth and home? Wouldn't that be pleasant?' She shook her head. 'It's something that you must straighten out alone.'

'There's nothing to straighten out!'

'Good, darling,' she said. 'Then I'll be back soon.'

She sat on the corner of the kitchen table.

'And another thing.' She looked at him. 'You should be cautious about confronting her with the truth immediately. Believe me, women can be unpredictable when their security is threatened.'

'She's got her own security in Zimbabwe. Her job, her home.'

'And you . . . whom she thinks she can always fall back on. I don't just mean financial security, but emotional, as well. Suddenly take that away from a woman, and she can turn frantic. And come running back, with every trick in the book.'

He said wearily, 'Not Shelagh. What are you suggesting?'

'*When* should you tell her? And how?' She sighed. 'She may only intend staying a few days before going to her parents. Maybe she's even got a boyfriend and she's meeting him in gay Paree. Maybe she's coming to tell *you* it's all over.' She smiled bleakly. 'In which case, don't tell her anything. It could change her mind.' She paused. 'But I doubt it. I think the lady believes she's on strong ground.' She gave him a little smile. 'And maybe she is?'

He felt his nerves getting tight. He said quietly, 'She is not, Tana.'

She roused herself. 'Hey Mahoney, shall we cheer up? It's not the end of the world. It's only for a few days.' She held out her arms. 'Come on, let's get drunk. Or laid. Or both.'

'Both.' He took her in his arms, and rocked her.

'Oh God, why did this have to happen now? . . .'

CHAPTER 55

He was still angry, all the way to Rome. By the time he returned to Gatwick, however, the anger was gone and he was tensely, recklessly calm. He didn't care any more. He was going to see how the land lay, judge his own timing. And then, no anguish. Especially not in front of Cathy. And no anguish *about* Cathy, either. She would always be his. He was completely under control.

It was eight o'clock when he got home. Lights were on and smoke was curling up the chimney. He opened the front door. 'Shelagh?'

He walked through into the kitchen. She was standing at the sink, back to him, the tap running. 'Hullo, Shelagh.'

She turned, with a start. Then her dazzling smile. 'Oh, hi!' But it was not the same warmth with which she had said goodbye to him four months ago.

He kissed her lightly on the mouth. And in that moment of contact he saw his whole marriage in a flash, the familiar feel of her, her mouth, her scent, and he felt his heart harden: for he also felt her familiar briskness, and he knew absolutely that it was all over. He felt a surge of happiness that she could not hurt him any more.

'You look well! Where's Cathy?'

'Upstairs, fast asleep, she's had a long trip. You'll see her in the morning.'

Of course he was disappointed. 'How was the flight?'

'Crowded. I'm about to have a bath. I bought you a half-bottle of duty-free whisky.' She waved at the counter. 'That's all I could afford, I'm afraid.'

He was touched. 'Thank you, Shelagh. Can I get you a drink?'

She smiled fliply. 'What's all this Shelagh business? You used to call me darling. Who is she?'

He smiled. 'Will you have a drink?'

'O.K., but I'll take it to the bath with me, it's getting cold. I intended looking more glamorous for you than this.'

He poured it. 'So how long are you here for?'

'Only until New Year. I'm taking a summer course at the university, I must get back for that. Cheers.'

'Is Cathy all right?'

'Fine. I'm hoping you'll pay for her ticket. I thought you'd like to see her. I'm sorry she's fallen asleep on you.'

She wasn't brittle like this in Zimbabwe. 'Of course. I've got a short flight to Malaga tomorrow.'

She smiled. 'And you're bringing back tomatoes? Your own cargo.'

'Right.'

She shook her head. 'Joseph Mahoney, Q.C. Occupation: Tomato Trader.'

'Good money, tomatoes in winter.'

She leant against the table. 'And what are you doing with it? Haven't painted the house, I see. Or done the garage. Or the garden.'

'I will, one day.'

She looked at him, then smiled. 'Oh, my, creature comforts aren't very important to you, are they?'

'I love this house. I'll get it finished.'

She conceded: 'It's a lot tidier than I expected. And the fridge well-stocked, I see. Are you coming to the Cotswolds for Christmas, with Mum and Dad?'

Here we go, Mahoney thought. But it wasn't the time.

'I don't think your parents are bursting a blood vessel to see me.'

'Please yourself.'

He said, to be kind, 'I'll be working, I'm afraid.'

344

'Working? I would have thought you could have put off work when your wife and child come for Christmas.'

'I may still be test-flying the airship at Christmas.' He had decided not to tell her about flying to Zimbabwe.

'*Test*-flying it? Really?' Then she put down her drink. 'Look, that bath's getting cold. Tell me about it afterwards.'

As she passed through the living-room she called, 'I've put dinner in the oven.' Then: 'Who's doing your cooking these days, all that elaborate food in the fridge?'

He called airily to the wall: 'Oh, me mostly.'

He walked quietly upstairs while she was bathing, to Cathy's room. The door was open. He looked down at his darling daughter.

She lay on her back, golden hair tousled, one little arm outflung, fast asleep. And she was perfect. Her little nose and mouth, her unmarked skin, his flesh and blood. He longed to just scoop her up, and feel her in his arms, her life, squeeze her, tell her he loved her and always would, that he was her daddy. Oh God, he did not want her to go away, but she had to, she had to . . . But, oh God, he was not going to have any showdown with her mother until he had had a little while in peace with his Cathy in the morning . . .

'Good night, darling,' he whispered. 'I love you.'

It was easy.

Sometimes, when she walked across the kitchen, he felt a wrench, at the line of her legs, the thrust of her breasts, and for an instant he knew why he had loved her so – then the feeling was gone, and it was easy to be calm and charmingly cool. He even enjoyed it. It was good to know with absolute certainty that he loved Tana, that Shelagh could not hurt him anymore, that this brief visit was the last step. And he did enjoy her company: it was nice to sit with her, talking about people they knew, remembering. He felt a real affection for her. She said: 'Now, tell me about the airship?'

'She's fantastic. She's being inflated at the moment.'

'*Really?* Congratulations.' She shook her head. 'I honestly never thought it would happen. When will she be flying?'

345

'In about ten days. Weather permitting.'

'Really! Can I come and watch?'

He said: 'You won't be allowed in her during the trials.'

'Oh, well.' She mused: 'Weather permitting? That's what worries me about these airships. How can a transport company only deliver "weather permitting"?'

'Airliners often cannot land because of weather conditions.'

She waved a hand wearily. 'I know all your arguments. But airships *must* be more vulnerable to bad weather.' He let that go and she said: 'And are you within your budget?'

'More or less.'

'What does that mean? A mere half-million pounds over budget?'

He smiled calmly. 'Much less than that, Shelagh.'

She sighed. 'Fourteen million pounds . . . Good God. What are you doing fooling with such a staggering sum of money? Lord, what one could do with *one* million, if you invested it in real estate.'

'The bank finally realized the world needs airships. Real estate developers are a dime a dozen.'

She smiled. 'And Joe Mahoney doesn't want to be one of a dime-a-dozen, does he? No, Joe Mahoney is *different*. He's *unique*.' Suddenly her eyes were glistening: 'You love to swim against the tide, don't you? Good God – you're a lawyer, not an entrepreneur!'

He smiled. 'An ex-lawyer. They're the worst kind.' He added mildly, 'I've made a success of Redcoat.'

She cried, 'But how? By living from hand to mouth – by running half a dozen little aeroplanes to support Redcoat. By buying Spanish tomatoes and Nigerian pineapples, for God's sake! By keeping two weeks ahead of bankruptcy all these years. And now you owe six million pounds!'

He said: 'I also own fourteen million pounds of airship that's going to make lots of money.'

She sighed in exasperation. 'Who'll pay fourteen million for it in a bankruptcy? Who trusts airships?'

'They will. After the publicity.'

She closed her eyes. 'You and your publicity . . . That's what Redcoat hangs together on. You're a showman at heart.

Maybe that's why you were such a whiz in the courtroom.' She looked at him. 'Oh, Joe. Why don't you go back to the law? That's what you promised me.'

'Maybe I will. When I've got these airships working for me.'

She cried, 'You'll be too bloody old! It's almost too late already – for the law *and* for me!'

She got up from the table and swept out of the room.

Mahoney sat where he was. He could hardly believe it. She still thought nothing had changed.

Five minutes later he followed her. She was already in bed, reading.

He showered, pulled on running shorts, which were his only pyjamas – when he wore pyjamas. He switched on his reading lamp, got into bed and started to read. She switched out her light.

'Good night,' she said.

'Good night.'

He lay on his side, trying to read.

After a minute she said: 'Is that it? Just "good night"?' He lay there. 'Is that a *very* good book?' She suddenly sat up. 'Is this what I've come six thousand miles for, bedside reading?'

He said: 'You came six thousand miles for a Christmas holiday, and to see your parents, Shelagh.'

'And to see you! Have you given up making love, along with the law and the remnants of your sense? Or don't I turn you on any more?'

He hesitated. But no, now was not the time. Tomorrow.

'You cannot turn these things on and off like a light-switch, Shelagh.'

She slumped and turned her back on him. 'Bullshit. You'd screw anybody, at the crook of a finger.'

Mahoney took a breath and lay back. He turned out his lamp.

She lay in angry silence.

'Who is she?' she said abruptly.

347

Mahoney lay in the dark. Amazed. That she thought she could just come back.

'Shelagh, we can have any discussions tomorrow. But not tonight, in this atmosphere of belligerence.'

She lay in seething silence. 'If you're under the impression you'll rekindle my interest by appearing hard-to-get, you're mistaken.'

Mahoney lay there. It was on the tip of his tongue to say that he cherished no such notion, but he kept his mouth shut. *No fighting.* But oh, how he longed for this to be over and done with, that she would just leave him with goodwill.

She said: 'In fact, I don't care. Sure, you've had a few fucks. Plenty probably – I know what you were like.'

He closed his eyes. Riding it out. Shelagh lay, waiting. Then she said, 'I could divorce you, you know.'

He was amazed all over again. That she genuinely thought that divorce would still be an emotional threat to him. She waited, then unveiled her last cannon.

'And take you for half of everything. Including your airship. Because I still own those shares in Redcoat. As many shares as you! You haven't paid me yet and they're still registered in my name.'

He felt himself go cold, with both anger and fear. He took a breath, then peeled back the duvet. He got up, put on his dressing gown.

'Where are you going?' she demanded in the dark.

And suddenly he was completely calm again. He even felt affection for her. He bent and kissed her forehead.

'Good night, Shelagh. I must rest. I'm flying tomorrow.'

He turned for the stairs, and the bed in his study below.

He was awake at six. He walked to the kitchen, switching on lights. He filled the kettle, turned back towards the door. And there stood Cathy.

'Hullo,' she grinned.

'Cathy!'

He ran to her joyously, and dropped to one knee and flung his arms around her. Then held her at arm's-length and looked

348

at her joyfully, then stood up, hugging her. He held her high and laughed up at her.

'Would you like a ride in your daddy's aeroplane today?'

'Yes!' Cathy shouted. '*Wow and yippee!*'

CHAPTER 56

They had an absolutely lovely day together. Shelagh packed them a lunch box. Cathy was beside herself with excitement, flying in her daddy's very own aeroplane, looking down awe-struck at the sea and the land. She sat beside Mahoney while Ed did the work, and he tried to explain to her how it flew, even let her steer for a moment. She shrieked, '*Wow and yippee! I can fly an aeroplane!*'

In sunny Malaga the Spanish officials made a great fuss of her while the cargo was being discharged, before Mahoney took her to the airport cafeteria and stuffed her full of ice-cream.

'*Wow* . . . Mommy never lets me have *so* much ice-cream.'

'Mommies never do,' Ed rumbled. 'But daddies? – *sure.*'

'Can I have another one?'

'*Sure,*' said Ed.

She fell asleep in the unused radio-officer's seat on the way home, exhausted by the excitement.

It was very sobering coming back to the dark clouds of England after such a lovely day, knowing what was going to happen tonight. But, please God, only after Cathy was safely in bed.

When he got to the Redcoat hangar, he telephoned Tana. 'Hullo, darling!' she cried.

He said: 'By tomorrow it'll be all over. Are you all right?'

'Yes! It's *you* who's got the problem, how're *you*?'

'I miss you, that's all.'

'Oh – I miss you! Mahoney?'

'Yes?'

She hesitated; then said: 'Nothing. I'll be thinking of you.'

*

When he got home, with a very sleepy little girl, there was nobody there. He was puzzled. He boiled Cathy an egg, which she couldn't eat, and he told her to skip her bath and go straight to bed. When he went upstairs five minutes later to kiss her goodnight, she was fast asleep.

He showered, opened a beer, and went to his study. But he could not work. Ten minutes later he heard a car arrive.

Shelagh walked straight into his study, with a newly lit cigarette. 'Hello,' he said. 'Whose car have you got?'

'Danish Erika's.' She sat down on the bed, puffed hard on her cigarette, looking at him. She said:

'I know all about you and Tana Hutton.'

He had been half-expecting it. He looked at her steadily. She said: 'Erika's told me everything. Your flights to Australia, like a dog on heat. That she's been living in this house. That she's in London now.'

He nodded. All he felt was grim amusement. Danish Erika, huh? Trust a bloody woman. He wondered if Erika had also confessed his adulteries with her.

'Well? What have you got to say?'

He said gently: 'Shelagh, let's talk about this calmly. Yesterday you said you didn't care.'

She said quietly, venomously: 'I'm going to divorce you, Joe. I want to know whether you admit it, to make it simpler – and cheaper, I might add. Or whether I have to call witnesses – which you'll pay for.' She glared. 'This divorce is going to cost you plenty as it is.'

'Really?' This was not the atmosphere in which he was prepared to discuss divorce. He stood up, and put his papers away. 'Come on. We'll talk about it over a drink. Come on.'

He started out of the room. She stared at him. She cried: 'I've taken legal advice! You don't own those shares because you haven't yet paid me for them! I own half of everything!'

He stopped at the door, and looked at her.

'I'm a lawyer, Shelagh. I own those shares, believe me. I haven't paid you yet because of the high price, but it's a valid contract of sale on credit.'

She jumped off the bed and swept past him. She strode to

the front door, and slammed it behind her. The car started with a roar.

Mahoney walked to the kitchen. He felt absolutely calm. And relieved that it was out. It had not come about as he had hoped, two adults who had reached the end of the road, kindly, even affectionately parting. But it was a relief.

He heard the front door burst open again, Shelagh striding through the living-room, running up the stairs. He listened. He heard her coming down again. The front door slammed again. He heard the car start.

He walked upstairs. To Cathy's room. Her bed was empty.

He went back down to the kitchen, and poured himself a stiff whisky. He went to the telephone and dialled. 'Hullo,' Tana said.

'Hullo,' he said. 'I'm coming up to see you.'

'Oh, *wonderful*!' She paused. 'Is everything all right?'

'Everything is fine,' he said.

He heard her sigh with relief. 'Oh, thank God. Joe? . . . I love you.'

'I love you too,' he said.

He parked the car in St James's Place and walked to her apartment block. He rode up in the elevator. He opened the door, walked into the living-room.

'Hullo,' Shelagh said coldly. She was sitting in an armchair.

He stared at her, confused. 'Where's Cathy?' he said.

'With Danish Erika.'

He breathed out. 'What are you doing here?'

'I need hardly ask you the same.'

'Where's Tana?'

She said, 'Putting on something more respectable. She came to the door in a rather transparent garment. Seems she was expecting someone.'

He turned, to go to the bedroom; but Tana was coming down the corridor. She was wearing a casual dress and she looked beautiful.

'Hullo,' she smiled. She turned brightly to Shelagh. 'Now then, are you sure you won't have a drink?'

351

'Quite sure.'

She turned smiling to Mahoney. 'What about you, Joe?'

'I'll get it,' he said grimly. He went to the cabinet and poured both Tana and himself a large whisky. Tana was saying, 'Now Mrs Mahoney – may I call you Shelagh?' Shelagh nodded. 'What can I do for you?'

'I'm sure', Shelagh said, 'that you can imagine. I simply want to know whether you will formally admit to having an affair with my husband? Or do I have to hire expensive detectives?'

Tana accepted her glass from Mahoney and took a large sip. She sat down elegantly. 'For the purpose of divorce?'

'How very perspicacious of you.'

Tana nodded. 'Well,' she said graciously, 'whether or not you get divorced is your decision, and Joe's, not mine. But if that is what you both want, anything I can legally do to help, I will.'

Mahoney almost wanted to laugh. He could tell that Shelagh was rattled. And, unaccountably, he felt sorry for her. 'For God's sake, of course we admit it!'

She said icily: 'Do you also admit that those shares are still legally mine?'

He was disgusted that money was what she was thinking about at a solemn moment like this. But he made himself speak calmly.

'No. You sold them to me. I owe you the money, that's all.'

Shelagh gave him a long, calculating look. Then stood up. 'Very well. We'll see.' She turned to Tana. 'Will you excuse me now? Goodbye.'

She walked to the door. She closed it quietly but firmly behind her.

Mahoney stood where he was. He looked at Tana. He felt numb. She looked at him sympathetically.

'Well,' he said, 'that's over.'

'Oh?' she said. 'Is it?'

'What do you mean?' he sighed.

She sighed too.

Then the doorbell rang.

Tana looked at him, raised her eyebrows. She got up and opened the door.

'Hullo,' she said.

'Hullo,' Shelagh smiled. 'May I change my mind and have that drink?'

Tana put on her most charming smile. 'Of course.'

Shelagh walked into the room again. She looked quite composed.

'Joe?' she said politely. 'Would you mind leaving Tana and me alone?'

Oh boy . . .

Maybe, he thought, that was a dumb move too, leaving them together. But it was done and he did not care. It was all a mess, and he had made it so, and he was just glad that he was not there right now. It was almost ten o'clock when he got back to the cottage. He was completely sober, and felt like getting completely drunk. He stuffed a handgrip with a few changes of clothing, stuffed his paperwork into his briefcase. Then he left the cottage again, with all the lights blazing.

First he drove to The Rabbit, to have a stiff drink for the road and to telephone Tana to make sure the coast was clear.

'Hullo, stranger,' Danish Erika said guiltily.

'A double Scotch, please.'

'Are you driving?' Erika said.

'I am.'

'Then we'll make that a single.'

He looked at her. It did not matter, but he felt like saying it. 'You're a real pal, Erika. What have I ever done to hurt you?'

She shrugged sullenly. 'I was in love with you.' She turned away and got the drink. 'And I don't want you to fly that airship.'

He stared at her. He could not believe women.

'And your interfering instead of letting me handle my wife my way is going to stop me flying it?'

'No,' she admitted guiltily. She added, 'I'm sorry now.'

He slapped the money on the bar. She pushed it back.

353

'That's on me, pal. In fact . . .' She took his glass away and added the second shot. 'Here, you'll need it. And you won't be driving far.'

'What do you mean?' he said.

She sighed. 'Shelagh was in here a minute ago – to fetch Cathy. Tana was in the car. They're on their way to your house.'

He was astonished. He threw back the whisky, banged down the glass, and turned. Erika grabbed his arm across the bar. 'Joe, I've got to tell you . . . *You mustn't fly that airship!*'

He stared at her. She pleaded: 'For God's sake – I'm a medium, I've *heard* the spirits. They've been crowding around to tell me . . .'

He pulled his arm free, and strode for the door.

He had no idea what to expect. And every idea. He angrily slammed the car to a stop. As he opened the front door he heard Shelagh laugh. He strode to the kitchen. They were seated at the table, like old friends.

'Joe!' Shelagh said pleasantly. 'I think you owe us an explanation.'

Tana looked at him steadily, a smile twitching the corners of her mouth. He could tell she was a little drunk.

He looked at them.

'I've been forewarned. By Erika. And if I have one interruption from either of you before I'm finished' – he pointed to the door – 'I'll leave.' He glared at them, then went to the refrigerator and snapped the cap off a beer. He looked at Shelagh. He said quietly:

'You left me, Shelagh. After a long, drawn-out struggle. With yourself. With marriage. With the airline business. With psychiatrists, with me, with your ambitions. You finally made your decision.' He paused. 'And so did I. I told you that if you left, our marriage was over. And you left.'

Shelagh was looking at him steadily. He went on: 'And I was heartbroken. Because, oh, how I loved you. I just wanted to turn my face to the wall. But do you know what I eventually found? I discovered I was attractive to women – I'd forgotten that, I was so demoralized. It was a revelation that there were plenty of women ready to pick up the pieces and jump into your side of the bed.'

'There were also plenty of men ready to jump into bed with me. But I didn't let them!'

He ignored the interruption. 'I'm telling you this because you left supremely confident you could come back when you chose. And for a long time you were right. But then I met Tana, and for the first time in a long while I was happy. Finally, I had to be sure that you could *not* come back. I'd reached a crossroad. So I flew to Rhodesia.'

'And told me what?' Shelagh said. 'I want Tana to hear. I was honest about what I was doing – *improving* myself! And you implied you understood.'

He said quietly, 'I did understand, perfectly. I also understood that our marriage was definitely over.'

She cried, 'Why didn't you *tell* me? Why did you make love to me?'

He said grimly, 'I think it was the other way round, Shelagh. But be that as it may. All I can say is that it was natural enough. I still felt for you. And I didn't have to say that our marriage was over because your decisions were clearly made. I didn't want to provoke any more emotional stress. If I simply went away the last of the marriage would die painlessly.'

Her eyes flickered. Then she snapped, 'So you choose Tana.'

'I was not aware until a few moments ago that I have a choice.'

She cried, 'I came to England believing that I was still married to you!'

'You came for a holiday, Shelagh. But to answer your question – yes, I choose Tana.'

She was ashen. Even to that last moment she had expected him to relent. She could not believe it. Then she jumped up from the table, her eyes suddenly bright with tears.

She turned and stormed out of the room. She ran across the living-room and up the stairs.

He looked at Tana. She was staring steadily in front of her. They heard Shelagh coming down again. Across the living-room. She burst back into the kitchen. She was dragging Cathy by the arm and the child's face was contorted in fright. '*What about this?*' she shrieked.

He was aghast. '*For God's sake, Shelagh!*'

'*Shelagh!*' Tana cried, standing shocked.

Shelagh backed away hysterically. '*What about this?* . . .'

Mahoney started after her. All he wanted to do was seize his child and rush her upstairs to safety. Shelagh backed around the table. '*Don't you come near her!*'

He stopped, shocked. Tana was aghast. Shelagh glared, panting. Then Tana said, 'Excuse me. Goodnight.'

She turned and walked out of the room. Mahoney looked at his wife furiously. 'Put Cathy back to bed!' He strode after Tana. He caught up with her outside the front door. He was shaking.

'I'm sorry.'

She said quietly, 'It's not your fault.'

He took a deep, shaky breath. 'I can't come tonight. I must stay and sort the last of this out.'

She nodded. 'Yes.' She touched his face. 'I'll take Erika's car back to her, then a taxi. Come when you're ready.'

He dragged his hands down his face. 'I'm flying to Accra tomorrow. I won't be back for two days.'

She looked at him, waiting for him to ask her to come with him. He understood, and oh God, God, he would regret the moment, but he desperately needed to spend those two days alone. She understood, and she said: 'Come when you're ready.'

He walked slowly back into the house. It was silent.

The kitchen was empty. He walked to the bottom of the stairs, and listened. Then he heard her sob once up there.

He took a deep breath, and began to climb the stairs.

He stood in the doorway. She lay on the bed, her arm across her eyes, her hair awry, shaking as she sobbed.

'Shelagh?'

She did not lift her arm from her eyes.

'Shelagh, I'm sorry it came to this.'

She lay still a long moment. Then whispered: 'Please leave me alone.'

He walked on down the passage to Cathy's room. The passage light shone in. She was lying on her back, the blankets pulled up to her chin, staring up at him with big eyes. He thought his heart would break. He sat down on the bed; then scooped her into his arms and clutched her tight. She put her little arms around his neck uncertainly. 'Daddy?'

He could feel her breath against his neck. 'Yes, my darling?'

She said tearfully, 'Mommy says you don't love us anymore.'

And he felt his heart break and he clutched her tight, his voice was thick as he whispered, 'Oh, my baby, I will always love you . . .' He held her out and looked into her little tear-stained face, her blue worried eyes, and he squeezed her arms. 'No matter what strange things grown-ups do, I will always love you. And I will always be here when you need me. *Always*.' The tears were burning. 'Will you remember that?'

She nodded her head earnestly.

And the grief swelled in his throat, and he just wanted to live with his child for ever, and he clutched her tight again, rocking her, kissing her little bewildered face.

He walked slowly down the passage. He did not pause at their bedroom. He walked down the stairs to his study. He stood there in the dark, suffering; then he began to undress. He climbed into the bed, and collapsed back, staring at the ceiling.

He was suddenly wide awake before dawn, at his lowest ebb, with the knowledge that somebody was in the room. The passage light was on. He saw Shelagh silhouetted against it, in her nightgown. She whispered:

'How could you do this to us?'

He put his arm over his eyes.

'Please, Shelagh, we've said it all.'

She stood there; then he felt her sit down on the bed. He lay racked with exhaustion and compassion. She whispered, 'I haven't slept.'

He breathed deep and said nothing.

Then he heard her sob. He lifted his arm. On her face was pure misery. She whispered: 'Oh God, what have I lost?' Her eyes were brimming. 'What a fool I've been.' She took a big juddering breath. 'Oh God, what a fool!'

He stared at her. She shook her head in her hand. 'I loved you . . . And oh God, I still do. I just thought . . .' She took a weepy breath: 'I just wanted to be my own *person* as well . . . Have my own work. My own money. My own identity.'

He said softly, 'You could have done all that here in England.'

She shook her head in grief. 'Oh, I see that now. But I didn't then . . . I didn't *try* hard enough. I just wanted my old life back.' She opened her eyes and looked at him. 'I wanted to be a full, liberated person. Not *just* a wife . . .' Her eyes were full of pleading. 'There's nothing wrong in that, is there?'

He said softly: 'No. But if you have to go away to achieve that, you can't have your marriage as well.'

She cried, 'Oh, I see that now! But *why* can't two people be – *equals*?'

'You were my equal.'

She sighed, deeply.

'Never . . .' She hesitated, then out it came. 'I wanted to *be* like you . . . Look at you! Everything you do turns out well. Even if it was the wrong thing in the first place! You were a successful lawyer – yet by your own admission you knew no law. How often have I seen you scrambling through the library at the last minute because you didn't know the law – then you sail into court. Then you chuck it all up and buy an aeroplane. You know *nothing* about aeroplanes. You don't even *like* aeroplanes. But *now* look at you.'

'I'm still broke,' he said gently.

She shook her head at him tearfully. 'And you don't *care* . . . Because you're so self-confident. All you care about is the challenge. You're never *afraid*.'

'I'm afraid sometimes,' he said.

For the first time she smiled, sadly. 'Oh no, darling – not like I'm afraid. Afraid of failure.' Her chin trembled. 'I've never done anything especially well in my *life*. Because . . .'

She closed her eyes, and her voice caught: 'Because I'm a loser!'

And oh, his heart went out to her. He knew what those words had cost her. 'You are *not*,' he whispered.

'I am! And now I've even lost you.'

Mahoney lay still, and closed his eyes tight. He could hardly believe what he was hearing. This was Shelagh? And, oh God, with all his heart he did not want her to feel her crushing sense of failure, did not want her to suffer the same despair he had when she had left him: but he lay there, rigid, not daring to say anything. She sobbed:

'Oh God, if you loved me at all, just *hold* me now . . .'

And he sat up, and he put his arms around her. She sat, sobbing, and he whispered: 'Oh Shelly, don't suffer.' She burst into racking sobs.

He lay back on the bed, and she clutched him tight. He whispered, 'Don't cry . . .' She sobbed against him.

'I thought you would come back to Rhodesia . . . I thought you'd give up this business and come home. I even thought . . . oh God, I don't know what I thought.' She shook her head in his shoulder. 'And all the time I was blind to your suffering . . . I even thought we could have some kind of "modern" marriage . . . where we live apart some of the time and together some of the time, and somehow stay married. I was stupid, don't you see! I was *blind* . . .' She stopped, and took a long, quavering, exhausted sigh. 'And now you love Tana.'

He lay there suffering for her, his whole body tense, and he knew she was desperately waiting for him to say he did not really love Tana; but he was not going to say that. She whispered miserably: 'She's so beautiful. I haven't got a chance against her.'

Oh God, her self-effacement tore at his guts.

'Oh Shelly, you musn't think like that. You're a *beautiful* woman, you know that.' He clenched his teeth and shook her gently, because he never wanted her to feel like he had. 'You're a beautiful woman!'

She lay stiff, holding him tightly; then he felt her go limp.

'Yes,' she whispered. Then she took a deep breath. 'Please make love to me,' she whispered.

He took a breath, and shook his head. 'No, darling.'

'*Please* . . . Just one last time.'

'No, Shelagh.'

'Why not?' she whispered.

He closed his eyes and did not answer.

'Because you're being faithful to her?'

'Because I'm being true to myself.'

She lay there, holding him tight.

'Because you still love me,' she whispered.

He took an anguished breath. He had to be brutal and say it.

'I don't love you like that any more, Shelagh. It's too late.'

She whispered ardently: 'You still love me.'

He felt anger through the anguish. 'It's too late, Shelagh. Too much has happened.'

She clung to him. 'It's not too late. I'm in your blood, like you're in mine. You will always love me, like I will always love you. And you love Cathy. We can all be happy together again. Happy . . .'

'We cannot.'

'We *can*. Don't you see? This whole thing was meant to bring me to my senses. It's the best thing that could have happened. And it's *over* now, and I'm *back*, I'm *back* . . . I'm going to be a wonderful wife to you from now on, the woman you always wanted me to be. Can't you feel it's true? Can't you feel it in my body? *Feel* me . . .'

'No.'

'*Yes.*' She slid her hand down to his loins. 'Oh yes, you can feel it, you're rock-hard for me.' She pulled her negligée off her shoulders and put his hand on her breast. 'Oh, please just feel me – feel how wet I am for you. Oh, please just love me once . . .'

'No.'

'Yes!' And she slid one long leg over him, and then she was crouching on top of him, and her mouth crushed against his, and she thrust herself down on him and he moaned in his throat at the blissful depths of her, and she kissed him and kissed him, and her face was wet with tears of happiness.

*

The dawn was breaking.

He lay, staring at the ceiling, her head on his shoulder, hair awry, one lovely leg still across his. He said quietly: 'I've got to go now.'

Her arm tightened on him for a moment: then she let go. He heaved himself up. He stood, his face gaunt. She looked up at him, and whispered: 'What are you going to do?'

He felt the anger again, through the anguish, but it was anger with himself. He said, 'I'm flying to Accra.'

She whispered, 'You know what I mean. Please don't be cruel.'

Oh, he did not want to be cruel to her, he wanted to punish himself, for confusing himself.

She said: 'Can I come with you to Accra?'

'No.'

She nodded, miserably, and closed her eyes. 'What do you want Cathy and me to do?'

Oh God, Cathy . . . And with the last of his common sense he wanted to tell her they must go; but also, God help him, he had to be truthful, to her and to himself.

'I don't know.'

Her eyes were bright with tears, and she smiled up at him with all her heart.

CHAPTER 57

He did not telephone Tana from the air – because of guilt, because of exhaustion, because he did not want to have to lie; because he didn't know what he had to say.

The plane droned on over the Mediterranean, then over the Sahara, and all he knew was guilt, and compassion, and confusion. Why had he not told her everything, months ago, in Zimbabwe? Why had he exposed himself to the pain of Cathy? And, oh, the things she had said, all words he had once so longed to hear, and the sweet feel of her in his arms

361

again. And all the time his darling Cathy asleep upstairs; and when he came back from Accra, there would be a light in the window, and smoke curling up the chimney, and she would come running out calling Daddy Daddy Daddy and he would scoop her up, her little arms around his neck, laughing and laughing.

Ed said: 'You look like death. Go on; I'll do your leg.'

'I'm all right.'

The desert droned on and on. Then way ahead the brown began to turn to mauve, and the real Africa, his Africa, was beginning.

Riding into town in the battered taxi to the broken-down hotel, through the bananas and goats and the tall green grass between the shanties and piccanins and the other battered traffic, he loved every turn and pothole in the road, and every black face. He sat drinking a row of luke-warm beers, looking at the sea from his hotel, the swimming pool filled with refuse, all the time the happy jabber of black voices.

'Suzie?' he said.

'I refuse to play this game,' she said. 'It's for you to decide.'

'But there's nothing to decide.'

'Isn't there? Then why are you suffering?'

'Isn't it perfectly natural?'

'So why are you being so hard on yourself?'

He dragged his hands down his face.

Yes, indeed. Why was he being so hard on himself? Was it not perfectly natural to still feel love for the woman you once loved so much, who bore your child, who broke your heart? Wasn't it natural to feel confusion when she suddenly comes back, sadness, even though you know it's no good, even though you love somebody else now? Wasn't it perfectly natural to look back over your shoulder at what might have been, at what you once yearned for? . . . And what about little Cathy? . . . So why was he being so hard on himself?

He sat there, trying not to think and suffer anymore, just drink. And then, slowly, a feeling began to build up in his chest, and it was relief; and then it was happiness. And he knew what he was going to do. He quaffed back his beer and strode through the beat-up hotel lobby.

'I want to telephone England, please.'

Two hours and five beers later he was still waiting for the call.

Then the operator told him: 'All-i lines out-i order.'

He was exasperated. But still happy. It did not matter. First thing tomorrow, from the air, he would telephone her.

At nine o'clock that brilliant morning the Britannia lifted off, and he spoke to Berna. An hour later they reported that there was no reply.

All the way back, Berna Radio tried to connect him with Tana's apartment, at half-hourly intervals. There was no reply.

He came hurrying down the steps of the Britannia, hunched against the rain, and piled into the Redcoat panelvan. They sped across the tarmac to Immigration. Then to the Redcoat hangar. He burst through the side door, into his dark office, snatched up the telephone and dialled. It rang and rang. Then a voice said: 'I don't think she's there.'

He spun round. Shelagh was sitting in the corner, looking beautiful. He stared. 'What are you doing here?'

She smiled: 'I'm the boss's wife. Come to welcome him home.'

He stared. She said: 'And I'm a shareholder. Come to look at the shop.' She got up and sauntered towards him, smiling seductively.

'Where's Cathy?' he demanded.

'At home, darling, with a baby-sitter. I thought you might take me out for dinner.' She laced her hands around his neck.

He stepped backwards. 'Why do you say Tana isn't there?'

She turned away.

'Because', she said soberly, 'I went to see her yesterday. And I told her that I intended resuming married life with you. Which, I told her, I had already done.' She took a breath. 'I asked her to leave.'

He stared at her, astounded. 'You had no right to do that!'

'I have every right. It's my marriage.'

363

His anger flared up, but he controlled it. 'The choice is not yours any more, Shelagh! You made your choice years ago.'

'Yesterday morning', she said, 'you made love to me.'

He took a furious breath. 'What else did you tell her?'

She looked at him steadily. 'Please don't let's fight. You were having understandable difficulty making up your mind. I simply made it up for you.' She smiled and stretched out her hand for his. 'Come . . .'

He turned and strode furiously out of the door, and across the hangar.

He scrambled into his car and gunned the engine. He tore on to the road for London.

The elevator was in use; he ran up the stairs. His heart was hammering. He rammed his key into the door, and opened it.

The apartment was in darkness. Complete silence. '*Tana!*'

He slammed on the lights. The living-room was neat. He strode down the passage to her bedroom, switched on the lights. He stopped.

All her things were gone, from the dressing table, the wardrobe, the bathroom. An envelope lay on the bed. He tore it open feverishly.

My darling,
      There's whisky in the cupboard.
      Now listen. Shelagh's explained it all. I understand most of what you're going through. I can imagine the rest. You're not out of the woods yet and, one direction or the other, only you can find the way.
      So I've gone away. To uncomplicate your life. And mine. To lick my own wounds. Nobody knows where, not even Vader, so don't waste valuable energy trying to find out – you've got enough to do. I'm not trying to punish you, I don't know myself where I'll go to clear my mind. Get your marriage clear in your heart and head. Get that airship flying and working for you. Good luck, good luck, good luck. And remember it's people like you who make dreams come true.

He crumpled the letter in his fist.

He wanted to bellow it to the sky so loud that she would hear: 'Oh, you *stupid* woman!'

He snatched up the telephone, and dialled.

'Hullo,' the old Erling Thoren said somberly, 'I've been expecting you to call. I am very sorry about this.'

'Do you know where she is?' he demanded.

'No,' the old man said. 'All I know is she telephoned me last night, saying she is leaving England. She explained why. She would not tell me where she was going. In case I told you, I suppose.'

Oh *Christ* . . . 'How did she sound?'

'She sounded – calm? But you know women, you can never tell. I am sure she was very upset, yes.'

'Where do you *think* she's gone?'

'She is a very independent woman, you know. Europe, I think – a hotel somewhere. She has no close friends there, to run crying to. She cannot come home yet, with her eyes all red.'

Mahoney said angrily: 'When she contacts you – and she will – will you get hold of me *immediately*? And *please* find out where she is?'

The old man hesitated. 'Well, that is up to her, you know. My first loyalty is to her. You know how bladdy stupid women can be.'

'But you *must*! And you've got to tell her that everything is straightened out now – *convince* her of that!'

The old man was silent a moment. 'Is this definite, now?'

'*Yes!* It always *was*, dammit!'

'Well, I will tell her when she contacts me, of course.' He added, 'I'm very sorry for you two young people, but maybe it is for the best, you know.' (Mahoney groaned furiously.) 'It was completely *im*practical to live twelve thousand miles away. All her responsibilities are in Australia. And, I told her, the wife always wins if there is a child, I must be honest with you.'

'Well, it's *not* the case!' He rubbed his forehead feverishly. 'She'll come back for the test-flight next week.'

'Maybe,' the old man said. 'She was always very excited about that.' He added: 'I will still be coming, if I may?'

'Of course,' Mahoney sighed. 'Of course.'

Five minutes later he was speaking to Dolores.

'If the airlines can't help try the travel agents. The big ones, like Cooks, American Express, near this apartment, then work outwards.'

'*Lord!*' Dolores said. 'But she might have bought an ordinary rail ticket to Paris!'

'Try, Dolores! Just *try!*'

An hour later he arrived at Roger's, the solicitor's, terraced house in Putney.

'Have you got a bed for me for a week? And a drink?'

PART 9

PART 9

CHAPTER 58

It was going to be a beautiful English winter day.

Mahoney watched the day breaking. *His* great day. Out in the centre of the field stood the big mast. There were the hundreds of chairs, rope cordons, a gay marquee, a dais. Today the Queen of England was coming to honour him by launching his airship . . . Today the world would be watching. It should have been the happiest day of his life. But he was aching, just irresistibly watching for her. Surely she would be unable to resist today? . . .

But the dawn was empty. A week of emptiness. He turned abruptly back into the clamorous hangar, to the excitement and activity.

Before sunrise they started arriving, hundreds of men of Bedford and Air Force volunteers, to walk the *Rainbow* out of her hangar. Malcolm addressed them over a loudhailer. He looked grey and exhausted and excited.

'Thank you all for coming! I hope you feel afterwards that it was worth it. Now, you practised yesterday, but I'll repeat the routine.' He pointed. 'The airship is tied down by ropes, to ringbolts on the floor. You are going to take the place of ringbolts. You are going to form two long lines down her hull and hang on to those ropes like billy-oh. The flight crew is aboard. The tow-truck will be attached to the bows. When I give you signal, you will begin to walk slowly – in step.' He turned sideways, holding an imaginary rope, and began to march: 'One, and two, and three. Got it?'

Mahoney stood on the flight deck beside Lovelock and Ed; his mouth dry, his whole body tense. Every few minutes he caught himself thinking she was out there, watching. Oh God, today, the day he had longed for and feared . . . And where was she, to rejoice with him, to share his fears?'

He felt gaunt, his chest rough from chain-smoking, and sick in his heart. And as for his magnificent, mighty airship – he was afraid of her. He did not want to touch the controls; theoretically he knew everything about her, every switch and button, but he did not want to touch her. He had lost all confidence. He only wanted Lovelock to touch his terrifying ship – and he did not want him to touch her either.

Malcolm's whistle blasted, and Mahoney's guts turned over.

The four big engines were purring in neutral pitch. From up here he could not see the lines of men holding on to the ropes. All he could feel was the slight sway as they earnestly slow-marched her, as the truck towed her. Ahead, in the early sunshine, Malcolm was walking backwards, in time with them. It was at the hangar doors that the danger would arise.

Mahoney measured the distance, heart hammering. Closer and closer the huge ship moved. She was only twenty feet from the door; now fifteen; now ten; now five. Now the nose was in the doorway. Malcolm gave two blasts, and the great ship came quick-marching into the cold light of day. And a cheer went up from the mass of people, and Mahoney prayed.

The men quick-marched the massive ship, and out she slowly came, enormous and gleaming. On and on she came, and now two hundred feet of her was in the bright sunshine. Now three hundred. Then she was two-thirds out; then three-quarters; now only a hundred feet of her was inside the hangar; now eighty; now sixty; and now only her big tail-fins . . . The crowd held its breath, and Mahoney prayed *Please God* . . . Then a spontaneous roar went up from the crowd, and Mahoney had a twitching smile, and the wind struck.

It came in a sudden swirling gust, and whipped round the end of the hangar and hit the high tail, and Malcolm blasted on his whistle, and the men broke into a run. The massive tail lurched sideways and Malcolm bellowed '*Heave!*' They lurched and heaved in a crab-run, the men up front running forwards and the men down aft staggering sideways. Mahoney

370

bellowed: *'Run!'* The huge ship lurched sideways again, but it was going to just make it, then a man tripped and fell.

He sprawled and the next man tripped over him, and the next. The tail swung up at the doorframe, and it was going to hit. Then the wind changed direction. Suddenly, as if teasing, it swept around the opposite side of the hangar, and the tip of the stern missed the door. It missed by a foot, and the great airship was out of her womb, under the sky, and another roar of applause went up.

Everything was ready. But there were two hours to wait.

The wind had gone. The *Rainbow* had made her ballast adjustments. Now she floated out there serenely, at her mast, gleaming, awe-inspiring, her great sweep of colours glistening. Thousands of people encircled her behind the cordons, in a gala mood. Cars and busloads of people were arriving all the time. There were scores of press and television men. The cordon made a wide avenue; people lined it, flags everywhere. At the end was the striped marquee where the official guests were gathering. A television reporter stood in front of his camera saying:

'Down that avenue Her Majesty will soon arrive, and it seems that Nature herself has resolved to help the courageous men who built the ship to put their best foot forward! We should have a fine view of her as she is put through her paces for at least two hours on the very first test flights. She will then return to her mast to take on board the official observers who will accompany her on the next exciting stage of her trials, namely her long romantic flight from here, across Europe, across Africa, all the way down to Zimbabwe, and back – a voyage of some fifteen thousand miles. During this journey the owners expect to encounter a wide range of conditions to prove her airworthiness. And now, here is the worthy man who built her!' The camera rolled back to take in a beaming Malcolm. 'Major Todd, how does it feel to see her floating out there?'

'Bloody marvellous,' Malcolm grinned.

'And are you confident she'll pass her trials?'

'Of course I am. She handled beautifully when we flew her to her mast. Everything's been tested, and treble-tested. The next stage, the two-hour flight this morning, is actually unnecessary, I'm sure, but the C.A.A. want a shake-down buzz-around before we take on the passengers. However, we're so confident that we've already loaded their luggage . . .'

The R.A.F. band was in position. Scores of bemedalled Air Force, Navy and Army officers sat with their wives and important-looking civilians. Mahoney stood in the principle cordoned area with the Admiral, Air Marshal Thompson, the Minister for Industry, the Director of Civil Aviation and his inspectors, their wives and some of the observers. The Chinese had arrived, as had the Canadians and the Ugandans, but not yet the Zimbabweans. Nor had Erling Thoren arrived. Mahoney was taken aback by the C.A.A. inspectors who were to accompany the trials. He had never met either. One was the dreaded Mr Perry he had dealt with by telephone: he was a short peppery man with lank hair greased back, a pencil-line moustache and a pinched, smug look of the little man in authority. The other inspector, Mr Carter, was plump, benign, freckled, and showed all his gums when he smiled. It was hard to imagine that they were expert airmen.

Mahoney had done his bit with the television and newsmen, but it had all sounded dead in his ears. Even his relief that his ship was safely out of that hangar had dissipated, his pride at her floating magnificently at her mast now overtaken by grief-stricken frustration that Tana was not beside him. Now he was anxious in case Dolores didn't bring his new uniform in time. He was desperate for Erling Thoren to come, please God, with news of Tana.

Just then a car pulled into the official parking area. A black man in a suit and fur hat got out. He was accompanied by a white man in an Air Force uniform. 'There're the Zimbabweans,' the Admiral said. Mahoney straightened and went forward with a forced public-relations smile to meet these important customers. He made sure he addressed the black man first. 'How do you do! Joe Mahoney, managing director of Redcoat Airshiplines.'

'Mr Moyo. And, I believe, you are captain of the airship?'

Mahoney laughed: 'No, Mr Lovelock is the experienced airshipman in command.' He turned to the Air Force officer, and his eyes widened. 'Good God!' he said. 'Bomber Brown!'

'Hullo, Joe.' The Air Force man gripped his hand warmly. 'Long time no see.'

'We knew each other in the services in the old days!' Mahoney exclaimed to Moyo.

'So I believe – the bad old days,' Moyo grinned. 'He's Acting Air Vice-Marshal now. Maybe you should have stayed in Zimbabwe, Mr Mahoney?'

'What – and give up the English weather?'

He led them to the others, thinking how nice it was to see Bomber.

'What the hell you doing messing with airships, Mahoney?' Bomber whispered. 'You couldn't even fly your Piper Comanche.'

'Anything to make a living,' Mahoney whispered. 'Air Vice-Marshal, huh?'

'*Acting*,' Bomber said. 'We've only got enough qualified men to put three planes up. Everybody's gone.'

'*Joe!*' a voice boomed.

Mahoney turned. There, steaming through the crowd, belly-first, was Tank O'Sullivan, lugging his little woman by the hand. '*Joe – I've got some wine I want stowed on board!*' he boomed from ten paces.

Mahoney took his hand, beaming at this very important customer. 'Tank, welcome, but we've got wine on board for you.'

'I want my *own*,' Tank boomed. 'I *only* drink wine . . .'

'All day,' his wife nodded up at Mahoney.

'Tank, around here the customer is always right. How much have you got?'

'Twenty cases,' Tank admitted, 'but it's a goddamn cargo ship, ain't it?'

'We're only going for ten days or so, Tank,' Mahoney grinned.

'That's ten cases for me, ten for you lot. Hate being short.'

373

Mahoney picked up his walkie-talkie, called Lovelock on the ship and told them to stand by to winch twenty cases of wine on board. The admiral said excitedly: 'The Americans are arriving.'

The car came rolling into the official parking area. Mahoney and the Admiral started towards it. A civilian got out, followed by a naval uniform. The Admiral made the introductions, beaming.

'This is Mr Casper P. Legget, of the Pentagon.'

'Call me Cas.'

'And this is Dwight J. Perkins, of the Navy.'

'Call me Dwight, Joe.' He was about fifty, thick-set with short-cropped hair. 'So you don't want me to play with your little bi-plane, Joe?'

'Later,' Mahoney smiled.

'Piece of cake,' Perkins smiled amiably, strolling with him towards the other guests. 'Your admiral, here-ah, and *my* admiral, they even want to play a few war games, drop a few bombs, strafe a few dummy targets to impress these guys – shee-it, nothin' to it. Just give me half an hour to get the hang of the machine.'

'I told you!' the Admiral beamed.

'I'll think about it,' Mahoney smiled.

The Admiral's radio crackled again. 'Here come the Australians.'

Mahoney turned, heart pounding.

The old man smiled bleakly as he shook his hand. Mahoney's heart sank. 'Not a word,' Erling Thoren said. 'I'm very sorry . . .'

Mahoney looked into the old blue eyes, and for a wild moment he thought the man was lying: then he saw the regret.

'Oh, that *stupid* woman! . . .'

'But she will show up somewhere soon. Women cannot keep their mouths shut for long, you know.' He put his hand on Mahoney's shoulder. 'Now forget about it, you have plenty to do, young man.'

Mahoney sighed bitterly.

A minute later, only twenty minutes before the Queen of England was scheduled to arrive, he saw Dolores's car coming and heaved a tense sigh of relief. He continued with his introductions, quickly.

Dolores's car stopped in the public car-park. Shelagh got out.

She lifted out Mahoney's new uniform. She went walking between the other cars, a beautiful blonde woman in a new, elegant suit and a handsome hat.

In a rented car ten spaces away, another beautiful woman sat, completely still, and watched her, with a sinking heart. She had a scarf tied around her head, to conceal her hair, and she was wearing big sunglasses. In the back of her car was a single suitcase.

From where she sat, Tana had a clear view down the cordoned avenue, of the marquee and the Queen's dais, the great airship beyond. She watched Shelagh Mahoney carrying her husband's uniform, and her heart was breaking.

Shelagh came towards him, smiling cheerfully: 'Hullo, darling!' Mahoney was astonished. The television men swung into action, to capture this touching domestic scene of the dutiful wife bringing her husband his uniform in which to greet his queen. Shelagh kissed the smile he had frozen on his face.

'This is a surprise,' he whispered grimly.

He took the uniform and hurried towards the marquee. She followed him, smiling and nodding at the official guests. Erling Thoren was looking at him with a fixed, regretful smile.

'Mr Thoren.' He stopped brusquely. 'This is my wife.'

Shelagh smiled dazzlingly. 'How do you do?' The old man gallantly took her hand and gave a slight bow.

'It is a great pleasure to meet you, Mrs Mahoney.'

'Equally,' she said, 'Mr Thoren.'

Mahoney turned and hurried angrily into the marquee. He hastily stripped off his old uniform and began pulling on the new one. She sauntered over to him with a bright smile.

375

'Dolores says good luck. I told her I'd bring your suit. She's minding Cathy in the office.'

'Thank you.'

She said airily, 'Where've you been staying this last week?'

'With a friend.'

'I figured that much. Male or female?'

He did not answer.

She waved a hand outside. 'Tana's not here, I see?' She faced him. 'Joe? After these trials, will you come home?'

He looked at her. 'No, Shelagh.'

She said: 'Please.'

He shook his head. 'I'm sorry, Shelagh.'

She took a deep breath, and turned aside. She said, 'I think you should.' She paused. 'You see, I've taken further legal advice. And those shares are still mine, because it was a sale subject to the condition that they were only yours, to register in your name, if you paid in full within a reasonable time. Which you haven't . . . So I can sell them to whoever I please.' She held up a hand, and went on casually, 'Tex Weston's been in touch again. He's in town. He badly wants to buy. He's offering me even more now.'

Mahoney felt cold fury. He said quietly, 'You're wrong, Shelagh.'

She looked at him with beautiful big eyes. 'If I sold to Tex, he would then control Redcoat – and the airship company.'

He felt white with anger. 'I'm a lawyer, Shelagh.'

'So is Tex's lawyer.' She turned aside again. 'You could find a nasty legal battle on your hands.' She turned back to him. 'You won't like that. By your own admission you don't know much law.' She looked at him. 'Don't make me do it. I will, you know. If I have to lose my husband I might as well be rich.'

He was shaking inside. 'You're rich with the money I'm paying you.'

'I might as well be *very* rich.' She pulled a photocopy document from her pocket. 'Here's Tex's offer. It only needs me to sign and he can take it to the Registrar of Companies and have the shares registered in his name.'

The Admiral's walkie-talkie rasped and he called excitedly:

'The Queen's coming! Everybody in the line-up, please!'

'May I?' Shelagh smiled dazzlingly at Mahoney. She took his arm.

Mahoney stood in line, his nerves stretched tight, a dry ache behind his eyes; he had a fluttering sensation in his chest; about his giant, bankrupting airship that he was about to test-fly, about Tana, about the terrible threat his wife had made. Anne Todd was on the other side of him. The Admiral's radio spoke again, the bandmaster gave a signal; the band struck up *God Save the Queen*, and Mahoney got gooseflesh. A big black car appeared, coming across the airfield, followed by another car, and a roar of welcome went up above the anthem, little flags waving. Mahoney's pulse was racing, and he felt his confused, battered heart swell with pride. Now the royal car was pulling up and he could actually see her . . . The Admiral and the Air Marshal stepped forward, the Air Marshal saluting.

Mahoney stood in the line-up, numbed, watching the Queen out of the corner of his eye coming closer and closer, shaking hands, smiling, saying a few words . . . Then she was shaking hands with Malcolm just two paces from him, talking; then with Anne . . . Then she was standing in front of him, smiling, and Mahoney felt his heart turn over.

In pure, patriotic love for the charming, attractive woman who was his queen, smiling up at him, and he just wanted to drop to one knee and kiss her hand and swear that he was her loyal subject, he would lay down his life for her and all she stood for —

'I beg your pardon, Ma'am?' he croaked.

'I said I believe you used to be one of my counsel in Rhodesia, as it then was.'

Mahoney could hardly believe it. *His queen knew he used to represent her? How did she know that?* . . . 'Yes – yes, I was, Ma'am.'

'Did you enjoy that?'

'Oh, I often wish I were still,' he lied shamelessly.

Her Majesty smiled. 'I really do congratulate you and wish you every success, Mr Mahoney.'

'*Thank* you, Ma'am.'

'I remember my father telling me about the Zeppelins of the First World War. I'm very much looking forward to seeing over your ship.'

Mahoney said fervently, 'I very much wish your Majesty were flying with us!'

Queen Elizabeth smiled: 'Maybe I will, one day.'

'Your Majesty,' Mahoney gushed, 'has a *standing* invitation . . .'

Everything was ready. The last checks and adjustments had been done, the list trembling in his hand as he read it off with Lovelock. With them were the two C.A.A. inspectors, Ed, Pomeroy, and Malcolm, flushed and nervous, his grey hair awry. Down below them, through the sweep of windows, was the sea of upturned faces. The Queen was standing on the dais, reading her speech into the microphone. And Mahoney was standing on air.

Walking on air. For almost an hour he had been in Her Majesty's company, showing her over his ship, and he was amazed. At all she knew about airships, about the economics of aviation, the Third World transportation problems: and he was so *proud*, of her, for knowing all that, which most people didn't, for *caring* . . . 'I was very interested in what you had to say about the environmental benefits, Mr Mahoney . . .' *His queen had read what he had to say?* . . . And she had thought his ship wonderful, 'and *such* an appropriate name. I hope there is indeed a pot of gold at the end of her journey!'

And Mahoney would have thrown down his cloak for her, fought all her wars for her, led the charge of the Light Brigade for her . . .

Now he stood at the controls beside Lovelock, and he had totally forgotten his wife's threat and he was no longer afraid of his ship, of her hugeness, of the dazzling array of instruments – he even wished that he was captain today instead of Lovelock. And he just wished with all his heart that Tana was down there watching, her heart bursting with pride too, and when he looked at Shelagh he was so happy and sure of himself that he felt a rush of compassion for what she might be suffering. Then Her Majesty was saying:

'I name this ship *Rainbow*. May God bless her and all who fly in her . . .'

The bottle of champagne swung through the air, smashed against the airship's nose, and a roar of applause went up as the Royal Air Force band struck up *Rule Britannia*. At the same moment the mooring was uncoupled, and the great airship rose.

She rose slowly, massively upwards, and a roar went up. Lovelock lifted the airship, fifty, a hundred, two hundred feet, the faces receding midst the blaring music; then he eased the engines into the horizontal, and the great ship surged foward and upwards. He was smiling.

Malcolm was grinning all over his face. 'This is what flying is all about, Malcolm!' Mahoney wanted to hug the man and dance around the flight deck with him, and he would have if the inspectors hadn't been there.

'Congratulations . . .' Mr Carter said. Mr Perry said nothing.

Mahoney just wanted to take over the controls and fly his wonderful ship himself. She climbed higher and higher, then slowly turned into a circle over the airfield, huge and silver. Now the band was playing *When The Saints Come Marching In*, and the green fields of Bedfordshire were rolling away to misty horizons.

The royal motorcade left in a mass of waving and cheering, then some of the crowd began to dissipate. In the marquee, the jolly Admiral rubbed his hands and said to the guests: 'What say we splice the mainbrace while we wait?'

Shelagh Mahoney said her goodbyes with great charm and walked away. But she did not go straight to the car-park. She walked into the huge open doors of the Redcoat hangar. She stopped, and looked about her. It was so vast she was not sure whether anybody was there. For a minute she stood, looking; and a tear began to glisten in each eye.

'Excuse me, madam, but the public's not allowed in here.'

She started, and turned to the workman. 'I am Mrs Mahoney. I would like to use a telephone, please.'

'Oh. This way, ma'am.'

He led her across the vast floor, to a glass cubicle. She went in, closed the door. She lit a cigarette, then dialled.

'Hullo?' Tex Weston said.

She pulled tensely on her cigarette. 'Tex, there are a few points about our proposed deal I'd like to clear up.'

'Of course,' Weston said eagerly. 'How about dinner tonight?'

'That would be very pleasant.'

Weston said, 'Tell you what – how about dinner in Paris? At the Ritz?' He smiled. 'My car will fetch you to the airport. No sweat, come as you are. I glimpsed you on television and you look absolutely stunning.'

She was smiling. 'Oh yes? – and what about a toothbrush?'

Weston laughed. 'I think the Ritz runs to toothbrushes.'

She smiled. 'Dinner in London will be fine, Tex.'

Weston sighed, then said ardently: 'Oh Shelagh, come *away* with me, godammit. Paris, New York, Tahiti – *any*where.'

She said firmly, 'Dinner in London, Tex. Send your car for me at eight.'

She walked slowly out of the vast hangar. She got into her car. She eased out into the stream of traffic.

Twenty yards away, Tana Hutton sat behind her steering wheel, and watched her go. Then she took a deep breath, lifted her sunglasses and wiped her knuckle under each eye. Then she started her car and eased out into the traffic also. To drive back to London, to her hotel. To fetch the rest of her luggage. To drive to Heathrow Airport. To board an aeroplane, to Australia.

The tears were running down her face.

CHAPTER 59

It was early afternoon when the *Rainbow* came sailing back
over the skies to Cardington. There were still over a thousand
people down there. Joe Mahoney, feeling gaunt, feeling battered, was elated. His ship had handled like a dream! All
systems had been briefly checked at various altitudes, and all
had been perfect.

'In these superb weather conditions,' Mr Perry said point-
edly. 'We haven't seen any wind yet. Or significant temperature variation. Or rain.'

'We'll try to find them for you in the next ten days, Mr
Perry.'

'Nobody *looks* for bad weather, sir,' Mr Perry said primly.

Mahoney smiled. 'Of course not.' It wouldn't be hard to get
into Mr Perry's bad books.

'Nor is she loaded,' Mr Perry further pointed out, as if she
should have been. Nevertheless he was 'prepared' to issue a
provisional certificate, enabling trials to be conducted with
observers aboard, subject to the ship being docked satisfac-
torily at her mast.

'By you, Mr Mahoney,' Perry said. 'Not by Mr Lovelock.'

Mahoney looked at him, astounded. The man was looking
ahead smugly, like a schoolmaster who had surprised a boy he
doesn't like. Mahoney wanted to protest that it was the ship
which was being tested, not his concessionary licence, that it
was not a fair test of the ship – but he kept his mouth shut.

He took over, his mouth dry and salty, and by God he
wanted a drink. Lovelock stood at the other controls. 'Piece
of cake,' he whispered.

Mahoney brought her into a wide circle over the airfield, to
get her measure, and his heart was knocking. He looked at
the wind indicator, then lined up his great sweep of bows with
the mast, into the small breeze. He eased the throttles down,
and then up again, up. . . . There was nothing but that mast
sticking up away over there and his huge, multi-million pound

ship, and he hated Mr Perry with all his heart. He clamped his mind shut to the whole goddamn lot of them and prayed Please God. . . . He eased the ship forward; fifty feet, forty, thirty. . . . 'Let go,' he ordered.

Lovelock pressed the button and mooring line came snaking down out of the bows. It hit the earth, and the Air Force boys ran for it, and they coupled it to the mast's line.

'Heave-in!'

The winch whirred and the slack came back in, and the great ship nosed, nosed up to the mast. And she was moored. Mahoney closed his eyes and Malcolm shouted *'Bravo!'* and Ed said, 'Well done!' Out there the crowds were cheering.

'Very well,' Mr Perry said.

An hour later all the official passengers were aboard. There was a holiday mood. The Admiral led them through the empty hold, up to the saloon. *'Now* then, gentlemen.' He rubbed his hands. The brass band burst into *It's a Long Way to Tipperary* and the crowd started singing. Lovelock said, 'Slip her,' and the mooring line crashed. He vectored the engines and the great ship lifted again into the afternoon. She circled the field midst the music and singing; then Lovelock turned her head for London, and the English Channel beyond.

Ahead was the Thames, St Paul's sitting bulbously, the Houses of Parliament, the Tower, Trafalgar Square, Buckingham Palace. . . . And down in the streets of London faces were upturned, traffic slowed. The airship circled low over the city in the winter sunshine, casting her big shadow, and the blare of the car horns rose up.

The suburbs of London slipped by below, then the rolling fields of Surrey and Sussex, the M24 motorway a broad swathe of black through the green. Mahoney stood on the bridge, his bruised heart full of pride, and full of sadness that Tana was not here beside him, to share the thrill of it, the beauty of the countryside just down there, the marvellous feeling of floating . . . and he was glad with all his heart that it was truly over with Shelagh. And he tried to push everything out of his mind except this ship and getting her airworthiness certificate. Ahead was the blue expanse of the Channel; then the French coast was looming, golden-brown sands with the surf rolling in, and the sea was changing colour. Over the coast they flew, the French countryside rolling by below, big fields dotted with solid homesteads, farmers and children waving: then ahead lay Paris, sprawling.

Down on the poplar-lined highway cars were honking and the people waving. They flew five hundred feet above the treetops, then there was the Seine winding through the famous city, the Eiffel Tower rearing up. They flew slowly along the Seine in the late afternoon, the noble Tuileries over there, the Sacre Coeur, and cars were following them. They sailed majestically down the Champs-Elysées, the honking following them all the way, over the Arc de Triomphe they flew; then they headed for the Eiffel Tower. They went sailing around the huge, graceful structure, six hundred feet of airship gleaming in the sun, all the colours of the rainbow, and Mahoney's heart was full thinking of that day almost ninety years ago when a brave young man called Alberto Santos-Dumont made history by flying around this tower on a De Dion tricycle and a bag of hydrogen. Oh God, he was proud to be making history again, and oh God he wished that Tana was here to share it with him, and Mr Perry said stiffly:

'This is enough showing off, Mr Mahoney. . . . Can we get on with the work?'

'Of course, Mr Perry.' He turned with formality: 'Over to you, Mr Lovelock.' He turned back to Perry. 'We'll be keeping a watch-system from now on. We'll work four hours on, eight hours off.'

'I know what watch-keeping is,' Mr Perry said.

'Of course. I'll be back on watch at midnight. But, of course, I am at your disposal twenty-four hours a day. And now, I wonder if you'd like to test our bar?'

'A *drink*?' Mr Perry said, scandalized.

Oh, Mahoney dearly wanted to tell Mr Perry the difference between aeroplanes and ships. He dearly wanted to tell Mr Perry that he was a prick.

'I meant a nice lemonade.'

Mr Perry made a mental note of this bare-faced lie. He turned, clasped his hand behind his back. 'No thank you, Mr Mahoney.'

Mahoney paused outside the saloon door. He felt haggard. He was not looking forward to facing Erling Thoren. He smoothed his hair; then walked in.

The saloon was jumping. There was a babble of talking and laughing and cigarette smoke. Behind the bar stood the Admiral in his best suit, flushed and jolly. Erling Thoren stood in the centre of a group, glass in hand, telling a funny story, his audience hanging on his words. Mahoney made his way to the bar, smiling and nodding. 'Hullo, young fella,' the Admiral beamed. 'What can we get for you?'

Mahoney beckoned and the Admiral leaned forward conspiratorially. 'A beer, in a teacup. Mr Perry thinks this is an aeroplane.'

'Aha-ha-ha!' the Admiral guffawed. 'I'll cover for you, young fella!' He put his hand over Mahoney's: 'Congrat*ulations* . . . Everything's gone *beau*tifully, jolly good show! That flip over London – they loved it! And around the Eiffel Tower – ooh, la! la!'

'Thank you, Admiral.'

'I say, young fella, don't you think you can call me Freddie, now we know each other?'

Mahoney smiled. 'Freddie doesn't sound quite right, Admiral. I kind of think of you as The Admiral.'

'Aha-ha-ha!' the Admiral guffawed. 'Jolly good show anyway!'

'Where's Malcolm?'

'Gone off to bed, drunk as a lord!'

'You're kidding!' Mahoney said, aghast.

'Gone off to bed, sober as a judge!'

'*Joe!*' Tank boomed, barrelling towards him with a beer-mug of wine in his hairy fist. 'This is a marvellous fucking machine—'

'You want your *own*?' Mahoney grinned.

'I want my fucking *own*!' Tank boomed.

*

Mahoney awaited his moment. 'May I have a word, Mr Thoren?'

Erling turned, with a little sympathetic smile. He took Mahoney's arm and led him to a window. Mahoney took a deep breath. 'I just want to say I'm so very sorry. I so badly wanted Tana to be here.'

'Young man, you do not have to explain yourself to me.'

Mahoney glared out of the window. 'There was no deception. Shelagh coming back was a complete surprise. For a day or two I was confused. But not any more. Her coming to Cardington today was a total surprise. It has no significance.'

The old man nodded. 'I've lived long enough to know that nothing is simple – certainly not triangles. The simple fact is they don't work. I am sorry for Tana, of course, because she was so happy. But it was quite impractical, and she will get over it. As you will.'

Mahoney sighed. 'There *is* no triangle,' he said.

The old man smiled. 'Never underestimate women, my friend. Your wife is not only very beautiful, and probably very nice too, but she is also very determined.' He put his hand on Mahoney's shoulder. 'Forget about Tana. She lives the other side of the world. Right now you have to worry about your customers, you know.'

Mahoney closed his eyes in exasperation. 'I want to telephone her. You know where she is, don't you?'

Earling looked at him, wondering what was for the best. Then he shook his head.

'I don't,' he said.

In the galley, the Air Force cook was preparing dinner. In the saloon, quite a party was developing. Tank O'Sullivan was trying to organize a quartet of Bomber Brown, Daniel Moyo, Air Marshal Thompson and himself to render *Red Sails in the Sunset* immortal. Erling Thoren stood at a far window, a pained expression on his face, trying to talk above the noise to Dwight

385

Perkins and Cas Legget. He said: 'I am very pleased you people are taking it seriously.'

Cas Legget said, 'Well, hang on, now. The U.S. Government is interested in anything to do with oil conservation and reducing our dependency on the Arabs – and NASA is interested in anything to do with the administration of space – but I don't think the Pentagon sees them as significant military vehicles, except for coastline surveillance.'

Dwight said, 'Then the Pentagon's wrong! You've been flying a goddamn desk too long, Cas. We could have done with airships in Vietnam, instead of shipping our troops by sea. We could have got them there in a quarter of the time.'

'What about the Falklands?' Erling said.

'What about the Falklands' war?' Dwight said aggressively. 'Shee-it, the British had to use the *QE II* as a troopship and how long did that take, compared to which this can dash at a hundred miles an hour? And the *QE II*'s a much bigger target than these things, Cas.' He turned to Erling with disgust. 'Goddamn bureaucrats.'

'And if an exocet sank the *QE II*,' Erling said earnestly, 'you'd lose hundreds of millions of pounds, but one airship costs only fifteen million.'

'*Exactly*,' Dwight said. 'You could afford dozens of airships for the price of one goddamn *QE II*!' He turned to Erling. 'That may impress him, bureaucrats are always impressed by money.'

'Dwight,' Cas smiled bleakly, 'you navy guys have a nostalgia for the old Akron airship-carrier, but remember. . . .'

'I have a nostalgia for common sense!' Dwight said. 'For the days when fighting men made the decisions, not a bunch of pen-pushers and vote-chasers in Washington!' He turned to Erling: 'I don't give a shit anymore, I'm retiring next year.' He turned back to Cas. 'I'm sick of this half-arsed attitude. We'd have won the Vietnam war if it weren't for goddamn politicians. We could have got the hostages out of Iran in one night if politicians minded their own business! We could knock off Kadaffi in five minutes – *and* Castro.' He shook his head. 'Shee-it, can you imagine the Russians tolerating a capitalist revolution in Poland? Yet we tolerate Castro's communist revolution right on our goddamn doorstep!'

'Exactly,' Erling Thoren said fervently. 'And now we tolerate Kadaffi building military airships.'

'There is no proof—' Cas began.

'A Trojan Horse,' old Erling interrupted earnestly. 'His airships fly across Africa. We think they are cargo ships. Out come troops and tanks. In one day he moves a whole army thousands of miles!'

'Shoot the bastard,' Dwight said. 'That's what I say.'

Mahoney leant against the bar, with Bomber Brown. He was on edge – he wanted to be back on his bridge, but the awful Perry was there. He knew he ought to rest. He had tried lying down but his mind was filled with Tana, and what Shelagh had said. Bomber was saying, 'Moyo is a fire-brand, but hell, it's the commercial role we want. I'm only here because I'm about the most senior airman the country's got now.' He took a mouthful of lemonade. 'With the airship, Zimbabwe hopes to trade easily with North Africa, West Africa, all the places where we've got no road or rail connections.'

'Right,' Mahoney said distractedly. He was sick of trying to sell airships. 'What's happenimg to those six Air Force officers who were acquitted?'

'Still in jail. I hear a rumour that three of them are going to be released soon because Britain is kicking up a fuss.'

'And the others?'

'God knows. Poor bastards!' He shook his head. 'Tortured. Give me a few hours with any man and I'll have him confessing to sinking the *Titanic*.'

'Who do you think did it?'

Bomber sighed. 'Classified information. But somebody who doesn't want a communist Zimbabwe to have an effective Air Force. That includes a lot of big business outfits, not necessarily government. And there're plenty of very professional gentlemen, like ex-Selous Scouts, ready, willing and able to do the job.' He added, 'You know a few of them.'

Mahoney wondered what he meant. 'Like Max?'

Bomber sighed. 'Classified. But there's going to be another war. All those angry Matabele soldiers taken to the bush?'

'But how can they mount a rebellion? They haven't got a base outside the country any more.'

'They've got friends.' Bomber sighed. 'I'm so sick of war. . . If you pull off this deal and you're training our crews down there, be bloody careful. You'll make a very interesting target.'

It was a strange feeling. He had to be charming to this very important customer, but he also wanted to like him, as a man, to let bygones be bygones. He answered Daniel Moyo's question: 'I was in the army. And you?'

'You men could fight,' Daniel Moyo said. 'I was a section commander on the Eastern Front.'

Mahoney said politely, 'Where did you train?'

'Outside Peking.'

'Did you enjoy that? How were the Chinese?'

Daniel Moyo glanced over his shoulder to ensure the Chinese observers could not hear, then said out of the side of his mouth: '*Bast*ards!'

Mahoney grinned. Moyo dropped a hand on his shoulder and grinned into his ear: 'More cheek than the white man!'

Mahoney threw back his head and laughed.

Erling Thoren whispered, 'Be nice to the general before he gets drunker.'

'Good evening, sir,' Mahoney said jovially to the bemedalled general of the Ugandan Army. 'Are people looking after you?'

The huge black man glowered at him with bloodshot eyes, then amiably held out his half-full glass. 'Death to Idi Amin!'

'*Absolutely*,' Mahoney beamed. He took the glass and headed for the bar. He came back, the glass stiff with whisky.

'Actually,' a lanky English aide was saying to Erling Thoren, 'Uganda's interest in the airship is purely commercial, not military.'

The general's big hand closed around the proffered whisky. 'Cheers!' He upended the glass and swallowed half of it. Then looked at Mahoney murderously. 'Did you go to Sandhurst, Captain?'

'No.' Mahoney grinned.

The general upended the rest of the glass. 'Kadaffi must die!' Erling Thoren was delighted.

A black hand slipped around Mahoney's arm and took the teacup of beer from his hand. 'Here comes Mr Perry,' Daniel Moyo whispered.

Mahoney turned guiltily. Mr Perry was striding through the smoke-filled saloon like a thoroughly disapproving Bantam rooster. He disappeared through the aft accommodation door, with a firm little bang. Mahoney bounded for the telephone on the bar and buzzed the bridge. 'Ed, anything wrong?'

'Yes,' Ed rumbled. 'It's all going too smoothly. This is the way to fly!'

It was really his last drink; then he had to try to sleep till midnight. He was just drunk enough to say it: 'Tell me, Daniel. Are you really a communist?'

The black man grinned with perfect teeth.

'Sure. Why not?' He put his hand on Mahoney's shoulder. 'You know the big mistake you whites made? . . . You just hit us over the head with your capitalism! You were superior. And you forgot that the army must be the fish swimming in the waters of the people, as Mao Tse-tung said.'

Mahoney looked at him.

'And were *you* the fish?' He wanted to add, Or the sharks?

Moyo grinned. 'We didn't have to be. You whites had made such a mess of it. Unintentionally, maybe. Because you were *honest* administrators. But you were so. . .' He was going to say 'stupid' but searched for a polite word.

'We didn't win the hearts and minds of the people?'

Moyo said: 'You know, if you had paid us a decent wage, I would never have joined up.' He jangled some coins in his pocket. 'That's what a man thinks with. But if he has nothing to lose?'

CHAPTER 60

The Alps reared up in the sunset, high above the airship, a great mass of black and white peaks: the airship sailed serenely down the Rhone Valley, glinting pink and dwarfed by the mountains. When the lights of Lyon were dropping astern, the first winds came.

They came from the north, across the plains towards the warm Mediterranean, funnelling down the valley, bending trees. Everybody felt the ship surge beneath them, drinks jolted: immediately the next rush came, and the ship surged again, stronger. Mahoney scrambled off his bed, and threw on some clothes. He bounded barefoot up the stairway and burst on to the bridge.

Mr Perry had his legs braced, holding the back of the pilot's seat. Mahoney grabbed the other seat-back. 'Take her up two thousand feet?'

'Doing that,' Ed muttered.

Mahoney watched the altimeter as the ship rose, the dark countryside dropping below. He noted the ground-speed.

The ship levelled out at her new altitude. Mahoney stood with bated breath, waiting for the next buffet, his heart beating fast. But it did not come. The ship seemed to have settled down. 'How does she feel, Ed?'

'O.K.,' Ed said guardedly. Then he remembered Mr Perry: 'Perfect!'

'Seventy-five knots,' Mahoney said. 'Try cutting the engines back.'

Ed eased the throttles back. The speedometer slowly dropped, then eased upwards again slowly, then settled at the original speed.

'Bloody marvellous,' Mahoney breathed.

Mr Perry was still clutching the seat-back. 'What is?' He waved his hand. 'We have just witnessed this airship's behaviour in low wind-gusts, and frankly I found it rather frightening.'

390

Mahoney turned to him. 'A little startling,' he agreed. 'But I've seen aircraft knocked around by vertical gusts more than that.'

'But they had the weight and the speed to carry them through!'

'It's our *size* that makes it seem frightening; it's psychological.'

'And the fact that she's weightless! If we'd been close to a mountain, and the winds were stronger, we could have been dashed against them!'

Was the man frightened, or not feeling well? Or just a prick?

'She is only "weightless" in the same sense that a ship at sea is weightless, Mr Perry. A ship floats because of the water she displaces, even though she weighs a hundred thousand tons – but once floating she "weighs" nothing. Same with this airship. She is floating on air, instead of water. But she still has the inertia of her *mass* – it takes a lot of wind to push her around, just like an ocean liner.'

'You will kindly not instruct me in elementary physics!'

'And nobody flies so close to a mountain that he hasn't a wide safety margin – like a ship doesn't sail too close to the rocks.'

Mr Perry glared at him. 'And you reckon you've got the reserve power to cope with seventy-knot winds trying to drive you against a mountain?'

'Of course. It's in the design, which was approved by your department.'

'My department, Mr Mahoney, hasn't seen an airship in fifty years! We know as little about them as you do.' He glared, then paced, his hands behind his back. 'What, pray, was so "bloody marvellous"?'

Mahoney controlled his irritation. 'We've caught a trade-wind. We were doing seventy-odd knots before. Now the wind's behind us, we're still doing seventy knots, with less throttle. We're saving fuel.'

Mr Perry nodded slowly.

'Fuel costs. Is that all you people think about? But economy at what price? At the cost of lives?'

Oh dear, Mahoney thought. The door opened and Lovelock

391

came on to the bridge, wearing trousers only, skinny and lanky and rubbing one eye. 'Everything O.K.?'

'Sure,' Mahoney said.

'That', Mr Perry said, 'is a matter of opinion.'

Mahoney told him what had happened. Lovelock looked at the instruments owlishly. 'O.K.,' he shrugged. 'I'll go back to bed.'

Mahoney was grinning.

It was nearly eight o'clock. Mahoney's off-duty period was half gone. Ed was about to come on duty. Mahoney should have been resting. He had gone back to his cabin, undressed, but he was unable to sleep. He was over-tired from days of strain. Finally he had got up, and gone back to the bridge out of sheer inability to leave the ship alone.

The Mediterranean was two thousand feet below, silvery black in the moonlight. Astern, shore lights were twinkling like jewels. There was not a breath of wind. That's what Mahoney was grimly hoping for, strong winds in which to demonstrate his ship for Mr Bloody Perry, far away from nasty mountains.

'I'm sorry,' he said. 'The wind's bound to pick up later, but you should get some sleep. We have to take on some ballast soon, so I suggest we do that test now.'

'I want', Mr Perry said, 'to see the ballast-suction tested in windy conditions, and near land.'

That was exactly what Mahoney did not want. 'As you wish. We'll be at the coast of North Africa later, I'll wake you, though it's a shame to disturb your sleep for such a simple exercise.'

'Oh, very well,' Perry said, 'let's get it over with now.'

'Thank you.' He smiled at Ed. 'Mr Hazeltine?'

Ed eased the lever, and a hundred yards astern the engines vectored, the tail flaps turned, and the giant began to ease down towards the silvery sea. Mahoney said: 'If there was wind, we'd have our bows into it, of course.'

Mr Perry said nothing. The ship was descending like a cloud.

'One hundred feet,' Ed said. 'Eighty. Seventy . . . Hovering.'

From the bows a stout hose began to drop down. At the end was a submersible electric pump. It sank beneath the glassy sea. A light shone on the panel. 'Activate.'

'Activate pump.' Mahoney flicked a switch. Gallons of water began to pulse upwards into the ballast tanks of the ship.

They waited, watching their gauges, the ship hovering.

'How long would you like this test to run, Mr Perry? We'll have to ballast up again anyway, before we start crossing Africa.'

Mr Perry clasped his hands behind his back.

'Until I am satisfied.' He looked at the instruments. 'In fact, I can tell you now that I am not satisfied. The sea is dead calm. If there were waves, and the pump sloshing about, maybe it would not work. If there were winds, the ship may be dragging.' He shrugged. 'So you may terminate the exercise, until the conditions I mention exist. Goodnight.'

'What a nice little guy,' Ed muttered.

Fifteen thousand miles away, over Antarctica, it was tomorrow's brilliant sunshine.

CHAPTER 61

Two thousand feet below, the Sahara stretched on, silvery, the dunes casting shadows. It was the coldest part of the night, just before dawn. Mahoney slept at last, having finished his second watch. The intercom buzzed. He was instantly awake. He snatched up the telephone. 'Will you come to the bridge, please?' Mr Perry said.

Mahoney grabbed at his clothes. He was still shucking on his jacket when he hurried up on to the bridge. 'What's wrong?'

Mr Perry turned to him calmly. 'The outside temperature is almost zero centigrade, I see. According to your manual, your lift should have increased with the cold. Why is it that this aircraft is only flying at two thousand feet?'

Mahoney was furious. He wanted to shout, *Do you realize my sleep is important?* But he swallowed it. His eyes swept the console. 'Because Mr Hazeltine is holding her at this altitude aerodynamically.'

'Right,' Ed said, mystified. 'I was at five thousand feet. But there're adverse winds up there.'

'Then that',·Mr Perry said, 'is where I want you to fly, please.'

Mahoney looked at him angrily. 'Find the winds,' he said to Ed.

He turned and strode off the bridge before he said anything indiscreet. He slung off his jacket, sat down on his bed and held his head.

God, he was tired. But it was no good, he was wide-awake. He got up angrily, went to the galley, made coffee. He took it back to the bridge.

The sun came up over the desert, fiery red, driving away the stars, glinting silvery gold on the airship. As the metal absorbed the sun's heat, the helium's temperature began to rise slowly. Mahoney pointed at the gauge and said: 'Helium is expanding. As helium expands, it increases its lifting power.'

'I know,' Mr Perry said. 'Superheat. If we're gaining lifting power, why are we maintaining the same altitude?'

Mahoney looked at the little man. He had been trying to make conversation. But Perry was treating him like an examiner.

'Because the outside air which we are floating on is also getting warmer, and therefore lighter, so for the moment a natural balance is being maintained.'

'Correct,' Mr Perry said. 'And when the ballonets are emptied by your expanding helium, and your helium is still expanding and you are still rising, what then?'

Mahoney knew he should not say it. 'Mr Perry. That Operations Manual you're referring to? – I wrote it.'

'And I', Mr Perry said, 'happen to have studied it. And I am charged with the responsibility of testing its efficiency.'

Mahoney took a deep breath. 'I'm sorry.'

'Accepted,' Mr Perry said. 'I never let personality differences interfere with the discharge of my statutory duties. Now, please answer my question?'

Mahoney pulled himself together.

'When superheat causes me to gain too much altitude, I would either have to valve off some of the helium to reduce the pressure, and so lose lift, or I would fly the ship downwards and maintain my chosen altitude aerodynamically.' He added: 'How's that?'

'And which', Mr Perry said, 'will you do? And please just answer the questions.'

Mahoney wanted to say, Both if you like, Mr Perry-sir, I'll stand on my fucking head if you like, Mr Perry-sir. 'Neither.'

'How so?' Mr Perry demanded.

'Because this is not my watch. Mr Hazeltine is in command at the moment and it'll be his decision.'

'I see,' Mr Perry said grimly. 'And which *would* you do?'

Mahoney said in a flat tone: 'Obviously, I would reduce height by flying downwards aerodynamically, rather than valve off helium.'

'Why? I want a full answer, please treat nothing as "obvious".'

'Because', Mahoney said flatly, 'valving off helium into the sky is expensive. This airship is presently pressurized with enough helium to make her fly at seven thousand feet maximum. Of course, she can fly at twice that height, but if she goes above seven thousand feet the helium will expand to bursting point, so I would have to valve off some in order to reduce the pressure. This is not only expensive, but also means I would lose lifting power for my cargo, so at some stage I would have to make the ship lighter by dumping water ballast, which I cannot recover until I fly over some more water. All unnecessary work.'

Mr Perry said, 'Unnecessary or not, it is my duty to ensure the ship can do both. Please keep her down to two thousand feet aerodynamically for the time being. Then, when she's adequately superheated, I want you to let her rise to seven thousand feet and valve off helium.'

'*You want me to waste helium deliberately?*'

395

'It is not a *waste*, Mr Mahoney – it's a *test*!' He smacked the manual. 'I intend to find out whether the theory works! And whether those valves work.' He glared at him. 'And when we see cloud, over the equator, I want you to fly into it and cool your ship, then fly back into the sunshine again to test the impact of sudden superheat!'

Impact, Mahoney thought. The man was hoping it would be a mortal blow. He did not care anymore. Mr Perry was very efficient. Mr Perry was a prick. Mr Perry was a very efficient prick.

The desert stretched on and on, shimmering brown and grey, the sun beating down on the flying ship. And the shimmering heat rose up off the sands in waves, creating pockets of hot, light air, and rising columns. Lovelock obediently drove the airship through them at two thousand feet, like a ship ploughing into waves, her bows plunging and surging up the other side. Mr Perry clung, his face grey, doggedly watching the ship's performance. Mahoney said cheerfully, 'Amidships, it's much steadier, of course. Or we could climb a few thousand feet and maybe fly over the worst of this.'

'That', Mr Perry replied bleakly, 'is not the point. I am testing this aircraft on the basis that it has to fly across this hot terrain at this low altitude, laden with cargo. Is she safe? Can she stand up to the stresses and strains?'

'Of course,' Mahoney said.

And, oh yes, she was safe, she could stand up to the stresses and strains. Lovelock ploughed her through the sky like a ship ploughing the seas, until Mr Perry's grim face began to go ashen, then suddenly he lurched around and stumbled away, down the stairs, with his hand over his mouth. Mahoney and Lovelock were laughing.

Five minutes later he came clutching his way back up the stairs, red-eyed. 'Very well,' he said, 'you may take her up now.'

'Up to five thousand?' Mahoney queried politely. 'Or do you want to go through the pressure ceiling of seven thousand and test those helium valves?'

'Tomorrow.' Mr Perry turned and lurched down the stairs again.

At mid-morning the heavy sales pitch began.

A few stayed in their bunks, nursing hangovers or airsickness, but most of the observers showed up in the saloon for the initial lecture. The Admiral was behind the bar to jolly them along. When everybody had a drink, Malcolm began his lecture on the economics of airships compared to other forms of transportation. This was followed, after an interval for more drinks, by a lecture from the Admiral on the naval role of the airship. Another interval, then Malcolm spoke on the military role. By then it was time for some real pre-prandial drinking, during a question-and-answer period. At the buffet lunch, wine flowed like water. After lunch, when nobody was feeling any pain, the tour began.

It started in the upper cargo hold. Lit, it was more impressive empty than full, the electric lights tapering away. Malcolm demonstrated the cargo hoists, showed them the enclosed man-way that led to the ship's topside. But the *pièce de resistance* came in the lower hold. For there, at the back, stood the only piece of cargo. Erling Thoren's gift of the old Curtiss aeroplane.

There were gasps when Malcolm switched on the lights, like a showman. They had been lectured on the aircraft-carrier capability of the airship, but there had been no hint of what to expect. The little aircraft stood businesslike, her machine-gun glinting, her bomb bays loaded with dummies.

The Ugandan general lumbered forward. He pointed at the aircraft with one hand, at the deck with the other. 'You mean', he boomed at Malcolm, 'this plane can fly *outside*, and come back *inside*?'

'That's it, General. Of course, these days we would do it with more efficient aircraft, but this makes the point.'

'Do it,' the General demanded.

'It would only be a pleasure,' Dwight Perkins smiled. Malcolm pointed out that they would have to get permission to penetrate somebody's air space, but he did the next best thing. While everybody watched, he removed the chocks from under the little aircraft's wheels and untied the webbing holding her down. 'Give us a push, please.'

They got behind the wings and trundled the aeroplane forward, almost to the central cargo hatch. Malcolm pressed a switch, and down from the ceiling eased the telescopic trapeze. He joined the trapeze to the hoop over the cockpit.

'Now everybody stand well back, please.'

He pressed another switch. There was a whirring noise. Suddenly the cargo hatch started opening, and daylight shone in. The desert below widened out before their eyes. The trapeze slid forward, and the aeroplane hung above space. Old Erling's eyes were shining.

'Now,' Malcolm said.

The shiny telescopic arms of the trapeze began to lengthen and swing downwards, and the little aeroplane began to lower through the hatch. Down, down she went. The telescopic arms reached their limit, and the little aeroplane was suspended below the airship, in the open sky. Everybody was staring.

'Now,' Malcolm shouted, 'the pilot starts his engine, unhooks from the trapeze, and flies off on his mission. When he's finished, back he comes, creeps up under the ship at the same speed she's doing, hooks on to the trapeze, and back aboard he comes.'

Dwight was smiling down at the little aircraft.

'You, Captain,' the general boomed, 'could you do it?'

'Only a pleasure, General. Eh, Bomber?'

'Just point me into the wind,' Bomber smiled.

They came on to the bridge in groups of six. Lovelock, Mahoney, Ed and Pomeroy were all present, in newly pressed uniforms.

Mahoney gave a brief welcoming speech, then handed them over to Lovelock, as commander, and to Pomeroy. First Pomeroy explained his job, in his improved accent.

'In an ordinary aircraft, if an engine packs in, like, there's not much the engineer can do about it until the plane is back on the ground – he can't climb out on the bleedin' wing, can

398

he?' But in the airship, a lot of the workin' parts are inside the hull. If something goes wrong, I can put on breathing gear, enter the hull, like, an' work to my heart's content. An' even if *all* the engines failed the ship would still float up there, while I went to work, for days if necessary. Whereas an ordinary aircraft would crash, like. . .'

Erling Thoren came up to Mahoney. 'They loved the little aeroplane,' he whispered.

'Thanks to you.' He sighed. 'I wish Tana were here.'

The old man said, 'Everything is going very well for you, young man. So rejoice and forget about Tana.'

Pomeroy was saying in answer to Daniel Moyo's question, 'If the trouble was outside, an' I had to repair it immediately, the ship would be slowed down, I would climb the ladder to the top of the ship, an' I'd be lowered to the engine in a cradle.'

'What about fuckin' snow?' Tank demanded. 'My mining claim's up there in Canada, where it pisses with snow.'

Pomeroy said, 'We can heat the helium sufficiently to melt the snow. Behind the engines is a scoop which catches the hot exhaust gas and pipes it through the hull, into a heat-exchanger jacket with a built-in fan which sucks cold helium in and blows it out heated.'

'Fuckin' *marvellous*,' Tank boomed.

'But snow can't collect while the ship's moving, because of the slip-stream.'

Mahoney said to Dwight Perkins: 'Erling Thoren tells me you're retiring next year, what are you going to do?'

Dwight smiled. 'Maybe fly for you?'

'May*be* . . . ,' Mahoney smiled back.

'Hell, this is neat.' He indicated the line of television screens which showed the pilot what was happening above, below, astern and on each side of the ship. 'Ain't got that on my jet. Comrade Walter Mitty can come screaming down on me out of the sun and I don't know it till he blows my ass off.'

Lovelock was saying, 'We have charts for the whole world aboard, both airways and admiralty. We navigate like an ordinary aeroplane, but because we expect to fly to parts of the world where there are no airports and navigation aids, we also navigate like a ship at sea, using *this*.' He touched an instrument. 'This is a satellite-navigation system. As you know, numerous man-made satellites are constantly orbiting the earth. They act as artificial suns. This sat-nav's computer has the sight-reduction tables programmed into it. As a satellite passes over, this sat-nav identifies which it is by its signal, measures the angle, does the arithmetic and tells me where I am, giving me a latitude and longitude accurate within a few hundred feet.'

'Fuckin' *marvellous*,' Tank boomed.

'And should the sat-nav break down,' Lovelock said, 'we have this.' He opened a drawer and lifted out a navigator's sextant.

Mahoney said to Dwight: 'Want to fly her?'

'Hell, yes! But what I really want to try is a launch with that little plane of yours.'

Mahoney smiled. He would never understand airmen.

The *Rainbow* sailed on. Way ahead, the shimmering brown horizon was beginning to turn hazy mauve.

Late that afternoon, the *Rainbow* approached the tropics. One thousand feet below was deep green stretching on, without a sign of human life, and the horizon was black with thunderstorm.

Then the sun was fading behind a haze. Soon there was only the blackness ahead, and flashes of lightning. Mahoney looked at it, and he dearly wished he could fly over it, or around it, failing which he dearly wished Lovelock were on watch.

'Nothing to it,' he said to Mr Perry.

'We'll see.' Mr Perry looked at it with bleak satisfaction.

Darker and darker the black stuff loomed. Then big wisps of cloud were flashing past the windows. Then drops of water were suddenly splatting. Suddenly all the light was gone and the blackness rushed over them. There was a blinding flash and a crack like cannon all about them, and the great ship lurched, and rain was smashing on the windows. Mahoney stood in the glow of his instruments, heart hammering, bracing himself. He glanced over his shoulder, then flicked the intercom switch and muttered: 'Lovelock? You still asleep?'

'Always talk in my sleep. Want me to come up?'

'No . . . Just don't go to sleep.'

The *Rainbow* ploughed through the lashing blackness and lightning for one hour: then it was thinning out and the rain grew lighter. She burst out of the thunderstorm into the sunshine again.

Mahoney's mouth was dry and his face clammy, and his heart elated. His ship had come through her first storm with flying colours. And down below him his Africa was beginning. Way ahead lay the Congo and the great Zambesi, with Rhodesia, the land of Monomatopa, beyond it.

CHAPTER 62

There were no bored travellers on the Fairwinds DC 10. Everyone had paid over seven hundred dollars for this one-day round-trip for one reason only – to see a thing of a lifetime, the Antarctic. There was animated conversation between the short lectures, and a lot of complimentary drinks.

It was a brilliant day. The sun shone low out of a cloudless sky. The Southern Ocean stretched on and on, blue-black; then, on the faraway horizon, a white dot appeared. Tana said over the loudspeakers: 'Ahead, on the left side, we are seeing our first iceberg.'

People crossed the aisle to peer. The iceberg grew bigger and bigger, until it was a solitary island, with bays and beaches of ice. And soon the horizon was studded with dots which grew into dazzling icebergs, an archipelago stretching across the horizon, gleaming white and streaked with blue, with high craggy peaks and flat plateaus, and valleys and gorges. Some of them were only the size of a house, some as big as mountains. Tana said over the loudspeakers:

'But what you see is only the tip. Eight-ninths of it is under the sea. That one over to the left is probably a thousand yards long and three or four hundred feet high. Multiply that by nine. . . .'

They could see the ice shelving away under the seas, pale,

then disappearing through turquoise into the blackness; and between the scattered icebergs lay the broken pack-ice, clogging and drifting. Tana said: 'And now, in the distance, we can see the mainland of Antarctica.'

The dark sea was giving way to solid pack-ice, jagged and lumpy, like a vast, white, rocky beach, jammed icebergs rearing up. They could make out the frozen mainland sloping upwards, cliffs and peninsulas of ice and rock and snow.

'What we see ahead is Victoria Land, with Mount Sabine sticking up. Beyond is the big bay of the Ross Sea, and the Ross Ice Shelf. Beyond that is the Queen Alexandra range. They average over twelve thousand feet, about as high as the Himalayas. We will be flying over them on our way to the South Pole, then crossing the South Polar Plateau, which averages about ten thousand feet above sea level, and we hope to follow the route taken by Scott. On our homeward-bound journey, we will be partly following another route, namely that taken by Sir Edmund Hillary in 1958.'

She put down the microphone. Her face was gaunt with heartache and fatigue. She had hardly slept in two days. She was suffering from jetlag, from the long flight to Australia. She did not feel like speaking at all, but it was better than being alone in her house with her thoughts. Or worse, going to the office, to those knowing looks.

Captain Hennessy flew the DC 10 over the white Adare Peninsula, then locked in on the radio beacon at the American base at McMurdo, on the edge of the Ross Ice Shelf. The icebergs of the Ross Sea came into his view. But the sea was obscured by cloud. Captain Hennessy identified himself to the McMurdo station, and requested permission to drop altitude and fly beneath the cloud base for the benefit of his sight-seeing passengers. McMurdo advised that the cloud was five thousand feet, and gave permission to descend to two thousand feet.

Captain Hennessy began his descent into the cloud, and the world disappeared in whiteness. In the passenger cabin, Tana was reading aloud extracts of the diaries of the polar explorers. At five thousand feet the Ross Sea burst into view again, thick

402

with icebergs. Tana interrupted her lecture to confer with Captain Hennessy, then said to her passengers: 'We are now at two thousand feet, and we'll be flying along the Scott Coast, passing the active volcano of Mount Erebus on our left. Then we'll be flying over the Ross Ice Shelf, up the Hillary Coast, and the Shackleton Coast, alongside the Queen Alexandra Range.' She pointed to the large map on the bulkhead. 'With luck, visibility will be good, and enable us to stay low and fly up the Amundsen Glacier, at an appropriate altitude, to the South Pole. Homeward bound, depending on the visibility, we hope to fly down the Beardmore Glacier.'

Captain Hennessy had never flown in polar regions before. He had read about the phenomen of 'white-out', where snowclad landscape and white sky join each other imperceptibly, leaving a pilot without a horizon and dangerously disorientating his senses: but that was not what he was experiencing now. He could see the ice mass below perfectly well, yet for the next moment his mind was confused. He couldn't co-relate distances and images. Then he would grasp it again. Something similar had sometimes happened to him flying over deserts, and particularly over the Red Sea. The heat haze was sometimes such that you weren't sure what you were seeing, sea or sky.

It was nothing like as bad as that now, but it was irritating. Under normal circumstances he would simply climb his aircraft well above the height of the mountains shown on his chart and keep his course; but his passengers had paid dearly to see the fabulous sights of the Antarctic.

The Ross Ice Shelf slid by below under cloud-ragged sunshine, jagged and beautiful and sparkling in spectrums, white and shadowed with dark fissures. The low-flying aeroplane cast a big shadow and down there penguins waddled frantically away, and seals looked up at them, then flopped along and dived into holes. The passengers pressed their faces against the windows, snapping photographs. Tana said: 'We are now approaching the point reached by Captain Scott in 1902.'

Captain Hennessy knew exactly where he was. His distance

measuring equipment clicked off the miles from his last way-point. From the surveyor's map on his knee, he could identify the names of the glaciers he was passing. He looked at the one coming up. 'That must be Beardmore.'

'Magnificent,' his co-pilot murmured.

Hennessy peered at the Beardmore Glacier. He was enthral-led by the huge swathe of ice, maybe a couple of miles wide at the mouth, a solid river of blue and white cascading out of mountains. He could see miles up it, the mountains on either side; and the cloud seemed to dissipate there, he could see clear sunshine sparkling on the peaks. 'That's the one to go up,' he said.

For another twenty minutes they flew alongside the mountain range over the wondrous ice-scape. Then Hennessy said to his co-pilot: 'Getting a bit thick ahead there, Mike.'

In front, up the range, where the Amundsen Glacier was, the cloud base seemed to lower.

'Don't like the look of that, Mike,' Hennessy said.

But he flew on for another few minutes. The cloud seemed to lower all the way. 'Call Mrs Hutton.'

When Tana came, he indicated the looming whiteness.

'We'll have to rise above it. Or circle back, and have a try at the Beardmore Glacier. It's sunny back there still, if we're lucky. Otherwise we have to go right over the top.'

'Oh, try the Beardmore if you can!' Tana said.

Captain Hennessy put his aircraft into a turn, to go back and find the Beardmore Glacier. Twenty minutes later he identified it.

Tana was saying to her passengers: 'Ahead is the Queen Alexandra Range, and in a moment we will be rising to negotiate them, following the Beardmore Glacier at an appropriate altitude. Remember that we are looking at a continent which is one and a half times bigger than the whole of Australia, and which is covered by an icecap hundreds and sometimes *thousands* of metres thick. . . . If that ice-cap were to melt, ladies and gentlemen, the sea level all over the earth would rise a hundred metres – over three hundred and thirty feet!

This means that most of the coastal cities of the world would be drowned.'

She paused for effect: and her heart ached. For what she was about to say she had taken from Mahoney's speech at the Dorchester Hotel: 'It is by no means far-fetched that the ice-cap could melt. Scientists have been warning us about this possibility for a long time. The cause is man's reckless pollution of the atmosphere. The industrial smoke which we daily pour into our skies, the exhaust fumes from car engines, ships and aeroplanes. In time, these will form a shroud around the earth which will create a hothouse effect, trapping the heat that comes off the earth. This would change all the climate patterns, and will melt the ice-caps of the polar regions, causing flooding of the seas. At the same time the sun's vital rays would be unable to penetrate this shroud. The sun makes the oxygen we breathe, along with the oceans' and the earth's vegetation, as well as making our rain. Without the sun the oceans will die, and a most terrible stench will rise up everywhere. There will be no rain to grow our crops, and no oxygen. And we will die, ladies and gentlemen – die, starving and gasping for breath midst the stink of rotting seas . . .'

The passengers pulled faces. Inwardly, Tana closed her eyes in exasperation. Would they ever do anything about it?

Captain Hennessy flew the aircraft towards the big white gap in the high white mountains. Ahead was a marvel of towering icy sunshine. He muttered to his co-pilot: 'Advise McMurdo.'

It is not known why that transmission to McMurdo was not made. There are only theories. Maybe the co-pilot misheard and thought his captain was saying that he would advise McMurdo: or maybe he was so concentrating on the remarkable flight, so enthralled by the wondrous sights, that he simply did not hear.

There is a device called the Black Box which records everything said on the flight-deck. It is the first thing aviation inspectors search for in a wreckage, to help them unravel what happened in the last moments of an aircraft's life. Eventually, the black box of the Fairwinds DC 10 was found, but it provided no concrete evidence as to what happened. The captain's order can be heard, but indistinctly. It is only certain that there was no anxiety on the flight-deck, no shouts of warning: on the contrary, the pilots commented to each other on the awesome beauty, the majesty and tranquillity of what they were seeing. For a moment Tana Hutton's indistinct but enthusiastic voice can be heard. For six minutes more there is only the droning of the engines and Captain Hennessy muttering 'Magnificent!' Then, suddenly, a loud bang and a long, terrible, screeching, metallic noise. Then nothing.

CHAPTER 63

Over central Africa it was the middle of a beautiful night. At midnight Mahoney came on to the bridge, to take over from Lovelock. He was feeling good for a change. For the first time in days he had slept solidly for eight hours, without the help of whisky. He had forced Tex Weston right out of his mind. His ship had sailed like a dream, and this very day he was arriving at the farthest way-point of his flight. For twenty-four hours thereafter they all had nothing to do but sleep some more, before demonstrating this marvellous ship to the prime minster of Zimbabwe. Then, come hell or high water, he was going to find his woman and drag her back to England. His determined good spirits were improved by finding Mr Carter on duty, who now almost bowled him over by saying, 'Mr Perry is very impressed with the ship. And so am I. I think it safe to say that if you don't blot your copybook in Zimbabwe, you're a long way towards getting your certificate.'

The officer at Hobart Air Traffic Control, in Tasmania, was saying slowly into his radio transmitter: 'Repeat we have received no transmission from you, please report your position immediately.'

He waited. His superior said: 'Ask McMurdo again.'

From the tower on the Ross Ice Shelf, an American voice

replied, 'Hobart, regret we have still have no communication. Repeat, we will report to you immediateley when we do.'

'And the weather?'

'The cloudbase is still lowering.'

The two Hobart men looked at each other. Half a minute later, exactly on time, the telephone rang.

'This is Fairwinds again, calling from Sydney,' the voice said. 'Have you any information for me?'

The officer said: 'Negative, I regret to say. We have been trying at regular intervals but nil result.'

Silence on the other end. Then: 'What do you think?'

'I think it's too early yet for panic. I've known a good few aircraft radios go on the blink.'

'There's a back-up radio. Captain Hennessy would listen for acknowledgement and when it doesn't come he would switch radios.'

'There could be an electrical failure.'

'There is a back-up system.'

'But both could fail.'

'Then he switches to his main electrical supply.' The Fairwinds man sighed grimly. 'At this moment they only have seven hours of fuel left. They should have flown back over McMurdo long ago.'

'Have you spoken personally to the Air Force, sir?'

'Yes, but it'll take a plane five hours just to get there, by which time it will be dark. They will send a plane to arrive there at sunrise.'

The Hobart man thought: To arrive where? They could be anywhere between the Ross Ice Shelf and the South Pole.

Hundreds of miles north, senior officers of the Royal Australian Air Force were saying exactly the same: *Where?*. And once the crash site were found – if the plane *had* crashed – it would be the work of helicopters to rescue any survivors. The helicopters would have to be taken there by aircraft-carrier.

The aircraft-carrier, HMAS *Dreadnought*, which was on routine exercises, was ordered to cruise south-west, in the direction of Antarctica.

Meanwhile the weather bureau was studying the latest meteorological photographs which had been transmitted by satellite. They depicted conditions near Antarctica, and indicated that a blizzard was coming.

CHAPTER 64

With the sunrise Mahoney stood on the bridge, his spirits soaring. Below lay the Zambesi Valley, mauve and gold in the early morning shadows. To the south the escarpment rose up, and beyond lay the plateau of bush that stretched all the way to faraway Limpopo, and South Africa beyond. And he, Joe Mahoney, was flying over the Zambesi, into his home country, in his airship that was going to make history and change the face of Africa. . .

In that sunrise the *Rainbow* came slowly down over the Zambesi, all her colours glinting, pumped on water ballast, then rose up again over the slopes of the escarpment. On it sailed, high and mighty; then far away on the horizon he could see the blur of his sprawling city. And Mahoney wanted to whoop and holler and sent his ship soaring up into the blue skies of Rhodesia with his loudspeakers blaring beautiful happy organ music. The *Rainbow* flew huge and gleaming over the suburbs, wide tree-lined avenues, gracious houses set in large gardens; then there was the city centre, streets wide enough to turn a wagon drawn by sixteen oxen. Mahoney sailed in a big circle over his old home town and his heart was filled with pride. He flew his airship low and slow over the African townships, over the teeming dusty lanes and broken-down backyards, and everywhere people were waving excitedly, and he waved down and he loved and pitied each one of them.

Lovelock was back at the controls.

The airport was black with people. In the far corner was the new mast, and the water tanker. Lovelock brought the airship into the wind, low, and gently throttled. The great ship came purring across the green grass; and the mass of black faces were staring, intent: when the bows were fifty yards from the tall mast, Lovelock vectored the engines, and she hovered. A rope ladder came furling out. Then came Malcolm. He clawed down the ladder, went scurrying under the ship, and out of the bows tumbled the mooring line. He snatched up the end and coupled it to the mast's rope. He waved, and Lovelock took up the slack. The ship winched up to the mast; and ululating applause and clapping went up.

And the *Rainbow* rode at her mast, shining under the African sun, at the end of her maiden voyage.

Mahoney turned to Mr Perry, a smile all over his face.

'Congratulations,' Mr Perry said uncomfortably.

'Thank you.' He looked around. Ed was holding a glass of brandy out to him. 'Thank you,' he beamed. But nobody was smiling. Mahoney gulped the brandy. He looked at them: he was about to ask what was wrong, but Ed poured his glass full again.

'Can I have a word with you, Joe?' He put his arm around his shoulder.

Mahoney let Ed lead him off the bridge, wonderingly; down into the crew's saloon. Erling Thoren was standing at the window. He turned, and Mahoney saw grief on his face. Ed said:

'We didn't tell you before – you have enough on your mind. But last night Mr Thoren received a phone call. From Australia.' He took a breath. 'Joe, Fairwinds' plane crashed somewhere in the Antarctic.'

Mahoney felt himself go white. He stared, his heart suddenly hammering. 'And Tana was aboard? . . .'

Ed said: 'I'm afraid so.'

Mahoney's mind was fumbling, aghast: then irrational fury flared. He turned on Erling Thoren, about to shout, *If you'd told me this wouldn't have happened!* He saw the old man's eyes wet with tears, his chin tremble. 'I didn't know she was going on the flight,' he said hoarsely. Ed went on quickly:

'The Australians have got an aircraft-carrier steaming to the area with helicopters, and the Americans at McMurdo sent their helicopter out searching, but it's night down there now, and there's a blizzard coming. . .'

Mahoney plunged up the stairs, on to the flight deck, and dashed to the navigation table. He swept the chart off, and snatched open the lid. He burrowed into the pile of charts feverishly. He pulled one out, opened it, flung it aside, grabbed the next one, and the next.

He found the chart he wanted, spread it on the table, his hands shaking. It was an admiralty chart, showing the southern part of Australia and Antarctica. He found the Ross Ice Shelf and snatched up the dividers. He measured off three hundred miles on the scale tremblingly, then walked the dividers across the chart, from the Great Australian Bight to McMurdo.

'Three thousand miles at least!' He demanded of the grim faces: 'How fast can an aircraft-carrier go? Admiral?'

The Admiral said bleakly, 'Say about twenty-five knots.'

Mahoney closed his eyes. 'God. . . That's. . . a hundred and twenty hours! Five days!'

The Admiral nodded. 'Without the blizzard,' he said quietly. 'And without icebergs to worry about.'

Mahoney was sick in his guts. He turned feverishly to Ed: 'And the Americans at McMurdo – what are they doing?'

Ed said, 'They've only one helicopter. And one plane. It's over a thousand miles from McMurdo to the Pole, with all those mountains in between. They need to establish fuel dumps along the way before any effective searches, to refuel the helicopter. That's the first thing the aircraft-carrier's choppers will have to do.'

Mahoney took an ashen breath. He said:

'Salisbury is about seventeen degrees south. That leaves seventy-three degrees of latitude to the Pole. Seventy-three times sixty miles? Admiral?'

'About four thousand four hundred miles,' the Admiral said. Everybody was staring at him. Mahoney still did not believe what was happening. 'At seventy knots, that's sixty-odd hours! Under three days.' He turned to Erling Thoren: 'We could be over the Pole the day after tomorrow. . .'

Mr Perry was looking aghast. 'Now, one moment. Are you proposing? . . .'

Mahoney turned on him and pointed south angrily: 'There're over two hundred people down there! And one of them happens to be my woman! And it's going to take the authorities at least a week to find them! And *you*' – he pointed at the airport building – 'can get off this ship if you think your bloody bureaucracy is going to stop me!'

'But', Mr Perry said, 'everybody may be dead! You may be risking everything in vain. . . .'

'*Shut up, Perry!*' Mahoney turned furiously to Ed: 'Get me Berna.'

'But, Joe!' the Admiral said. 'We aren't *insured* below Latitude Twenty-two.'

'*To hell with insurance!*' Mahoney cried. 'If we don't get back none of us is going to be alive to collect it, are we! Malcolm – can this ship make it across the South Pole?'

'But the demonstration's tomorrow!' the Admiral said.

'Explain it to the prime minister! Bomber and Moyo can come with us. Malcolm?'

'Of course she can make it,' Malcolm said. 'She can go anywhere. But what about those mountains? How high are they?'

'We can valve off helium and go to fourteen or fifteen thousand feet, for God's sake!'

Malcolm said worriedly, 'We'd have to valve a lot of helium to go that high, we'd lose a lot of lift.'

'We'll only be taking on board two hundred people – less than twenty tons. We'll still lift that much. And helium's lifting power increases with the cold.'

Malcolm rubbed his chin. 'But it's never been tried. When the *Graf Zeppelin* flew over the North Pole it was using hydrogen – and there are no mountains at the North Pole.'

Mahoney said feverishly, 'We'll find a way *round* the highest mountains, we're a *ship*, not a plane!' He turned to Lovelock. 'Charts! Get on to the South Africans and tell them we need every chart they've got of the Antarctic – naval, aerial and ordinary surveyor's charts showing elevations. And ask them for a couple of navy doctors and medical orderlies.'

'Oh, Lord. . . ,' the Admiral groaned. 'Have we got the fuel range?'

411

'Yes,' Malcolm said. 'Just. . .' He looked at the chart. 'Take off from Durban with maximum fuel, eighty-one tons. No ballast. We'll be about eleven tons heavy. Burn a ton of fuel every seventy-five miles. Start reballasting here.' He pointed a thousand miles to sea from Durban.

'We can probably refuel off the aircraft carrier,' Mahoney snapped. 'Don't the Americans also have an air base actually at the South Pole?'

'Yes,' Malcolm said, 'but it's tiny. Only big enough for little planes, like Twin Otters. Forget them, they won't have any fuel for us.'

The Admiral closed his eyes. 'What about our satellite navigation? At that low latitude most of the satellites will be too low on the horizon for the sat-nav to pick up. And compasses go crazy at the poles. Navigation systems have to be specially programmed. I've heard of something called the "grid-system" for polar regions—'

'For God's sake,' Mahoney cried, 'so the compass tries to point downwards! Does it *explode*? When you cross the Pole it *must* swing around and show you where north .s. We've got dead reckoning! We've got distance measuring equipment! Even *I* think I can figure it out!'

'What about all these observers and customers?'

'They can wait here till we get back! I want Bomber and Dwight Perkins to come, the more airmen aboard the better.' He turned, ashen, to Erling Thoren. 'What are you going to do?'

The gaunt old man looked at him, his eyes moist.

'I am going to pay all your costs.' He added: 'I'm not afraid of going with you. Besides, my life is nearly over. But I'll be of more use to you now in Australia.'

Mahoney still couldn't believe it. He wanted to bellow his grief and outrage to the sky.

PART 10

CHAPTER 65

The DC 10 lay spreadeagled in the glacial snow. It was completely silent. Her whole head was crumpled, like a concertina. One wing was torn off. The icy mountains towered up on either side of her, the sun glinting across them in slowly moving spectrums, reflecting off them into the sky.

It was completely still.

Then came the first snow. It fell lightly at first, settling on the silver fuselage; then thicker, and thicker. A little later came the winds.

First only gusting across the polar plateau, driving the snow, piling it up against icy outcrops: then harder and harder, until the snow was lashing along in great eddys. It hurtled against the high mountains, went swirling up over them, and between them; the snow came pounding down the glaciers, and beat against the silent wreckage. The wind went howling down on to the Ross Ice Shelf, beating on over the ice-clogged sea, so the icebergs surged before it, grinding and wallowing in the troughs of icy waves.

That night three Australian Air Force planes had taken off. In the early morning they were over the Ross Ice Shelf. All the pilots could see was swirling snow. They rose to fifteen thousand feet to climb over the Queen Alexandra Range, fighting the headwinds, and at that height they could see nothing of the myriad of valleys and glaciers below. They had thousands of square miles to search. After two hours they turned back, to await a break in the weather.

The aircraft carrier, HMAS *Dreadnought*, was steaming into strong headwinds too. The seas were great running troughs.

The coast of South Africa was dropping far astern, a dark line on the horizon. Below, the deep blue swells of the Indian Ocean rolled. Way to the south, the Roaring Forties were roaring eastwards, making seething swells sixty feet high. If the *Rainbow* swung eastwards when she reached the Forties, the winds would carry her joyfully to Australia. But she was going to fly across them.

Mahoney stood with Pomeroy on the bridge. The ship was flying on automatic, locked on one hundred and eighty degrees, due south. He stared at the sea, his face haggard. He was over the awful, incredulous shock of it now. He had thrust all that aside in his frantic preparations. He desperately refused to acknowledge that she may be dead. If he thought that, it would drive him mad. The only thing in the world right now was to get down there and find her before she perished. Nor could he let himself think of failing. *She is alive.* . . Sometimes he glimpsed his awful nightmare, the thunder of falling seas, his ship sailing off the end of the earth. Sometimes he remembered what the witch-doctor and Danish Erika had said – but he ruthlessly pushed these thoughts aside, and fiercely thought of *her* down there, *alive*. And he prayed: *God, please help us, now.* . .

He turned to the chart table. All the naval and air charts of Antarctica, and surveyor's maps, had been rushed by the South African government to Durban last night, where he had refuelled, taken two naval doctors and orderlies on board, and hard rations. It was the surveyor's maps of the Queen Alexandra Range that he was looking at now.

He had the details of the Fairwinds flight-plan. Captain Hennessy had filed a plan for a flight at sixteen thousand feet all the way to the South Pole and back. Bullshit! No sightseeing at that altitude would be worth it. So Hennessy would have bent the rules. Mahoney had spoken to McMurdo.

'Affirmative,' the American had said, 'I gave him permission to descend to two thousand feet. I picked him up on radar. Then saw him visually, flying past Mount Erebus. He proceeded on, over the Ross Ice Shelf, off the radar screen. His flight-plan indicated—'

'Forget his flight-plan, what did he *say*?'

'That he intended flying parallel to the mountains, up to the Amundsen Coast. Then, visibility permitting, turn south again, over the mountains, following the Amundsen Glacier

416

at a safe altitude, appropriate for sight-seeing. He would report to me at that way-point.'

'And he didn't report?'

'No. If visibility deteriorated, he would advise me of his plans.'

'And he didn't advise that, either?'

'No, sir. Cloud can lower very rapidly down here.'

Mahoney's mouth was dry. 'In your opinion, which glaciers are the most spectacular for him to fly-up?'

'There are so many. . .'

Mahoney closed his haggard eyes. The maps showed so many big glaciers pouring out of the mountains on to the Ross Ice Shelf. Hennessy could have turned back to investigate any number before advising McMurdo. Or he might have turned for Amundsen to investigate, and crashed before reporting the way-point.

Mahoney desperately racked his memory for anything Tana had said. Suddenly he remembered her letters. A minute later he was speaking to Berna.

'Redcoat,' Dolores said tensely.

'Dolores – in my desk are Tana's letters. *Read them.* I want to know the names of any glaciers she mentions. Call me back immediately.'

An hour later Dolores called back. 'She mentions three: Amundsen, Beardmore, and Byrd.'

Mahoney feverishly consulted the map. They were five hundred miles apart. . . With dozens of other glaciers between each. He dragged his hands down over his face.

South Africa was gone over his horizon, the midday sun glinting on the solitary airship, when he listened to the B.B.C. news.

'Gale-strength winds, causing blinding snowstorms, continue to halt all efforts by the Australian Government to send aircraft to the Antarctic to search for the missing aeroplane belonging to the charter-airline, Fairwinds, which is believed to have crashed in the Queen Alexandra Range, close to the South Pole. Similarly, the aircraft-carrier, HMAS *Dreadnought*, which is en route to the Antarctic to act as a fuelling base for search-aircraft, is being held back by stormy seas inducing widespread drifting of icebergs. . .'

'To where?' The Commander of HMAS *Dreadnought* had said.

'To the South Pole, from South Africa, sir.'

'How the *hell* can an airship fly into an Antarctic blizzard?'

Now the commander stared out his window. The Southern Ocean crashed over his bows, spray hurtled across his decks like grapeshot, lashing his windows. There was no snow this far north, but visibility was down to a few hundred yards, the heaving sea disappearing into howling, flying spray. There were icebergs beyond the horizon, being driven north, huge and treacherous: but just as treacherous were the smaller growlers, as big as a tram but hardly showing above the water. The *Dreadnought* was sixty degrees south, one hundred and sixty degrees east – about halfway between Macquarie Island and the Belaney Islands, executing endless squares, waiting for the weather to improve.

'Well, I'm damned. An airship in this lot?'

Well, if it could hang in there above the weather until it cleared, maybe it made sense. The thing could hover almost indefinitely. Whereas *he* was down here risking life and limb just to get helicopters close enough to fly ashore and establish fuel bases for more helicopters to make sorties into the mountains. . . Well, this airship caper was O.K. with Bruce Greenfield. *He* didn't like it down here at the Ice. If this guy could save him sweat, hoo-bloody-ray, mate. Good on yer. There was a knock on his door. 'The latest met report, sir.'

He read the meteorological report gloomily. There was no sign of improvement in the weather.

Down there the dark-blue swells were getting bigger, the troughs deeper, running high before the fringe winds of the Roaring Forties: they could see the long shadows cast by the running crests, white sheets of spray flying, and they could feel the winds on the ship's side. The *Rainbow* sailed southwards, crabbing into the winds to keep her course. Mr Perry,

Malcolm, Pomeroy and Lovelock stood at the console, watching sensors. Mr Perry made a note in his book.

The sun was getting low when the big winds struck. They came out of the west, and the ship suddenly lurched. Lovelock corrected the rudder and she heaved her nose more into the wind.

The lurch woke Mahoney. He scrambled out of bed and wrenched on his trousers. He came bounding barefoot up the stairs. 'What's happening?'

Lovelock said: 'Roaring Forties.'

'What's your altitude?'

'Five thousand. I'm climbing.' He added, 'We're going to have to valve off some helium soon, if we go through seven thousand feet.'

Mahoney took a deep breath. Valving off precious helium, the stuff that kept his ship afloat. . . And that means losing lifting power. He stood over the console, taking in the mass of dials. The ship lurched again and he braced himself. 'How high are you taking her?'

Malcolm was watching the console, his calculator in his hand. 'About ten thousand feet. We've got to go that high, anyway, to cross the South Polar plateau.'

'How much lift are we going to lose?'

'Theoretically, not enough to worry us yet.'

Mahoney snatched up the binoculars and looked west, into the sunset. Cloud, tinged golden red. He swung the binoculars south. He could hardly tell where the darkening sky met the windlashed dark of the running sea. And beyond that horizon? The very end of the earth. For a moment he felt again the primitive dread of flying off the edge of the world, the thunder of falling seas.

He screwed up his eyes fiercely: '*She's alive. . .*'

The *Rainbow* ploughed upwards into the gathering darkness, the winds beating against her, helium venting out into the roaring sky.

It was breakfast time on the *Dreadnought*, but a hundred and forty degrees further west it was still last night.

Ed stood at the sat-nav with Bomber Brown. He noted the latitude and longitude, then made a mark on the admiralty chart, with the time and date. With dividers, he measured the distance to the nearest Antarctic coast, and onwards to the South Pole. About two thousand miles to go.

Ed sighed deeply. He sure as hell hoped Malcolm was right about airships' fuel consumption. You didn't have to be a mathematical genius to see that if he was wrong, they were all going to be very wrong indeed.

'*Rainbow*, this is *Dreadnought*, do you read us?'

'This is *Rainbow*, come in, *Dreadnought*.'

A new voice said: 'G'day, this is Greenfield speaking. Where are you?'

Ed told him. 'That's about halfway across the Roaring Forties.'

'Crikey. In an airship. And are they roaring?'

'We're at ten thousand feet, above the worst of it, but we're taking some drift. What's it doing down your way?'

'Roaring down here. Force ten, from the south.'

'Then it may be in our favour crossing Antarctica.'

'You need something in your favour. What's your E.T.A. at the Pole?'

'Reach the Pole day after tomorrow. No news on the aircraft?'

'Nothing,' the Australian said. 'The Americans can't send up any planes, can't see their noses. What's your fuel range?'

'Eight thousand miles.'

The Australian did a little thinking. 'South Africa is about three thousand miles from the Pole? About the same as Australia. So that's six thousand. That gives you less than two thousand to play with.'

'We may be able to refuel at McMurdo.'

'Right now you couldn't even *see* McMurdo.'

'Or we can refuel off you.'

'Sure, but the Australian Navy is having plenty trouble as it is. Conserve your fuel.'

CHAPTER 66

The Roaring Forties were gone. Below lay the Southern Ocean; scattered across it were the icebergs, reddy gold and sparkling white and crystal blue and green, reflecting the rising sun up into the sky. Some were as big as city blocks, with fjords and valleys.

Mahoney was speaking to McMurdo on the radio.

A faraway voice answered: 'Hardly reading you, *Rainbow*, but situation unchanged. Force ten southerly, visibility nil.'

Lovelock was going over his calculations again. They showed how much fuel the *Rainbow* had burnt since leaving South Africa, how much ballast she had to take on now to compensate before her flight across this continent of howling ice, having regard to distance and the altitudes she'd have to climb. Suddenly it was snowing.

'All right, we'll ballast here before the icebergs get too thick.'

He nosed her into the breeze, then eased her down, down under the grey sky. The icebergs loomed upwards, closer and closer. Lovelock vectored the engines and the ship hovered, fifty feet above the dark sea. The hose came down. Mahoney watched it on the television screen. The pump disappeared under water. He turned and looked grimly over Lovelock's calculations.

'Thirty-three tons we've burnt since Durban. How much ballast are you taking on, having regard to the helium we've lost?'

'The maximum. We can always dump some of it if we're too heavy, but we can't get more unless we shovel up snow.' He watched the ballast gauge.

Mahoney pressed his fingertips to his eyes. The icebergs towered above them. Lovelock muttered, 'She's not pumping.'

'*What?*' Mahoney exclaimed.

Lovelock pointed at the gauge. 'She's not pumping water. Wake Pomeroy – and Malcolm.'

Mahoney bounded for the telephone. 'Pomeroy, get your ass up here!'

Pomeroy burst on to the bridge in his underpants, Malcolm in his pyjamas.

'Airlock,' Pomeroy said. 'Can't be electrical.'

'But how can the pump be sucking air? It's a submersible sealed unit!'

'Get the bleedin' thing back on board!'

Pomeroy hurried off the bridge. The hose and pump began to whirr up again. Lovelock said, 'Maybe, if the intake valve were jammed open, the prime would get lost and you'd get air in.'

'Are we going to hover here or get the hell out of this snow?' Mahoney demanded hoarsely.

Malcolm said, 'Waste of fuel, it'll be snowing everywhere. We've got plenty of room here.'

Mahoney closed his eyes, his nerves stretched tight. *Please God Pomeroy fixes it quickly* . . . He looked exhaustedly out of the windows. The snow was falling thickly now.

'Malcolm, please go and see what Pomeroy's doing.'

An interminable twenty minutes later Malcolm came on the intercom. 'The valve was jammed, he's bleeding the air out now.'

'Thank God,' Mahoney breathed.

They waited, and waited. 'Lower the pump,' Malcolm ordered.

Mahoney breathed out and threw the switch. The hose dropped down to the sea again.

'She's pumping!' Lovelock said.

'Thank God!'

An hour later the pump was winched back aboard. The airship began to climb up into the snowy sky.

'O.K.,'Mahoney breathed. 'This is it.' His ship was about to take on Antarctica. With forty-eight tons of fuel. There was no turning back now. He closed his eyes and prayed fiercely, *She's alive.*

Within two hours the sea had given way to pack-ice, jagged and craggy, the bergs locked solid amongst it, a desert of ice stretching on and on. Far ahead, the solid coastline began to show, bleak icebound cliffs and frozen bays: and beyond the wilderness of Antarctica began, mountains and plateaus rising up to ten thousand feet and more. The *Rainbow* was going to have to go twice as high as seven thousand feet, and she was going to have to valve off a lot of helium to make it.

Mahoney peered, haggard, through his binoculars: and he saw the long wisps of snow drifting up the white, rocky slopes. The *Rainbow* climbed higher, and higher, and now the snow was moving in streaks and furls; more, and more, until all the ice was hazy. And the sky was white where it met the white horizon of Antarctica.

CHAPTER 67

Mahoney was suddenly wide awake, with the awful knowledge that something was wrong. He scrambled off his bed and hurried up to the bridge.

Out there was a hurtling white world. The *Rainbow* rode through whiteness. He could not see the frozen landmass below. Ed was bent over the console, with the Admiral and Mr Perry. 'We're flying heavy.'

Mahoney's mind fumbled. *How could she be heavy?* It was five hours since they had ballasted, in that time she would consume five tons of fuel. 'She should be light!'

'Well, we ain't.'

Mahoney turned desperately to the fuel gauge. It was right – so was the ballast – their combined weight should leave them light. He looked feverishly at the altimeter. 'Is this as high as she'll fly?'

'The helium valves aren't working so I can't go higher or we'll burst.'

'*Wake Malcolm and Pomeroy and Lovelock!*' He looked feverishly at the Doppler. It showed seven hundred feet. Just seven hundred feet below was the frozen landmass!

'Ice!' She must be heavy because she had taken on ice! And the helium valves were iced over. But how could she have collected ice – the slip-stream over the hull made it impossible

423

for snow to collect! And if she had somehow accumulated snow, why weren't the heaters melting it? . . .

The Admiral pointed grimly at the television screens. They were a blur. 'The cameras must be iced over.'

'But *how*?' Then he realized. 'While we were ballasting!' Was it snowing hard?'

'Yes. But we were only hovering a couple of hours at most. The heaters should have melted it when it landed!'

'Turned it to water,' Mr Perry said. There was nothing petulant about his tone now. 'Which froze, if your heating isn't strong enough for these temperatures.'

Pomeroy came bounding up on to the bridge in his underpants again, followed by Malcolm. 'The topside helium valves are clogged,' Mahoney rasped. 'Snow collected while we were ballasting.'

Lovelock appeared, blinking. Malcolm stared at the dials. 'But the heating system is so simple. . .'

'Unless that bleedin' fan ain't workin',' Pomeroy said, 'in the heat-exchanger.'

'But', Malcolm protested, 'even a little heat would melt it.'

'Not five bloody tons of it, Malcolm! If the under part melts, the rest is still on top of us like a saddle!'

Malcolm said worriedly, 'If we descend five hundred feet, that will reduce the pressure of the helium and the hull may flex just enough to crack the ice off—'

'*Blind into a blizzard over uncharted terrain?*' Mahoney cried.

'That's O.K.,' Lovelock muttered, 'we've got radar and Doppler.'

Mahoney rasped: 'Three hundred feet – that's all you're allowed to descend!' He turned to Pomeroy. 'Get inside that hull and check that heat-exchanger. I'm going up top to see what's happening. Tell Dwight and Bomber to get up there.'

He turned and clattered down the stairs. He feverishly pulled on boots and three sweaters, windbreaker, gloves. He plunged down the stairs to the storeroom. He grabbed a canister of de-icing fluid, hefted it on to his back.

*

Mahoney climbed up the long vertical ladder, his heart thudding from the exertion and from the dread-filled fear of his ship coming down under the weight of terrible ice, crashing down on to that wilderness, the wind bowling her over and over, her hull splitting open and spewing her helium out, and they would all die down here – and *Tana would die in this terrible frozen land*. . . Mahoney desperately climbed and climbed towards that tiny square of light way up there, taking deep breaths. Then he was entering a cone of unearthly daylight. He clambered on to the platform, gasping.

He was surrounded by ghostly daylight, his head inside the perspex observation dome. He looked out, over the top of his ship.

God, it was a frightening sight. . .

The topside was so big that it looked like a white field. It disappeared in a curve into white sky and flying snow. He looked aft feverishly. All he could see was ice in all directions. It was well over an inch thick against the perspex dome. Was that uniform? How many tons?

He frantically unbolted the locks and shoved up the dome, with a cracking of ice. He stuck his head out, into the Antarctic sky. He stretched the nozzle of the de-icing canister outside, and squirted.

The fluid sprayed, and melted a hole the size of a soup plate. But there was no place for the water to drain away to. Oh God, this wasn't going to work unless he made channels for the water to run out by – but the hull's surface was almost flat here! He snatched up the intercom.

'Tell Daniel Moyo to get up here with plenty of rope. And two shovels. We've got to go out and clear those valves.'

'What's happening?' Mahoney yelled over the intercom.

Malcolm answered, 'The switch boxes are O.K. Pomeroy's gone inside the helium to check the wiring. I'm going with him.'

'How long will it take?'

'If it's the lower wiring, no problem. If it's the fan itself at the top, Pomeroy must go up in the bosun's chair. And I've got to winch him up.'

Oh God. . . *'Get in there, Malcolm!'*

He tied the rope around his waist, lashed three turns around the rung of the ladder. He gave the end to Daniel. 'Feed it out to me. *Slowly.*'

Oh, he was frightened. . . He clambered shakily up out of the hatch, into the Antarctic sky.

He crouched on the rim. And though he had known it theoretically he was amazed that there was no wind, because of the slipstream created by the hull. Absolute silence, but for the hammering of his heart. Only the silent whiteness out there, the icy topside curving away into terrible space. He crouched, eyes fixed on the flatness, desperately ignoring the curvature beyond. Then he carefully, desperately carefully, began to straighten his shaky legs. Up, up, he straightened. Still no wind. He slowly lifted his hand. When it was six inches above his head the icy wind hit it.

He lowered himself into a crouch again. Then he placed one foot on to the ice. He tested it for slip. He took a deep trembly breath, then he began to creep carefully out, down the icy spine of the airship.

He put one tentative foot forward, testing, then the other. The girder-spine of the airship was only three feet wide under the aluminium skin: on either side, that skin was only millimeters thick over the framework. If he slipped off the spine on to that skin he would plunge through it to his death and helium would come gushing out into the sky. He kept his eyes down, not daring to look at the terrible void beyond the ship. He crouched ten, fifteen, twenty trembling feet: then he could stand it no longer. He carefully lowered himself on to his hands and knees.

Mahoney crawled over the ice, eyes down. The buried valve was about fifteen feet further. He stopped where he estimated it was. He raised himself shakily, sat back on his heels. He reached for the canister's hose. He sprayed the fluid down the spine. The ice melted in a strip a yard long. Yes, beneath the water was the round valve.

He feverishly sprayed all around it. But the water could not drain away. He began to scoop it out by hand. He turned and shouted to Dwight, '*Go and clear the other valve. Scoop the water out!*'

Dwight clambered out the hatch, a rope around his waist. He started walking upright down the spine towards the stern.

Mahoney scooped and scooped. It was desperately slow work. No way would he get all the water out. He heard Daniel shout: 'He's cleared it!'

Mahoney turned. He shouted, 'Tell Lovelock to try them!'

Mahoney crouched at the valve, waiting. Suddenly it opened with a loud hiss and the remnants of the water flew in a spray. 'Yes!' he shouted. He looked back at the hatch. Daniel was looking back at Dwight, then shouted, 'O.K.!'

Thank God! 'Tell Dwight to come back!' He started crawling back to the hatch.

Mahoney rasped to Dwight: 'The heating system won't melt all this ice – it'll melt the underpart but the rest will just sit on top like a saddle. But if we cut the ice in half by melting a path down the spine, it may fall off when the heater gets to work.'

'Gotcha.'

'Start near the stern, where it curves, so the water can run away, and work back to the hatch. I'll start at the bows. And try with a shovel. The more we crack, the faster the heaters will melt it. And clear the ice off that aft television camera.'

Mahoney started crawling along the icy spine of his airship, a shovel clutched in one hand, eyes down, terrified. Then he could feel the hull begin to curve. He crawled on desperately carefully. He could see the camera ahead, down the slope, a little mound of ice. He crawled on. Then he stopped. The slope was getting more pronounced now.

He lowered himself on to his stomach, gasping. The camera was twelve feet ahead. Slowly, teethclenched, he worked his way towards it, down the curve. Closer, and desperately closer.

He reached behind his back, got the hose. He squirted it.

The ice fell off the camera. He looked back at the hatch.

Daniel Moyo spoke into the intercom. Then held up his thumb.

'Thank God!'

But, oh God, he had to go further.

He began to work his way forward, down the slope. He wriggled and shoved desperately carefully. Then he could make himself go no more.

He got to his knees shakily. He sprayed the fluid towards the bows. The ice melted, the water ran slowly away. He sprayed more, sideways. But that would not drain. He picked up the shovel, feverishly, worked it under the ice, and levered. A chunk of ice came away, with a crack. He sprayed into the new hole. Then wedged the shovel again. A sheet of ice two feet long crunched up. It went sliding down the slope.

He got fearfully to his feet, crouching. His mouth was dry. He dared not look at the sky. He was whimpering from cold. He tested himself shakily, then worked the spade under the ice again. Another chunk came up. Then the spray again. The ice melted and the water slowly ran away. But it was so slow. He started with the shovel again.

He shoved a big piece of loose ice towards the curvature. It slid, then stopped, blocking the drainage channel.

He looked at it, gasping. Then he sat down. He wriggled on his buttocks, feet first, down the curvature, his heart pounding. He eased himself on to his back, and gave the ice a kick. It went slithering across the hull, then suddenly it was gone into the Antarctic sky. He closed his eyes.

Pomeroy crouched through the vast darkness of the hull. On his back was an airtank, the breathing valve in his mouth. His flashlight was following the electric cable of the heat-exchanger. If he did not find the fault down here, he had to get his arse right up there in a bosun's chair.

Charming. Absolutely fookin' charming. . .

Mahoney worked, blue with cold, whimpering, spraying, then feverishly wedging his shovel, levering. Sometimes the ice came away easily, sometimes it broke. Dwight was working from the stern forwards. Mahoney was desperately keeping his centre of gravity low, not daring to look out in to the void, but Dwight worked standing up, like a suburbanite shovelling snow off his sidewalk.

Inside the hull Pomeroy swung his canvas chair, grunting

through his respirator, his bucket of tools swinging from his belt, his head back, following the electric cable that led to the heat-exchanger. Below, Malcolm winched him upwards manually.

Pomeroy had thirty minutes of air left in his tank. He had to get up there, fix that heat-exchanger, get back down, and get outside this hull in thirty minutes: thirty-one minutes, and he was very dead.

Mahoney lay on his stomach, gasping. The bows sloped away before him, fading into nothingness. He could not bear to look out there, but he had to. He had gone as far as he dared down the slope. If he had the guts, like Dwight, he could go further, but he was terrified he would go sliding over the edge, clutching at thin air, then hurtling through space until the rope stopped him with a wrench that would break his back. He looked over his shoulder. He could not even see the hatch. He wriggled round on his stomach, then began to crawl back to the hatch.

Inside the ghostly hull, suspended high up in his bosun's chair, Pomeroy was feverishly working on the heat-exchanger. He had found the fault, in the fan, and he had eleven minutes of air left in which to fix it and make it to the bottom and into the shaft. He worked frantically, clenching his respirator in his teeth, desperately trying to take shallow breaths. Down below, Malcolm feverishly waited at the winch, holding the rope, and Pomeroy's life, in his hands. He took a breath, snatched the respirator from his mouth and bellowed:

'Hurry up!'

Pomeroy whimpered, working with his screwdriver. He got the last screws in, then slapped the cover on the plastic jacket and screwed it down. With only three minutes of air left, he yelled around his mouthpiece, 'Down!'

Frantically Malcolm began to let the rope slide around the winch-drum, controlling it with his palm, holding his breath as long as he could. Pomeroy was coming slowly, jerkily down with each slide of the rope over the drum. His life was entirely in Malcolm's hands, and in Malcolm's airtank. If Malcolm let go that rope, Pomeroy would come hurtling down out of the darkness and crash to his death on the machinery below. Malcolm was going as fast as he could without losing control of the rope. Down and down Pomeroy came, and there was now one minute left in Malcolm's tank. Now thirty seconds. Now twenty. Now ten, and Pomeroy was still forty feet up there, dangling desperately. When Pomeroy was thirty feet off the deck, Malcolm's tank ran out and he sucked on nothing. He clutched wildly at his throat, and Pomeroy lurched. Malcolm threw himself wildeyed back at the winch to seize the rope, and Pomeroy came plummeting down.

He came hurtling down through the dark helium with a gargled scream, and he crashed on top of Malcolm. They sprawled on the deck, airless, choking, stunned. For a second Pomeroy was senseless, gasping helium into his lungs, then he scrambled up, choking, and he wildly lunged at Malcolm. But his arm was broken. Malcolm collapsed onto his stomach, mouth agape, sucking in helium, his face turning purple. Pomeroy lunged at him frantically with his good arm, and grabbed his collar, and blindly heaved him towards the shaft-door, staggering, wildeyed, and his broken arm groped uselessly for his respirator. And he dropped Malcolm and grabbed the respirator with his good arm and rammed it into his mouth and sucked and then into Malcolm's gaping mouth and croaked, '*Suck, you bastard!*' – but Malcolm was unconscious. Pomeroy seized him again and wildly dragged him to the shaft-door, wrenched it open, and he slung Malcolm headfirst into the open shaft. He collapsed on top of him and rammed his mouth over his, and blasted air into the man's lungs; and gasped more air and blasted it again, whimpering, frantic.

Mahoney wriggled furiously up the sloping spine, his nerves almost finished. He shoved himself forward yard by yard, his legs spread to give himself maximum purchase. Then an edge of ice gave way under his foot, and he felt himself go.

His heart lurched in the purest terror and he clawed wildly at the aluminium. Slowly he went, his scrabbling feet ploughing up ice. Then he came to the end of his rope, and suddenly stopped. He gargled in terror and clawed at the aluminium and tried to scramble; and the ice gave way and he began to slide again. Sideways this time, slowly, his rope dragging like a pendulum across the hull, ploughing up ice: then faster and faster as he gathered momentum, his hands clawing and terror all over his face, ice cascading down on him, then the hull was disappearing beneath him as he ploughed faster and lower, swinging down on his terrible pendulum, his arms spreadeagled trying to claw up into a blinding cascade of crashing ice. Then there was suddenly nothing, and he was flying through thin air. Nothing but terrible space about his hurtling body as Mahoney parted company with the hull, and all he knew was the heart-stopping terror of clutching at air and the terror of the propellors that were going to slice him to ribbons. In those terrible seconds he saw himself cloven and splayed out to the sky in a mass of flying blood and flesh and bone, and he screamed from the bottom of his lungs.

'*Daniel!*'

And the propellors hurtled towards him and there was nothing in the world but their roaring; then they disappeared. Mahoney went screaming under them, then he was swooping under the belly of the airship. He was wrenched to a bone-jarring stop for an instant, then he was swinging back again.

Mahoney swung in the freezing Antarctic sky, shocked witless, contorted, desperately trying to clutch the rope above him to take the weight, desperately trying to scream for help, and it was blasted to nothing in the roar of the propellors, and all he saw was the belly of the ship and the terrible whirling whiteness.

Mahoney swung, clutching, croaking, and way up there Daniel Moyo was astride the hatch, trying to heave on the rope, hand over gut-wrenching hand. Below him midst the roaring Mahoney swung, gasping and clinging, and through the terror he knew that no way could anybody pull him two hundred feet up against the friction of the hull, and he was crying to the howling sky:

'*Put me down – bring the ship down!*'

His cries were torn away to nothing. He did not see the ice

431

coming up to meet him until his feet suddenly hit it, and his legs buckled and he collapsed, into the snow, up to his hips. Then there was his ship, hovering fifty feet above him, huge and wonderful, and the cargo hatch was opening, the winch-hook coming down.

CHAPTER 68

For the first time in many years he had prayed constructively: for her; to give thanks that he and Malcolm and Pomeroy were alive; that the heat-exchanger had been repaired and the ice had fallen off the ship. Now he prayed for the blizzard to stop, for sunshine to see by – and that nothing mechanical would go wrong that Pomeroy could not fix with one arm. And he fiercely *knew* that she was alive. . . .

But the blizzard did not stop, and the winds kept sweeping the snow across the icy plateau, driving the *Rainbow* before them in an unearthly glow. Eventually Mahoney fell into an exhausted sleep in a chair on the bridge. He awoke with Pomeroy's hand on his shoulder. Pomeroy's arm was in a sling, and his face looked waxen with pain, but he was smiling. Mahoney sat bolt upright. He scrambled up, blinking, strode to the window.

The sun was shining! . . .

Down there the ice sparkled and the snow only wisped lazily across it. The blizzard was gone!

'We're crossing the South Pole.'

'Oh thank you, God,' he whispered.

The South Pole! And suddenly it changed from today to tomorrow, from thirty degrees east to one hundred and fifty degrees west, the compass heading from due south to due north, from one-eighty to three-sixty. . .

'The Amundsen Glacier is about three hours away,' Ed said.

Mahoney breathed deeply. 'Just keep helping us now, God!' He said: 'Get everybody up now, to keep lookout.'

*

Everybody was assigned a position along the windows on both sides of the saloon and bridge, to look for the aircraft.

The Queen Maud Range reared up, white, knotted in black rock. A thousand feet below the airship lay the South Polar plateau. It dazzled in the low sun, white flecked with blue with iced ravines and outcrops casting shadows. Snow still wisped across it, though the big winds had gone. But on the other side of the high mountains, down on the Ross Ice Shelf, it was a different story.

'Negative,' the American said emphatically from McMurdo. 'Visibility is practically zero, winds are gusting up to fifty knots. Under present conditions you definitely could not refuel at McMurdo.'

'But how long do these conditions last after a blizzard?'

'I've seen it last for days. And there is a serious risk of white-out.' He repeated with emphasis: '"White-out", sir? Where everything's white, you think maybe you're flying upside down?'

'Yes,' Mahoney breathed. 'Please keep reporting. So will we.'

He knew that three Royal Australian Air Force planes had left Hobart. They would be over the mountains in a few hours, with photography. That encouraged him. But what would cameras pick up in white mountains after a blizzard? And the film still had to be returned to Australia for experts to interpret. And the weather still precluded the deployment of helicopters off the *Dreadnought*. She was still a thousand miles away in the Ross Sea, fenced in by wind-driven icebergs.

Mahoney stood at the chart table and dragged his trembly hands down his face. *She is alive.* . . .

On the map he had drawn in pencil a rectangle over the mountains, roughly five hundred miles long by one hundred miles wide. It started at the Amundsen Glacier and straddled the mountains, to the Byrd Glacier, with Beardmore Glacier in the middle. Those were the three glaciers Tana had mentioned. Five hundred miles multiplied by a hundred made fifty thousand square miles they had to search. If he halved the area, because the Beardmore Glacier was in the middle, it was still about twenty-five thousand square miles. In how many hours, before they'd have to run for fuel? Theoretically, ten hours – unless they could refuel at McMurdo, or off the *Dreadnought*. They could do neither in this weather.

Twenty-five thousand square miles in ten hours? At fifty knots his airship could cover one side of the smaller rectangle, two hundred and fifty miles, in five hours. It was all theoretical, but with, say, a ten-mile visibility range on either side of the ship, their eyes would cover roughly five thousand square miles in five hours. The very least he needed, therefore, was twenty-five hours. He only had ten.

It was impossible, unless the *Dreadnought* steamed north now, away from the bad weather, so the *Rainbow* could refuel off her: but he could not give orders to the Australian navy. The Australian navy was there to rescue survivors of a crashed aircraft, not to rescue the *Rainbow*.

'Lovelock?' Lovelock came and bent over the map with him. Mahoney drew a line from the Pole, across the Amundsen Glacier to the Ross Ice Shelf.

'According to McMurdo, that's the route Captain Hennessy was going to take, visibility permitting. It's an easy route. The surrounding mountains are pretty low, there's only Mount Astor here, seven-odd thousand feet, this one here, ten thousand, and Mount Nansen, thirteen thousand. But they're well apart. You can fly us down the Amundsen Glacier at a reasonable altitude pretty easily, giving us a fair chance to search?'

Even Lovelock looked gaunt. 'And if we don't see them?'

'Visibility is bad on the Ross Ice Shelf – no point searching along that side of the mountains. So we should cut back here, up the Bowman Glacier, next door. In fact, they might have flown up that one, it seems to join Amundsen at the mouth. It's also low and easy.'

Lovelock nodded. 'And then?'

Mahoney traced an 'S' with his finger, from the mouth of the Amundsen, over the mountains, back to the South Polar Plateau, and on to the Beardmore Glacier. 'That's the route we're going to fly.' He tapped the Beardmore Glacier. 'If I were Hennessy, and I couldn't go up the Amundsen, I would have turned back for the Beardmore. It's about the biggest and widest. And that's one of the glaciers Tana mentioned.'

'And the most crooked,' Lovelock said.

'Easy enough for an aeroplane. The highest mountain seems to be Dickenson, fourteen-odd thousand feet, and it's well clear. These others, only ten thousand feet, miles away.'

'But', Lovelock said, 'there're all these other glaciers they might have taken before reaching Beardmore – Liv Glacier, Ramsey, Shackleton.'

'We'll be covering part of them in our S route. But they're all much narrower, and Tana doesn't mention them. Malcolm?'

Malcolm came from the window. The Admiral followed him. 'Please, Admiral,' Mahoney said, 'you must keep look-out.'

The Admiral put his hands to his temples. 'I must know what you're doing.'

'All right.' Mahoney pressed his eyes. Impotent, that's how those mountains made him feel. He explained it again. 'The Amundsen's easy. But can we fly this ship down the Beardmore?'

Lovelock stooped to the chart again. 'Sure. But safely? . . .'

'No,' the Admiral whispered. He turned to Mahoney with exhausted eyes. 'For God's sake, Joe! We can do a figure of eight over the mountains to search. But fly down a *canyon* of icy mountains? . . .'

'The *Graf Zeppelin* did it when she crossed the Rockies fifty years ago!'

'But why take the *risk*? Joe, we're doing our best! Why fly into that glacier when there are so many other areas to search?'

Mahoney became angry. It was unreasonable, but his nerves were going. He slammed his hand flat on the map. 'We've only got ten hours!' He hit the Beardmore Glacier. 'I think they're in there! Malcolm – can we fly this ship down that glacier? Lovelock says yes.'

Malcolm said worriedly, 'It depends on the winds.'

'*Exactly*,' the Admiral said. 'The winds will be funnelling into the glacier! You're sailing a ship lighter than air down a crooked tunnel. . .'

Mahoney cried, '*Look* at those mountains. Like looking for a needle in a haystack! With ten hours to do it in!' He turned to Lovelock. 'Do it! Start on the Amundsen. Then loop back, to Beardmore. I'll tell McMurdo.'

'Joe, we have a suggestion to make.'

Mahoney turned. Dwight and Bomber were standing there. 'Yes?' he snapped.

Dwight said, 'We've been figurin'. When you fly down the glaciers, we could fly ahead of you in the little aeroplane. That would serve two purposes. Firstly, we could warn you of any dangers ahead. Secondly, we will be more manoeuvrable than you, so if we see something we'll be able to buzz down and look at it, and even go back up the glacier for a second look while you're still coming down it.'

Mahoney said tersely, 'That aeroplane only carries a few hours of fuel. When you come back to us, we've got to manoeuvre and that'll cost *us* a lot of fuel. We're desperately short.'

Bomber said, 'But between us we'd search the glacier at least twice, once by you, once by us.'

Mahoney closed his eyes. Oh God, he didn't trust that little aeroplane. He said, 'And if you *can't* get back on board, you crash. We're here to rescue other people, not you guys.'

Bomber said angrily, 'With all due respect, you are not a very experienced airman! Dwight and I—'

'*Are you prepared to be left out there to die if we can't get you back aboard?*'

Dwight said grimly: 'We'll get back aboard. But if it comes to that, yes.'

Mahoney shut his eyes. He thought of Tana somewhere down there.

'Thank you, gentlemen. Sincerely. We'll do it when we go down the Beardmore glacier. Not now. We'll save you guys as a last resort.'

CHAPTER 69

When you love somebody and she lies dying somewhere down there in twenty-five thousand square miles of icy, mountainous wilderness, and you have only ten terrible hours in which to find her, then only nine, then only eight. . . And you do not even know if this vehicle can make its way over these terrible mountains or whether it is going to get blown against them and go crashing down on to the ice also. . . But, oh God, when you love somebody and she lies dying you do not care, you will do it.

The *Rainbow* flew towards the mountains, her siren booming out a mournful *whoop – whoop* every few minutes, a huge silver elipsoid that was tiny against the vast icy range looming up. At the big windows everybody stood, searching the whiteness, blinking, searching.

The whiteness played tricks on their eyes. They had to squeeze them shut frequently, then focus again. Peering through binoculars disorientated them. And what were they looking for in that jumbled mass of whiteness? The aeroplane was silver, almost white. Possibly scattered in several pieces. Over how big an area? They could not see into distant gullies and ravines.

At the end of the first hour they identified the start of the Amundsen Glacier, flowing off the polar plateau. Mount Wyatt on their right, Mount Astor ahead. The winds were wisping snow across the ice, but the sun was shining.

The Amundsen was an easy glacier, mountains low and spread out. The *Rainbow* entered high, and the glacier was so wide that they did not even feel the suction of the winds. She sailed slowly down the broad icy swathe, six hundred feet above it. The river of ice tumbled away below, smooth and jagged and white and blue, with the snow wisping down. Mahoney feverishly swept his binoculars across the mountains on either side, and he just knew the aircraft was not there. He could see no topographical reason why an aircraft might crash.

Unless the pilot suffered total white-out. At the end of the second hour, they saw the first Australian Air Force plane flying towards them.

It was the friendliest sight, another aircraft helping them, expert airmen with their cameras; but then Mahoney's heart sank again. How could they see anything from that altitude and at that speed? The aircraft was cruising up the middle of the mountain range. Mahoney spoke to it by radio. 'What's your visibility like up there?'

'Fair, sir, but everything's so white. We're filming all the time.'

'How are conditions over the Ross Ice Shelf from what you've seen?'

'Low cloud, right up to the mountains.'

Oh Lord . . . 'Have you copied that, McMurdo?' Mahoney said.

'Copied, Rainbow,' the American said. 'And confirm cloud.'

'And what's your sector?' Mahoney sighed bitterly.

The Australian said, 'I'm covering from the Amundsen to the Beardmore. Call-sign Two is covering Beardmore to Nimrod Glacier. Call-sign Three, from Nimrod to Byrd Glacier. Do you want map references.'

'Yes.' Mahoney feverishly noted them down. 'Have you covered Beardmore yet?'

'Affirmative, on the first leg of my section. Visibility fair to poor, wind blowing quite a lot of snow, also deep shadows.'

Beardmore, he wanted to say, *go back to the Beardmore and look again.* 'Will your other plane also cover Beardmore?'

'Affirmative, when he reaches that leg of his section.'

'And so will I.' He spelled out his proposed route. 'How long before you have to return to refuel?'

The Australian said: 'Less than one hour, now, sir. . .'

The *Rainbow* sailed on down the Amundsen Glacier, her siren going *whoop . . . whoop . . .* then cloud was wisping past her windows, and Lovelock eased the bows up, rising above it. Then he turned her head, to start the first swing of the S over the treacherous mountains.

*

438

Mount Fridtjof Nansen dropped astern, almost fourteen thousand feet high: Mount Wade, higher still, slid by on their starboard side: below was the myriad of lesser mountains and valleys and glaciers, Shackleton, Koska beyond, Ramsey. All the time the mounting despair as the minutes ticked by. Oh God, how vast the whiteness and craggy blackness stretching on and on, yawning valleys and towering peaks, what chance of seeing one broken aeroplane, one tiny figure weakly waving? . . .

'Six hours' fuel left,' the Admiral announced hoarsely. 'The Dominion Mountains about sixty miles ahead.'

Navigation was by dead reckoning, and Mahoney had asked Lovelock to put the Admiral in charge of that.

Silence. Then the Admiral spoke up again:

'Mr Mahoney, I must urgently suggest you now ask *Dreadnought* to re-position herself. To steam north, out of bad weather, so we can refuel off her.'

Mahoney stood at his window, his mouth clamped shut. *The Dreadnought is here to get rescue helicopters ashore, not to rescue us! In the next five hours the weather may clear and we can refuel at McMurdo or off the Dreadnought where she is!* He looked grimly at the Dominion Mountains, way ahead.

Those were the mountains he had to fly over, to get back on to the South Polar plateau, to enable him to approach the entrance of the Beardmore. They would push the *Rainbow* to her very limits of height. He feverishly pushed them and time and fuel out of his mind, and forced his aching eyes to keep searching.

The icy mountains loomed ahead. The *Rainbow* sailed towards them, her nose up. Closer and closer the mountains loomed, and upwards and upwards the *Rainbow* flew. Mahoney forced himself to ignore the altimeter, not to look at the mountains, to keep his eyes sweeping the snow. Up and up the airship flew, and now the craggy slopes were right in front of them, the crest up there, the snow furling off it; and, oh God, it looked as if she was not going to clear it. The ragged peaks were now two hundred yards away and still higher than the bridge: now a hundred and fifty, and the *Rainbow* was straining up and up: now one hundred, and the sharp icy rocks were still higher, closer and closer they came, and Mahoney's nerves were about to break – and then the mountain tip was sliding under the nose. And over the top the great ship flew, the white crags gliding by just below, bursting into view again.

CHAPTER 70

The surveyor's map was clear. To the west of the Dominion Mountains was the Beardmore Glacier, running in long, wide, jagged curves down into the Ross Ice Shelf. Measuring distances on the map with dividers, it was clear that the *Rainbow*, six hundred feet long, could negotiate the glacier, avoid the jutting mountainsides, and sail around the curves with plenty of room to spare.

Mahoney pressed his fingers to his exhausted eyes.

In theory. But what about winds? The Australian pilot had seen wind-driven snow flying. Theoretically, winds would be rushing through that steep divide, into a funnel, sucked through by other winds moving across the Ross Ice Shelf which were strong enough to be giving the Australian Navy trouble. And the winds were stronger now. The snow wisped thickly across the plateau, flew off the looming mountains in streaks and furls, making them hazy. Looking at the map and looking for the big gap in the mountains were two very different things. The map was a cartographer's bird's-eye view, but the icy mountains unfolded white and hazy and shadowed, outlines blurred and overlapping. And all the time the long tails of snow were swirling.

The *Rainbow* flew along the edge of the mountains, looking for the start of the Beardmore Glacier. She had less than three hours of fuel left before she had to run. Mahoney screwed up his aching eyes.

This was it. . . If they did not find her now. . .

Ten minutes later they saw the opening. 'There! . . .'

Mahoney took a big, tense breath. 'Dwight?' he said. 'Bomber? You guys still prepared to go out there?'

Daniel Moyo spoke up: 'I've got good eyes. I'll go with one of them.'

'Thanks, Dan,' Mahoney said. 'But no. Two pilots are better than one.' All right,' he said to the airmen, 'get on with it.'

The big doors in the belly opened. The little aeroplane hung on the trapeze above the yawning opening, with Bomber and Dwight strapped into the cockpits, wrapped in as much heavy gear as they could wear. Pomeroy pressed the button and down they began to go, and the icy air hit them. Down they went, to the limit of the telescopic arms; and they hung above the Antarctic. Dwight turned over the engine and it kicked to life. He throttled up, then he held up his thumb. He slipped the hook off the bar, and the aircraft lurched. She dropped from the airship with a stagger. Then her wings gripped the air, and she went roaring away underneath the belly.

Mahoney watched her go, a tiny machine heading straight into the great, white Antarctic mountains. Diminishing, diminishing. Then she was gone, and the *Rainbow* was on her own.

The big glacial gap loomed closer and closer, the mountains rearing up on each side, steep and white. Mahoney's mouth was dry, his hands clammy, his nerves stretched tight. Closer and closer the airship flew, engines slowly turning; bigger and closer the mountains loomed, huge and treacherous.

They could not yet feel the wind of their huge bulk, but they were desperately waiting for it. Mahoney tried not to watch Lovelock steering his ship towards that terrible opening; his eyes were darting, heart pounding, his nerves stretching tighter and tighter; and those tails of flying snow whipped faster and faster into the glacier creaming out of the plateau, a frozen river of white and grey, humps of blue sticking up, and cones and knife-edges of ice. Closer and closer the white and black mountains loomed, and now the mountain sides were towering up in front of them; and the ship nosed into the icy canyon, and they felt the winds hit.

They felt the airship lurch, and Lovelock corrected and

441

eased back the throttles; and the ship steadied. Then she
surged forwards again as the wind caught her afresh. She
went billowing straight into the icy canyon, the mountainsides
towering above her and the jagged glacier skimming past five
hundred feet below: faster and faster the airship went, the icy
sides surging past her great flying bulk. And now, miles ahead,
the first bend was coming, blocking their flight-path. Mahoney
rasped: '*Look for that aircraft – let Lovelock worry about the
ship!*' He turned feverishly to the chart table.

From the map it was clear that there was a bend ahead of
forty-five degrees: but looking down this glacier, desperately
looking for that turn, for the life of him he could not see it.
He feverishly measured the width of the bend again with his
dividers: *Plenty of room. But where was it?* He turned back to
the window.

The mountain loomed ahead, much higher than the ship,
completely blocking the glacier. The ship sailed down the
canyon towards it, engines turning as slowly as they would
and still give steerage, the wind pushing from behind. Closer
and closer the mountain came, the glacier tumbling by below,
fierce and jagged, and Lovelock's face was set in tense concentration.

'Oh Lord,' the Admiral breathed, 'where is it? . . .'

Oh Lord. . . And then Mahoney saw it. Just a faint line in
the side of the canyon, almost invisible against the whiteness
beyond. '*There it is!*' The mountain jutted out, the glacier
curved away, more white mountainsides looming beyond. The
snow was whipping in confusion around the point. Mahoney
heaved a tense breath.

'*Eyes on the snow, everybody! Let Lovelock do the flying!*'

Lovelock eased the ship across the glacier, to the right. The
wind would catch her broadside on when she reached the
bend, and try to force her the other way, across the canyon.
He felt the wind hit her side and try to shove her nose around
again: but she held. The jutting mountain was five hundred
yards ahead, and now the sides of the canyon were just three
hundred feet off his right side, steep rocky whiteness flashing
past the windows. Closer the point loomed, then suddenly the
full curve of the glacier sprang into view, and the wind hit the

ship. She lurched, surging into the bend, skidding sideways through the air. Lovelock feverishly opened the throttles. The wind caught the stern and the huge machine lurched again, then she straighened out.

'Thank the Lord,' the Admiral breathed.

Mahoney went limp with relief. 'Well flown,' Mr Perry said.

'We aren't at the end of it yet.'

But ahead the glacier opened out wide, as far as they could see. The giant ship sailed down the middle of the icy canyon, between the towering mountains.

'*Search, everybody!*' Mahoney turned feverishly to the chart table. Miles ahead the glacier went into another bend. And so on, all the way down to the Ross Ice Shelf. It was very difficult to estimate how wide each bend was, and nobody knew what the winds would be doing on those curves.

'About a hundred and twenty miles to go,' he said.

He turned from the chart table, his face gaunt. He smacked his hands together. 'Eyes on the ice! Ed, keep blowing that horn.' He snatched up the transmitter. 'Rainbow to Bomber, what do you see?'

Bomber's voice came crackling back: 'Rainbow, winds looking stronger down there, visibility poor. Deep shadows. We're about two-thirds the way down. Will go down to the bottom then turn around and come back up for a second look, passing you on the way. Will you roger that?'

'Roger,' Mahoney sighed tensely. 'Just give us a wide berth. Out.'

He took a deep breath. And forced his eyes to search.

They had two hours of fuel left before they had to run.

CHAPTER 71

She is alive, She is alive. . . . Only that refrain kept his stretching nerves from breaking. Oh God, when you love somebody and she lies dying somewhere in these frozen wastes, and she doesn't know you are looking for her, and maybe you won't even see her if you're looking right at the place where she lies dying – it is the most desperate feeling in the world.

Mahoney stood at his station, gaunt eyes fiercely searching, every nerve desperately willing somebody to shout, for the radio to speak. But nothing. Only the ship's horn blasting, the long mournful whoop-whoop, and in his desperation he was sure the mountains deadened it. Every few minutes his heart leapt as his eye caught something. But it was always just a shape of the ice, a trick of the light.

'One and a half hours of fuel left,' the Admiral said softly.

She did not hear the little aeroplane droning down the glacier; she did not hear it come droning back again up the glacier half an hour later, although it flew within half a mile of her; she did not hear the mournful wail of the airship as it flew over her twenty minutes later.

She lay rigidly, curled on the freezing deck of the shattered aircraft on the tattered mass of seat stuffing, her frozen fingers clutching the blanket around her. The *Rainbow* flew slowly past only half a mile away, whooping, and nobody saw the broken aircraft lying half-buried in the white snow over there.

The airship was another half mile past when she heard it in her sleep, drugged by hunger so deep that she no longer felt it, by cold so deep she no longer felt it. Her ears registered the distant sound, but it just became part of her dream, the low, mournful wail of a distant ship setting out to sea. Then in her dream she was on the ship, and she was warm and eating wholesome food. And it was the most wonderful feeling, and then Joe Mahoney was with her as she frantically feasted, smiling at her, and she was filled with absolute joy . . . then it turned to fear, because they could not reach each other, and she struggled and struggled and stretched frantically. Then the ship hooted again, long and mournful as it steamed down towards the sea, and now she was no longer on the warm ship. For a long moment she lay there, rigid, staring at the gloom, her heart pounding, wondering if she had dreamed it: then she scrambled.

Her frozen fingers desperately scrabbled in the box of flares, then she ripped aside the blanket that blocked the hole in the fuselage and she plunged wildly out into the snow, looking desperately, dazedly upwards. She sank to her knees in snow, and stumbled, gasping, eyes screwed up, desperately searching the sky all around. She searched, and she searched, her heart pounding in dread that she was too late, that it was just part of her dream. Then she heard it again, a distant, receding sound which made her reel around with a cry, and then she saw it.

She did not grasp what she was seeing. She was looking for a helicopter or an aeroplane, and she saw instead a circle in the sky, slowly disappearing down the mountains. She gave a frantic cry and stumbled forwards to show herself, trying to wrench open the flare, and she fell. She sprawled face downwards and the flare shot out of her hand. She clawed frantically after it, and scrambled to her feet again; she held the flare above her head and tugged the ring. There was a whooshing noise and the rocket went blasting up, trailing a thick tail of orange smoke: then the wind caught it and swept it away, wide and faint. She crouched in the flying snow, staring aghast at her flare being blown to nothing. Then she tried to shout again, and she went floundering after the disappearing aircraft, gasping, her heart pounding with exhaustion, her stomach wrenching. She got another flare above her head, jerked the ring, and she lost her balance and fell. The flare went blasting off horizontally over the ice like a cannonball, gushing its orange smoke. And the aircraft was gone.

She lay sprawled, her face contorted, the wind whipping over her, the tears running down her frozen face. Then she dropped her face into the freezing snow, and sobbed with all her exhausted heart and guts and anguish.

She did not hear her little aircraft coming back down the glacier; she did not see it through the flying snow.

It was as Bomber was saying, 'We only got half an hour of fuel left,' that Dwight shouted over the radio, *'I see something! Over there! Rainbow, I've seen orange smoke! It's gone now but I definitely saw it!'*

Mahoney was dashing to the television screens yelling joyfully at Lovelock, *'Up – get us up and turn around!'*

CHAPTER 72

Mahoney rasped: 'But will you be able to identify the mountainside again?'

Bomber's calm voice came back, 'Affirmative, but can't see anything down there because of flying snow and Dwight's bearing may be out by miles, and we've only got twenty minutes of fuel.'

'Come back now! We're clear of the mountains. We'll keep circling until we see you then we'll head into the wind. The trapeze will be out. Roger that!'

'Roger, you'll circle, we'll report when we see you. Out.'

Lovelock was bringing the airship round again. Mahoney stood by the television screens, fiercely praying *Please God keep helping us now*, his heart pounding with joy, and in fear that they would not find the place, that something terrible would happen now. Lovelock brought the ship into the wind, and Mahoney prayed, *Please God they find us quickly.* . . . Lovelock flew back towards the mountains, all eyes searching feverishly for the little aircraft. Lovelock muttered, 'I'll have to take her round again.' Then the radio crackled:

'We see you, Rainbow. You are bearing three four zero from us.' And Mahoney cried, *'There they are! About one six zero degrees!'* They saw the tiny airplane, just a speck against the towering whiteness, flying towards them.

Lovelock said, 'I've got to turn around again.'

Mahoney cried, 'We see you, Bomber, we've got to turn around because we'll be too close to the mountain, so follow us and come up under our stern when we're back into the wind. Roger that!'

Lovelock brought the giant ship slowly around. Now the little aircraft was out of sight behind them. They searched for it on the television screen. Now Mahoney was tensed with fear that they would not hook up.

446

'There they are!'

There it was, on the aft television screen, flying towards their stern, tiny against the mass of whiteness. Lovelock said, 'We're almost back into the wind. Tell them to get ready.'

It was a living nightmare. Mahoney stood before the television screens, mouth dry, his nerves screaming. Closer and closer, the little bi-winged Curtiss came, getting bigger and bigger, until he could make out Dwight, then Bomber behind him. Oh God, it looked as if they were approaching too low – they were going to miss the trapeze and they'd have to come around and try again! . . . And then it looked as if they were coming too high. Oh God, they were going to smash into the trapeze and go screaming down to their deaths! . . . Then the Curtiss was jerkily filling the whole screen *and they were going to smash into the airship* – and there was a jolt, and Pomeroy shouted over the intercom, '*They're hooked on!*'

And Mahoney could have wept for joy and bellowed his praises to the Lord.

CHAPTER 73

Dwight and Bomber stood at the windows, frozen, directing Lovelock. Mahoney stood beside them, desperately searching, his heart hammering in hope, his heart hammering in dread at what they may find.

Every man stood at his station. Down on the glacier the bitter wind blew the snow in sheets. Lovelock rode low, ploughing the *Rainbow* back up the Beardmore Glacier, into the wind the horn blasting its urgent *whoop . . . whoooop. . .*

'Twenty minutes of fuel left,' Pomeroy said.

Mahoney did not care if he did not have enough fuel to get back to Australia, he did not care if he had to try to refuel off the *Dreadnought* in an Antarctic gale, did not care how Lovelock was going to hold this ship steady in this glacial canyon in this wind – all he cared about was that they find that aircraft.

'*Search! Search!*'

They were doing thirty knots into this wind. They had

covered nearly eight miles since they had turned around, so they must be approaching the area where Dwight had seen the smoke. But Dwight's visual bearings could be out by miles.

'*Look*, you bastards! *Look!*'

Then Dwight shouted, '*There!*' and they all saw it; the sudden streak of orange smoke shooting up above the flying snow, two miles ahead, scattering in the winds, and Mahoney shouted, '*Oh yes!*'

And he blew the horn, blaring his joy out over the Antarctic.

Lovelock forced the ship down towards the snow-driven ice. Mahoney's gut was a knot with joy and dread. *She is alive. . .* Down Lovelock pushed the ship, and the lower she came the harder the winds beat her. He brought her down to two hundred feet, before he levelled off, and now they could see the jumble of ridges and cracks in the great, solid river.

'Oh Lord . . . ,' Mr Perry said.

And oh Lord, yes, this was the most dangerous thing the *Rainbow* had yet tried to do, a flying ship as big as the Albert Hall trying to squeeze herself down towards that howling, jagged ice between those mountains, but Mahoney did not care about anything except that they had found her. On and on the airship flew up the glacier into the winds, her horn blasting. Then another streak of orange smoke shot up into the sky in a dissipating plume.

He did not recognize her. Her snow-packed blanket was clutched over her head, her desperate face, contorted to tears and laughter, trying to shout above the swirling snow. Mahoney looked in the direction this figure was pointing, up the swathe and flying snow, but he could see no sign of a crashed aeroplane. *How much further?* Then suddenly he saw another figure lurching down the snowswept slope, then another, and another, stumbling and floundering. Then his eye caught it, another three hundred yards up the glacier, the dim white outline of the crashed hulk.

'*There it is! Hold her here!*'

The *Rainbow* hung seventy feet above the snow-driven ice, her bows grinding into the wind, snow flying past her windows. The cargo doors opened in her belly, icy wind and snow rushed in, and the hoist began to come down. Mahoney and Bomber and Dwight and Malcolm and Daniel and Mr Perry were in it. Down they came, Malcolm signalling up to Pomeroy who was operating the winch above. Tana was floundering down the glacier towards them. The cargo hoist hit the snow and the men leapt out, up to their knees.

'*In!*' Mahoney bellowed at her. '*In!*'

She was staggering towards him, then she sprawled. She clambered up again, gasping, her face covered in snow, and Bomber grabbed her arm. Mahoney went struggling past her towards the crashed aeroplane. Bomber heaved her, reeling, towards the hoist, and she wrenched free and shrieked, 'Mahoney!'

He turned. He saw the snow-covered figure lurching towards him, desperately trying to claw the snow off her frozen face, the wind blowing her ice-matted hair like rope. She staggered towards him, her frozen arms outstretched, laughing and crying – then he recognized her. His heart leapt in desperate joy, and he started towards her, the snow grabbing at his legs, and she floundered, laughing, weeping, and they clutched each other.

The rest was very confused. All she knew was the joy, and the dreadful fear that something would go wrong now, that some terrible accident would bring this ship crashing down out of the sky, some terrible blast of wind would dash this wonderful machine against the mountainsides and hurl it broken and buckled down the glacier and they would all die after all. And all the time the lashing snow flying, the shouting, the exhaustion. He tried to make her stay at the hoist but she floundered blindly after him, back to the fuselage to fetch the passengers – *her* passengers. The confusion of people staggering down the glacier, slipping and sliding and crashing, gasping and crying, exhausted by cold and hunger, desperately stumbling their way down to the huge machine hovering above them. She hardly remembered the gut-wrenching eternity of slogging back to the awful fuselage, the pandemonium, people trying to struggle up, old people too exhausted to move, their terror of being left behind. She did not think of the frozen lines of dead laid out in the snow. She would remember her own dazed weakness, as in a nightmare, frantically trying to pull people to their feet and not having the strength, falling down herself, struggling up again and falling down again, feet trampling over her: and all the time the desperate need to hurry, hurry. She came staggering out of the fuselage for the last time, trying to support an elderly woman but she collapsed and just lay there in the snow. Then a hand was wrenching her to her knees, shouting, then she was stumbling drunkenly, half dragged by Daniel Moyo, half dragging Mrs Jorgen. There was the ship towering above her, the cargo hoist going up. Then it was coming down again and she was lurching on to it, clinging, and Mahoney was shouting above the wind, and the hoist was rising through the flying snow, then the yawning opening was closing around her.

She did not remember the rest. She did not feel the deck suddenly rising under her frozen, lurching feet: she would not remember the saloon like a battlefield, bodies sprawled everywhere, steam rising, the floor sodden with melting snow and the air dank, she would not remember reeling up a corridor, protesting that she had to help, nor the wonderful feeling of the weight coming off her buckling legs as he picked her up, the complete exhausted surrender and trust in this wonderful machine. She did not remember him stripping the sodden clothes off her, pulling the blankets over her: she did not feel the agony of the blood returning to her frozen skin. She slept.

And the joyful word went out to the world.

It had taken over two hours to load all the people aboard. The *Rainbow* did not have nearly enough fuel to reach Hobart, Tasmania: she was over five hours of fuel shy. She would run dry four hundred miles out over the sea. But, seven hundred miles away, HMAS *Dreadnought* turned about and began to steam north, away from the icebergs and the wind, so that the *Rainbow* could refuel off her.

Mahoney clambered up the stairs on to the bridge. He was utterly exhausted, utterly joyous. The *Rainbow* was well clear of the mountainsides, sailing towards the ocean of cloud above the Ross Ice Shelf.

Only Lovelock and Ed and Malcolm were on the bridge: the rest were helping the doctors look after the survivors. Lovelock was slumped in his seat, eyes closed: Ed was at the controls. Malcolm turned to Mahoney, and looked at him, pride all over his face. Mahoney just grinned, then put his arms around him, and they hugged each other.

'Marvellous ship, Malcolm.'

He walked slowly and happily to Lovelock. He dropped his hand on his shoulder. 'Go to bed, Martin. It's plain sailing now.'

'He's asleep,' Ed said. 'Leave him.'

Lovelock opened his red eyes. 'It's easy, now,' he mumbled. He heaved himself up and shuffled off the bridge.

'He should sleep properly, in his bunk. You go to bed, too, Ed.'

'I'm all right for two hours,' Ed said. 'Go to your girl.'

Malcolm went down to the crew's saloon and came back with three cans of beer. 'Hope Mr Perry doesn't see this.'

'Mr Perry', Ed said, 'can go take a running jump at himself.' He lifted the beer to his bristly mouth.

'Mr Perry', Mahoney said, 'is O.K.' He upended the beer, and swallowed, and swallowed, and the lovely stuff glugged down into his empty stomach like food. 'You're O.K., too, Ed.'

'Go to your girl,' Ed smiled.

All he could think of was his beautiful, exhausted, dirty, beautiful woman asleep down there, and his marvellous ship flying high and mighty and triumphant, the joyous relief that they were all safe, that right this minute the wonderful *Dreadnought* was steaming hard away from icebergs to help them. All he wanted to do was walk down to his dark cabin

451

and lay himself carefully down and just take her exhausted sleeping body in his arms, and surrender to happiness and sleep sleep sleep. But it was not fair to leave Ed alone on the bridge, and suddenly he was not exhausted anymore, he was joyfully wide-awake.

He slapped Ed on the shoulder: 'Go to bed.'

Ed turned from the console: then creakily lowered himself to the carpet, and stretched out. 'I'll rest here a while. In case you need me.'

'Malcolm?' Mahoney said. 'How about three more beers?'

Ed was already asleep when Malcolm came back with the beers. So Mahoney drank his for him. He had never felt happier in his life.

Ed woke four hours later. Mahoney was having difficulty remembering what day it was. He kept thinking in terms of yesterday's time, before they crossed the Pole, but now today here *was* yesterday, here tomorrow was already today. It would have played havoc with his navigation if the Admiral had not come back, a little drunk, and reprogrammed the sat-nav for him.

'Like a madhouse down there. But now everything's quietened down, the doctors are doing a great job.'

Mahoney was fuzzy with tiredness when he handed over to Ed. He did not go down to the saloon to check it out. He opened his cabin door carefully; and an exhausted smile spread across his face. The bed was empty, and he could hear the gush of the shower.

He went back to the crew's saloon. He got a can of beer and a bottle of champagne. He ripped the cap off the beer and upended it to his dry, salty mouth, and swallowed it down, down. Then he turned back to his cabin.

He was not exhausted anymore. His heart was beating with delicious excitement and laughy happiness. He untwisted the wire off the champagne bottle, the cork popped and shot to the ceiling. He filled a glass, and started for the bathroom door, a grin all over his face.

She was standing under the shower, eyes closed, steam

452

billowing, long hair hanging sodden, the water beating into her upturned face. He closed the door behind him, and she opened her eyes. Her wide Tana smile spread over her face, and he stepped under the shower in his clothes, and she flung her joyful arms around him.

And the shower beat down on them, champagne and all.

PART 11

PART II

CHAPTER 74

The clouds were gone, but the wind was still howling, whipping the snow off the icebergs. So the *Rainbow* flew with the winds, at four thousand feet and low throttle, to save fuel and to give *Dreadnought* time to steam north. On the evening of the next day they saw her on the horizon. She was still many miles away, still in heavy seas, though the icebergs were fewer. Lovelock cut the throttles back further. But the Roaring Forties were only one day ahead and the weather reports said that they were still roaring.

Admiral Anderson had offered it, Admiral Pike had urged it, Erling Thoren had said he would pay for it: but when all had been said, Malcolm and Mahoney and Lovelock had decided not to have the engineers aboard the *Dreadnought* try to erect a mooring mast on her stern. Doubtless the engineers could have done it. But Malcolm had visions of it tearing out of the deck as the ship heaved in the heavy swells, wrenching the *Rainbow* with it, and Mahoney agreed. Mahoney reposed his faith in God, Malcolm Todd and Lovelock, not always in that order.

HMAS *Dreadnought* turned into the wind, her bows heaving up the running hills of sea, then seething down, and the *Rainbow* followed her, Lovelock desperately trying to keep level with the surging stern so he could drop his mooring lines and fuel pipe. But it was too dangerous, and the *Dreadnought* had to heave her bows around and head north again, towards the Roaring Forties and the calmer seas beyond.

And the word went out to the world that it had been impossible for the gallant *Rainbow* to refuel, that she was battling across the Roaring Forties to try again on the other side.

The *Rainbow* rode high over the Roaring Forties, crabbing into the wind. Far behind, the *Dreadnought* ploughed across

457

the running swells of sea, the waves thudding, the spray flying over her decks in sheets. For two days the aircraft-carrier battled across the Forties; and by now the *Rainbow* was gone over the horizon, away ahead to get beyond the winds.

In the dawn of the second day, when the *Dreadnought* was only halfway across, the *Rainbow* sailed into the soft airs of the Pacific Ocean. The sun came up red and gold on to a beautiul day, glinting on the airship, and the sea down there was blue and flat. The *Rainbow* cut her engines.

It was still over a thousand miles to Australia, almost twenty hours away; the *Dreadnought* was over twenty-four hours behind, and the *Rainbow* had less than fifteen hours' fuel left.

And Lovelock shut down all engines and the great ship free-floated in the sunrise above the south Pacific, drifting gently with the wafting breezes. On board there was not a single sensation of movement. They rolled down the windows and let the fresh air waft in, marvelling, and they saw the dark flitting shapes of whales down there, and sharks and shoals of fish. It was completely quiet.

'Show me any other aircraft that can do this!' Malcolm exclaimed.

And Mr Perry, sitting in his deckchair, took another sip of his sherry and nodded, smiling, and dutifully made a note in his little book.

They had a wonderful, dreamy time those twenty-four hours, Tana Hutton and Joseph Mahoney.

Floating on air – that's how it was. They had been apart for three weeks and a hundred terrible years; they had been to the very gates of death, whence never in their sound senses could they have believed they would come back, and they had found each other, and now here they were, in each other's arms, and it was all a wondrous joy after the long nightmare.

But there was still the horror of what had happened. She lay tight in his arms and she said, 'I've got to talk about it. I've got to get it out. . .'

He held her, and out it came, slowly, fragmented, tumbling, bleakly. He got the whole awful picture: the plane flying serenely up the magnificent glacier, the passengers excitedly filming and photographing; then the sudden shocking blinding jolt, cameras flying and people sprawling, the screaming, then the long terrifying plunging, engines roaring, down, down; then the earthshaking jolt, and another, and another, then the long, mind-blacking skidding and bouncing and ploughing, snow flying up past the wndows, to the final bone-jarring halt.

Then the horrific silence. Then the hysterical whimpers, the cries, the weeping, people picking themselves up. She staggered forward to the flight-deck, to a terrible sight: the blood, the heads hanging on broken necks, the flight-deck a mangled bloodsoaked shambles. Then the shocking, terrible, macabre, desperate business of trying to make the shattered radio equipment work, working amongst those bodies. The final acceptance of the awful fact that nothing worked. *Nothing*. . . And not knowing what Captain Hennessy had said to McMurdo. The stunned, hopeless business of going back to those shattered passengers and trying to instil hope into them, the confidence that McMurdo knew where they were, that tomorrow they would hear search-planes buzzing overhead. Meanwhile they had to go about the desperate business of first-aid, carrying the dead outside, building up a wall in front of that gaping hole, organizing men to make a big cross of seat cushions in the snow. There was still a lot of unsmashed booze, and food for two days if they rationed it. They spread the cushions on the floor and huddled close together to keep warm. But the search planes did not come, and the blizzard did. First the moaning and then the lashing, snow flying and the fuselage shaking; and the desperation in their eyes, the clutching and huddling, and the dreadful, icy hand of death.

But the awful story was out, and now there was the pure joy of being alive, *alive*, of being restored to each other. All that day and into the beautiful night the *Rainbow* floated free: her sat-nav told them where she was, and they kept in touch with the *Dreadnought* by radio. Before dawn they saw her lights steaming over the southern horizon.

At daybreak the *Dreadnought* turned her bows into a gentle wind, all lights blazing, and the *Rainbow* came up on her stern. Lovelock brought her in low and slow; the floodlit deck loomed, closer and closer. Then the *Rainbow*'s nose was over the big flat stern, down came the mooring line on to the deck with a crash. Then down came her fuel hose, and the sailors coupled it to the carrier's.

Two hours later it was all over. The *Rainbow* hovered above the carrier's stern, her colours shining in the new day, her tanks full; then she rose up into the glorious morning, and a cheer went up from the decks, and both ships' hooters sounded over the ocean.

CHAPTER 75

It was a hero's welcome. It seemed the whole world was there, at Sydney International Airport, to see the *Rainbow* come in. The car-parks were full, the surrounding roads jammed for miles, the airport packed with people. There were television crews and pressmen from all around the world. In the middle of the afternoon the first aeroplanes and helicopters took to the skies to welcome the great airship.

There were the long white lines of breakers curling in. The *Rainbow* flew up the Australian coastline, high and gleaming and triumphant: and then the aeroplanes and helicopters started appearing.

Out of the blue sky they came, joyful little aeroplanes buzzing through the southern summer sunshine, radios crackling with good wishes and congratulations. They swarmed around the big airship like bees, and now down there was Botany Bay, the outskirts of Sydney, the pretty homes and winding roads, and then the famous harbour, the bridge spanning it, and ships were blasting up their welcome, and all the time the helicopters and aeroplanes buzzing about, escorting and filming. The world was watching the *Rainbow* come in to Sydney.

It was a gala day.

For three days Erling Thoren and the authorities (in that

order) had been erecting the mast at the end of the airport. For fifteen minutes the crowds watched the *Rainbow* come in, growing larger and larger. Then she was circling over the airport, huge and beautiful, to a roar of welcome, and the naval band struck up. First they played *Rule Britannia*, to salute her flag: then *When The Saints Come Marching In*, and the whole crowd was singing it, hands clapping to the beat. The joyful roar of it rising up to the sky. A television reporter stood in front of his camera with tears in his eyes:

'Listen to that! And are they not saints? Tens of thousands of people think so who have turned out to salute these men and their beautiful and wonderful ship! It is a great day for them and for the survivors they rescued – indeed for the whole world! Because aviation history has been made again, a new era of travel is being ushered in. The hearts of the world are reaching out to these men who braved the Antarctic in their untried ship, risked their lives in a mission of mercy when the rest of the world stood helpless. The whole world is rooting for them and singing along with us and wishing them well! Oh, it is a well-deserved day of triumph. This is their day of vindication, of years of work and enormous courage, the courage to mortgage their lives for vision, for a theory that will save the world enormous quantities of fuel-oil, from pollution, from poverty, as their new machines reach into parts of the world that never can be reached economically by conventional transport. Today they have won their place in history as much as the first pioneers of flight did, because they had the *guts* to tackle and rework the failures of the past, to go *against* history, against the conventional aviation and financial establishment, against the whole doubting Thomas world! And above all they had the sheer common-o'-garden *guts* to put their precious machine to the greatest of tests, to risk their very lives and fortunes to fly on a mission of mercy over the very edge of the world, into the frozen wastes of the Antarctic, flying a machine twice the length of a football pitch blind through snowstorms, out into the great unknown, knowing full well they were stretching their fuel to the very limits. . . knowing, indeed, that they may never come back. They put themselves and their wonderful airship to that greatest test, and they *passed* it with flying colours!

'And now here they are, ladies and gentlemen, circling mighty proud over Sydney International Airport to *When The Saints Come Marching In*, her colours of the rainbow gleaming from nose to tail, and it's very easy to believe that there's a pot of gold for her. We certainly hope so. She's coming down now on the last part of her turn, about a hundred feet off the ground – and, my word, the size of her! The sheer *enormity* of her. And so beautiful! She's lining up with her mast now, going very slowly. Now we can see the crew standing at the windows, the survivors waving. Oh, my word, what a sight she is! Here she comes. . . Approaching her mast now, and the gound crew are waiting to catch her ropes. Now they're running for it! Now they're joining it to the mast's rope. Meanwhile there she hangs in the air, under perfect control. Now she's inching forward to her mast. Closer, and *yes* – she is moored! And just *listen* to that roar from the crowd!'

CHAPTER 76

Millions of enthralled people across the world watched those historic pictures of the triumphant *Rainbow*, heard the roar of the crowds and the thumping of the band, saw the survivors coming down on the cargo hoist, the tearful, joyful reunions. For over an hour Mahoney and Malcolm and the crew were interviewed on the bridge, while the ship was topped-up with helium, refuelled, reballasted and made ready to fly back across the ocean to Africa. Malcolm had radioed the Australian government asking them to make helium available. It had been flown out from America in a Thoren Pacific aircraft.

'But,' old Erling Thoren protested, *'must* you leave tonight?'

'I'm afraid so.' Mahoney smiled. 'I'm already a bit late for an appointment with the prime minister of Zimbabwe.'

'But I want to throw a big party for you tomorrow. And I want to take you to Canberra to meet our prime minister.

He spends money like water, you know, he'll probably buy half-a-dozen of your airships!'

Mahoney smiled. 'I'll come back for that, I promise. But right now we've got all those observers waiting for us in Zimbabwe.'

'Yes, you'll have plenty of money to come back,' the old man agreed. 'You'll have no difficulty now. But what about my crazy daughter?'

Tana put her arm around Mahoney. 'I'll have to stay here for a few weeks, for the air crash enquiries. Then I'm going back to England.'

'Yes, you must hurry back to England,' the old man twinkled, 'these separations are becoming quite impractical.'

Millions of television viewers watched *Rainbow*'s departure, heard the naval band playing *Will ye no come back again?*, saw her circle Sydney in the sunset, then turn her head towards the darkening west, and the Indian Ocean beyond. And it was not only a story of heroes, it was a story of lovers. For the word was out about the dashing young man with the flying machine and his beautiful Australian lady. And the world sighed.

For the past twenty-four hours the press and television men had been descending on Zimbabwe, to report the arrival of the famous airship, and to witness her demonstrations to the Zimbabwe government. The airport was black with people. There was a police band to play what was now the *Rainbow*'s tune, *When the Saints Come Marching In*, until somebody remembered that it had also been the signature tune of the Rhodesian Light Infantry: *Rule Britannia* was ruled equally inappropriate, and so the *Marseillaise* was decided upon. Just before noon the prime minister and his entourage arrived at the airport to greet the brave ship and her gallant crew. It was a nice gesture, and the two national newspapers were even claiming Mahoney and Pomeroy as sons of Zimbabwe.

Just after noon *Rainbow* appeared on the horizon, a distant shape that grew and grew, coming high and mighty over the mauve of Africa. Millions of television viewers the world over saw what happened next. For many years afterwards the words of the television reporter were remembered.

'Magic carpet' were words he used, and 'like clockwork'. 'Everything has gone like clockwork for this wonderful ship and the wonderful men who built her! She has sailed out of the winters of the northern hemisphere and all the way down the summers of Africa on time, and then down over the bottom of the world through howling blizzards, and all the way back, and now here she is – *on time* and larger than life and very, *very* beautiful! . . .'

Then the world gasped – at first uncomprehending, then aghast; and then came the horrified words:

'Oh my God, I don't believe it . . . Oh Christ no, this is not what was meant to happen! Oh God no, this is not happening. . .'

The shell that struck the *Rainbow* was fired from the bush surrounding the airport by a group of four dissidents, ex-guerillas, hostile to the prime minister and his party. They bore no grievance against Joe Mahoney and his magnificent *Rainbow*; it was simply a spectacular target on a spectacular day when the prime minister himself would be watching. The weapon was a conventional piece of anti-aircraft equipment, supplied by Russia, capable of being launched by one man. It was not a heat-seeking missile, which would have zeroed in on the nearest engine, but an ordinary incendiary shell, which sliced through the great flank of the *Rainbow* and would have passed right through without exploding if it had not hit the bottom of a girder. The shell exploded and the great ship shuddered, a fuel pipe was sliced and kerosene began to spew down into the cargo space, on fire. A yellow ball of fire ballooned in the cargo hold and the television reporter cried:

'Oh God this is terrible! Oh God, the flames! She's just hanging there in the sky with those huge tongues of flame leaping out her windows. Yet she's not coming down! . . . She's got a great hole in her side and the helium must be rushing out but she's hanging in the sky. And still her engines are turning and she seems to be

flying on towards us. Oh my God, who could have done this terrible thing? Oh God what a tragedy! . . .'

The kerosene cascaded down the man-way into the upper hold, the flame galloping along after it, and the black smoke billowed. Malcolm and Bomber and Daniel burst through the door, their fire-extinguishers gushing into the dense fumes, burning kerosene gushing down from above. The burning liquid ran down the accommodation alleyway, and the flames took on the sodden carpeting and on the fibreglass partitions, killer smoke billowing, and then the cabins were on fire, and the bedding and the furniture. Malcolm and his men stumbled backwards down the alleyway, their extinguishers spewing into the dense smoke.

The television reporter said: *'I can hardly believe this! . . . She's not falling out of the sky! This is absolutely extraordinary! She's got a bloody great hole blown in her side, fire is raging, smoke pouring out of her, but she is not plummeting to the earth! There she still is, ploughing through the air, and she is going to come in to land! Yes sir, she is hanging up there, and she is coming in to land! She's still afloat and apparently under control! . . .'*

The saloon was an inferno of burning fibreglass and fabric, the suffocating smoke barrelling up the corridor leading to the bridge, but the kerosene could spread no further because the bridge was higher. Down on the ground a red fire-engine had come just out of its garage, but no closer. Malcolm rasped into the radio: 'We can't cut off the whole fuel supply until the ship is on the ground because we need the engines, so we're going into the hull to isolate the broken pipes. *Do you understand?'*

'I think so,' the voice said.

'All you've got to understand is that this ship is not going to blow up because helium does not burn and kerosene does not explode, it only burns – so send that fire-engine to break open the door and send your men in to fight this fire. Do you understand?'

465

'I will ask the fire engine,' the voice said.

'*I think so.*' Malcolm yelled. '*Call the prime minister.*'

Mahoney flung open the saloon door and black smoke billowed out. He could not even see the flames as he lumbered feverishly into the inferno.

He moved stiffly in the fire-suit, feeling with his feet. Now he could see the fire leaping off the carpet, the furniture. He crossed the saloon, the flames beating against the suit. He kicked open the accommodation door. The bulkheads were aflame behind the belching fires. He lurched down the corridor, and kicked open the door at the end.

It was a ghastly sight. There was nothing to burn in here, but the whole huge space was aflame, the kerosene awash, like a lake on fire. Mahoney stared, heart pounding, aghast; then he shoved himself into it.

He lumbered flat out, the flames leaping up to his knees. Kerosene was pouring down the vertical manway, under the door. He flung open the door and gallons flooded out over his boots. He looked up, horrified. The shaft was flickering with flames, the very rungs on fire. He grabbed a flaming rung in his gloved hand, began to climb. His gloves were on fire, wet with running kerosene; he scrambled blindly up the flaming, smoke-filled manway, then his helmet smacked the hatch. He fumbled it open, and gallons of kerosene cascaded down on to him, and now his head and shoulders were on fire. He clambered frantically up the last rungs, fumbled at the airtight door, then flung open the hatch into the hull.

He burst into the black hull, a man on fire, a terrible human torch lighting up the cathedral darkness. He heaved the door closed behind him, gasping, and stared down at himself aghast. Before his eyes the flames flickered out on his suit, and died, just as Malcolm had promised him, because there was no oxygen in here to feed the flames.

For a second he stood collecting his wits, wrestling the torch out of his pouch; then he lumbered across the hull towards the big fuel tank.

He could see daylight through the hole in the hull. He

crouched, his torch shaking as he traced the fuel pipes. He found the right valve, and turned it.

Down on the ground the television reporter had tears running down his cheeks as he said: *'She's coming in now. Her wheels are lowered. She's ten feet off the ground now. Oh God, the smoke! Those men! . . . Here she comes, only six feet up now – now a yard . . .'* And in a choking voice he cried: *'She's down. . . .'*

CHAPTER 77

The sun had gone down. The crowds had been sent home by the army, who were encircling the entire airport. Out in the bush a new manhunt had started, in the African townships a new police sweep midst sounds of fury. Most of the press had returned to town to send their dramatic stories home, but a few were still at the airport bar, talking to Mahoney and Malcolm and Dwight and Pomeroy. Mahoney was exhausted, drained, numb, but he could not bring himself to leave his ship yet, he just wanted to stay near her. He had placed an international telephone call, reversed charge, and he was also waiting for that. He had drunk half a bottle of whisky aboard the *Rainbow* and he intended drinking a hell of a lot more. He felt deadly, dreamy, reckless calm. Dwight said: 'What was the prime minister like?'.

Mahoney said, 'How do you expect him to be? Furious.'

'Did you like him?' a reporter demanded.

Mahoney was sick, sick, sick of reporters. 'I don't like communists. But I liked him.'

'Can I print that?'

'You can print any bloody thing.'

'Because now the deal has fallen through?'

Mahoney looked at the man. 'Of course the deal's fallen through! He won't buy until he's seen it work in terms of our agreement! And he's not going to buy if his political enemies can pot it down out of the sky.'

Malcolm was hunched over the bar, staring into space, his

467

flushed face tear-stained and streaked with ashes. He did not turn, but muttered: '*Any* goddamn aircraft is easy to shoot these days.'

Mahoney had found a ten-pound sterling note in his pocket but after it was spent he had no more money in the whole wide world. He slapped it on the bar. 'Whiskies, please.'

'No more whisky, sah,' the barman said apologetically. 'Bottle finished.'

Mahoney sighed angrily. 'Is· this or is this not an international airport?'

'Brandies,' Dwight said to the barman. 'They're on me.'

'O.K.,' Mahoney said. 'But when you're bankrupt to the tune of millions of pounds, ten more quid makes no difference.'

'But are you really bankrupt? Shee-it, what about insurance?'

Mahoney sighed. 'My insurance specifically excludes acts of ·sabotage and damage done by weapons of war. Everything I goddamn own, and everything my airline owns, is hocked to pay for that smoking wreck out there. I still morally owe this guy' ‑ he jerked his head at Malcolm – 'about a million pounds.'

Malcolm came out of his reverie, his flushed face streaked. 'Forget about that,' he said.

Mahoney stared at the man a moment, then threw back his head and laughed tearfully. '*Forget* about that? . . . Forget about a million pounds! Oh, Malcolm, I love you. . .' He reached out and shook the older man's shoulder. 'No wonder you're broke and build airships!'

Malcolm muttered: 'She'll fly again. We can patch up those holes.'

'And what's that going to cost?'

Malcolm shook his weary head, and shrugged.

'Exactly,' Mahoney said. He wanted to laugh and cry.

'So what are you going to do?' the reporter demanded.

Mahoney had answered all these questions before. He jerked his thumb at Malcolm. 'Ask the mad scientist.'

'Do?' Malcolm said absently, his face suffused. 'Build another one.'

Mahoney wanted to roar with laughter. '*For whom?*'

Malcolm said: 'For you.' He waved his hand. 'For us.'

Mahoney was half-laughing, tearfully. 'Except this time we'll have fans to pump the helium down into the gondola as a built-in fire extinguisher? . . .'

'Right.' Malcolm said. 'Listen, we've proved the airship hands down. . .'

'Exactly!' Dwight cried. 'You've been shot by a bloody great cannon that would have sent any other aircraft screaming down out of the sky, but you brought her down to a soft landing! Kee-rist, you've proved your airships to the whole world!'

Mahoney looked out the window at the African night. Way down at the end of the runway was his smoking airship, the soldiers surrounding it. And he did not care any more. He did not care about his ruined airship, all he cared about was what it represented. It represented Africa. The whole mess of Africa, all the mistakes and the mindlessness of Africa. Give them a whole country, and they will become poor. Give them freedom and they will become enslaved. Give them democracy and they will fight each other. Give them peace and they will make war on themselves. He felt dreamy reckless calm as he said: 'They're not *my* airships. They're Malcolm's. He's the genius, not me.'

'If it hadn't been for you—' Malcolm began.

'But what are *you* going to do?' Dwight demanded.

The telephone rang. Mahoney started for it, but the reporter picked it up. 'Hullo?' he said. 'Yes?' He put his finger in his ear and listened intently. Then he said, 'I'm coming now.' He put down the telephone, and looked at them.

'That was the Quill Bar. The prime minister has turned the Fifth Brigade loose. On Matabeleland. . . It's mayhem.'

Mahoney stared at him. Then he closed his eyes. 'Oh God!' he breathed.

'What's this?' Dwight demanded.

'The prime minister's private army,' the reporter said. 'Under North Korean officers.' He looked at them. 'It's bloody murder. In the towns and in the bush. Dragging out the dissidents. Even the police are running.'

'Because of this afternoon?' Dwight demanded.

And Mahoney could almost hear the sounds of fury. 'No,' he whispered angrily. 'This afternoon was just the last straw.'

The reporter said to Dwight: 'There's been a lot of trouble down there, the Matabele and the Shona hate each other.' He quoted from his telephone conversation: '"Bury your dead and run." That's what the police said to people who came running to the station for protection.' He looked at them. 'Right, I must go and chase this story – goodbye.' He turned and strode out of the bar.

Mahoney hung his head and groaned. 'Oh, Africa. . .'

'There's nothing you can do about it,' Dwight said grimly. 'What about this airship?'

'Do?' Mahoney said. And he could hear the screaming and the thuds of flesh and bone and the crack of guns. And suddenly he knew loud and clear what he was going to do. He felt sick in his guts, deadly calm. It was a relief. Almost a wonderful feeling. He said: 'Somehow get this ship back to England. And then. . .' He took a big breath and pointed at the floor. 'I'm coming right back here.'

They all stared at him.

'And do what?' Malcolm sighed wearily.

He said: 'Go back to politics. And try to shout some sense into them. Stop them committing suicide.'

There was amazed silence.

'But', Pomeroy protested, 'it's going to be a one-party state, mate!'

'If you can't lick 'em, join 'em.'

'*Join* them?' Pomeroy echoed.

Mahoney said angrily: 'How else can we try to influence what kind of a one-party it is – what kind of state?'

'*Join* 'em?'

Mahoney sighed. 'If it comes to that, yes! That's what I always said we should do, isn't it? *Get 'em on our side*, I said. Well, it's too late for that now, Pomeroy. So now we've got to join *their* side. Because that's the only way we can exert any influence. From the inside. And', he sighed, 'maybe a one-party state is what they goddamn need.' He snorted bitterly. 'Has any government in Africa done differently? Can the African handle a Westminster-style democracy? Maybe a one-party state is what they goddamn *need* – just one big boss with a big stick to tell them what to do! Give 'em a choice, and they'll fight each other – give them one boss and they'll do as they're told. That's the way it's always been in Africa. That's the way their chiefs ruled them since time began, that's the way the white man ruled them, that's the story of Africa, and will be for the next thousand years. That's how long it's taken us to develop our Westminster-style democracy, isn't it? Why should it take these guys any less?' He spread his hands. 'That's what our tragic war was all about – one-party rule. The White Party. So we went to war about it, and we lost. So now it's the Black Party's turn.'

'But' – Dwight protested – 'they're *communists*! They're going to start nationalizing industry and all. . .'

Mahoney said tersely, 'That's where the likes of me come in, Dwight. To stop them doing that. To shout some sense into them. To stop them committing economic suicide.'

'*But*', Pomeroy protested incredulously, 'they'll screw it up anyway!'

Mahoney spread his hands again. 'And didn't we whites screw it up first? By not giving them their fair share of the sun? By not *grooming* them to take over in their own country? By not including enough of them in government to satisfy their political ambition, little by little, so we would *control* the inevitable transition – instead of *defying* the inevitable? Defying world opinion, instead of being clever about it? Didn't we screw it up by making ourselves outlaws by declaring independence? By not practising the Partnership we preached? By failing to win the hearts and minds? And thereby losing everything. Wasn't *that* a screw-up? . . . Were we *smart*?'

Pomeroy was looking at him, unbelieving. 'You'll be a bleedin' voice in the wilderness, mate. They won't want a white man.'

Mahoney shook his head wearily.

'Maybe they won't. But I can still be a voice to be reckoned with. And this prime minister's no dummy.' He looked at him. 'What's our duty? To *all* our countrymen, black and white? How can we try to preserve the standards we profess to cherish if people like us don't get ourselves into positions of influence? And hold the country's hand.' He shook his head. 'Shelagh's dead right about that – the country *needs* her, and people like her. What's the alternative? Just sit back in England and watch the whole continent go to rat-shit?' He gestured impatiently. 'Just take one example – the wildlife of this country. The Wankie Game Reserve. The Zambesi Valley. . . What's going to happen to all that wonderful wildlife, if people like us don't stay to hold their hand? Because once they are gone, they are *gone*.' He glared, then sighed. He said: 'The white man has got to come back to Africa. To the *whole* of Africa. In strength. Africa can't make it alone. That's been proved time and again. That's why Britain and America have to pour billions in aid into the continent – to try to do by proxy-money what the white man used to do by himself. But aid alone isn't any good either. It just gets maladministered. So the white man must come back. . . Give 'em good roads, and they'll start to crumble. Well, the roads in this country haven't started to crumble yet. And I'm coming back to say something about it before they do.' He nodded at them. Then jerked his head at Malcolm. '*He* can build the airships. I'm going to stay in Africa and see that they don't get shot down out of the sky. . . .'

The telephone rang suddenly rather shrilly. The barman picked it up, then called: 'Mistah Mahoney?'

He walked down the bar and took the telephone.

'Hullo, darling,' he said.

'*Hullo, darling!*' Shelagh cried.

She wept into the telephone. 'Oh it's so wonderful! You've survived! The radio, the television, they're all full of it, tomorrow you're going to be across the front page of every newspaper in the world again. The telephone hasn't stopped ringing. Dolores says the cargo is pouring in! Oh darling, how right you were all along, I see that now. Darling? – can you hear me?'

Mahoney stood slumped against the bar. 'Yes.'

She half-laughed, then blurted: 'And there's something else I want to tell you. . .' She hesitated. 'About those shares?

472

Well, I want to set your mind at rest. I have not sold them to Tex Weston. You're right, I really did sell them to you, gentleman's agreement, and all that. You' – she gave an embarrased half-laugh – 'you just owe me the rest of the price, that's all.'

Mahoney closed his eyes in relief. 'Yes, of course.'

'So', she blurted on, 'today I gave a letter to your lawyer, acknowledging the deal, and authorizing him to register the shares in your name forthwith.' Her voice caught. 'I felt such a heel. . . There you were, down at the Antarctic, a goddamn hero, and I was threatening you!'

Two tears squeezed out of his closed eyes. 'Thank you, darling.'

'I know you think it's no more than your legal right – and it is – but I just want you to know that I've done that.'

'Thank you, Shelagh.'

She sniffed. 'Well,' she sob-laughed – 'what do you say?'

'About what?'

She said, 'Well – when are you coming home? Or shall I jump on a plane and come out to you?'

His voice felt thick. 'Where are you speaking from?'

'From home! I've been trying for hours to trace you! Oh darling, the cottage is so cozy – and it's crying out for you to be in it! Listen, here's Cathy. She wants to say hullo to her famous daddy!'

There was a shuffling sound; then Cathy's little voice: 'Hullo, Daddy. . .'

Mahoney felt the tears rolling down his cheeks.

'Hullo, darling,' he said.

He heard Shelagh say something in the background, then Cathy piped: 'You're famous, Daddy!'

'Am I, darling? . . .'

He heard Shelagh say something else and Cathy piped: 'You must come home at once, Daddy!'

The tears were salty on his mouth.

'Must I, darling?' Then: 'Thank you, my baby. Let me speak to Mommy now. Your daddy loves you. . .'

'Mommy speaking!' Shelagh cried.

'Shelagh?' Mahoney said, and his throat was thick. He took

473

a deep breath that shook, then he said: 'I'm sorry, but I'm not coming home.'

And he quietly put down the telephone.

He did not go back to the others. He turned and walked out the glass doors on to the verandah, under the African sky. He stood there, looking up at the stars, feeling the warm, rich, night air of Africa on his sweaty, tearful face. He closed his eyes and listened. Yes, there they were: the crick-cricking of the night insects. And, oh, the balm of them.

'Hullo, Suzie,' he whispered.

And Suzie said, 'Hullo there.'

A smile spread across his tearful face.

'I'm right, Suzie,' he whispered.

He was sure he heard her chuckle.

And her chuckle turned into the ring of the telephone; then the barman was shouting: 'Mistah Mahoney?'

He turned and walked back into the bar. He wiped his hand across his eyes and picked up the telephone.

'Hullo, darling,' he said.

'Hullo,' old Erling Thoren said, 'I suppose you want to speak to the other darling, but as you're using my telephone I have some rights too, you know, and I just want to tell you not to worry about money to fix your ship – your ship will fly again soon and you are going to be a very rich crazy young man, because everybody thinks your airship is wonderful and you will get many contracts. But now I better give this telephone to my daughter, you know, before she has hysterics. . . .'

'*Hullo, darling!*' Tana yelled joyfully.

The tears were running down his face. Oh God, he was ridiculously happy. Out there under the African sky his airship lay smoking, and he was happy. He said, 'We're coming back here, Tana.'

She laughed: 'And what about these airships of yours, now you're a goddamn millionaire?'

And suddenly it was all very funny and very joyful and nothing else mattered, nothing else in the whole wide world, not money, not fame: all that mattered was love and that smoking airship out there and all that it stood for, the whole of smoking Africa. It was all terribly clear and dear and he loved one woman in the whole wide world. He laughed.

'Millionaires make the best politicians. . . I'll still own Redcoat, and Redcoat will still fly airships, and airships are going to change the face of the world – but *I* don't have to fly them *personally*, do I? Besides, I don't like heights.' He added: 'We'll get that *Noah's Ark* cranked up again. Bring lots of mushroom spore, and your pretty hat.'

'*Hat?*' she laughed. 'Did you say *hat?*'

'Your garden-party hat,' Mahoney said. 'I suppose politicians still have to go to garden parties, if there're any gardens left.'

She laughed, '*Oh, there'll be gardens, Mahoney. . .*'